PRAISE FOR

Daughter of Regals & Other Tales

"Stephen R. Donaldson demonstrates new breadth and range in his first book of short stories . . . There is no doubt that Donaldson remains the reigning master of epic fantasy." —*The Atlanta Journal-Constitution*

"He has a versatility that few had previously guessed . . . [The] stories are fresh, original, and, in a couple of cases, simply superb . . . Exciting fare for Donaldson fans and the uninitiated alike." —*Rocky Mountain News*

"Donaldson proves himself at home in a surprising number of story genres . . . Of those stories that are fantasies, 'The Lady in White' and 'Ser Visal's Tale' are exceptional . . . Overall, *Daughter of Regals* is a good collection." —*The Columbus Dispatch*

"The best tales here (both written for this collection) are the title story, a real good twist on magical power achieved at the proper time and place, and 'Ser Visal's Tale,' on betrayal and ultimate triumph . . . An interesting overview on Donaldson's style and the turnings of his imagination." —*Los Angeles Times*

"This collection leaves one intrigued about what Donaldson will try next. Meanwhile, his many readers should appreciate this chance to broaden their picture of him and his work." —*Publishers Weekly*

PRAISE FOR

Against All Things Ending

"Maintains the high standards of the first two volumes . . . Donaldson remains a romantic who believes in lovers who will risk all for each other." —*Booklist*

"A fascinating fantasy . . . Fast-paced." —*Midwest Book Review*

"There's much to like in Donaldson's latest installment in the multivolume Thomas Covenant epic series." —*Kirkus Reviews*

continued . . .

"A long and complex tale, with many different forces and magical objects, strange words, prophecies, betrayals, and the fate of the whole world at stake."

—*The Wooster (OH) Daily Record*

"This final installment does more than merely entertain. It brings the reader into intimate acquaintance with loss, sorrow, rage, self-doubt, and, ultimately, despair."

—*Western Morning News* (UK)

PRAISE FOR

Fatal Revenant

"Thought provoking . . . This complicated and emotional continuation of the Thomas Covenant saga is exactly what Donaldson's fans have been hoping for."

—*Publishers Weekly*

"The real testament to Donaldson's storytelling ability is that he makes readers interested in spite of his protagonists' shortcomings . . . Many readers around the world are waiting for the third installment in the final series of a fantasy creation that rivals *The Lord of the Rings* in scope and imagination."

—*Onyx reviews*

"The ending is the kind of cliff-hanger that should have readers returning to see how it and the remaining adventures play out."

—*Booklist*

"Donaldson continues to weave a complex tapestry in *Fatal Revenant* . . . An engaging tale."

—*Warren County Report*

"A complex, poignant epic fantasy . . . Stephen R. Donaldson is a great world-builder as he makes his characters—even the monsters—seem real, but it is the poignancy of relationships that makes him one of the best fantasists today."

—*Midwest Book Review*

"There simply are not enough stars to award this book. It is not a lightweight fluff piece but an intense, mentally stimulating, and utterly satisfying read . . . It breaks my heart to finish a story like this."

—*The Eternal Night*

"[Donaldson has] managed to expand on an already-detailed world with a rich imagination unique in modern fantasy."

—*The Science Fact & Science Fiction Concatenation*

Reave the Just & Other Tales

Stephen R. Donaldson

ACE BOOKS, NEW YORK

THE BERKLEY PUBLISHING GROUP
Published by the Penguin Group
Penguin Group (USA) LLC
375 Hudson Street, New York, New York 10014

USA • Canada • UK • Ireland • Australia • New Zealand • India • South Africa • China

penguin.com

A Penguin Random House Company

Ace Books are published by The Berkley Publishing Group.
ACE and the "A" design are trademarks of Penguin Group (USA) LLC.

Library of Congress Cataloging-in-Publication Data

Donaldson, Stephen R.
[Short stories. Selections]
Reave the Just & other tales / Stephen R. Donaldson. — Ace trade paperback edition.
pages cm
ISBN 978-0-425-25703-6 (Trade)
I. Title.   II. Title: Reave the Just and other tales.
PS3554.O469R42 2014
813'.54—dc23
2013041888

PUBLISHING HISTORY
Bantam Spectra hardcover edition / January 1999
Bantam Spectra mass-market edition / January 2000
Ace trade paperback edition / February 2014

PRINTED IN THE UNITED STATES OF AMERICA

10 9 8 7 6 5 4 3 2 1

Cover art by John Jude Palencar.
Cover design by Sarah Oberrender.
Interior text design by Laura K. Corless.

"What Makes Us Human"—
First appeared in *The Magazine of Fantasy & Science Fiction*, 1984.
Subsequently appeared in *Berserker Base*, edited by Fred Saberhagen, Tor, 1985.
Later appeared in one of DAW's "Year's Best" collections.

"The Djinn Who Watches Over the Accursed"—
First appeared in "World Tales," the souvenir booklet of the 1985 World Fantasy
convention, © Stephen R. Donaldson.
Later appeared in *Arabesques 2*, edited by Susan Shwartz, Avon, 1989.

"Reave the Just"—
First appeared in *After the King*, edited by Martin H. Greenberg, Tor, 1992.

"The Woman Who Loved Pigs"—
First appeared in *Full Spectrum 4*, edited by Lou Aronica, Amy Stout,
and Betsy Mitchell, Bantam, 1993.

"The Kings of Tarshish Shall Bring Gifts"—
First appeared in *The Book of Kings*, edited by Richard Gilliam
and Martin H. Greenberg, Roc, 1995.

TO JOHN HUMPHREYS—

FOR GOOD THINGS WHICH WOULD NEVER

HAVE BEEN POSSIBLE OTHERWISE

CONTENTS

INTRODUCTION

As I think about it, I realize that fourteen years have passed since I last published a collection of short fiction. I'm not quite sure how that happened. Apparently I've spent more time than I realized writing novels.

By contrast, all the fiction in my previous collection, *Daughter of Regals and Other Tales*, was composed over a six-year span, from 1977 to 1983—with the obvious exception of "Gilden-Fire," a novel fragment originally conceived as a part of *The Illearth War*.

However, the fact that I took fourteen years to produce these eight novellas and short stories does have an advantage or two for the reader.

The first—and less interesting—benefit is that the present work was quite naturally done under more diverse conditions and circumstances than those which obtained during the writing of *Daughter of Regals and Other Tales*. In essence, all my previous stories came to me between the completion of *The Chronicles of Thomas Covenant the Unbeliever* and the publication of *White Gold Wielder*. They were all composed, in a manner of speaking, under Thomas Covenant's ambiguous influence. Not so the stories here. The earliest of them predates *The Mirror of Her Dreams*; the most recent were completed two years after I finished work on *This Day All Gods Die*. For that reason, they were produced to meet a greater variety of needs and aspirations. My career as well as my life went through more changes in fourteen years than in six.

For example, two of these stories were written "on demand"—which is emphatically not my usual approach. I wrote them not because I felt particularly inspired by them, but because I'd accepted the responsibility of writing *something*. In one case, "The Djinn Who Watches Over the Accursed," I was overtaken by career concerns: I'd agreed to be a guest at the World Fantasy Convention, and my hosts wanted an original story for the program book. In the other, "What Makes Us Human," my ego impaired my judgment: Fred Saberhagen had asked me to contribute to a "shared-world" *Berserker* novel he had in mind, and I wanted to prove that I belonged in the company of other writers he'd approached—among them Roger Zelazny, Poul Anderson, Ed Bryant, and Connie Willis.

I include these two stories as examples of craft, not of art. Everything else I've ever written—here, in *Daughter of Regals and Other Tales*, and in my novels—I've written because I fell in love with it, believed in it, and couldn't imagine writing anything else, not because someone asked me (or paid me) to write it.

But there were other variables as well that didn't impinge on my previous collection. "The Kings of Tarshish Shall Bring Gifts" came to me while I was skidding down into a catastrophic divorce; "Reave the Just" played a crucial role in my recovery afterward. "The Woman Who Loved Pigs" helped me regain my balance when I'd begun to founder in the Gap novels—specifically, between *A Dark and Hungry God Arises* and *Chaos and Order*. "By Any Other Name" brought me back from the worst case of writer's block I've ever experienced.

In retrospect, the man who produced *Daughter of Regals and Other Tales* seems to me to have had a remarkably uncomplicated existence.

As it happens, the autobiographical dimension of fiction holds limited interest, at least for me. Any true storyteller draws on life to create fiction; but the interaction is so oblique, and goes through so many sea changes, that it defies explication. (A brief demonstration: which of the stories in this book responds to a lawsuit impugning my honor, both as a writer and as a father? None that I've mentioned so far can be excluded—although I admit that "The Djinn Who Watches Over the Accursed" and "What Makes Us Human" are unlikely candidates.)

More interesting, I think, is the second advantage of the time span occupied by the composition of these stories. It is that the reader receives here a better glimpse of the ways in which I'm developing my gifts and skills. With experience—both personal and creative—any artist ambitious for excellence inevitably changes. And the distance between, say, "The Kings of Tarshish Shall Bring Gifts" and "The Killing Stroke" is greater than any comparable interval in *Daughter of Regals and Other Tales*. Fourteen years should allow enough time for the stages of the journey to reveal themselves.

What all those changes might be, I don't pretend to know. My sense of perspective about my work might politely be called imprecise. I suspect, however, that they will be more apparent to the reader. Nevertheless, I'm aware that my aspirations as a storyteller have gradually shifted focus, especially in the past decade. To repeat a comment I've made elsewhere: "I want all my characters to have dignity." Of the many elements which combine to make up a work of fiction, I've been known to attend more closely to design than to character. This was particularly true in the six *Covenant* books. But not anymore. I'm good at design, and I no longer worry about it. Instead, I strive as carefully as I can to penetrate the hearts of my characters, so that I'll be able to see and value them for who they are.

I am—if I may be forgiven the expression—the only God they've got.

One practical point in conclusion: the order in which these stories now appear is not the order in which they were written. I've rearranged them, shamelessly, for effect. The actual sequence of composition was:

"What Makes Us Human"
"The Djinn Who Watches Over the Accursed"
"The Kings of Tarshish Shall Bring Gifts"
"Reave the Just"

"The Woman Who Loved Pigs"
"By Any Other Name"
"The Killing Stroke"
"Penance"

The first two have been very slightly revised for this edition.

Reave the Just

Of all the strange, unrelenting stories which surrounded Reave the Just, none expressed his particular oddness of character better than that concerning his kinsman, Jillet of Forebridge.

Part of the oddness was this—that Reave and Jillet were so unlike each other that the whole idea of their kinship became difficult to credit.

Let it be said without prejudice that Jillet was an amiable fool. No one who was not amiable would have been loved by the cautious people of Forebridge—and Jillet was loved, of that there could be no doubt. Otherwise the townsfolk would never have risked the unpredictable and often spectacular consequences of sending for Reave, merely to inform him that Jillet had disappeared. And no one who was not a fool would have gotten himself into so much trouble with Kelven Divestulata that Kelven felt compelled to dispose of him.

In contrast, neither Reave's enemies—of which his exploits had attracted a considerable number—nor his friends would have described him as amiable.

Doubtless there were villages across the North Counties, towns perhaps, possibly a city or two, where Reave the Just was admired, even adulated: Forebridge was not among them. His decisions were too wild, his actions too unremitting, to meet the chary approval of the farmers and farriers, millers and masons who had known Jillet from birth.

Like a force of nature, he was so far beyond explanation that people had ceased trying to account for him. Instead of wondering why he did what he did—or how he got away with it—the men and women of Forebridge asked themselves how such an implausible individual chanced to be kinsman to Jillet, who was himself only implausible in the degree to which likable character was combined with unreliable judgment.

In fact, no one knew for certain that Reave and Jillet were related. Just recently, Jillet had upon occasion referred to Reave as "Reave the Just, my kinsman." That was the true extent of the information available in Fore-bridge. Nothing more was revealed on the subject. In an effort to supply the lack, rumor or gossip suggested that Jillet's mother's sister, a woman of another town altogether, had fallen under the seduction of a carnival clown with delusions of grandeur—or, alternatively, of a knight-errant incognito—and had given Reave a bastard birth under some pitiful hedgerow, or perhaps in some nameless nunnery, or conceivably in some lord's private bedchamber. But how the strains of blood which could produce Reave had been so entirely suppressed in Jillet, neither rumor nor gossip knew.

Still it must have been true that Reave and Jillet were related. When Reave was summoned in Jillet's name, he came.

By the time Reave arrived, however, Jillet was beyond knowing whether anyone valued him enough to tell his kinsman what had become of him.

How he first began to make his way along the road to Kelven's enmity was never clearly known. Very well, he was a fool, as all men knew—but how had he become enmeshed in folly on this scale? A few bad bargains with usurers were conceivable. A few visits to the alchemists and mages who fed on the fringes of towns like Forebridge throughout the North Counties were conceivable, in fact hardly to be wondered at, especially when Jillet was at the painful age where he was old enough to want a woman's love but too young to know how to get it. A few minor and ultimately forgettable feuds born of competition for trade or passion were not only conceivable but normal. Had not men and women been such small and harmless fools always? The folk of Forebridge might talk of such matters endlessly, seeking to persuade themselves that they were wiser. But who among them would have hazarded himself against Kelven Divestulata? Indeed, who among them had not at one time or another suspected that Kelven was Satan Himself, thinly disguised by swarthy flesh and knotted muscle and wiry beard?

What in the name of all the saints had possessed Jillet to fling himself into such deep waters?

The truth—which no one in Forebridge ever divined—was that Jillet brought his doom down on his own head by the simple expedient of naming himself Reave's kinsman.

It came about in this fashion. In his early manhood, Jillet fell victim to an amiable, foolish, and quite understandable passion for the widow Huchette. Before his death, Rudolph Huchette had brought his new bride—foreign, succulent, and young—to live in the manor house now occupied by Kelven Divestulata, thinking that by keeping her far from the taints and sophistication of the cities he could keep her pure. Sadly for him, he did not live long enough after settling in Forebridge to learn that his wife was pure by nature and needed no special protection. And of course the young men of the town knew nothing of her purity. They only knew that she was foreign, young, and bereaved, imponderably delicious. Jillet's passion was only one among many, ardent and doomed. The widow Huchette asked only of the God who watched over innocence that she be left alone.

Needless to say, she was not.

Realistically considered, the only one of her admirers truly capable of disturbing her was dour Kelven. When she spurned his advances, he laid siege to her with all the cunning bitterness of his nature. Over the course of many months, he contrived to install himself in the manor house which Rudolph had intended as her lifelong home; he cut off her avenues of escape so that her only recourse was to accept the drudgery of being his housekeeper since she steadfastly refused the grim honor of being his wife. And even there he probably had the best of her, since he was no doubt perfectly capable of binding and raping her to satisfy his admiration.

However, Jillet and the other men enamored of the widow did not consider her circumstances—and their own—realistically. As men in passion will, they chose to believe that they themselves were the gravest threat to her detachment. Blind to Kelven's intentions, Jillet and his fellow fools went about in a fog of schemes, dreaming of ways to persuade her to reveal her inevitable preference for themselves.

However, Jillet carried this scheming farther than most—but by no means all—of his peers.

Perhaps because of his amiability—or perhaps because he was foolish—he was not ordinarily successful in competitions over women. His face and form were goodly enough, and his brown eyes showed pleasure as openly as any man's. His kindness and cheery temper endeared him throughout Forebridge. But he lacked forthrightness, self-assertion; he lacked the qualities which inspire passion. As with women everywhere, those of Forebridge valued kindness; they were fond of it; but they did not surrender their virtue to it. They preferred heroes—or rogues.

So when Jillet first conceived his passion for the widow Huchette, he was already accustomed to the likelihood that he would not succeed.

Like Kelven Divestulata after the first year or so of the widow's bereavement—although no one in Forebridge knew at the time what Kelven was doing—Jillet prepared a siege. He was not wise enough to ask himself, Why am I not favored in the beds of women? What must I learn in order to make myself desirable? How may I rise above the limitations which nature has placed upon me? Instead, he asked, Who can help me with this woman?

His answer had already occurred to a handful of his brighter, but no less foolish, fellows. In consequence, he was no better than the fifth or sixth man of Forebridge to approach the best-known hedgerow alchemist in the County, seeking a love potion.

According to some authorities, the chief distinction between alchemists and mages was that the former had more opportunities for charlatanism, at less hazard. Squires and earls consulted mages; plowmen and cotters, alchemists. Certainly, the man whom Jillet approached was a charlatan. He admitted as much freely in the company of folks who were wise enough not to want anything from him. But he would never have revealed the truth about himself to one such as Jillet.

Charlatan or not, however, he was growing weary of this seemingly endless sequence of men demanding love potions against the widow Huchette.

One heartsick swain by the six-month or so may be profitably bilked. Three may be a source of amusement. But five or six in a season was plainly tedious. And worrisome as well: even Forebridge was capable of recognizing charlatanism when five or six love potions failed consecutively.

"Go home," the alchemist snapped when he had been told what Jillet wanted. "The ingredients for the magick you require are arduous and expensive to obtain. I cannot satisfy you."

But Jillet, who could not have put his hand on five farthings at that moment, replied, "I care nothing for the price. I will pay whatever is needed." The dilemma of cost had never entered his head, but he was certain it could be resolved. The widow Huchette had gold enough, after all.

His confidence presented an entirely different dilemma to the alchemist. It was not in the nature of charlatans to refuse money. And yet too many love potions had already been dispensed. If Providence did not inspire the widow to favor one of the first four or five men, the alchemist's reputation—and therefore his income—would be endangered. Perhaps even his person would be endangered.

Seeking to protect himself, the alchemist named a sum which should have stunned any son of a cotter.

Jillet was not stunned. Any sum was acceptable, since he had no prospect of ever paying it himself. "Very well," he said comfortably. Then, because he wished to believe in his own cleverness, he added, "But if the potion does not succeed, you will return that sum with interest."

"Oh, assuredly," replied the alchemist, who found that he could not after all refuse money. "All of my magicks succeed, or I will know the reason why. Return tomorrow. Bring your gold then."

He closed his door so that Jillet would not have a chance to change his mind.

Jillet walked home musing to himself. Now that he had time to consider the matter, he found that he had placed himself in an awkward position. True, the love of the widow Huchette promised to be a valuable investment—but it was an investment only, not coin. The alchemist would require coin. In fact, the coin was required in order to obtain the investment. And Jillet had no coin, not on the scale the alchemist had mentioned. The truth was that he had never laid mortal eyes on that scale of coin.

And he had no prospects which might be stretched to that scale, no skills which could earn it, no property which could be sold for it.

Where could a man like Jillet of Forebridge get so much money?

Where else?

Congratulating himself on his clarity of wit, Jillet went to the usurers.

He had had no dealings with usurers heretofore. But he had heard rumors. Some such "lenders" were said to be more forgiving than others, less stringent in their demands. Well, Jillet had no need of anyone's forgiveness; but he felt a natural preference for men with amiable reputations. From the honest alchemist, he went in search of an amiable usurer.

Unfortunately, amiable, forgiving usurers had so much kindness in their natures because they could afford it; and they could afford it because their investments were scantly at risk: they demanded collateral before hazarding coin. This baffled Jillet more than a little. The concept of collateral he could understand—just—but he could not understand why the widow Huchette did not constitute collateral. He would use the money to pay the alchemist; the alchemist would give him a love potion; the potion would win the widow; and from the widow's holdings the usurer would be paid. Where was the fallacy in all this?

The usurer himself had no difficulty detecting the fallacy. More in sorrow than in scorn, he sent Jillet away.

Other "lenders" were similarly inclined. Only their pity varied, not their rejection.

Well, thought Jillet, I will never gain the widow without assistance. I must have the potion.

So he abandoned his search for an amiable usurer and committed himself, like a lost fish, to swim in murkier waters. He went to do business with the kind of moneylender who despised the world because he feared it. This moneylender feared the world because his substance was always at risk; and his substance was always at risk because he required no collateral. All he required was a fatal return on his investment.

"One fifth!" Jillet protested. The interest sounded high, even to him. "No other lender in Forebridge asks so much."

"No other lender in Forebridge," wheezed the individual whose coin was endangered, "risks so much."

True, thought Jillet, giving the man his due. And after all, one fifth was only a number. It would not amount to much, if the widow were won swiftly. "Very well," he replied calmly. "As you say, you ask no collateral. And my prospects cannot fail. One fifth in a year is not too much to pay for what I will gain, especially"—he cleared his throat in a dignified fashion, for emphasis—"since I will only need the use of your money for a fortnight at most."

"A *year?*" The usurer nearly burst a vessel. "You will return me one fifth a *week* on my risk, or you can beg coin of fools like yourself, for you will get none from me!"

One fifth in a week. Perhaps for a moment Jillet was indeed stunned. Perhaps he went so far as to reconsider the course he had chosen. One fifth in a week, each and every week— And what if the potion failed? Or if it were merely slow? He would never be able to pay that first one fifth, not to mention the second or the third—and certainly not the original sum itself. Why, it was ruinous.

But then it occurred to him that one fifth, or two fifths, or twenty would make no difference to the wealth of the widow Huchette. And he would be happy besides, basking in the knowledge of a passion virtuously satisfied.

On that comfortable assumption, he agreed to the usurer's terms.

The next day, laden with a purse containing more gold than he had ever seen in his life, Jillet of Forebridge returned to the alchemist.

By this time, the alchemist was ready for him. The essence of charlatanism was cunning, and the alchemist was nothing if not an essential charlatan. He had taken the measure of his man—as well as of his own circumstances—and had determined his response. First, of course, he counted out Jillet's gold, testing the coins with spurious powders and honest teeth. He produced a few small fires and explosions, purely for effect: like most of his ilk, he could be impressive when he wished. Then he spoke.

"Young man, you are not the first to approach me for a potion in this matter. You are merely the first"—he hefted the purse—"to place such value on your object. Therefore I must give you a magick able to supersede all others—a magick not only capable of attaining its end, but in fact of doing so against the opposition of a—number—of intervening magicks.

This is a rare and dangerous enterprise. For it to succeed, you must not only trust it entirely, but also be bold in support of it.

"Behold!"

The alchemist flourished his arms to induce more fires and explosions. When an especially noxious fume had cleared, he had in his palm a leather pouch on a thong.

"I will be plain," said the alchemist, "for it will displease me gravely if magick of such cost and purity fails because you do not do your part. This periapt must be worn about your neck, concealed under your"—he was about to say "linen," but Jillet's skin clearly had no acquaintance with finery of that kind—"jerkin. As needed, it must be invoked in the following secret yet efficacious fashion." He glared at Jillet through his eyebrows. "You must make reference to 'my kinsman, Reave the Just.' And you must be as unscrupulous as Reave the Just in pursuing your aim. You must falter at nothing."

This was the alchemist's inspiration, his cunning at work. Naturally, the pouch contained only a malodorous dirt. The magick lay in the words *my kinsman, Reave the Just*. Any man willing to make that astonishing claim could be sure of one thing: he would receive opportunities which would otherwise be impossible for him. Doors would be opened, audiences granted, attention paid anywhere in the North Counties, regardless of Jillet's apparent lineage, or his lack of linen. In that sense, the magick the alchemist offered was truer than any of his previous potions. It would open the doors of houses. And conceivably, if the widow Huchette were impressionable enough, it would open the door of her heart; for what innocent and moony young female could resist the enchantment of Reave's reputation?

So, of course, Jillet protested. Precisely because he lacked the wit to understand the alchemist's chicanery, he failed to understand its use. Staring at his benefactor, he objected, "But Reave the Just is no kinsman of mine. My family is known in Forebridge. No one will believe me."

Simpleton, thought the alchemist. *Idiot.* "They will," he replied with a barely concealed exasperation born of fear that Jillet would demand the return of his gold, "if you are bold enough, *confident* enough, in your actions. The words do not need to be true. They are simply a private incantation, a way of invoking the periapt without betraying what you do. The magick will succeed if you but *trust* it."

Still Jillet hesitated. Despite the strength which the mere idea of the widow Huchette exercised in his thinking, he had no comprehension of the power of ideas: he could not grasp what he might gain from the idea that he was related to Reave. "How can that be?" he asked the air more than the alchemist. No doubt deliberately, the alchemist had challenged his understanding of the world; and it was the world which should have answered him. Striving to articulate his doubt, he continued, "I want a love potion to change the way she looks at me. What will I gain by saying or acting a thing that is untrue?"

Perhaps this innocence explained some part of the affection Forebridge felt for him; but it did not endear him to the alchemist. "Now hear me," *clod, buffoon, half-wit,* said the alchemist. "This magick is precious, and if you do not value it I will offer it elsewhere. The object of your desire does not desire you. You wish her to desire you. Therefore something must be altered. Either she must be made to"—*stifle her natural revulsion for a clod like you*—"feel a desire she lacks. Or you must be made more desirable to her. I offer both. Properly invoked, the periapt will instill desire in her. And bold action and a reputation as Reave the Just's kinsman will make you desirable.

"What more do you require?"

Jillet was growing fuddled: he was unaccustomed to such abstract discourse. Fortunately for the alchemist's purse, however, what filled Jillet's head was not an idea but an image—the image of a usurer who demanded repayment at the rate of one fifth in a week, and who appeared capable of dining on Jillet's giblets if his demands were thwarted.

Considering his situation from the perspective not of ideas but of images, Jillet found that he could not move in any direction except forward. Behind him lurked exigencies too acute to be confronted: ahead stood the widow Huchette and passion.

"Very well," he said, making his first attempt to emulate Reave's legendary decisiveness. "Give me the pouch."

Gravely, the alchemist set the pouch in Jillet's hand.

In similar fashion, Jillet hung the thong about his neck and concealed the periapt under his jerkin.

Then he returned to Forebridge, armed with magick and cunning—and completely unshielded by any idea of what to do with his new weaponry.

The words *trust* and *bold* and *unscrupulous* rang in his mind. What did they mean? *Trust* came to him naturally; *bold* was incomprehensible; *unscrupulous* conveyed a note of dishonesty. Taken together, they seemed as queer as a hog with a chicken's head—or an amiable usurer. Jillet was altogether at sea.

In that state, he chanced to encounter one of his fellow pretenders to the widow Huchette's bed, a stout, hairy, and frequently besotted fletcher named Slup. Not many days ago, Slup had viewed Jillet as a rival, perhaps even as a foe; he had behaved toward Jillet in a surly way which had baffled Jillet's amiable nature. Since that time, however, Slup had obtained his own alchemick potion, and new confidence restored his goodwill. Hailing Jillet cheerfully, he asked where his old friend had been hiding for the past day or so.

Trust, Jillet thought. *Bold. Unscrupulous.* It was natural, was it not, that magick made no sense to ordinary men? If an ordinary man, therefore, wished to benefit from magick, he must require himself to behave in ways which made no sense.

Summoning his resolve, he replied, "Speaking with my kinsman, Reave the Just," and strode past Slup without further explanation.

He did not know it, of course, but he had done enough. With those few words, he had invoked the power, not of the periapt, but of ideas. Slup told what he had heard to others, who repeated it to still others. Within hours, discussion had ranged from one end of the village to the other. The absence of explanation—when had Jillet come upon such a relation? why had he never mentioned it before? how had *Reave the Just*, of all men, contrived to visit Forebridge without attracting notice?—far from proving a hindrance, actually enhanced the efficacy of Jillet's utterance. When he went to his favorite tavern that evening, hoping to meet with some hearty friend who would stand him a tankard of ale, he found that every man he knew had been transformed—or he himself had.

He entered the tavern in what was, for him, a state of some anxiety.

The more he had thought about it, the more he had realized that the gamble he took with Slup was one which he did not comprehend. After all, what experience had he ever had with alchemy? How could he be sure of its effectiveness? He knew about such things only by reputation, by the stories men told concerning alchemists and mages, witches and warlocks. The interval between his encounter with Slup and the evening taught him more self-doubt than did the more practical matter of his debt to the usurer. When he went to the tavern, he went half in fear that he would be greeted by a roar of laughter.

He had invoked the power of an idea, however, and part of its magick was this—that a kinship with Reave the Just was not something into which any man or woman of the world would inquire directly. No one asked of Jillet, "What sort of clap-brained tale are you telling today?" The consequences might prove dire if the tale were true. Many things were said about Reave, and some were dark: enemies filleted like fish; entire houses exterminated; laws and magistrates overthrown. No one credited Jillet's claim of kinship—and no one took the risk of challenging it.

When he entered the tavern, he was not greeted with laughter. Instead, the place became instantly still, as though Reave himself were present. All eyes turned on Jillet, some in suspicion, some in speculation—and no small number in excitement. Then someone shouted a welcome; the room filled with a hubbub which seemed unnaturally loud because of the silence that had preceded it; and Jillet was swept up by the conviviality of his friends and acquaintances.

Ale flowed ungrudgingly, although he had no coin to pay for it. His jests were met with uproarious mirth and hearty backslappings, despite the fact that he was more accustomed to appreciating humor than to venturing it. Men clustered about him to hear his opinions—and he discovered, somewhat to his own surprise, that he had an uncommon number of opinions. The faces around him grew ruddy with ale and firelight and pleasure, and he had never felt so loved.

Warmed by such unprecedented good cheer, he had reason to congratulate himself that he was able to refrain from any mention of alchemists or widows. That much good sense remained to him, at any rate.

On the other hand, he was unable to resist a few strategic references to *my kinsman, Reave the Just*—experiments regarding the potency of ideas.

Because of those references, the serving wench, a buxom and lusty girl who had always liked him and refused to sleep with him, seemed to linger at his elbow when she refreshed his tankard. Her hands made occasion to touch his arm repeatedly; again and again, she found herself jostled by the crowd so that her body pressed against his side; looking up at him, her eyes shone. To his amazement, he discovered that when he put his arm around her shoulders she did not shrug it away. Instead, she used it to move him by slow degrees out from among the men and toward the passageway which led to her quarters.

That evening was the most successful Jillet of Forebridge had ever known. In her bed and her body, he seemed to meet himself as the man he had always wished to be. And by morning, his doubts had disappeared; what passed for common sense with him had been drowned in the murky waters of magick, cunning, and necessity.

Eager despite a throbbing head and thick tongue, Jillet of Forebridge commenced his siege upon the manor house and fortune and virtue of the widow Huchette.

This he did by the straightforward, if unimaginative, expedient of approaching the gatehouse of the manor and asking to speak with her.

When he did so, however, he encountered an unexpected obstacle. Like most of the townsfolk—except, perhaps, some among his more recent acquaintance, the usurers, who had told him nothing on the subject—he was unaware of Kelven Divestulata's preemptive claim on Rudolph's widow. He had no knowledge that the Divestulata had recently made himself master of the widow Huchette's inheritance, possessions, and person. In all probability, Jillet would have found it impossible to imagine that any man could do such a thing.

Jillet of Forebridge had no experience with men like Kelven Divestulata.

For example, Jillet knew nothing which would have led him to guess that Kelven never made any attempt to woo the widow. Surely to woo was the natural action of passion? Perhaps for other men; not in Kelven's case. From the moment when he first conceived his desire to the moment when he gained the position which enabled him to satisfy it, he had spoken to the object of his affections only once.

Standing before her—entirely without gifts or graces—he had said bluntly, "Be my wife."

She had hardly dared glance at him before hiding her face. Barely audible, she had replied, "My husband is dead. I will not marry again." The truth was that she had loved Rudolph as ardently as her innocence and inexperience permitted, and she had no wish whatsoever to replace him.

However, if she had dared to look at Kelven, she would have seen his jaws clenched and a vein pulsing inexorably at his temple. "I do not brook refusal," he announced in a voice like an echo of doom. "And I do not ask twice."

Sadly, she was too innocent—or perhaps too ignorant—to fear doom. "Then," she said to him gravely, "you must be the unhappiest of men."

Thus her sole interchange with her only enemy began and ended.

Just as Jillet could not have imagined this conversation, he could never have dreamed the Divestulata's response.

In a sense, it would have been accurate to say that all Forebridge knew more of Reave the Just, who had never set foot in the town, than of Kelven Divestulata, whose ancestral home was less than an hour's ride away. Reave was a fit subject for tales and gossip on any occasion: neither wise men nor fools discussed Kelven.

So few folk—least of all Jillet—knew of the brutal and impassioned marriage of Kelven's parents, or of his father's death in an apoplectic fury, or of the acid bitterness which his mother directed at him when her chief antagonist was lost. Fewer still knew of the circumstances surrounding her harsh, untimely end. And none at all knew that Kelven himself had secretly arranged their deaths for them, not because of their treatment of him—which in fact he understood and to some extent approved—but because he saw profit for himself in being rid of them, preferably in some way which would cause them as much distress as possible.

It might have been expected that the servants and retainers of the family would know or guess the truth, and that at least one of them would say something on the subject to someone; but within a few months of his mother's demise Kelven had contrived to dispense with every member of his parents' establishment, and had replaced them with cooks and maids and grooms who knew nothing and said less. In this way, he made himself as safe from gossip as he could ever hope to be.

As a result, the few stories told of him had a certain legendary quality, as if they concerned another Divestulata who had lived long ago. In the main, these tales involved either sums of money or young women who came to his notice and then disappeared. It was known—purportedly for a fact—that a usurer or three had been driven out of Forebridge, cursing Kelven's name. And it was undeniable that the occasional young woman had vanished. Unfortunately, the world was a chancy place, especially for young women, and their fate was never clearly known. The one magistrate of Forebridge who had pursued the matter far enough to question Kelven himself had afterward been so overtaken by chagrin that he had ended his own life.

Unquestionably, Kelven's mode of existence was secure.

However, for reasons known only to himself, he desired a wife. And he was accustomed to obtain what he desired. When the widow Huchette spurned him, he was not daunted. He simply set about attaining his goal by less direct means.

He began by buying out the investments which had been made to secure the widow's future. These he did not need, so he allowed them to go to ruin. Then he purchased the widow's deceased husband's debts from the usurer who held them. They were few, but they gave him a small claim on the importing merchantry from which Rudolph Huchette's wealth derived. His claim provided him with access to the merchantry's ledgers and contacts and partners, and that knowledge enabled him to apply pressure to the sources of the merchantry's goods. In a relatively short time, as such things are measured, he became the owner of the merchantry itself.

He subsequently found it child's play to reveal—in the presence of a magistrate, of course—that Rudolph Huchette had acquired his personal fortune by despoiling the assets of the merchantry. In due course, that fortune passed to Kelven, and he became, in effect, the widow Huchette's landlord—the master of every tangible or monetary resource on which her marriage had made her dependent.

Naturally, he did not turn her out of her former home. Where could she have gone? Instead, he kept her with him and closed the doors to the manor house. If she made any protest, it was unheard through the stout walls.

Of all this, Jillet was perfectly innocent as he knocked on the door of the manor's gatehouse and requested an audience with the widow. In consequence, he was taken aback when he was admitted, not to the sitting room of the widow, but to the study of her new lord, the Divestulata.

The study itself was impressive enough to a man like Jillet. He had never before seen so much polished oak and mahogany, so much brass and fine leather. Were it not for his unprecedented successes the previous evening, his aching head, which dulled his responses, and his new warrant for audacity, he might have been cowed by the mere room. However, he recited the litany which the alchemist had given him, and the words *trust*, *bold*, and *unscrupulous* enabled him to bear the air of the place well enough to observe that Kelven himself was more impressive, not because of any greatness of stature or girth, but because of the malign and unanswerable glower with which he regarded everything in front of him. His study was ill-lit, and the red echo of candles in his eyes suggested the flames of Satan and Hell.

It was fortunate, therefore, that Kelven did not immediately turn his attention upon Jillet. Instead, he continued to peruse the document gripped in his heavy hands. This may have been a ploy intended to express his disdain for his visitor; but it gave Jillet a few moments in which to press his hand against his hidden pouch of magick, rehearse the counsel of the alchemist, and marshal his resolve.

When Kelven was done with his reading, or his ploy, he raised his grim head and demanded without preamble, "What is your business with my wife?"

At any former time, this would have stopped Jillet dead. *Wife?* The widow had already become Kelven Divestulata's *wife?* But Jillet was possessed by his magick and his incantation, and they gave him a new extravagance. It was impossible that Kelven had married the widow. Why? Because such a disappointment could not conceivably befall the man who had just earned with honest gold and courage the right to name himself the kinsman of Reave the Just. To consider the widow Huchette Kelven's wife made a mockery of both justice and alchemy.

"Sir," Jillet began. Armed with virtue and magick, he could afford to be polite. "My 'business' is with the widow. If she is truly your wife, she will tell me so herself. Permit me to say frankly, however, that I cannot understand why you would stoop to a false claim of marriage. Without the sanction of the priests, no marriage can be valid—and no sanction is possible until the banns have been published. This you have not done."

There Jillet paused to congratulate himself. The alchemist's magick was indisputably efficacious. It had already made him *bolder* than he had ever been in his life.

In fact, it made him so *bold* that he took no notice of the narrowing of Kelven's eyes, the tightening of his hands. Jillet was inured to peril. He smiled blandly as the Divestulata stood to make his reply.

"She is my wife," Kelven announced distinctly, "*because* I have claimed her. I need no other sanction."

Jillet blinked a time or two. "Do I understand you, sir? Do you call her your wife—and still admit that you have not been wed?"

Kelven studied his visitor and said nothing.

"Then this is a matter for the magistrates." In a sense, Jillet did not hear his own words. Certainly, he did not pause to consider whether they would be pleasing to the Divestulata. His attention was focused, rather, on alchemy and incantations. Enjoying his new boldness, he wondered how far he could carry it before he felt the need to make reference to his kinsman. "The sacrament of marriage exists to protect women from those who are stronger, so that they will not be bound to any man against their will." This fine assertion was not one which he had conceived for himself. It was quoted almost directly from the school lessons of the priests. "If you have not wed the widow Huchette, I can only conclude that she does not choose to wed you. In that case"—Jillet was becoming positively giddy—"you are not her husband, sir. You are her enslaver.

"You would be well advised to let me speak to her."

Having said this, Jillet bowed to Kelven, not out of courtesy, but in secret delight. The Divestulata was his only audience for his performance: like an actor who knew he had done well, he bowed to his audience. All things considered, he may still have been under the influence of the previous evening's ale.

Naturally, Kelven saw the matter in another light. Expressionless except for his habitual glower, he regarded Jillet. After a moment, he said, "You mentioned the magistrates." He did not sound like a man who had been threatened. He sounded like a man who disavowed responsibility for what came next. Having made his decision, he rang a small bell which stood on his desk. Then he continued, "You will speak to my wife."

The servant who had conducted Jillet to the Divestulata's study appeared. To the servant, Kelven said, "Inform my wife that she will receive us."

The servant bowed and departed.

Jillet had begun to glow inwardly. This was a triumph! Even such a man as Kelven Divestulata could not resist his alchemy—and he had not yet made any reference to Reave the Just. Surely his success with the widow was assured. She would succumb to his magick; Kelven would withdraw under threat of the magistrates; and all would be just as Jillet had dreamed it. Smiling happily at his host, he made no effort to resist as Kelven took him by his arm.

However, allowing Kelven to take hold of him may have been a mistake. The Divestulata's grip was hard—brutally hard—and the crush of his fingers upon Jillet's arm quickly dispelled the smile from Jillet's lips. Jillet was strong himself, having been born to a life of labor, but Kelven's strength turned him pale. Only pride and surprise enabled him to swallow his protest.

Without speaking—and without haste—Kelven steered Jillet to the chamber where he had instructed his wife to receive visitors.

Unlike Kelven's study, the widow's sitting room was brightly lit, not by lamps and candles, but by sunshine. Perhaps simply because she loved the sun, or perhaps because she wished herself to be seen plainly, she immersed herself in light. This made immediately obvious the fact that she remained clad in her widow's weeds, despite her new status as the Divestulata's *wife*. It also made obvious the drawn pallor of her face, the hollowness of her cheeks, the dark anguish under her eyes. She did nothing to conceal the way she flinched when Kelven's gaze fell upon her.

Kelven still did not release Jillet's arm. "This impudent sot," he announced to the widow as though Jillet were not present, "believes we are not wed."

The widow may have been hurt and even terrified, but she remained honest. In a small, thin voice, she said, "I am wed to Rudolph Huchette, body and life." Her hands were folded about each other in her lap. She did not lift her gaze from them. "I will never marry again."

Jillet hardly heard her. He had to grind his teeth to prevent himself from groaning at Kelven's grip.

"He believes," Kelven continued, still addressing the widow, "that the magistrates should be informed we are not wed."

That made the widow raise her head. Sunlight illuminated the spark of hope which flared in her eyes—flared, and then died when she saw Jillet clearly.

In defeat, she lowered her gaze again.

Kelven was not satisfied. "What is your answer?" he demanded.

The widow's tone made it plain that she had not yet had time to become accustomed to defeat. "I hope he will inform the magistrates," she said, "but I believe he was a fool to let you know of his intentions."

"Madam—my lady." Jillet spoke in an involuntary gasp. His triumph was gone—even his hope was gone. His arm was being crushed. "Make him let go of me."

"Paugh!" With a flick of his hand, Kelven flung Jillet to the floor. "It is offensive to be threatened by a clod like you." Then he turned to the widow. "What do you believe I should do when I am threatened in this fashion for your sake?"

Despite her own distress, Rudolph's widow was still able to pity fools. Her voice became smaller, thinner, but it remained clear. "Let him go. Let him tell as many magistrates as he wishes. Who will believe him? Who will accept the word of a laborer when it is contradicted by Kelven Divestulata? Perhaps he is too shamed to tell anyone."

"And what if he is not shamed?" Kelven retorted instantly. "What if a magistrate hears him—and believes him enough to question you? What would you say?"

The widow did not raise her eyes. She had no need to gaze upon her *husband* again. "I would say that I am the prisoner of your malice and the plaything of your lusts, and I would thank God for His mercy if He would allow me to die."

"That is why I will not let him go." Kelven sounded oddly satisfied, as though an obscure desire had been vindicated. "Perhaps instead I will put his life in your power. I wish to see you rut with him. If you do it for my amusement, I will let him live."

Jillet did not hear what answer the widow would have made to this suggestion. Perhaps he did not properly hear anything which the Divestulata and his *wife* said to each other. His shame was intense, and the pain in his arm caused his head to throb as though it might burst; and, in truth, he was too busy cursing himself for not invoking the power of alchemy sooner to give much heed to what was said over him. He was a fool, and he knew it—a fool for thinking, however briefly, that he might accomplish for himself victories which only magick could achieve.

Therefore he struggled to his feet between Kelven and the widow. Hugging his arm to his side, he panted, "This is intolerable. My kinsman, Reave the Just, will be outraged when he learns of it."

Despite their many differences, Kelven Divestulata and the widow Huchette were identical in their reactions: they both became completely still, as though they had been turned to stone by the magick of the name *Reave the Just*.

"My kinsman is not forgiving," Jillet continued, driven by shame and pain and his new awareness of the power of ideas. "All the world knows it. He has no patience for injustice or tyranny, or for the abuse of the helpless, and when he is outraged he lets nothing stand in his way." Perhaps because he was a fool, he was able to speak with perfect conviction. Any man who was not a fool would have known that he had already said too much. "You will be wiser to come with me to the magistrate yourself and confess the wrong you have done this woman. He will be kinder to you than Reave the Just."

Still united by the influence of that name, the widow and Kelven said together, "You fool. You have doomed yourself."

But she said, "Now he will surely kill you."

His words were, "Now I will surely let you live."

Hearing Kelven, Jillet was momentarily confused, misled by the impression that he had succeeded—that he had saved the widow and himself, that he had defeated the Divestulata. Then Kelven struck him down, and the misconception was lost.

When he awakened—more head-sore, bone-weak, and thirst-tormented than he had ever been in his life—he was in a chamber from which no one except Kelven himself and his own workmen had ever emerged. He had a room just like it in his ancestral home and knew its value. Shortly, therefore, after his acquisition of the manor house he had had this chamber dug into the rock beneath the foundations of the building. All Forebridge was quite ignorant of its existence. The excavated dirt and rock had been concealed by being used in other construction about the manor house—primarily in making the kennels where Kelven housed the mastiffs he bred for hunting and similar duties. And the workmen had been sent to serve the Divestulata in other enterprises in other Counties, far from Forebridge. So when Jillet awakened he was not simply in a room where no one would ever hear him scream. He was in a room where no one would ever look for him.

In any case, however, he felt too sick and piteous to scream. Kelven's blow had nearly cracked his skull, and the fetters on his wrists held his arms at an angle which nearly dislocated his shoulders. He was not surprised by the presence of light—by the single candle stuck in its tallow on a bench a few feet away. His general amazement was already too great, and his particular discomfort too acute, to allow him the luxury of surprise about the presence or absence of light.

On the bench beside the candle, hulking in the gloom like the condensed darkness of a demon, sat Kelven Divestulata.

"Ah," breathed Kelven softly, "your eyes open. You raise your head. The pain begins. Tell me about your *kinship* with Reave the Just."

Well, Jillet was a fool. Alchemy had failed him, and the power of ideas was a small thing compared to the power of Kelven's fist. To speak frankly, he had lived all his life at the mercy of events—or at the dictates of the decisions or needs or even whims of others. He was not a fit opponent for a man like the Divestulata.

Nevertheless he was loved in Forebridge for a reason. That reason went by the name of *amiability*, but it might equally well have been called *kindness* or *openheartedness*. He did not answer Kelven's question. Instead, through his own hurt, he replied, "This is wrong. She does not deserve it."

"'She'? Do you refer to my wife?" Kelven was mildly surprised. "We are not speaking of her. We are speaking of your kinsman, Reave the Just."

"She is weak and you are strong," Jillet persisted. "It is wrong to victimize her simply because she is unable to oppose you. You damn yourself by doing so. But I think you do not care about damnation." This was an unusual insight for him. "Even so, you should care that you demean yourself by using your strength against a woman who cannot oppose you."

As though Jillet had not spoken, Kelven continued, "He has a reputation for meddling in other men's affairs. In fact, his reputation for meddling is extensive. I find that I would like to put a stop to it. No doubt his reputation is only gossip, after all—but such gossip offends me. I *will* put a stop to it."

"It is no wonder that she refuses to wed you." Jillet's voice began to crack, and he required an effort to restrain tears. "The wonder is that she has not killed herself rather than suffer your touch."

"*Simpleton!*" spat Kelven, momentarily vexed. "She does not kill herself because I do not permit it." He promptly regained his composure, however. "Yet you have said one thing which is not foolish. A strong man who exerts his strength only upon the weak eventually becomes weak himself. I have decided on a more useful exercise. I will rid the world of this 'Reave the Just.'

"Tell me how you propose to involve your *kinsman* in my affairs. Perhaps I will allow you to summon him"—the Divestulata laughed harshly—"and then both you and my wife will be rescued."

There Jillet collapsed. He was weeping with helplessness and folly, and he had no understanding of the fact that Kelven intended to keep him alive when the widow Huchette had predicted that Kelven would kill him. Through a babble of tears and self-recrimination and appeals for pity, he told the Divestulata the truth.

"I am no kinsman of Reave the Just. That is impossible. I claimed kinship with him because an alchemist told me to do so. All I desired was a love potion to win the widow's heart, but he persuaded me otherwise."

At that time, Jillet was incapable of grasping that he remained alive only because Kelven did not believe him.

Because Kelven did not believe him, their conversation became increasingly arduous. Kelven demanded; Jillet denied. Kelven insisted; Jillet protested. Kelven struck; Jillet wailed. Ultimately Jillet lost consciousness, and Kelven went away.

The candle was left burning.

It was replaced by another, and by yet another, and by still others, so that Jillet was not left entirely in darkness; but he never saw the old ones gutter and die, or the new ones set. For some reason, he was always unconscious when that happened. The old stumps were not removed from the bench; he was left with some measure for his imprisonment. However, since he did not know how long the candles burned he could only conclude from the growing row of stumps that his imprisonment was long. He was fed at intervals which he could not predict. At times Kelven fed him. At times the widow fed him. At times she removed her garments and fondled his cold flesh with tears streaming from her eyes. At times he fouled himself. But only the candles provided a measure for his existence, and he could not interpret them.

How are you related to Reave?

How do you contact him?

Why does he meddle in other men's affairs?

What is the source of his power?

What *is* he?

Poor Jillet knew no answer to any of these questions.

His ignorance was the source of his torment, and the most immediate threat to his life; but it may also have saved him. It kept Kelven's attention focused upon him—and upon the perverse pleasures which he and the widow provided. In effect, it blinded Kelven to the power of ideas: Jillet's ignorance of anything remotely useful concerning Reave the Just preserved Kelven's ignorance of the fact that the townspeople of Forebridge, in their cautious and undemonstrative way, had summoned Reave in Jillet's name.

Quite honestly, most of them could not have said that they knew Reave had been summoned—or that they knew how he had been summoned. He was not a magistrate to whom public appeal could be made; not an official of the County to whom a letter could be written; not a lord of the realm from whom justice might be demanded. As far as anyone in Forebridge could have said for certain, he was not a man at all: he was only a story from places far away, a persistent legend blowing on its own queer winds across the North Counties. Can the wind be summoned? No? Then can Reave the Just?

In truth, Reave was summoned by the simple, almost nameless expedient of telling the tale. To every man or woman, herder or minstrel, merchant or soldier, mendicant or charlatan who passed through Forebridge, someone sooner or later mentioned that "Reave the Just had a kinsman here who has recently disappeared." Those folk followed their own roads away from Forebridge, and when they met with the occasion to do so they told the tale themselves; and so the tale spread.

In the end, such a summons can never be denied. Inevitably, Reave the Just heard it and came to Forebridge.

Like a breeze or a story, he appeared to come without having come *from* anywhere: one day, not so long after Jillet's disappearance, he was simply *there*, in Forebridge. Like a breeze or a story, he was not secretive about his coming: he did not lurk into town, or send in spies, or travel incognito. Still it was true that he came entirely unheralded, unannounced—and yet most folk who saw him knew immediately who he was, just as they knew immediately why he was there.

From a certain distance, of course, he was unrecognizable: his clothing was only a plain brown traveler's shirt over leather pants which had seen considerable wear and thick, dusty boots; his equally dusty hair was cropped to a convenient length; his strides were direct and self-assured, but no more so than those of other men who knew where they were going and why. In fact, the single detail which distinguished him from any number of farmers and cotters and wagoneers was that he wore no hat against the sun. Only when he drew closer did his strangeness make itself felt.

The dust showed that he had walked a long way, but he betrayed no fatigue, no hunger or thirst. His clothing had been exposed to the elements a great deal, but he carried no pack or satchel for food or spare garments or other necessities. Under the prolonged pressure of the sun, he might have developed a squint or a way of lowering his head; but his chin was up, and his eyes were open and vivid, like pieces of the deep sky. And he had no knife at his belt, no staff in his hand, no quiver over his shoulder—nothing with which to defend himself against hedgerow robbers or hungry beasts or outraged opponents. His only weapon, as far as any of the townspeople could see, was that he simply appeared *clearer* than any of his surroundings, better focused, as though he improved the vision of those who looked at him. Those who did look at him found it almost impossible to look away.

The people who first saw him closely enough to identify him were not surprised when he began asking questions about "his kinsman, Jillet of Forebridge." They were only surprised that his voice was so kind and quiet—considering his reputation for harsh decisions and extreme actions—and that he acknowledged the implausible relation which Jillet had claimed for the first time scarcely a week ago.

Unfortunately, none of the people questioned by Reave the Just had any idea what had become of Jillet.

It was characteristic of the folk of Forebridge that they avoided ostentation and public display. Reave had the effect, however, of causing them to forget their normal chariness. In consequence, he did not need to go searching for people to question: they came to him. Standing in the open road which served Forebridge as both public square and auctioneer's market, he asked his questions once, perhaps twice, then waited quietly while the slowly growing crowd around him attracted more people and his questions were repeated for him to the latecomers until a thick fellow with the strength of timber and a mind to match asked, "What's he look like, then, this Jillet?"

The descriptions provided around him were confusing at first; but under Reave's influence they gradually became clear enough to be serviceable.

"Hmm," rumbled the fellow. "Man like that visited my master t'other day."

People who knew the fellow quickly revealed that he served as a guard for one of the less hated usurers in Forebridge. They also indicated where this usurer might be found.

Reave the Just nodded once, gravely.

Smiling as though they were sure of his gratitude, and knew they had earned it, the people crowding around him began to disperse. Reave walked away among them. In a short time, he had gained admittance to the usurer's place of business and was speaking to the usurer himself.

The usurer supplied Reave with the name of the widow Huchette. After all, Jillet had offered her wealth as collateral in his attempt to obtain gold. Despite his acknowledged relation to Jillet, however, Reave was not satisfied by the information which the usurer was able to give him. Their conversation sent him searching for alchemists until he located the one he needed.

The alchemist who had conceived Jillet's stratagem against the widow did not find Reave's clarity of appearance and quietness of manner reassuring: quite the reverse. In fact, he was barely able to restrain himself from hurling smoke in Reave's face and attempting to escape through the window. In his wildest frights and fancies, he had never considered that Reave the Just himself might task him for the advice he had sold to Jillet. Nevertheless, something in the open, vivid gaze which Reave fixed upon him convinced him that he could not hope for escape. Smoke would not blind Reave; and when the alchemist dived out the window, Reave would be there ahead of him, waiting.

Mumbling like a shamed child—and inwardly cursing Reave for having this effect upon him—the alchemist revealed the nature of his transaction with Jillet. Then, in a spasm of defensive self-abnegation, attempting to deflect Reave's notorious extravagance, he produced the gold which he had received from Jillet and offered it to Jillet's "kinsman."

Reave considered the offer briefly before accepting it. His tone was quiet, but perfectly distinct, as he said, "Jillet must be held accountable for his folly. However, you do not deserve to profit from it." As soon as he left the alchemist's dwelling, he flung the coins so far across the hedgerows that the alchemist had no hope of ever recovering them.

In the secrecy of his heart, the alchemist wailed as though he had been bereft. But he permitted himself no sound, either of grief or of protest, until Reave the Just was safely out of hearing.

Alone, unannounced, and without any discernible weapons or

defenses, Reave made his way to the manor house of the deceased Rudolph Huchette.

Part of his power, of course, was that he never revealed to anyone precisely how the strange deeds for which he was known were accomplished. As far as the world, or the stories about him which filled the world, were concerned, he simply did what he did. So neither Jillet nor the widow—and certainly not Kelven Divestulata—were ever able to explain the events which took place within the manor house after Reave's arrival. Beginning with that arrival itself, they all saw the events as entirely mysterious.

The first mystery was that the mastiffs patrolling within the walls of the manor house did not bark. The Divestulata's servants were not alerted; no one demanded admittance at the gatehouse, or at any of the doors of the manor. Furthermore, the room in which Jillet was held prisoner was guarded, not merely by dogs and men and bolted doors, but by ignorance: no one in Forebridge knew that the chamber existed. Nevertheless, after Jillet's imprisonment had been measured by a dozen or perhaps fifteen thick candles, and his understanding of his circumstances had passed beyond ordinary fuddlement and pain into an awareness of doom so complete that it seemed actively desirable, he prised open his eyelids enough to see a man standing before him in the gloom, a man who was not Kelven Divestulata—a man, indeed, who was not anyone Jillet recognized.

Smiling gravely, this man lifted water to Jillet's lips. And when Jillet had drunk what he could, the man put a morsel or two of honeycomb in his mouth.

After that, the man waited for Jillet to speak.

Water and honey gave Jillet a bit of strength which he had forgotten existed. Trying harder to focus his gaze upon the strange figure smiling soberly before him, he asked. "Have you come to kill me? I thought he did such things himself. And liked them." In Jillet's mind, "he" was always the Divestulata.

The man shook his head. "I am Reave." His voice was firm despite its quietness. "I am here to learn why you have claimed kinship with me."

Under other conditions, Jillet would have found it frightening to be confronted by Reave the Just. As an amiable man himself, he trusted the amiability of others, and so he would not have broadly assumed that Reave meant him ill. Nevertheless, he was vulnerable on the point which Reave mentioned. For several reasons, Jillet was not a deceptive man: one of them was that he did not like to be *found out*—and he was always so easily *found out*. Being discovered in a dishonest act disturbed and shamed him.

At present, however, thoughts of shame and distress were too trivial to be considered. In any case, Kelven had long since bereft him of any instinct for self-concealment he may have possessed. To Reave's inquiry, he replied as well as his sense of doom allowed, "I wanted the widow."

"For her wealth?" Reave asked.

Jillet shook his head. "Wealth seems pleasant, but I do not understand it." Certainly, wealth did not appear to have given either the widow or Kelven any particular satisfaction. "I wanted her."

"Why?"

This question was harder. Jillet might have mentioned her beauty, her youth, her foreignness; he might have mentioned her tragedy. But Reave's clear gaze made those answers inadequate. Finally, Jillet replied, "It would mean something. To be loved by her."

Reave nodded. "You wanted to be loved by a woman whose love was valuable." Then he asked, "Why did you think her love could be gained by alchemy? Love worth having does not deserve to be tricked. And she would never truly love you if you obtained her love falsely."

Jillet considered this question easy. Many candles ago—almost from the beginning—the pain in his arms had given him the feeling that his chest had been torn open, exposing everything. He said, "She would not love me. She would not notice me. I do not know the trick of getting women to give me their love."

"The 'trick,'" Reave mused. "That is inadequate, Jillet. You must be honest with me."

Honey or desperation gave Jillet a moment of strength. "I have been honest since he put me in this place. I think it must be Hell, and I am already dead. How else is it possible for you to be here? You are no kinsman of mine, Reave the Just. Some men are like the widow. Their love is worth having. I do not understand it, but I can see that women notice such men. They give themselves to such men.

"I am not among them. I have nothing to offer that any woman would want. I must gain love by alchemy. If magick does not win it for me, I will never know love at all."

Reave raised fresh water to Jillet's lips. He set new morsels of honeycomb in Jillet's mouth.

Then he turned away.

From the door of the chamber, he said, "In one thing, you are wrong, Jillet of Forebridge. You and I are kinsmen. All men are of common blood, and I am bound to any man who claims me willingly." As he left, he added, "You are imprisoned here by your own folly. You must rescue yourself."

Behind him, the door closed, and he was gone.

The door was stout, and the chamber had been dug deep: no one heard Jillet's wail of abandonment.

Certainly the widow did not hear it. In truth, she was not inclined to listen for such things. They gave her nightmares—and her life was already nightmare enough. When Reave found her, she was in her bedchamber, huddled upon the bed, sobbing uselessly. About her shoulders she wore the tatters of her nightdress, and her lips and breasts were red with the pressure of Kelven's admiration.

"Madam," said Reave courteously. He appeared to regard her nakedness in the same way he had regarded Jillet's torment. "You are the widow Huchette?"

She stared at him, too numb with horror to speak. In strict honesty, however, her horror had nothing to do with him. It was a natural consequence of the Divestulata's lovemaking. Now that he was done with her, he had perhaps sent one of his grooms or servingmen or business associates to enjoy her similarly.

"You have nothing to fear from me," her visitor informed her in a kindly tone. "I am Reave. Men call me 'Reave the Just.'"

The widow was young, foreign, and ignorant of the world; but none of those hindrances had sufficed to block her from hearing the stories which surrounded him. He was the chief legend of the North Counties: he had been discussed in her presence ever since Rudolph had brought her to Forebridge. On that basis, she had understood the danger of Jillet's claim when she had first met him; and on that same basis she now uttered a small gasp of surprise. Then she became instantly wild with hope. Before he could speak again, she began to sob, "Oh, sir, bless Heaven that you have come! You must help me, you must! My life is anguish, and I can bear no more! He rapes me and rapes me, he forces me to do the most vile things at his whim, we are not wed, do not believe him if he says that we are wed, my husband is dead, and I desire no other, oh, sir! you must help me!"

"I will consider that, madam," Reave responded as though he were unmoved. "You must consider, however, that there are many kinds of help. Why have you not helped yourself?"

Opening her mouth to pour out a torrent of protest, the widow stopped suddenly, and a deathly pallor blanched her face. "Help myself?" she whispered. "Help myself?"

Reave fixed his clear gaze upon her and waited.

"Are you mad?" she asked, still whispering.

"Perhaps." He shrugged. "But I have not been raped by Kelven Divestulata. I do not beg succor. Why have you not helped yourself?"

"Because I am a woman!" she protested, not in scorn, but piteously. "I am helpless. I have no strength of arm, no skill with weapons, no knowledge of the world, no friends. He has made himself master of everything which might once have aided me. It would be a simpler matter for me to tear apart these walls than to defend myself against him."

Again, Reave shrugged. "Still he is a rapist—and likely a murderer. And I see that you are not bruised. Madam, why do you not resist him? Why do you not cut his throat while he sleeps? Why do you not cut your own, if his touch is so loathsome to you?"

The look of horror which she now turned on him was unquestionably personal, caused by his questions, but he was not deterred by it. Instead, he took a step closer to her.

"I offend you, madam. But I am Reave the Just, and I do not regard who is offended. I will search you further." His eyes replied to her horror with a flame which she had not seen in them before, a burning of clear rage. "Why have you done nothing to help Jillet? He came to you in innocence and ignorance as great as your own. His torment is as terrible as yours. Yet you crouch there on your soft bed and beg for rescue from an oppressor you do not oppose, and you care nothing what becomes of him."

The widow may have feared that he would step closer to her still and strike her, but he did not. Instead, he turned away.

At the door, he paused to remark, "As I have said, there are many kinds of help. Which do you merit, madam?"

He departed her bedchamber as silently as he had entered it, leaving her alone.

The time now was near the end of the day, and still neither Kelven himself nor his dogs nor his servingmen knew that Reave the Just moved freely though the manor house. They had no reason to know, for he approached no one, addressed no one, was seen by no one. Instead, he waited until night came and grew deep over Forebridge, until grooms and breeders, cooks and scullions, servingmen and secretaries had retired to their quarters, until only the hungry mastiffs were awake within the walls because the guards who should have tended them had lost interest in their duties. He waited until Kelven, alone in his study, had finished readying his plans to ruin an ally who had aided him loyally during a recent trading war, and had poured himself a glass of fine brandy so that he would have something to drink while he amused himself with Jillet. Only then did Reave approach the Divestulata's desk in order to study him through the dim light of the lamps.

Kelven was not easily taken aback, but Reave's unexpected appearance came as a shock. "Satan's balls!" he growled shamelessly. "Who in hell are *you*?"

His visitor replied with a smile which was not at all kindly. "I am grieved," he admitted, "that you did not believe I would come. I am not as well known as I had thought—or men such as you do not sufficiently credit my reputation. I am Reave the Just."

If Reave anticipated shock, distress, or alarm in response to this announcement, he was disappointed. Kelven took a moment to consider the situation, as though to assure himself that he had heard rightly. Then he leaned back in his chair and laughed like one of his mastiffs.

"So he spoke the truth. What an amazing thing. But you are slow,

Reave the Just. That purported kinsman of yours has been dead for days. I doubt that you will ever find his grave."

"In point of fact," Reave replied in an undisturbed voice, "we are not kinsmen. I came to Forebridge to discover why a man of no relation would claim me as he did. Is he truly dead? Then I will not learn the truth from him. That"—in the lamplight, Reave's eyes glittered like chips of mica—"will displease me greatly, Kelven Divestulata."

Before Kelven could respond, Reave asked, "How did he die?"

"How?" Kelven mulled the question. "As most men do. He came to the end of himself." The muscles of his jaw bunched. "You will encounter the same fate yourself—eventually. Indeed, I find it difficult to imagine why you have not done so already. Your precious reputation"—he pursed his lips—"is old enough for death."

Reave ignored this remark. "You are disingenuous, Kelven. My question was less philosophical. How did Jillet die? Did you kill him?"

"I? Never!" Kelven's protest was sincere. "I believe he brought it upon himself. He is a fool, and he died of a broken heart."

"Pining, no doubt," Reave offered by way of explanation, "for the widow Huchette—"

A flicker of uncertainty crossed Kelven's gaze. "No doubt."

"—whom you pretend to have married, but who is in fact your prisoner and your victim in her own house."

"She is my *wife!*" Kelven snapped before he could stop himself. "I have claimed her. I do not need public approval, or the petty sanctions of the law, for my desires. I have claimed her, and she is *mine.*"

The lines of Reave's mouth, and the tightening about his eyes, suggested a variety of retorts, which he did not utter. Instead, he replied mildly, "I observe that you find no fault with my assertion that this house is hers."

Kelven spat. "Paugh! Do they call you 'Reave the Just' because you are honest, or because you are 'just a fool'? This house was awarded to me publicly, by a *magistrate,* in compensation for harm done to my interests by that dead thief, Rudolph Huchette."

The Divestulata's intentions against Reave, which he had announced to Jillet, grew clearer with every passing moment. For some years now, upon occasions during the darkest hours of the night, and in the deepest privacy of his heart, he had considered himself to be the natural antagonist of men like Reave—self-righteous meddlers whose notions of virtue cost themselves nothing and their foes everything. In part, this perception of himself arose from his own native and organic malice; in part, it sprang from his awareness that most of his victories over lesser men—men such as Jillet—were too easy, that for his own well-being he required greater challenges.

Nevertheless, this conversation with his natural antagonist was not what he would have wished it to be. His plans did not include any defense of himself: he meant to attack. Seeking to capture the initiative, he countered, "However, my ownership of this house—like my ownership of Rudolph's relict—is not your concern. If you have any legitimate concern here, it involves Jillet, not me. By what honest right do you sneak into my house and my study at this hour of the night in order to insult me with questions and innuendos?"

Reave permitted himself a rather ominous smile. As though he were ignoring what Kelven had just asked, he replied, "My epithet, 'the Just,' derives from coinage. It concerns both the measure and the refinement of gold. When a coin contains the exact weight and purity of gold which it should contain, it is said to be 'just.' You may not be aware, Kelven Divestulata, that the honesty of any man is revealed by the coin with which he pays his debts."

"*Debts?*" Involuntarily, Kelven sprang to his feet. He could not contain his anger sitting. "Are you here to annoy me with *debts?*"

"Did you not kill Jillet?" Reave countered.

"I did *not!* I have done many things to many men, but I did not kill that insufferable clod! *You,*" he shouted so that Reave would not stop him, "have insulted me enough. Now you will tell me why you are here—how you *justify* your actions—or I will hurl you to the ground outside my window and let my dogs feed on you, and *no one* will dare criticize me for doing so to an intruder in my study in the dead of night!"

"You do not need to attack me with threats." Reave's self-assurance was maddening. "Honest men have nothing to fear from me, and you are threat enough just as you stand. I will tell you why I am here.

"I am Reave the Just. I have come as I have always come, for blood—the blood of kinship and retribution. Blood is the coin in which I pay my debts, and it is the coin in which I exact restitution.

"I have come for your blood, Kelven Divestulata."

The certainty of Reave's manner inspired in Kelven an emotion he did not recognize—and because he did not recognize it, it made him wild. *"For what?"* he raged at his visitor. "What have I done? Why do you want my blood? I tell you, *I did not kill your damnable Jillet!"*

"Can you prove that?"

"Yes!"

"How?"

Shaken by the fear he did not recognize, Kelven shouted, "He is still alive!"

Reave's eyes no longer reflected the lamplight. They were dark now, as deep as wells. Quietly, he asked, "What *have* you done to him?"

Kelven was confused. One part of him felt that he had gained a victory. Another knew that he was being defeated. "He amuses me," the Divestulata answered harshly. "I have made him a toy. As long as he continues to amuse me, I will continue to play with him."

When he heard those words, Reave stepped back from the desk. In a voice as implacable as a sentence of death, he said, "You have confessed to the unlawful imprisonment and torture of an innocent man. I will go now and summon a magistrate. You will repeat your confession to him. Perhaps that act of honesty will inspire you to confess as well the crimes you have committed upon the person of the widow Huchette.

"Do not attempt to escape, Kelven Divestulata. I will hunt you from the vault of Heaven to the pit of Hell, if I must. You have spent blood, and you will pay for it with blood."

For a moment longer, Reave the Just searched Kelven with his bottomless gaze. Then he turned and strode toward the door.

An inarticulate howl rose in Kelven's throat. He snatched up the first heavy object he could find, a brass paperweight thick enough to crush a man's skull, and hurled it at Reave.

It struck Reave at the base of his neck so hard that he stumbled to his knees.

At once, Kelven flung himself past his desk and attacked his visitor. Catching one fist in Reave's hair, he jerked Reave upright: with the other, he gave Reave a blow which might have killed any lesser man.

Blood burst from Reave's mouth. He staggered away on legs that appeared spongy, too weak to hold him. His arms dangled at his sides as though he had no muscle or sinew with which to defend himself.

Transported by triumph and rage and stark terror, the Divestulata pursued his attack.

Blow after blow he rained upon Reave's head: blow after blow he drove into Reave's body. Pinned against one of the great bookcases which Rudolph Huchette had lovingly provided for the study, Reave flopped and lurched whenever he was struck, but he could not escape. He did not fight back; he made no effort to ward Kelven away. In moments, his face became a bleeding mass; his ribs cracked; his heart must surely have faltered.

But he did not fall.

The utter darkness in his eyes never wavered. It held Kelven and compromised nothing.

In the end, Reave's undamaged and undaunted gaze seemed to drive Kelven past rage into madness. Immersed in ecstasy or delirium, he did not hear the door of the study slam open.

His victims were beyond stealth. In truth, neither the widow Huchette nor Jillet could have opened the door quietly. They lacked the strength. Every measure of will and force she possessed, she used to support him, to bear him forward when he clearly could not move or stand on his own. And every bit of resolve and desire that remained to him, he used to hold aloft the decorative halberd which was the only weapon he and the widow had been able to find in the halls of the manor house.

As weak as cripples, nearly dying from the strain of their exertions, they crossed the study behind Kelven's back.

They were slow, desperate, and unsteady in their approach. Nevertheless, Reave stood patiently and let his antagonist hammer him until Jillet brought the halberd down upon Kelven Divestulata's skull and killed him.

Then through the blood which drenched his face from a dozen wounds, Reave the Just smiled.

Unceremoniously, both Jillet and the widow collapsed.

Reave stooped and pulled a handkerchief from Kelven's sleeve. Dabbing at his face, he went to the desk, where he found Kelven's glass and the decanter of brandy. When he had discovered another glass, he filled it as well; then he carried the glasses to the man and woman who had rescued him. First one and then the other, he raised their heads and helped them to drink until they were able to sit and clutch the glasses and swallow without his support.

After that, he located a bellpull and rang for the Divestulata's steward.

When the man arrived—flustered by the late summons, and astonished by the scene in the study—Reave announced, "I am Reave the Just. Before his death, Kelven Divestulata confessed his crimes to me, in particular that he obtained possession of this house by false means, that he exercised his lusts in violent and unlawful fashion upon the person of the widow Huchette, and that he imprisoned and tortured my kinsman, Jillet of Forebridge, without cause. I will state before the magistrates that I heard the Divestulata's confession, and that he was slain in my aid, while he was attempting to kill me. From this moment, the widow is once again mistress of her house, with all its possessions and retainers. If you and all those under you do not serve her honorably, you will answer both to the magistrates and to me.

"Do you understand me?"

The steward understood. Kelven's servants were silent and crafty men, and perhaps some of them were despicable; but none were stupid. When Reave left the widow and Jillet there in the study, they were safe.

They never saw him again.

As he had promised, he spoke to the magistrates. When they arrived at the manor house shortly after dawn, supported by a platoon of County pikemen and any number of writs, they confirmed that they had received Reave's testimony. Their subsequent researches into Kelven's ledgers enabled them to validate much of what Reave had said; Jillet and the widow confirmed the rest. But Reave himself did not appear again in Forebridge. Like the story that brought him, he was gone. A new story took his place.

This also was entirely characteristic.

Once the researches and hearings of the magistrates were done, the widow Huchette passed out of Jillet's life as well. She had released him from his bonds and the chamber where he was imprisoned; she had half carried him to the one clear deed he had ever performed. But after Rudolph Huchette she had never wanted another husband; and after Kelven Divestulata she never wanted another man. She did one thing to express her gratitude toward Jillet: she repaid his debt to the usurer. Then she closed her doors to him, just as she did to all other men with love potions and aspirations for her. In time, the manor house became a kind of nunnery, where lost or damaged women could go for succor, and no one else was welcome.

Jillet himself, who probably believed that he would love the widow Huchette to the end of his days, found he did not miss her. Nor, in all candor, did he miss Reave. After all, he had nothing in common with them: she was too wealthy; he was too stringent. No, Jillet was quite content without such things. And he had gained something which he prized more highly—the story; the idea.

The story that he had struck the blow which brought down Kelven Divestulata.

The idea that he was kinsman to Reave the Just.

The Djinn
Who Watches Over
the Accursed

Fetim of the al-Hetal made a serious mistake when he allowed himself to be caught in the bed of Selmet Abulbul's youngest and most delectable wife. The mistake was not instantly obvious, however. Selmet was old and infirm: there was nothing physical he could do to Fetim, who was at least as strong as he was handsome. Furthermore, Selmet was unpopular, being a usurer: he had no friends he could call on to fight for him. Public opinion, in fact, would have applauded Fetim's choice of cuckolds. And, sadly, the Abulbul clan was in decline. Selmet had no relations or children who might be persuaded to view Fetim's action as a matter of honor. In short, he did not appear to be a man who could avenge insults.

But Selmet Abulbul the usurer knew how to curse.

While Fetim preened himself beside the bed, lacking even sufficient decency to be frightened, and the young wife pretended to cower among the sheets, Selmet called upon a few names which I am not permitted to record. He uttered several phrases which it would be sacrilege for me to repeat. Then, his voice quaking with rage, he explained what he wished the powers whose attention he had invoked to do to Fetim of the al-Hetal.

"In the name of the great father of djinn, let all those he loves be killed. Let him be readily loved—and let all those who love him die in anguish. Let all his seed and all his blood be brought to ruin. Let horror cover the heads of all who befriend him. Let his friendship be a surer sign of death than any plague-spot.

"And let the djinn who watches over the accursed protect him, so that his sufferings cannot end."

From such a curse, Selmet's youngest wife was safe: she loved no one but herself. But the clan of the al-Hetal was prosperous in that town. Hearing his doom, Fetim should have found it in his heart to be frightened.

He did not. "Are you done?" he asked politely. "We are taught that it is rude to leave a room while our elders are speaking."

Selmet's youngest wife also did not understand curses. A snicker at her husband's expense escaped from the sheets.

"Go!" Selmet shouted as well as he was able. "From this day forward, you will never forget that you would be happier dead."

Bowing with sardonic grace, Fetim left the house of Selmet Abulbul. Although his sport with the woman had been interrupted, his spirits were gay. It was gratifying that others knew of his successes. And the vengeance which Selmet might take upon his youngest wife was amusing to contemplate. In such benign good humor, Fetim turned his steps toward the high mansion where he lived with his mother, who thought him flawless, his father, who doted upon him, and his brothers, who worked harder than he did.

To his vast astonishment, he saw over the intervening rooftops that the mansion was in flames.

Fetim of the al-Hetal was not a notably selfless young man. Nevertheless, he had a warm place in his heart for anyone who loved him as much as he loved himself. In a frenzy which resembled concern for his parents and family—and which did indeed include some concern among its other considerations—he tore his hair and ran to see what was happening to his home.

Turmoil gripped the neighborhood. Men, women, and children raced in all directions, wailing. For some reason, the thought of water did not enter their heads, despite the fact that a history of fire had taught the town to respond promptly and efficiently. No one fought the blaze which tore at the walls and flailed from the windows of the fine mansion.

The destruction of Fetim's house was not a pleasant sight; but it was more pleasant than some of its details. He heard his mother scream and saw her in flames on the rooftop. Two of his nephews fell like stones to the street when one of the brothers' wives in desperation threw them out a window. A favorite servant who had cared for Fetim and taught him a great deal of fun as a boy died trying to descend the outer wall.

"Where is the fire brigade?" roared Fetim. But no one answered him. Everyone in the street was too busy running and yelling.

Then Akbar of the al-Hetal, Fetim's father, appeared before him. Akbar's clothes were still afire, and his eyes were mad. Inspired by the curse, he cried, "This is your doing!"

Fetim was so surprised that he did not defend himself when his father swung a cudgel at his head.

I deflected the blow, and he was no more than stunned. He recovered his wits in time to see Akbar die in front of him.

On this signal, the neighborhood commenced shouting:

"There he is!"

"He started the fire!"

"He killed his own family!"

"Stone him!"

Stones began to fly. None of them struck him seriously—although I was confident that he would not soon forget the bruises they left on his body—but they were enough to make him flee.

Led only by a desire to get away from the stones, he left the neighborhood and soon found himself at the gates of the town with a howling mob on his heels. The gates were open, as was customary on occasions of fire, in case the flames spread. The mob needed only a moment to drive Fetim out of the town where he had lived all his life—out onto the bare road which led into the desert.

There it became clear to me that he would not be able to run much farther. His life of self-indulgence had not prepared him for these exertions. And the mob would surely tear him limb from limb when he faltered. Therefore I caused his pursuers to lose sight of him. Shortly, they retraced their steps and set to work quelling the fire.

In the aftermath of the blaze, the neighborhood discovered that the damage had been confined to the clan of the al-Hetal, its dependents and friends. But of that sizable group of people, Fetim was the only survivor.

Because he did not know what else to do, he continued trudging along the road until nightfall. Then he threw himself down in order to bemoan his lot.

"It is unjust," he protested. "I am blameless. Any man would have accepted the invitation that woman gave me. Am I to be punished because she gave the invitation to me rather than to another? Selmet should not have married that heartless trollop. Yet his folly is inflicted upon me."

"Has there ever been a man as unfortunate as I am?"

"Actually," I replied, "it seems to me your family and friends are considerably more unfortunate." I spoke thus to provoke him. "You're merely accursed. They're all dead."

Apparently, he had believed himself alone. He gaped foolishly about him, as though I might be visible. "Who are you?" he asked.

"Think about it. You'll figure it out."

Who I was did not yet interest him, however. "You are wrong," he said. "Their deaths were painful, perhaps, but swift. And I will be blamed for it, although I am blameless. Also, they are free from misery. I must die slowly, alone and lost. I have neither food nor water. I have no camel. I know not where to go. I am entirely pitiable, and my sorrows are greater than any man has ever suffered."

"If you keep talking like that," I said, "I'm going to get bored in a real hurry."

"You cannot fault me! It was not I who pronounced the curse. It was Selmet Abulbul, punishing me for his own errors."

"'His own errors,' indeed. Do you want me to believe he forced you into his wife's bed against your will?"

"She invited me!"

"You accepted."

"It is not my fault!"

"So you keep saying."

Pretending to ignore me, Fetim of the now-defunct al-Hetal wept for a while to prove how miserable he was. Then, instead of dying, he slept.

The next day, he continued down the road. After all, he was young and handsome. Surely the world loved him too well to prolong his travail. And, in fact, this seemed to be true. Before midmorning, an entire caravan caught up with him. By that time, he was dirty and tired, and in no good humor; but the caravan master chanced to like handsome young men with a thick sweat on them, and he offered Fetim a ride to the city of Niswan.

If Fetim had bothered to think about his circumstances, he might have believed that I had arranged this fortuitous offer for him. He would have been mistaken, however.

He did not find the caravan master's attentions especially pleasant, but he endured them. On the one hand, he preferred women personally. On the other, he could not be surprised by the fact that he had been found attractive. And he had no money—as well as no taste for work. How else was he to travel in comfort? It was only a journey of some few days to Niswan, he had been assured. Then the unpleasantness would be over, and he would have the whole city before him in which to make his fortune. The prospect excited him boyishly.

Unfortunately, some few days were all the caravan master required to conceive intentions of his own concerning Fetim. His name, when he chose to use it, was Rashid, and a number of years had passed since he had last shared a bed with a young man whom he considered as succulent as Fetim. Being neither shortsighted nor weak-minded, he grew jealous well in advance of Fetim's opportunities to merit such a reaction. First he began to plot ways to keep the young man with him when Niswan was reached. Then he began to consider how he might keep other men away.

The outcome was that, after the caravan had wound its dusty way past the gates and the guards of Niswan deep into the city's teeming bazaar, and the camels were at last stopped for unloading and profit, Rashid knocked Fetim on the head and sequestered him.

At first, this was a highly successful arrangement from Rashid's point of view—less so from Fetim's. The caravan master now had at his whim a handsome young man made even more tasty by the occasional savors of truculent resistance and abject beggary. Nevertheless, Fetim's sequestration was not long. The multitudes who thronged the bazaar naturally included many men and women of dubious virtue, individuals who reflexively coveted anything which anyone else kept hidden. One night, Rashid leaped out of bed and grabbed at his knives too late to prevent himself from being gutted like an ox in an abattoir. A remarkable amount of blood splashed onto Fetim. Then he was dragged away.

Before dawn, he found himself sold into slavery as a desirable—if temporarily blood-sotted and noxious—catamite.

His purchasers tolerated no resistance. In any case, he had little to offer, being accustomed to seek his own pleasure rather than willingly to undergo pain. Therefore he submitted. It seemed conceivable that with the right degree of complaisance and cunning his life could still be quite pleasurable. Perhaps freedom was not too high a price to pay for homage to his desirability. A few baths, a few perfumes, a few hints, and he was set to work at love in a luxurious stable of young men resembling himself.

The resemblance was only superficial, of course: the other young men had not been cursed by such a proficient as Selmet Abulbul. Rich merchants, minor sheiks, and occasional grande dames discovered in Fetim an attractiveness which plucked at their hearts. They were less aware of the fact that after a night or two with Fetim they were prone to die horribly.

For some time, this caused him no difficulty. He was more conscious that as an object of lust he found lust to be less and less interesting. He was constrained to humble himself: the practices which brought him love took on the flavor of degradation. This, he thought, was the true meaning of the old usurer's curse.

He was mistaken, however. In the same irrational way that Akbar of the al-Hetal had pronounced his son responsible for the ruin of the clan, the family, friends, supporters, and adherents of Fetim's butchered patrons concluded that the stable which owned him was to blame for the deaths. One night when he was especially miserable, a throng of sheiks, swordsmen, and rabble burst into the richly appointed establishment and began slaughtering everyone present.

This was naturally not an action which the owners of the stable could permit to pass unchallenged. In the bazaars of Niswan, no man or woman dared make a shekel's profit without guarding it in some way. At once, forces which had been retained for precisely this sort of emergency were called out. The conflict quickly escalated, and in a short time the gauze-curtained cubicle where Fetim had pleased his patrons became the effective center of a fervid and bloody battle.

Maimed and dying boys and women and bystanders screamed. And Fetim screamed as well, although he was unhurt. He knew almost nothing about defending himself. In any case, he was unarmed. I was forced to work quickly to keep him from being cut apart at any moment.

When I opened a corridor for him through the bloodshed, he found his legs and ran.

As he did so, both sides of the battle turned their enmity in his direction and followed.

By this time, the entire city had been roused. The King's forces marched to suppress the conflict—and joined Fetim's pursuit. Brigands and looters sought to take advantage of the chaos—and found themselves chasing a young man they had never seen. In self-defense, good men and respectable families armed their servants—who immediately snatched up torches and plunged into the tumult.

The great father of djinn himself must have been listening when Selmet Abulbul had cursed Fetim of the al-Hetal. I was hard-pressed to keep my charge alive.

I accomplished it by driving him into the sewer, which an enlightened king of a previous generation had caused to be dug under the length of the city.

The stench and density of Niswan's effluvium eventually proved to be stronger than the curse. While I dragged Fetim through the sewage—keeping his head above the surface largely without his assistance—his pursuers one by one lost interest in what they were doing and retreated. Before we passed under the wall and emerged into the fetid swamp which Niswan used as a cesspit, we had left behind everyone who wanted him dead.

Unceremoniously, I dredged him from the far end of the swamp. Then, because he still did not wish to make an effort on his own behalf, I let him fall to the dirt.

Once again, he sobbed like a girl. This time, however, his emotion was composed of revulsion and fear: his grief was for himself. After a while, he raised his head and said, "They deserved what happened to them. I wish I could have stayed to watch them die."

"Deserved it?" I asked. "What makes you say that?"

He blinked his eyes stupidly for a moment. "You are the djinn who watches over the accursed."

"Good for you. I knew you would figure it out eventually."

"I wish that you had rescued me sooner."

I ignored this inane remark. "Now that you know who I am, why don't you explain how all those dead and damaged people back there came to deserve what happened to them?"

"They enslaved me. They forced the most disgusting acts upon me. They took advantage of my loneliness and my helplessness to sate their foul lusts. Do not accuse *me*, djinn. I know my innocence."

"Good for you again. How did you resist them?"

"How could I resist them? They were many and strong. I am alone and weak."

"It's easy," I insisted. "You just say no. Then you keep saying no until they give up."

"Easy!" He snorted derision.

"All right, for you it wouldn't have been easy. You're too weak and helpless. What about Rashid?"

"Rashid?" Fetim had already forgotten the caravan master.

"Did you tell him you didn't want to be his catamite? Did you offer to work for your ride to Niswan? You did not. You saw that gleam in his eyes, and you thought, 'Here is another who will do all I wish and ask nothing because I am adorable in his sight.' He would have treated you honestly if you had done anything to deserve honesty from him. And then all those poor people in Niswan would still be alive."

"Go away," he replied, cutting to the heart of the matter. "Go away and let me die. Then you will have no more cause to reproach me."

He did indeed appear pitiable as he huddled upon the verge of the swamp. Though I knew it to be a false kindness, I granted him silence.

In fact, he could have died. He was ignorant of any roads—and little able to care for himself. After a long and rancid night, he took to his feet with the dawn and walked out into the desert as though intending to exhaust himself and thereby hasten the end of his sufferings. Soon he was thirsty. And soon thereafter he was hungry. He had come away from Niswan without sandals, and the pressure of the sand began to wear sores on his feet. The sun blistered him. His needs took on the strength of rage. They expanded until they filled the horizons. Under the weight of the desert sun, his misery increased until it became as great as his self-pity. Then he collapsed into the sand.

Nevertheless a great journey lay ahead of him, which he must not shirk. It was not my task to make him comfortable. I did not permit his thirst to kill him, however. I kept his hunger within limits his flesh could bear. I did not allow the sores on his feet to become infected enough to threaten his life. And when he lay himself down with the avowed intention of not rising again, I reached into his mind and found enough fears to goad him back to his feet.

Gradually, his physical distress ground his self-pity and his revulsion and even his pride away: he had no strength for them. He had only his pain, his fear of death, and me.

After a number of days which he could not have counted—and which I had no interest in counting for him—he came to the River Kalabras. Falling on his face among the reeds at the riverbank, he drank enough of the muddy water to ensure himself a fever.

While he drank, I observed a large felucca riding the current nearby. Confident that he would be rescued, I permitted him to lose consciousness.

The craft, called *Horizon's Daughter* by its master, proved to be a vessel of commerce which plied the River Kalabras, carrying trade and passengers wherever they wished to go. As soon as the felucca's master, Mohan Gopal, saw Fetim fall among the reeds, he put about, anchored *Horizon's Daughter* against the current, and commanded two of his men into the river to bring Fetim aboard.

By this time, Fetim's condition would have aroused pity in a heart of stone. Far from having a heart of stone, however, Mohan Gopal was a man of such kindness that he would willingly have accepted a diminution of his profits in exchange for an opportunity to do a good deed. And on this voyage he was accompanied by his only child, Saliandra, a woman whose instincts of compassion exceeded his own. When Fetim had been dragged from the Kalabras, Mohan and Saliandra were so struck by his tattered garments and mangled feet, his emaciation and his look of madness, that they at once vacated their cabin under the felucca's stern for his use and devoted all the resources of *Horizon's Daughter* to his care.

As it chanced, Saliandra was not a beautiful woman. For that reason—and because her father loved her extremely—she was unwed. On the other hand, she was not ill-favored. Though her features were plain, her form was comely. When Fetim first opened his eyes and turned on Saliandra a gaze bright with illness, he believed that he had at last been lifted out of perdition into the realm of the houris.

"Be at rest," she cautioned him gently. "You are among friends."

Prostrate and feverish, he replied, "You are the only friend I will ever desire."

Had I been mortal, I would have gnashed my teeth and torn my hair.

Unable to do otherwise, however, I watched as *Horizon's Daughter* slid down the River Kalabras, and Saliandra tended the young man's broken health, and Mohan Gopal and his men made Fetim of the lost al-Hetal welcome among them as though he were an honored comrade.

The felucca was on its way downriver to great Qatiis, the storied and corrupt city of the Padisha, bearing a nearly priceless cargo of saffron—a cargo which had been entrusted to Mohan Gopal rather than to a flotilla of defencers by reason of his honesty, and also in hopes that *Horizon's Daughter* would not attract the notice of the river pirates.

Of this Fetim knew nothing, of course. To do him justice, it must be admitted that he had never felt an unreasonable interest in wealth. And now he was simply an invalid, scarcely able to hold his head up unassisted—deaf and blind to other considerations. His experiences in Niswan had taught him a deferential manner; his days in the desert had taught him gratitude. These qualities made him a satisfying invalid for whom to care. By the time he became able to sit up on his pallet and sip a bit of soup, he was so well regarded aboard the felucca that Mohan Gopal had begun to consider offering him a share of the cargo's profits to help set him on his feet when *Horizon's Daughter* reached Qatiis.

The master's regard was reciprocated. The comradely feelings of the crew were shared—a bit shyly, perhaps, but not insincerely. And Salian-dra's attentive concern was welcomed. To all appearances, Fetim was not the man he had been.

Now he noticed that Saliandra was not indeed a houri. Recovering enough strength to stand on his legs and converse, he also recovered enough clarity of vision to perceive that she was plain. But, oddly, this did not disconcert him. For the first time in his life, he considered that a woman's virtues might be of more importance than her face. And he was flattered by the fact that she was unmistakably smitten with him. Because of her great kindness, she thought highly of all things that needed her. Addition-ally, his sufferings had given his handsomeness a pensive and poetic cast, which she found impossible to resist. She would willingly have laid down her life for him. This was not lust; it was love. It was not surprising that she soon went to his bed. The surprise lay in the tenderness with which he accepted the sweets of her body.

Yet even that was not as surprising as his approach to Mohan Gopal the next morning, asking for permission to wed Saliandra.

The felucca's master considered that his daughter's acquaintance with Fetim was too brief to support a decision of marriage. And he went farther: he ousted Fetim from the cabin, so that he and Saliandra could resume their normal sleeping arrangements—in other words, so that Saliandra's nights would be properly chaperoned. Nevertheless, he did these things with such obvious benevolence, with such a distinct intention to relent in a reasonable time, that his decrees caused no offense. Having once slept with Fetim, Saliandra was secretly amused by her father's unnecessary protectiveness. And Fetim only looked on his prospective father-in-law with more respect.

My task was unchanged, however, and I prepared myself for battle.

When it came, the attack of the pirates was perplexing. On the one hand, it appeared to be founded on general principles, rather than on any specific awareness of *Horizon's Daughter*'s cargo. On the other, it lacked the usual ferocity of the curse. Indeed, it was beaten off with relative ease. Fetim himself flailed a cutlass, drew some blood, and suffered a minor cut. And Mohan Gopal's men were sturdy and determined, familiar with the perils and exigencies of trade: they defended their vessel with both stubbornness and skill. The pirates were soon daunted and withdrew.

In consequence, Fetim raised his estimation of himself. He also dismissed any lingering qualms he may have felt concerning his fate.

To celebrate the victory, Mohan Gopal exercised a master's prerogative by commanding his men to broach a consignment of wine destined for a merchant in Qatiis—Haroon el-Temud, a man of great wealth and unsavory reputation. "Let his count be short a cask or two," pronounced Mohan Gopal with a certain unworthy satisfaction: he had accepted el-Temud's consignment to disguise his more serious cargo; but he disliked carrying goods for a man whose honesty he did not trust. "If he complains, I will pay for the difference."

The crew cheered heartily and obeyed.

During the afternoon and the early evening, the mood aboard *Horizon's Daughter* became convivial. Having sampled good wines in Niswan, Fetim was not impressed by Haroon el-Temud's taste. Nevertheless, he drank a comfortable excess among his comrades. Mohan Gopal did not refuse a cup or two. Accustomed to the company of men, Saliandra also enjoyed a modest libation.

But as night closed over the River Kalabras, and the stars shone coldly from the heavens, first one and then another of the felucca's men began to scream.

For numerous excellent reasons, Haroon el-Temud had enemies; and his enemies had poisoned his wine. A slow acid ate at the vitals of all who consumed it. Clutching his stomach, the first victim fell overboard. The river seemed to swallow him without a sound. Howling in agony, the second flung himself at Fetim.

Taken by surprise, and inspired by his elevated opinion of himself—as well as by wine—Fetim snatched up his cutlass and cleft his shipmate from shoulder to breastbone. Then he heard Saliandra's wail and realized what he had done.

No one reproached him, however. Instead, his companions sought to kill him. *Horizon's Daughter*'s people were being driven mad with pain. Blades flashed; screams beat against the darkness. Having drunk less than his men, Mohan Gopal remained himself long enough to defend Fetim as well as he could. Then he, too, fell prey to the poison. Turning, he knotted his fingers around Fetim's throat and attacked the young man's handsomeness with his teeth.

Saliandra hung from her father's back, trying to pull him away from her lover. I kept Fetim alive, but did not feel compelled to preserve him from injury. He was bleeding from several wounds when Mohan Gopal finally stumbled into convulsions and died.

Everyone died. More from malice than from any wish to spare him pain, I did not let the poison touch Fetim: I wanted him to watch the way his friends were taken.

Saliandra was the last, of course. The wine let her live long enough to experience the ruin of her life and everything she had loved. Although her suffering was extravagant, however, it could not turn her against her lover. She expired in his arms, with his name on her lips.

For that reason, he felt the loss of her all the more severely.

Alone on the River Kalabras, covered by darkness, in a vessel peopled by corpses, he rose to his feet and cried out at the stars, "The fault is mine!"

I peered at him more closely. "Say what?"

"They were my friends. She would have married me. He would have been proud to call me his son-in-law. And I am the cause of their deaths. There is no one more despicable. Knowing what would befall them, I allowed them to make me the object of their goodness. Truly, I deserve to be accursed."

"Well." This was gratifying. "I was wondering when you were going to see the truth."

Instead of answering, he took a fallen dagger from the deck and plunged it toward his breast.

I turned the blade. He bruised himself, but did not pierce the skin.

"You are the worst of the curse," he said brokenly, "the most malefic of all djinn. If you had permitted me to die, only the clan of the al-Hetal would have paid the price of my folly. Because of you, the graveyards of Niswan are crowded with my victims, and the honest and loving people of *Horizon's Daughter* have been slaughtered. By preserving my life, you wreak abominable evil."

Recognizing the justice of what he said, I demanded nonetheless,

"Whose fault is that? It wasn't me who tried to take advantage of Rashid. It wasn't me who preferred slavery to resistance. I'm not the one who said, 'You are the only friend I will ever desire,' when what he should have done was jump ship as soon as he could stand."

Again he did not answer. Rather, he took a length of line and climbed to one of the felucca's yards. There he bound the line to the yard and also to his neck, then cast himself down.

I caused one of the knots to fail. Additionally, I adjusted his impact on the deck so that he was not seriously harmed.

"Help me," he beseeched. "I must put an end to myself, or I will cover the world with ruin wherever I go."

"You know who I am," I replied. "I'm part of the curse. I can't help you. If I tried, the great father of djinn would tear me apart and scatter every portion of my being to the four winds." After a moment, I added foolishly, "You've got to stop thinking like a normal man. You've got to start thinking like one of the accursed."

He drank a large flagon of the tainted wine while he considered what I had said. His bitten features seemed to undergo a number of changes, passing from self-pity and anger to emotions which were more obscure. Then he commanded peremptorily, "Repeat the curse."

I complied. "'In the name of the great father of djinn, let all those he loves be killed. Let him be readily loved—and let all those who love him die in anguish. Let all his seed and all his blood—'"

"Enough. I have heard enough." He consumed more of the wine. Now it seemed to have no effect upon him. "I have received both decency and love aboard this vessel, and those who gave it to me have been poisoned. I must 'start thinking like one of the accursed.' Very well. Do your work, djinn. I will do mine."

He did not speak again that night. The River Kalabras bore the ship of the dead through the dark, and he rode the vessel alone, as though he were its rightful master.

Two days later, the current carried *Horizon's Daughter* past the teeming waterfront of Qatiis, the crystal city where the Padisha devoted himself alternately to civic virtue and imaginative perversion. Hailing assistance in the name of Haroon el-Temud, Fetim achieved a berth for his felucca among the wharves of the great merchants. The state of the vessel's crew—by then as rank as the waters of the city—aroused considerable comment, and there was talk of summoning the Padisha's civil guard; but Fetim deflected this threat by invoking Haroon el-Temud's name with alarming freedom. This in turn incurred the rancor of the merchant's adherents. They made Fetim their prisoner and hauled him up into the rich city, where they threw him at Haroon el-Temud's feet as a suspected murderer.

Piqued by Fetim's fearless manner and his air of knowledge, the merchant allowed the young man to speak. At once, Fetim revealed that Mohan Gopal and his crew had been killed by wine intended for Haroon el-Temud himself.

"Yet you survive," the merchant observed. "It might be reasonable to assume, therefore, that the wine was poisoned by none other than yourself."

"That assumption would be understandable, but faulty," replied Fetim. "Your men will tell you that the felucca's crew has been dead long enough to permit me an easy escape, which would have freed me forever from suspicion. I have risked your distrust because the name of Haroon el-Temud is known as far away as Niswan, and I have that to offer you which can profit us both."

"What is it?"

With an eloquent shrug, Fetim indicated his bonds.

Haroon el-Temud considered. Surely it would be madness for a poisoner of wine to remain in the company of his victims as Fetim had done. And if Fetim were innocent, he had done the merchant a great service by making him aware of the death his enemies plotted for him. To this service Fetim added an offer of profit. And he was a remarkably handsome young man. The rapidly healing scars on his face, far from marring his features, served to give his appearance piquancy. Even the Padisha, in one of his lascivious phases, might be interested in such a man.

Nodding approval of his thoughts, Haroon el-Temud commanded Fetim's release. Then he and Fetim reached a bargain favorable to them both: Fetim was granted a well-remunerated place in the merchant's service; the merchant was made aware that *Horizon's Daughter* carried unprotected saffron, which had not yet been delivered to its rightful buyer.

The profits which accrued to Haroon el-Temud from so much stolen saffron greatly increased his goodwill toward his new protégé.

Fetim had no particular aptitude for his work; he had no aptitude for any work. But he was pleasing in manner, at once unafraid and certain, deferential and modest. And he plied his attractiveness to good effect. He soon found himself accepted and busy among the merchant's many adherents—accountants, clerks, couriers, and guards; odalisques and assassins, opium peddlers and spies—whose lives were devoted to taking advantage of the Padisha's outbreaks of virtue and vice.

He was watched with suspicion, of course: Haroon el-Temud had not achieved such wealth through a lack of caution. But what was in Fetim's heart was more convoluted than the malice which the merchant knew and understood. Haroon el-Temud's spies remarked on the ease with which Fetim accumulated lovers; but neither the spies nor their master feared it.

Fetim, however, found the opportunity when his lovers were sated and happy to ask them interesting questions. And as more and more people chose to make him the repository of their secrets, he gained more and more knowledge. With a celerity which would have frightened the merchant, had he been aware of it, Fetim learned the names of Haroon el-Temud's principal enemies, the locations and characters of their strengths, the parts they played in the balance of conflict which preserved the Padisha's bizarre rule. Then, almost without discernible effort, he began to extend his amorous sphere beyond the circle of Haroon el-Temud's adherents.

In fact, he began to extend his amorous sphere into the domains of his patron's enemies. The knowledge he sought with such diligence was simple: he wished to know who had poisoned Haroon el-Temud's wine.

Initially, he was baffled to learn that the merchant knew the name of this particular foe—and declined to act on the information. This seemed improbable to Fetim: Haroon el-Temud was neither forgiving nor forbearant. Nevertheless, persistence brought the young man better understanding.

In cycles of both virtue and vice, the Padisha enjoyed games of power. He played the strong men of Qatiis against each other, setting one merchant at another, shifting favor between traders, hatching treacheries back and forth. Thus he deflected challenges to the manner in which he reigned over his city.

Haroon el-Temud's wine had been poisoned by a trader who by that gambit rose high in the Padisha's munificence.

Fetim's expression became increasingly difficult to interpret. Armed with his knowledge, he formed a resolution. Then he approached his master and offered to put the extensive network of his lovers at the merchant's service.

Haroon el-Temud greeted the suggestion with relish. After only a moment's consideration, he asked the young man to glean a certain piece of information.

For the first time since he had joined the merchant's adherents, Fetim showed a spark of passion. It was unsettling to witness because it seemed to arise from a wildness which Haroon el-Temud had not expected and did not know how to read. Nevertheless, the young man did and said nothing wild. Instead, with his strange blend of boldness and modesty, he began to bargain. In exchange for using his bed to his patron's advantage, he desired neither money nor position. Rather, he desired Haroon el-Temud himself in that same bed.

Accustomed to buying love instead of receiving it, the merchant was at once flattered by and suspicious of Fetim's proposition. He let himself be persuaded, however, by the spice of Fetim's handsomeness and desire— and by that hint of wildness, which augured well for Haroon el-Temud's particular lusts. He and Fetim kissed to seal their bargain. Then the young man went away.

That night, after the call to prayers had echoed over the gilt minarets and crystal domes of great Qatiis, the merchant went to Fetim's bed. There, after a bout of love which left Haroon el-Temud nearly insensible, he was roused by the arrival of one of the men on whom he had wished Fetim to spy.

"We had an assignation!" this man cried to Fetim in jealous chagrin.

"You arranged this?" demanded Haroon el-Temud.

"Yes," Fetim replied. "Your wine killed the woman I would have wed."

In a rage, the merchant struck at Fetim. The new arrival drew a blade to defend his lover. Haroon el-Temud only had time to shout for his waiting guards before his blood was spilled on the bed.

The guards charged into Fetim's quarters. The jealous lover in turn called out for help. More men came to the fray. Qatiis was a city in which no man or woman dared pass out of earshot of assistance. Cries echoed into the streets. Realizing the location of the struggle, Fetim's lovers converged on each other, each bringing strength for battle. Shortly Haroon el-Temud's house and the houses of his enemies were engaged in full-scale war.

Amid this war sat Fetim, contemplating havoc. Because of the curse, much of the violence turned toward him; but he made no effort to defend himself or flee. While blades flashed at him from all sides, and blood gushed everywhere, he murmured only, "Do your work, djinn," and remained where he was.

My work was not easy. It would have been simplified if he had been willing to move. Or—since I must speak honestly—if I had been willing to coerce him to move. I chose, however, to let him be. I covered him with myself and turned every blade and blow aside.

Before the night was over, Qatiis had been cleansed of several powerful merchants who had traded upon the vices of the rich and the flesh of the weak. When at last the Padisha's civil guard was able to beat back the turmoil, they found Fetim still seated on his bed. From that vantage, he surveyed the bloodshed as though he had become accustomed to it.

Naturally, the guards raised their scimitars to strike him down. But it was not his intention to destroy civil rule in Qatiis; his plans were more insidious. He spared the guard by raising his hands and saying in a voice of command, "Hold. What I did, I did at the command of Babera, the Padisha's vizier."

Because the vizier Babera had a hand in suggesting and effecting many of the Padisha's treacheries and counter-treacheries, Fetim's assertion was plausible enough to be dangerous. The men drew back their swords. Instead of attempting to butcher the cause of so much death and damage, they took him prisoner. While conflicting forces sought to find a new balance by defeating each other, and most of the city's strength concentrated on protecting Qatiis itself from riot and ravage, and beggars and pickthieves scurried to loot the undefended warehouses, Fetim was dragged ungently through the streets toward the gold palace of the Padisha.

His ploy succeeded: he was hauled before the vizier Babera rather than the vizier Meyd.

The Padisha was served by two viziers, whose fortunes rose and fell as his phases alternated. The function and protection of the city, the command of the civil guard, the regulation of the marketplace to preserve at least a semblance of honesty, all were the province of the vizier Meyd, whose loyalty and probity were the qualities which kept the Padisha on his throne. Conversely, the vizier Babera was the master of the Padisha's revels and plots. He it was who conceived the vices and debaucheries, the extravagances and perversions, which gave the Padisha's life its exotic flavor.

Presented to the vizier Babera, Fetim acted swiftly: he spat in the vizier's face.

Babera's instant reaction was to order Fetim's head lopped from his shoulders. A moment's reflection, however, suggested a better fate. In recent days, the Padisha had developed a taste which was difficult to satisfy, even for the cunning vizier: the Padisha desired fornication with someone—man or woman, as occasion supplied—while that individual's neck was being broken. The snapping of the spine and the spasm of death brought him to climaxes which were greatly coveted. Seeing that Fetim was handsome, Babera concluded that he would make an appropriate victim for the Padisha's concupiscence.

Therefore Fetim's death was not attempted. Instead, he was drugged into a state of languor and acquiescence, and presented to the Padisha.

The Padisha met the vizier Babera's offering with intense approval. At once, he called women to arouse him, boys to toy with him. He consumed aphrodisiacs to make him manly. He inhaled incenses which heightened the senses; he drank herbs which sensitized the skin. At the same time, Fetim was bound hand and foot into an upright frame designed so that the Padisha might penetrate from one side while his bodyservant, a hugely muscular eunuch, clasped the victim's neck from the other.

Drugged, Fetim suffered this indignity without alarm. He only murmured at intervals, "Do your work, djinn. I will do mine."

When the Padisha was ready, he began to exercise himself upon Fetim's body. Swiftly, the moment of climax approached. The eunuch wrapped his great hands around Fetim's throat.

But when the Padisha was engorged and aching, and the signal was given, the eunuch's hands unaccountably jerked from one neck to the other. It was the Padisha himself who met death in the moment of bliss.

Horrified by the consequences of what had just happened, the eunuch fled for his life, rampaging like a maddened bull through the palace. The vizier Meyd entered the Padisha's disporting chamber, took one look at his master's body, and commanded his men to arrest the vizier Babera.

Babera's supporters resisted; the civil guard was called into action. While violence echoed in the halls of the palace, propelling the vizier Meyd to the rule of Qatiis whether he desired it or not, I released Fetim from his bonds, swept the drugs from his mind, and guided him to a safe egress.

As we journeyed together away from the changed city, I said, "You learn well."

"Learn?"

"You learn to think like one of the accursed."

"Thank you," he said. He did not sound notably happy. Yet he faced the desert ahead of us without quailing.

"You fill me with pride," I said. "You have exceeded all my expectations."

"Give me time," he returned. His tone suggested mockery of my former manner of speaking. "I might have some more surprises for you. The world has a lot of opportunities."

Had I been mortal, I would have laughed. If he continued to learn at this pace, he would eventually become one of the djinn.

The Killing Stroke

When he was returned to the cell we shared, he retained nothing except his short, warrior's robe and his knowledge of *shin-te*. The years of training which had made him what he was despite his youth had not been taken from him. Everything else was gone. His birthplace and family, his friendships and allegiances, his possessions and memories—all had been swept aside. The faces of his masters and students had vanished from his mind. He could not have given an account of himself to save his life—or ours. Not even his name remained to him.

I was familiar with his plight. As was Isla. We had experienced it ourselves.

The look of bereavement in his eyes did not augur well for him. It had settled firmly into the strained flesh at his temples and the new lines of his cheeks, causing him to appear almost painfully youthful and forlorn. He might have been a small boy who had grown so accustomed to blows he could not avoid that he had learned to flinch and duck his head reflexively.

Weariness clung to his limbs, burdened his shoulders. His ordeal had been immeasurably arduous.

Still his skill, and the rigor behind it, showed in the poise with which he carried himself, in the quick accuracy with which he saw and noted everything around him. He had presumably been dealt a killing stroke, with blade or fist. Yet he remained lithe of movement, prompt of gaze— and centered in his *qa*.

So he had returned on previous occasions. That he could continue to move and attend as he did, in spite of defeat and death, moderated his air of bereavement.

His throat was parched from his various exertions. Studying us with his incipient flinch, he tried to speak, but could not find his voice at first. With an effort, he swallowed his confusion and fear in order to clear his mouth. Then he asked faintly, "Where am I?"

It was the same question he had asked each time he entered. With repetition, his voice had grown husky, thick with doubt, but his mind continued to arrange its inquiries in the same order.

That also did not augur well.

As she had each time before, Isla shrugged, glowering darkly from her smudged features.

As I had each time before, I spread my hands to indicate the cell. Its blind stone walls and eternal lamps, its timbered ceiling, its pallets and cistern and privy, were the only answer we could give.

Frowning fearfully, he asked his second question. "Who are you?"

Isla turned her glower toward me. Behind its grime, her face might have been lovely or plain, but she had long since forgotten which, and I had ceased to be curious. The shape of her mouth was strict, however, and the heat of her *qa* showed in her eyes. "Does he never get tired of this?" she demanded.

Her protest was not a reference to the young man standing before us.

"Or she?" I retorted. The debate was of long standing between us. It meant nothing, but I maintained it on the general principle—oft repeated by my masters—that we could not escape our imprisonment by making unwarranted assumptions.

The young man swallowed again. "He? She?"

That question, also, he had asked more than once.

No doubt deliberately, Isla chose to violate the litany of previous occasions. "You answer," she ordered me. "I get tired, if he doesn't."

Simply because I enjoyed variations of any kind, I tried to provoke her. "How are you tired? You do nothing except pace and complain."

"Tired," she snapped, "of being the only one who cares."

Her defeat had predated mine—although neither of us could measure the interval between them. In fact, she had preserved my heart from despair. I could not have borne my own ordeal alone. But my gratitude did neither of us any good.

And she was not the only one who cared.

Smiling ruefully, I faced the young man. "I am Asper." For entertainment's sake, I performed a florid bow. "This uncivil termagant is Isla. We are here to serve you. However," I admitted, "we have not yet grasped what aid you might need."

Isla snorted, but refrained from contradiction. She knew I spoke the truth.

A small tension between the young man's brows deepened. He may have been trying to anticipate the next blow. For him the litany remained unbroken. He had not moved from the spot where he had appeared in the cell.

"Have we met before?"

Since Isla had elected to vary the experience with silence, I continued alone. "Several times."

He did not ask, How is that possible? His masters had trained him well. He remained centered in his *qa*—and in his thoughts. Instead he observed hoarsely, "A mage has imprisoned us."

This was not an assumption. If it were, I might have challenged it. His conclusion was inescapable, however, made so by the perfect absence of a door through which any of us could have entered the cell. And by the fact that we yet lived.

Keeping my bitterness to myself, I shrugged in assent.

His sorrow augmented the weariness which burdened his spirit. In the unflinching lamplight, he appeared to dwindle.

Sadly, he asked, "What are you?"

The same questions in the same order.

"By the White Lords," Isla swore, "he learns nothing."

There my temper snapped. My own memory had been restored to me after my last defeat. I recalled too much death. "And what precisely," I demanded of her, "is it that *we* have learned?"

She answered at once, crying at the walls, "I have learned hatred! If he makes the mistake of letting me live, I will extract the cost of this abuse from his bones!"

I understood her anguish. We both knew that neither of us would ever see the light of day again, if this *shin-te* master did not win our freedom for us.

Still I was angry. I did not allow her to leave her place in the litany.

Smiling unkindly at the young man, I performed a small circular flick with the fingers of one hand—a gesture both swift and subtle, difficult to notice—and at once a whetted dagger appeared in my palm. Without pausing to gauge direction or distance, I flipped the bladepoint at Isla's right eye.

My cast was true. Yet the dagger did not strike her. Instead it flashed upward and embedded itself with a satisfying thunk in one of the ceiling timbers.

She adjusted the sleeve of her robe.

We both gazed at the young man.

Curling his hands over his heart, he accorded us the *shin-te* bow of respect. *"Nahia,"* he said to me. And to Isla, *"Mashu-te."*

In our separate ways, we also bowed. We could not do otherwise. He had named us, although he remembered nothing.

"Your mastery is plain," he observed unhappily. "You must have answered better than I."

Opening his hand, he indicated what lay beyond our cell.

"If that were true," Isla snapped, "you wouldn't be here."

For myself, I added, "Neither would we."

There was nothing for which we could hope if his mastery did not prove greater than ours.

Fortunately, he appeared to understand us without more explanation.

We had none to offer. Nothing had been revealed to us. If our captor had placed any value on our comprehension, we would not have been deprived of our memories while we fought and failed.

Shouldering his dismay as well as he could, he asked the question which must have given him the most pain.

"Who am I?"

Because we were familiar with his distress, both Isla and I faced him openly so that he could see that we had no reply for him. We knew only what he had told us—and he remembered only *shin-te*.

For the first time, he varied our litany of question and response himself. Slowly, he raised his hands to wipe tears from his eyes. His struggles had exhausted his flesh. Now his repeated return from death had begun to exhaust his spirit.

That also did not augur well.

When he spread his hands to show us that they were empty—that he was defenseless—we recognized that he had come to the point of his gravest vulnerability. So softly that he might have made no sound, he voiced the question which haunted us all.

"Why?"

We would have answered him kindly—Isla even more than I, despite her hate. We knew his pain. But any kindness would have been a lie.

"Presumably," she told him, "it is because you failed."

As we had failed before him.

Despite his training, he allowed himself a sigh of weariness and regret. That, too, was a slight variation. He had sighed before. With repetition, however, it had begun to convey the inflection of a sob.

His last question contained little more than utter fatigue.

"Is it safe to rest?"

I might have answered sardonically, "We survive the experience, as you see." But Isla forestalled me.

"We will ward you with our lives," she assured him. "While you are here, we have no other hope."

He nodded, accepting her reply. Carefully, he moved to the nearest pallet and folded himself onto it. Within moments he had fallen asleep.

As before, I found no satisfaction in his willingness to trust us. I knew as well as he did that his weariness left him no alternative.

He had endured altogether too much death.

————

Folk like myself might have said that we had already seen enough to content us. After simmering and frothing for the better part of a decade, the Mage War had at last boiled over three years ago, spilling blood across the length and breadth of Vesselege until all the land was sodden with it. For reasons which few of us understood, and fewer still cared about, the White Lords had scourged and harried the Dark until only one remained—the most potent and dire of them all, it was said, the dread Black Archemage, secure among the shadows and malice of his granite keep upon the crags of Scarmin. Even then, however, the victories of the White Lords, and the withdrawal of the Archemage, did not suffice to lift the pall of battle and death from the land. The reach of a mage was long, as we all knew. During that war, we learned how long. A hundred leagues from Scarmin's peaks and cols, hurricanes of fire and stone fell upon Vess whenever—so we were told—Argoyne the Black required a diversion to ward him from some assault of the White Lords, and of Goris Miniter, Vesselege's King.

Vess was Miniter's seat, the largest and—until the Mage War—most thriving city in the land. So naturally I lived there, within a whim of destruction every hour of my days. By nature, I think, I had always enjoyed the proximity of disasters—as long as they befell someone else. Certainly, I had always been adept at avoiding them myself. And that skill had been enhanced and honed by my training among the *nahia*.

My poor father, blighted by poverty and loss, had gifted me there after my mother's death. Though I had squalled against the idea at the time, I had learned to treasure it. When my masters had at last released me, I was a gifted pickthief, an impeccable burglar, and an artist of impossible escapes and improbable disappearances. I was also a true warrior in the tradition of the *nahia*. Faced by a single antagonist, I might leave him dead before he realized that I was not the one being slain. Confronting a gang of ruffians, I could dispatch half of them while the other half hacked at each other in confusion and folly.

Despite the visitations of power which blasted one section of the city or another at uncertain intervals, I lived rather well in Vess, I thought. Unfortunately, late in the third year of the War, some mischance or miscalculation must have brought me to the attention of one mage or another. The life I knew ended as suddenly as if I had severed it at the base of the neck. Without transition or awareness, I found myself in a stone cell with Isla and no door. When my memory was restored, I recalled days or weeks of bitter combat. I felt myself die again and again, until my spirit quailed like a coward's. Yet I remembered nothing of how I had been taken from Vess—or why. And I had nothing but assumptions, which my masters abhorred, to tell me where I was.

Isla's story, as I learned it after my memory had been returned, was completely different than mine—and entirely the same.

Her father and mother, her brother and sisters, her aunts and uncles—her whole family, in fact—had dedicated their lives to the *mashu-te*, the Art of the Direct Fist. As a young girl, fiery of temper, and quick to passion—or so I imagined her—she had been initiated in the disciplines and skills of those masters, and she had studied with the clenched devotion of a girl determined to prove her worth. The study and teaching of *mashu-te* had consumed her, and in all her years she had never left the distant school where her masters winnowed acolytes to glean students, and students to glean warriors. When she spoke of that time, I received the impression that she had never tested her skills against anyone not already familiar with them.

Still, her skills were extraordinary. It was said around Vesselege that a *mashu-te* master could stop a charging bull with one blow. I doubted that—but I did not doubt that Isla was a master. I had slipped once with her, and my *qa* still trembled in consequence.

From time to time, I had assured her that I could slay her easily, if I permitted myself to use my fang, the *nahia* dagger secreted within my robe. But that was mere provocation. I did not believe it. The truth was that I feared her—and not only because of her vehement excellence.

She had endured alone an ordeal which had nearly broken me despite her companionship.

Like mine, her life had simply ended one day, without transition or explanation, and she had found herself here. Like me, she had faced countless opponents and death, and had remembered nothing until her captor had given up on her. Yet she was whole. She was bitter, and she had learned hatred, but she was whole. I could not have said the same of myself. Without her, I would have succumbed to despair—that death of the spirit which all the Fatal Arts abhorred. She possessed the strongest *qa* I had ever encountered, surpassing even the greatest of my masters. I had never seen the like—until the young *shin-te* warrior joined us.

For three years, we had both ignored the Mage War, after our separate fashions. Now, however, we considered it a personal affront. For that reason, among others, we did what we could to aid the new prisoner.

After a time, he awakened. When he did so, there was food. There was always food when we needed it. He ate sparingly, respectful of his *qa*. Then he performed the ablutions and devotions of the *shin-te*, centering himself in meditation. Isla and I passed the time as we had on previous occasions, watching him with the tattered remnants of hope.

Rest and nourishment had restored him somewhat, as they had in the past. His air of bereavement had been diminished, and the pallor of death had receded from his cheeks. After meditation, he asked us to train with him. His manner as he did so was curiously diffident, as if he considered it plausible that we might refuse—that if we aided him we would do so out of courtesy rather than desperation.

So we trained with him, although our previous efforts had not done him any discernible good.

The exercise was little changed from other occasions. Isla and I feinted and attacked, or attacked and feinted, as our inclination took us, but we made no impression on him. He altered his tactics in accordance with our assaults, varying his blocks and counters easily, deflecting us without effort. Despite his youth and forlornness, he seemed impervious to our skills, and our cunning. Behind his fluid movements and light stances, his *qa* had a staggering force. In truth, I feared him as much as I feared Isla. Although we challenged him furiously, he did us no harm. But the harm he could have done was extreme.

How, I wondered, had such a very young man become so strong? And how was it possible that he had been slain so often?

When he had thanked us for our exertions, he meditated again, perhaps on what he had learned, perhaps on nothing at all. No word or glance from him suggested that we had in any way given him less than he needed from us. Yet we knew better. We were not his equals, but we were masters, able to recognize the truth. And we could see it in the deepening sorrow which underlay every turn of his gaze, every shift of his mouth.

Again and again, we failed to prepare him for his opponents. Or for his death.

"We should stop holding back," Isla muttered to me sourly. "This polite exercise is wasted on him."

She had said the same more than once.

Earlier, I had argued with her. What if by some chance we injured or weakened him? What became of our hope then? But that debate had lost its meaning, and I gave it up. Matching her tone, I replied, "I will follow your example. When I see the full strength of the Direct Fist turned against him, I will do what a *nahia* can to emulate it."

She snorted in response, but I knew that her disgust was not directed at me. The training of the *mashu-te* had penetrated her bones. She would have considered it a crime to put all the force of her *qa* into blows struck against a training partner.

The *nahia* spared themselves such prohibitions. I was restrained, not by conscience, but by understanding. If I slew him, my last hope would die with him. And if I attempted his death and failed, he might well break my spine.

I was quite certain that if I died now I would not live again. No doubt that was just an assumption. Still, I believed it.

Neither Isla nor I witnessed his disappearance. In some sense, neither of us noticed it. Nothing in the cell—or in our own minds—marked the moment. He was among us. Then he was not. Without transition or summons. He was removed from the cell with the same disdain for continuity with which we had been removed from our lives.

This was precisely as it had been on any number of previous occasions.

———————

"I had thought," Isla remarked with no more than ordinary asperity, "that the *nahia* were adept at escape. I must have been misinformed."

I sighed. "Give me a door, and I will open it. Give me a window—give me a gap for ventilation—give me somewhere to begin." I had long since scrutinized the walls and ceiling and even the floor until I feared my heart would break. "The *nahia* are not mages, Isla."

"But we came and went," she protested. "He comes and goes." She meant the young man. "There must be a door."

"As there was among the *mashu-te*?" I inquired gently. "As there was on the streets of Vess? A door from those places to this? No doubt you are right. But it is a mage's door, and I cannot open it."

Attempting to lighten her mood—or my own—I continued, "However, it may be that some among these stones are illusions." I gestured at the walls. "Perhaps if you aim the Direct Fist at them all, one will shatter, revealing itself to be wood."

She avoided my gaze. "Do not mock me, Asper," she said distantly. "I have no heart for it."

That did not augur well for any of us.

———————

He staggered as he returned, barely strong enough to remain on his feet. We saw differences he could not recognize, having no memory. As before, he breathed and moved among the living. As before, his wounds and bruises had been healed. Apparently, our captor wished to spare him the obvious consequences of death. Yet his exhaustion came near to overwhelming him. A glaze of forgotten pain clouded his eyes as he searched the cell, and us.

But his thoughts had not been altered. Weary as he was, how could he have considered anything new? When he had recovered his balance, he began the litany of our doom.

"Where am I?"

We had no answer for him.

"Who are you?"

Suppressing fury or despair, Isla told me, "This must change. We are lost otherwise."

"How can he change it?" I countered. "Look at him." I was less than she, and endangered by my own despair. "He has nothing left."

"Have we met before?"

I would have given him an exact answer if I could. But the magery of his disappearances and returns foiled me. Although Isla and I could remember what we had said and done, neither of us was able to keep a count of the days, or the deaths.

"Your mastery is plain. You must have answered better than I."

Neither Isla nor I suspected him of mocking us.

This time, however, he did not ask "Why?" He seemed to understand that he had failed. Perhaps his own weakness made the truth evident.

At last he settled himself to sleep. Isla spread a blanket over his shoulders, then stooped to kiss his forehead. The gesture was uncharacteristic of her. There were uncharacteristic tears in her eyes. His bereavement had become infectious.

Her voice thick with sorrow, she said, "Asper, it must change. If he cannot change it, then we must. Someone must."

I dismissed the idea that our captor's intentions would alter themselves. "How?" I asked. Her gentleness frightened me more than her grief.

"I do not know." For the first time, she sounded like a woman who might surrender.

———

She was right, of course. It must change. And I was a *nahia* master, adept—or so I claimed—at impossible escapes and improbable disappearances. The burden was mine to bear.

While the young man slept, she and I neither rested nor watched.

Instead, I questioned her closely, searching her knowledge of the other Arts for any insight the *nahia* did not possess.

I hoped that the *mashu-te* might have some true understanding of *shin-te*.

Shin-te. Nahia. Mashu-te. Here were represented three of the five Fatal Arts of Vesselege. Only *ro-uke* and *nerishi-qa* were needed to complete the tale of combative skills in all our land. And of the two, *ro-uke* was widely considered too secretive—too dependent upon stealth and surprise—to equal the others in open conflict. It was the Art of Assassination. As for *nerishi-qa*, it was said to be the most fearsome and pure of all the Five. The Art of the Killing Stroke, it was called. Indeed, legend claimed that every deadly skill contained in the other four derived from *nerishi-qa*.

If legend could be believed, Isla and I had not been joined by a *nerishi-qa* master because no mage was sufficiently powerful to subdue one.

That was an assumption, however—so ingrained that I hardly noticed it. My masters had respected all the Arts, but they feared only *nerishi-qa*.

Unfortunately, Isla was well schooled in legends, but owned less practical knowledge than I. She spoke of *shin-te* masters who broke wooden planks with their fists while holding soap bubbles in their palms, but she had not been taught how such feats might be accomplished. If indeed they were possible at all. Her isolated life among the *mashu-te* had been more conducive to the proliferation of mythologies than to a detailed awareness of the world. *Nahia* was called the Art of Circumvention. Our skills and our *qa* were rooted in use. And the masters of the Direct Fist were so very scrupulous—

If I desired understanding, I would have to gain it from the young man.

As before, he roused himself at last, broke his fast, performed his ablutions and meditations. This time, however, he had slept in the grip of troubled dreams, and had awakened unrefreshed. His gaze remained dull, and the hue of his skin suggested ashes. Still he did not diverge from his pattern. When his meditations were complete, he asked us to train with him.

I refused, in Isla's name as well as my own.

He seemed to flinch as if he had received another blow. His dreams had left him weaker than before—younger, and more lost. "You say that I failed," he murmured. "Without training, I will surely fail again."

He had not regained his memory. By that sign, we knew that the mage was not done with him.

"You have trained enough," I informed him. "You need rest, not more exertion." More than rest, he needed insight. "And we are already familiar with our limitations.

"With your consent"—he was a master, and deserved courtesy—"I will question you."

"Concerning what?" Isla protested irritably. "Have you forgotten that he remembers nothing? What do you imagine he will tell us?"

I ignored her, and instead watched doubts glide like shadows across his bereavement. In his eyes, I seemed to see his desire to trust us measure itself against his failures, or his dreams. And he may have guessed that I desired to probe the secrets of his Art. At last, however, he nodded warily.

"I will answer, if I can."

Isla wanted me to account for myself, if he did not. But I wasted no effort on explanations. In fact, I had none to offer. I was simply groping, as my masters had taught me, hunting the dark cell of my ignorance for some object or shape or texture I might recognize.

Stilling Isla's impatience with a gesture, I began at once.

"What," I asked him, "are the principles of *shin-te?*"

Having made his decision, he did not falter from it. Without hesitation, he replied, "Service to *qa* in all things. Acceptance of that which opposes us." He remembered his training, if nothing else. "There is no killing stroke."

I stared at him witlessly. All the Fatal Arts were given to obscure utterance—it was one of the means by which we cherished our own, and deflected outsiders—but this seemed extreme, even to me. I pursued him as best I could.

"Please explain. Your words will give us no aid if we do not understand them."

Politely, he refrained from observing that we were not intended to understand. The urgency of our plight was plain.

"*Qa*," he began, "is the seat and source of self. It is the power of self, and the expression. Without self, there is no action, and no purpose. To deny service to the self is to deny existence."

So much I could grasp. It was not substantially different than the wisdom of my masters. They expressed themselves more concretely, but their meaning was much the same.

"*Qa* draws its strength from acceptance," he continued. "To reject that which opposes us is death. Life opposes us. Nothing grows that is not contained. And life will not alter itself to satisfy our rejection. Without acceptance, there is no power."

Privately, I considered this mystical nonsense. He was worse than the *mashu-te*. I was *nahia* by nature as much as by training. I kept my opinion to myself, however. It was as useless to us as his oblique maxims.

"That there is no killing stroke," he concluded, "is self-evident. No man or woman slays another. There is only the choice to live or die."

In response, I laughed softly, without humor. I might have asked him if he denied the existence of *nerishi-qa*, but I did not. I wished to circumvent misunderstanding, not enhance it.

Was not *shin-te* one of the Fatal Arts?

"There we differ," I told him. "I myself have shed blood and caused death. Do you call this illusion? Are the men I gutted still alive?"

Isla nodded sharp agreement, although I was certain that she would argue in other terms.

He appeared to regard my challenge seriously. Yet he gave no sign that it disturbed him. Rather, he considered how he would answer. After a moment, he stepped near to me and touched the place where I had secreted my dagger.

"Strike me," he instructed simply.

I hesitated. Naturally I did not wish to slay him—or to harm him. But I felt a greater uncertainty as well. That he knew my fang's resting place troubled me. As I had been taught, I varied its location frequently. And I took pains to ensure that I was not observed when I concealed it.

"The *shin-te* teach that there is no killing stroke," he insisted. "Show me that this belief is false."

"Asper—" Isla murmured in warning. Her wish to see blood spilled here was even less than mine.

I understood him, however. He might have been a *nahia* master, reminding me to affirm nothing which I could not demonstrate.

By no hint of movement or tension did I announce my intent. I had studied such moments deeply. Without discernible transition—or so I believed—I transferred my *qa* from rest to action. More swiftly than the blinking of an eye, my hand projected my fang into the arch between his ribs.

Yet my fang bit air, not flesh. Wrist to wrist, he had deflected my attack.

I did not pause to admire his counter. Following the line of his deflection, I turned my stroke to a disemboweling slash.

Again I found air rather than my target. He had shifted aside, guiding my hand so that my own motion helped him drive my wrist against the point of his knee.

My grip loosened. Before I could secure it, he knocked the fang from my fingers.

By that time, I had already directed a jab at his face, seeking to gouge him blind. But the motion was a mere formality, nothing more. With a negligent flick of his elbow, he knocked my arm aside.

Then he stood a pace beyond my reach, holding my dagger lightly by its blade. I could not see that my efforts had inconvenienced him in any way. I told myself that I might have pressed my attack more stringently—that I might perhaps have retrieved my fang in a way which threatened him—but I did not believe it. He had made his point in terms I could not contradict by skill alone.

When I had bowed to show my acquiescence, he restored the dagger to me and bowed in turn.

At once, Isla advanced. Her desperation she expressed as anger so that it would not turn to despair. With the compact force of the Direct Fist, she flung a blow at him which caused my own *qa* to quake, although I was now a bystander.

Her speed did not exceed mine, of that I was certain. However, the efficiency of the *mashu-te* had the effect of enhanced quickness. Her first strike touched his robe—as mine had not—before he turned it. And even then her fist focused so much *qa* that he was forced to recoil as if he had been hit.

As easily as oil, she followed one blow with another.

He did not deflect her again. Rather, he met her squarely, palm to fist. I hardly had time to see the flex of his knees, the set of his strength. When their hands met, I flinched, thinking that she had shattered his bones.

Yet it was Isla who gasped in pain, not the *shin-te*. Her own force had nearly dislocated her shoulder. If the blow had betrayed any flaw, she would have ruined her arm.

He waited, motionless, until she had mastered her distress enough to bow. Then he replied gravely, with such respect that if I had not seen the event I would not have known he had humbled her, "Have I harmed you?"

Glaring, she dismissed his concern. "This proves nothing," she retorted. "You are greater than we. Your skill surpasses ours. So much we already knew. You have not demonstrated that there is no killing stroke."

"Still," he assured her, "it is the truth."

"I disagree," she protested. "A master may strike at a farmer, and the farmer will die. He can neither counter nor evade the blow. Is he then responsible for it? Is it not a lie to say that he chooses his death? Is the blow not murder? The *mashu-te* teach that the burden and the consequences belong to the one who strikes. How otherwise," she concluded, "do the *shin-te* call themselves honorable?"

He was young and bereft—and apparently better content to contest his beliefs with actions than with words. Yet he did not shirk her demand.

"Service to *qa* precludes murder," he answered. "Acceptance of that which opposes us necessitates responsibility. There is no killing stroke.

"Consider the farmer. Do you contend that the master struck him without cause? Is that the act of a master? Do the *mashu-te* conduct themselves so?" He shook his head. "If you wish to say that the farmer did not choose his death, you must first consider the cause of the blow."

"That is specious," Isla snapped. "Maybe mages reason so. Warriors do not.

"No cause is sufficient," she insisted. "Despite whatever lies between them, they are unequal in skill and force. Therefore the blow is murder."

Unswayed, he lifted his shoulders delicately. "Since you do not name the cause," he murmured, "I cannot answer you. The truth is there, not in the conclusions you draw from it."

Although he had been slain several times, he knew how to render the teachings of the *shin-te* unassailable.

He disturbed me. I found suddenly that I feared for him more than I feared his skills, or the distilled potency of his *qa*. Isla was right. His words, like his actions, proved nothing. I was *nahia* to the core. I knew—as he did not—that any belief which placed itself beyond doubt nurtured its own collapse. A warrior who did not risk despair could not master it.

Again, he was no longer among us. Neither Isla nor I saw how he was taken from the cell. We could not name the moment of his disappearance. We only knew that while she wrestled with her own beliefs, and I considered my fears, the object of our concern ceased to share our imprisonment.

"Asper," she said when she had recognized his absence, "we're beaten." She may have meant "broken." "We can't help him. And he can't help himself. If he can't remember what happens to him, he can't get past what he's been taught. And all that *shin-te* training has already failed him."

She had endured her own testing without aid or companionship. She had strength enough for any contest, even though it killed her. But she could not suffer helplessness.

I, on the other hand—

I could not have borne repeated death alone. But I was *nahia*—oblique of heart as well as of skill. I had been trained to impossible escapes and improbable disappearances. My masters had made a study of helplessness.

I did not attempt to answer her. She was too pure—no answer of mine would touch her. Instead I turned my attention to the walls.

As ever, there was no door, no window, no gaps at all. Faceless granite confronted me on all sides. But I did not allow myself to be daunted.

Raising my fists, I cried as though I believed I would be heard, "Are you stupid as well as cruel? Does magery corrupt your wits as it does your heart? Or are you only a fool? He cannot succeed this way!"

Isla gaped at me, but I took no heed of her chagrin. I was certain of nothing except that our captor needed this *shin-te* master as sorely as we did.

"He remembers nothing," I called to the blind stone. "He learns *nothing!* Death after death, he fails you. If you do not let us teach him, he will always fail you. And we cannot teach him if we do not know what he opposes!"

The walls answered with silence. Isla stared at me in shock. After a moment, she breathed, "Asper—" but no other words came to her.

"Hear me!" I demanded. "They say that the Black Archemage is malefic beyond belief, but even Argoyne himself could not be this *stupid!*"

An instant later, I was stricken dumb by the sudden vehemence of the reply. From out of the air, a voice clawed with bitterness replied, "And what in the name of the Seven Hells makes you think I can *spare*—?"

As abruptly as it had begun, the response was cut off. A soundless tremor filled the cell as though the stone under our feet had flinched.

"Asper," Isla whispered, "what have you done?" She stood ready for combat.

I swallowed a moment's panic. Adjusted the fang in my grasp. "Apparently," I said, feigning calm, "I have insulted our captor."

"Oh, well," she answered between her teeth. "If *that's* all—"

Without transition, we became aware that one of the walls was gone. Its absence revealed a corridor I knew too well—a passage as wide as the cell, leading from nowhere to nowhere, and fraught with death. Like the cell, it was endlessly lit. And it showed no intersections or doorways through which it might be entered. Still it held perils without number, threats as enduring as the light.

It was the arena in which Isla and I had been slain too often.

In the center of the space stood the young *shin-te* master, waiting. His back was toward us, but his stance showed that he was ready, poised for challenge. No sound came from his light movements, or from the faceless walls—or from the warrior advancing behind him.

The warrior held a spear, which he meant to drive into the young man's back.

I made no attempt to help or warn him. The silence stilled me. I remembered sounds from that corridor, a host of small distractions hampering awareness—the distant plash of water, the rustle of unnatural winds, the grinding of shifted stones. And I did not believe that we had suddenly been given our freedom. But Isla immediately hastened forward, perhaps thinking that she would be allowed to aid the young man.

At once, she encountered the wall of the cell, and could not pass it. The scene before us was an image, mage-created, showing events which transpired elsewhere. Apparently my demand had been heeded.

"By the White Lords!" she swore. "What—?"

I ignored her confusion. It would pass.

That warrior looked to be the same one who had slain both of us until we were entirely beaten. I saw no reason to think otherwise. I had killed him occasionally myself, as had Isla, but death had not hindered him significantly. When my memory was restored, I had concluded that he was not a man at all, but rather a creature of magery, returned to life whenever he fell by the same power which had first created him. If he had a man's features—or even a man's eyes—I could not recall them.

From a distance of no more than five strides, he cocked his spear and flung it.

Warned by the sensitivity of his *qa*, the young *shin-te* turned, snatching the spear from the air. With the ease of long familiarity, he whirled the weapon as if it were a staff, and confronted his assailant.

By some means which I could neither observe nor understand, the warrior held another spear. Flipping his weapon swiftly end for end to disguise the moment when he would strike, he attacked.

The young man countered smoothly with the shaft of his staff. Foot and knee, hip and arm, at every moment his stances were flawless, apt for attack or defense, advance or retreat. The fast wheel of his assailant's blows he parried or slipped aside, adjusting his distance from the warrior at need.

Then he saw his opening. Stabbing his staff between the warrior's arms, he slapped its shaft against both of the warrior's wrists at once. The spear spun from the warrior's grasp.

A quick thrust would end the contest, at least momentarily.

"Now!" Isla commanded sharply, although the young man could not hear her.

He did not thrust. Instead, he stepped back, holding his staff ready.

"Fool," Isla groaned.

I agreed mutely. That warrior could not be defeated by death. Still, a living assailant was always more dangerous than a dead one. That the young man seemed to have no use for his spear's point disturbed me. To my eyes, the *shin-te* carried their denial of the killing stroke to unfortunate extremes.

Surely these contests were being staged to test his ability to master living opponents? If they had some other purpose, I could not fathom it.

Already the warrior had retrieved his weapon. Now he held it by its balance in one hand, bracing it along his arm so that it extended his reach. With his free hand, he warded away the young man's staff. To my eye, this method of attack seemed awkward, but the warrior employed it smoothly. Feinting forward, he flicked his fingers at the young man's eyes. In the same motion, he kicked rapidly to draw the staff downward, then jabbed with his spear.

The young *shin-te* countered, retreating. A line of blood appeared on his cheek before he knocked the spear aside and spun out of reach. The staff blurred with speed in his hands. Undaunted, his assailant advanced. An abrupt slap of the spear broke the staff's whirl. Precise as a serpent, rigid fingers struck at the young man's throat. I felt rather than saw the spear follow the blow.

The young man saved himself by dropping his staff. Simultaneously, he blocked the spear with one palm, the blow with the other. An instant later—so swiftly that he astonished me—he collapsed one arm and struck inward with his elbow, catching his opponent at the temple hard enough to splinter bone.

The warrior flipped away to diminish the force of the impact.

The *shin-te* pursued without hesitation. But the warrior landed strongly—and in his hands he now held both weapons, their points braced for bloodshed. Again the young man was forced to retreat.

I hardly saw the warrior settle both spears into his awkward-seeming grasp. The young man commanded my attention. His poise betrayed no uncertainty, and the cut on his cheek was small—dangerous only if the spearpoint had been poisoned. Still he alarmed me. Although he fought well, his eyes held a flinch of defeat. Repeated death had eaten its way into his heart. When his opponent attacked again, weaving both spears in a pattern intricate with harm, he could find no opening through which to repay the assault.

"Asper," Isla breathed suddenly, "he needs a champion."

I ignored her. I could not look away from the *shin-te* master's grief.

"The mage," she insisted. "He needs a champion. That's what he's testing us for. He's trying to find someone good enough to fight for him."

Without thinking, I murmured, "That is an assumption."

A rent appeared in the young man's robe, showing blood on his skin. He countered at the warrior's knees, but failed to penetrate the weaving of the spearpoints.

"I'm sure of it." In her excitement, she turned her back on the scene before us in order to confront me. "Forget your *nahia* rigor for a moment. Listen to me.

"Why else does a mage do this?" She gestured at the young man's battle. "A mage so beleaguered he has no power to spare? If he were not already embattled for his life, he would have no need to treat us this way. What does he gain?"

I found myself looking at her rather than at the contest. She had thought of something which had eluded me. Her assumption exposed my own. Without realizing it, I had simply believed that the motives of mages surpassed our capacity to explain them—that no guess of ours could hope to approach the truth. But we had been given a hint when the mage spoke. And she had made better use of it than I.

"Why doesn't he return us to our lives?" she continued. "Or simply kill us? Or let us remember? Because he can't spare the power. These trials are all he can manage.

"He needs someone," she stated as if she were certain, "to fight for him."

Behind her, the *shin-te* went to the floor in a flurry of spear strokes. I thought him finished, but he recovered. Scissoring his legs, he flung out kicks which cost him a jab to one thigh, but which succeeded at breaking apart the warrior's attack. For an instant, he appeared to spin on his back among the spears. Then he arched to his feet, facing his opponent.

Now he held one of the spears. I had not seen him acquire it, could hardly imagine how he might have wrested it from the warrior's grasp. Nevertheless he had restored a measure of equality to the struggle.

Although his leg had been wounded, his stance remained sure. His air of strength was an illusion, however. His new weakness revealed itself in diminished quickness, diminished focus. Pain and damage disturbed the concentration of his *qa*.

And still he used the spear as a staff—a defensive weapon. While his opponent sought to kill him, he appeared to desire only the warrior's defeat.

He had said that *there is no killing stroke*, but he was wrong. And I believed that he knew it, although he might not have been able to name the truth. The anguish in his eyes did not arise from his wounds. Mere hurt could not exceed him.

I knew to my cost that the killing stroke was despair.

For a moment, I had the sensation that my mind had closed itself, shutting out thought. I felt only panic. Who else but Argoyne might require a champion in the midst of the Mage War? Black Argoyne, Archemage of the Dark Lords? All others like him were dead. And everyone in Vess—everyone in all Vesselege—knew that the White Lords were winning. They had no need of a champion.

Isla had not yet pushed her assumption to that conclusion. When she did, what would she say? Impelled by the scruples of the *mashu-te*, would she insist that we must pray for the young man's failure, so that Argoyne would receive no aid from us?

I was *nahia* to the bone. The violation of such a sacrifice would burst my *qa* entirely, leaving me empty and lost.

While she returned her gaze to the contest, the warrior again changed his tactics. Now he held his spear by its butt with both hands, whirling it about his head as though it were a bolus. To my eye, this seemed an implausible assault. Surely it left him exposed to counterattack? Yet apparently it did not. The young *shin-te* found no way past the wheeling spearpoint.

At first this baffled me. And the more closely I studied him, the more confused I became. Why did he not strike *now*—or *there*? But then, despite my panic, I glimpsed the truth. The warrior varied his stance, distance, and pace in ways which exactly mirrored the young man's *qa*. Every shift of the young man's energy or intention was reflected by the whirling spear. He could not counter because the warrior's weapon matched each movement.

The truth was that I had concentrated my attention on the wrong combatant. Thinking that I must understand the young man's skills and limitations and mistakes in order to aid him, I had missed the real point of Isla's assumption. His mastery was not at issue. Rather, he needed to grasp the nature of his opponent.

If it was true that Argoyne required a champion, then it must also be true that the warrior we watched had been mage-made to mimic an opposing champion. The champion of the White Lords, and of Goris Miniter, Vesselege's King.

"Where—?" I tried to ask Isla. But my voice stuck in my throat. I swallowed, breathing deeply to clear my *qa*. "Where," I began again, "have you seen a spear used in that way before?"

I feared her reply almost as much as I feared her scruples.

However, she answered softly, "I haven't." Then she added, "The *mashu-te* distrust weapons. I know less than you."

Indeed. No doubt the *mashu-te* believed that any weapon diminished the personal responsibility of its wielder. In contrast, the *nahia* studied weapons without number. But ours was the Art of Circumvention. We studied all weapons—apart from the fang—in order to counter or defeat them. We did not wish to become dependent upon them. And I had never encountered tactics such as the warrior used.

"Do the *ro-uke* fight so?" I pursued, although I did not expect a response. I was merely thinking aloud.

"If they do," she muttered, "they do it in secret."

I understood more than she said. The *ro-uke* did nothing publicly. In Vess, however, I had watched such masters at work. Once or twice I had measured myself against them, when one escapade or another had brought us into conflict. Theirs was not an art of direct confrontation.

In addition, the tactics this warrior now used were ill suited to the stealthy work of assassination. They demanded great skill, but lacked both quickness and subtlety.

Still they were effective against the young man. I knew how I would attack in his place. Thrown at the warrior's foot, my fang might serve me well. And I could guess at Isla's counter. Direct in all things, she would attempt to catch the spearpoint—or break the shaft. But I could not imagine how the *shin-te* would meet such a challenge.

Service to qa *in all things.* He may have been handicapped by the strengths of his Art.

Abruptly I received my answer. Amid a flurry of feints and deflections, the young man struck.

All the Fatal Arts made a study of *qa*, and I was a master—yet I saw no hint of his intent, no concentration of purpose or projection of energy, until he had carried it out. A blow like his would have felled me where I stood.

Whirling his staff, he swung it against his opponent's spear a span or two below the point. I felt the crack of impact before I truly saw what he had done.

Apparently, however, this was the opening which the warrior sought. Using the young man's force to accelerate his own motion, he reversed the spear in his hands so that its butt punched down onto the *shin-te*'s crown. Less than an instant later, his foot hooked the young man's ankle, jerking away his support.

Stunned, the *shin-te* dropped to his back.

Before his spine touched stone, his opponent had reversed the spear again. Both Isla and I winced as the point drove deep into the young master's chest.

Our only hope was dead before his limbs had settled themselves to the floor.

―――――――

"I'm not sure that was a good idea," she observed when she had composed herself. "What do we gain by watching him die? I don't think any master can beat that—that whatever it is—that creature."

Certainly she and I had both failed often enough.

Pacing the cell, she continued bitterly, "It's inhuman. None of us can defeat magery. That's not what the Fatal Arts are for.

"If our captor wants a champion to fight an enemy like that," she avowed, "let him create one."

"Again you make assumptions," I sighed. "Your conclusion does not follow from your observation."

I had no wish to argue with her. More than that, I actively wished to avoid speaking of my own assumptions. I did not know how I might counter her reaction to Argoyne's name. But the young man's death had restored my knowledge of despair. I contradicted Isla simply so that I would not succumb.

"That our captor uses an inhuman test," I explained, "does not necessarily imply that he intends his champion to fight an inhuman opponent. It suggests only that he cannot persuade or coerce an appropriate master to serve him." If he could have done so, he would have had no use for us, and our lives would have been left undisturbed. "Lacking any man or woman who fights as the opposing champion does, he is unable to test us fairly. This is the best he can do. With the power at his disposal."

A power which was itself being tested to its limits.

"Are you defending him now?" she protested. But her objection was not seriously meant. "Who is he, anyway?" she asked more plaintively. "Who in all the White Hells needs a champion at a time like this?"

I spread my hands. "Does it matter? If our captor cannot obtain a fit champion—and if his champion does not win—we will die. Nothing else has significance."

She snorted. "Of course it matters." Apparently she felt a *mashu-te* contempt for the ambiguities of the *nahia*. "All this must have something to do with the Mage War. Why else does a mage need a champion? Are you saying that you see no difference between the White Lords and the Dark?"

In Vesselege it was believed that the White Lords were the servants of light and life, while such men as Black Argoyne devoted themselves to havoc and cold murder. For that reason—it was believed—Goris

Miniter had allied his reign and his kingdom against the Dark Lords, and the Archemage.

I shared such assumptions. If I distrusted them, I did so on principle, not from conviction.

"That is not how you reasoned with the *shin-te*," I countered wearily. "Then you claimed that only the blows mattered, not the context." More than my companion, I had been broken by my defeats. "Who we are asked to serve will mean nothing to us if we are dead."

I prayed that this thin argument would suffice. I lacked a better one—except that I was *nahia*, and my loyalties did not much resemble the abstract purity of the *mashu-te*.

Fortunately, Isla was silenced while she considered the contradictions of her beliefs.

Once again, he returned from death to the cell, remembering nothing. The sight of him wrung my heart, for his sake as well as my own. The bereavement in his eyes had deepened until it seemed to swallow hope. For the second time, he staggered as he appeared. And he was slow to recover, as though he were unsure where his balance lay.

Still his thoughts followed their familiar path. When he could summon his voice from his parched throat, he asked, as he had always asked, "Where am I?"

Neither Isla nor I attempted a reply. Instead we stared in dismay at the blood which drained from his lips with each word, dripping from his chin to spatter his robe with failure.

Then he was gone. We observed his departure no more clearly than we had witnessed his arrival. We only knew that he had been given back to us—and taken away again.

"By the Seven—!" Isla cried. "Asper, what's happened to him?"

The young man's blood might have been my own. I had grown tired of speculation. I did not like where it led me. But I did not need to assume much in order to answer.

"Our mage grows weak." According to the stories told in Vess, Argoyne had fought alone against the assembled might of the White Lords for the better part of a year. "He could not spare the power which allowed us to witness the contest. For that reason, the *shin-te* was inadequately restored from death."

She accepted this explanation. "Who is he?" she asked again. "Asper, I do not know what to wish for." She was close to despair herself. "I want to live. I want to repay what this mage has done to us. He has taught me hate, and that I will not forgive. But I cannot desire victory for such as the Black Archemage.

"I need to know who it is that requires a champion."

Behind the grime on her face, her anguish was plain. Until then, I had not fully appreciated how costly the scruples of the *mashu-te* might be. During my own trial, she had saved my spirit. Now she threatened to crush it within me.

"Isla," I replied as gently as I could, "I am *nahia*. We have taken no part in this war because it surpasses us." Tales were told of *mashu-te* who fought for Goris Miniter, and of *ro-uke*, but never of *nahia*. "Who are we to stake our allegiance"—our honor—"on a struggle we cannot understand?" Honor was a word which my masters did not use lightly. "I want to live. And I want to repay this mage. Other concerns do not trouble me."

Mine was the Art of Circumvention.

I expected more *mashu-te* contempt, but Isla surprised me. She regarded me, not with scorn, but with wonder and pity. "You're avoiding the truth," she breathed. "You know who he is. And you don't want to name him."

Her *qa* confronted me as though she readied a blow.

"You believe he's Argoyne," she said softly. "And you're willing to help him. You believe we'll die here if we don't help him defeat the White Lords, and you're willing to do it."

I would have preferred being struck. Stung by despair, I cried, "Because it does not matter!" Against her scruples and her purity, I protested, "*I* matter. To me. *You* matter to me. The *shin-te* matters to me. But this war of mages and kings—" I could not explain myself to one who was not *nahia*. "It requires too many assumptions."

Her reply might have finished me. Before she could utter it, however, we became aware that the young man had returned.

————————

The blood was gone from his lips. He appeared stronger—perhaps better rested. This time more magery had been spent on his restoration. But it did not soften his loss and bafflement. Mere power could not heal the aggrievement of his young heart.

"Where am I?"

Mere power could not make him other than he was.

"Who are you?"

This could not go on. If Argoyne was scarcely able to heal those he tested, his crisis must not be far off. And despair was not cowardice. Although I feared Isla in several ways, I did not allow her to daunt me.

Only memory would be of any use to him.

Instead of answering the young man, I faced Isla squarely.

"Stop me now," I told her. I was certain that she could do so. "If you mean to abandon your life"—and your hate—"for the sake of guesses, do so now. Or stand aside, and let me do what I can."

The young man appeared to think I meant to attack him. His stance shifted subtly, focusing his abused *qa*.

She glared at me from the depths of her begrimed face. The *mashu-te* placed great value on achieving their ends through sacrifice—in this case, obtaining Argoyne's defeat at the cost of her life. But to sacrifice my life, and the young man's, for the sake of her purpose troubled her. And if she played only a passive part in the Archemage's death, her hate would not be appeased.

Deliberately she withdrew. From the distance of a few paces, she fixed a gaze hungry with anger on the *shin-te*.

In haste, I turned to the young man. I could not know when Argoyne's crisis would overtake him.

Recognizing his apprehension, however, I paused to bow. I wished him to see that I meant no challenge—that I regarded him as a respected comrade, not as an opponent.

As he bowed in reply, he softened his stance somewhat. But he did not set aside his readiness.

"Young master," I began, "you have been imprisoned by a mage. As have we. He has deprived you of your memory. For that reason, you cannot recollect your circumstances, or your name. You do not remember us. But we remember you. We are your allies."

I could not imagine why he should believe me. In his place, I would not have done so. Certainly I had mistrusted Isla long enough—until death and isolation had forced me to set aside suspicion. Nevertheless I spoke with all the conviction I had learned from my plight.

"Our captor," I continued, "is Argoyne the Black. The Dark Archemage. Somewhere beyond this place, the Mage War rages, and he intends you to play a part in it, if you are able."

I studied the *shin-te* for a reaction, but he betrayed none. His expression revealed only courtesy and grief, nothing more. Lacking memory, he could attach no significance to Argoyne's name. Doubtless the Mage War itself meant nothing to him.

Perhaps that simplified my task. I could not tell.

Stifling a sigh, I informed him, "The Archemage desires a champion. By some means which we do not understand and cannot fathom, this war has become a matter of single combat. Both Isla and I have been tested to serve as Argoyne's champion, but we failed. You are all that remains of hope for the mage—and for us.

"*You* have not failed," I insisted, fearing that Isla would contradict me, although she made no move to speak. "You have met certain setbacks." This was difficult to explain. "They account for your weariness and confusion. The magery which restores you exacts a toll. But you have not failed. The *shin-te* teach that you must give 'service to *qa* in all things,' and you have done so."

The young man received this assurance as he had all I said—sadly, without acknowledgment. Though he had no memory of the experience, he appeared to understand in his bones and sinews—in his *qa*—that he had indeed failed.

Breathing deeply to quell my alarm, I pursued my purpose. "However," I announced, "you have not grasped the nature of the champion who opposes you. The champion you are asked to defeat. And your ignorance has caused your setbacks."

At last I saw a hint of interest in the *shin-te*'s eyes. He found it easy to credit that he was ignorant—and that ignorance was fatal.

I summoned my *qa*. "The challenge before you is the true test," I told him, "simple and pure. The *shin-te* believe that 'there is no killing stroke.' You will face a master of the *nerishi-qa*. The Art of the Killing Stroke."

There I stopped. I saw in the sudden flaring of the young man's eyes that he knew more of the *nerishi-qa* than I.

Isla could not silence her surprise. Advancing, she demanded, "*Nerishi-qa*, Asper? How do you know?" At once she added, "How long have you known? Why haven't you said anything?"

"I do *not* know," I replied without disguising my vexation. "I am making an assumption." An exercise I did not enjoy. To the young man, I said, "We were permitted to watch the contest from which you have just returned. In it, you were slain. And restored by magery. At the cost of your memory. Your opponent fought in ways unfamiliar to me. I am *nahia*. Isla is *mashu-te*. I have seen the *ro-uke*. And you are *shin-te*. Your opponent's skills belong to none of these. Therefore he is *nerishi-qa*."

From the first, the *shin-te* had met death with sorrow, remembering nothing except his loss. Now, however, there was another light in his gaze. Strictures shaped the corners of his eyes, the lines of his mouth. A sensation of anger emanated from him.

"The *nerishi-qa*," he pronounced softly, "teach a false Art."

Isla rounded on him. "How so?"

"Legend teaches," I put in, "that *nerishi-qa* is the first and most potent of the Fatal Arts. All others derive from it."

The young man shook his head. There was no doubt in him. "It is false.

"You have called it 'the Art of the Killing Stroke,' yet there is no killing stroke." The strength of his conviction shone from him. "The *nerishi-qa* claim for themselves the power and the right to determine death. But he who determines death also determines life, and that they cannot do. Life belongs to the one who holds it. It cannot be taken away. There-fore no killing stroke exists. There is only choice."

In my urgency, I had no patience for such mystical vapor. And Isla felt as I did, apparently. Nearly together, we objected, "We saw you die."

Direct as a fist, she added, "That champion nailed you to the floor with a spear."

"Did you choose *that*?" I demanded.

Uncomfortably, he answered, "I do not remember."

A moment later, however, he shouldered the burden of his beliefs. "Yes. I did."

Then his earlier sorrow returned to his gaze—a bereavement shaded by shame. "You say that I was ignorant. I did not know him for *nerishi-qa*."

I accepted his assumption. I feared to weaken him with doubt. But Isla did not.

"Or you knew," she countered, "and that's why you chose to die. You knew you couldn't defeat him." *Mashu-te* to the core, she accepted the risk of what was in her heart. "You surrendered to despair."

Anxiously I watched the young man for his response.

"I do not remember," he repeated. "Perhaps I did." The flinch had returned to his eyes, although he did not look away. "If so, I do not deserve to be named among the *shin-te*."

Seeking to help him if I could, I asked, "Are you acquainted with the *nerishi-qa*? Would you recognize that Art?"

He considered for a moment, then shook his head. "There are scholars among the *shin-te*, preserving our knowledge of all the Arts. I have studied the texts. But they are old. And what is written conceals as well as reveals what it describes. I have never seen the *nerishi-qa*."

I sighed privately, keeping my relief to myself.

Isla was plainer. "Then perhaps," she said, "we can still hope."

"I do not know," he said as if admitting the true source of his sorrow. "Every year, my masters send one of us to carry a challenge to the *nerishi-qa*, so that we may test our skills—and our beliefs. But the messengers are always spurned. The *nerishi-qa* disdain to measure themselves against us."

I was sure that Isla retained her wish for Argoyne's destruction. For the present, however, she had apparently accepted that life was better than death. There may have been a hint of the *nahia* in her nature. Rather than merely assuming that the Black Archemage would be ruined by the young man's defeat, she hoped to witness that ruin herself—and to participate in it if she could. And for that purpose sacrifice would not serve.

———

As on previous occasions, the young *shin-te* needed rest. Both death and restoration had been arduous for him, as I remembered well. Despite my eagerness to know what he had read in the texts of his scholars—and my belief that Argoyne's crisis was near—I urged him to his pallet.

He acquiesced readily enough. But he was not granted an opportunity for sleep. As he uncoiled his fatigue upon the pallet, a tremor shook the cell. In the distance, we heard a mutter of stone, as though the crags of Scarmin ground their teeth.

"Earthquake," Isla suggested when the tremor had passed.

"Do you believe that?" I asked sourly. I did not.

A second tremor followed the first, stronger and more prolonged. In its aftermath, dust sifted from the ceiling, filling the constant light with hints of peril. Again we heard from afar the rumor of crushed rock.

We were on our feet, the three of us, instinctively keeping our distance from the walls—and watching the timbers above us, in case they should start to crack.

For the second time, a voice spoke in the air. "Now," the mage said harshly. "It must be now."

Then the young man was gone. Neither Isla nor I saw his departure.

———

She reacted while I stood motionless in consternation. In the wake of Argoyne's bodiless utterance, she protested, "He's exhausted! He hasn't rested!" Furiously, she cried, "By the White Lords, do you *want* him to fail?"

There was no answer. Instead a third tremor jolted us. It struck the cell harder than the first two combined, endured longer. I staggered, despite my training, and Isla fought for balance. Above us, timbers shrieked against each other. A disturbing unsteadiness afflicted the lamps.

Argoyne's peril was more desperate than I had imagined. He had expended too much of his power testing us—and lost too much time.

When the convulsion eased, I saw that its force had stricken a crack up one wall from floor to ceiling beside the door.

The door—

Isla did not see it. The straining timbers consumed her attention. "Asper!" she shouted. "The keep is falling! We'll be crushed!"

The door. At last. Argoyne's magery had failed him. Or he no longer needed it. Or our imprisonment served no further purpose in his designs.

"I think not." Between one heartbeat and the next, my dismay vanished. Some sleight of circumstance transferred it to her, and I was freed. "These quakes will cease as soon as Argoyne announces his champion."

I had already turned my fang to the challenge of the door.

Now she noticed it. "Asper—" she gasped. "What's happening? How did this—?"

"Compose yourself," I snapped, "and let me work." Her questions, and my own, would answer themselves soon enough.

I was *nahia*, a master of Circumvention. No mere door could hold me if I bent my will to escape. But could I bypass this obstacle quickly? That was another matter altogether. The more strictly the door had been secured, the more time and skill would be needed to open it.

I did not care why Black Argoyne's concealment of the door had failed. Rather, I wished to know how much trust he had placed in that concealment.

"This changes everything, Asper," Isla insisted at my back. "The White Lords must have beaten him. He can't protect his keep. Why don't they press their advantage? Why risk this war on a champion when they can tear his power stone from stone?"

"Am I a mage?" I snarled without interrupting my efforts. I had no patience for her. "Do I understand these things?"

I understood bolts and locks, staples and bindings. Estimating the actions of mages required too many assumptions. Words were also a form of circumvention, however, and they could cut as well as any blade.

"Perhaps," I continued while I tested the door, "the effect of their attacks is hidden from the White Lords. Or perhaps the Archemage has other uses for his power. The truth—"

Abruptly I sighed. It appeared that Argoyne relied more upon magery than upon physical restriction. My fang found the doorbolt and turned it so that its hasp left the staple. Carefully I began to slip the bolt aside.

"The truth," I repeated as I pulled the door open, "will be revealed when we find him."

Between her teeth, Isla remarked, "Asper, you amaze me." But she did not pause to admire my handiwork. "Come on," she commanded at once. Ahead of me, she hastened from the cell. "I have a debt to repay."

I followed without hesitation. I, too, had a debt to repay—although it did not much resemble hers.

For the first time in uncounted days, we were free of imprisonment. Therefore we were also free of Argoyne's purposes, and could now choose our own way—or so she apparently believed.

I did not make that assumption.

———————

We found him with relative ease. The corridors and chambers within the keep were simply arranged, one level above the next. On each, a large hall filled the center of the structure, surrounded by a wide passageway. Smaller rooms were arrayed between the corridor and the keep's walls. A broad stair climbed from floor to floor. We might have spent days at it if we had attempted to search the outer chambers, but by tacit agreement we concentrated on the central halls. I was content to believe that the Archemage would need space around him in order to wield his power. On each level, we opened massive doors to look inward, discovered nothing, and proceeded to the next stair.

None of the passages we traveled resembled the one in which we had been tested.

At another time, I would have been fascinated by the apparent absence of any servants, retainers, companions, or defenders. Argoyne the Black, it seemed, desired no human service—or had been abandoned by it. In addition, I would have been intensely interested in the possessions with which the outer rooms were filled, as well as in the uses to which the inner halls were put. Much of what I saw served no purpose I could recognize. Now, however, I was in too much haste for curiosity. Refusing investigation, I kept pace with Isla.

Five levels above our cell, we came upon the Archemage.

In a stone chamber lit by the keep's ceaseless lamps, he sat at a long trestle table scattered with scrolls and charts, his back to the door. More scrolls curled outward from the stool on which he perched, in reach of ready reference. And still more, texts by the hundreds, were piled upon row after row of shelves propped against all the walls—scrolls in profusion, of every description, some plainly ancient, others still gilt and gleaming. Together they held more knowledge than I had ever seen, or indeed imagined, in one place.

At the sight, I experienced an eerie pang. Where the *mashu-te* valued purity and scruples, the *nahia* prized knowledge. Granted the opportunity, my masters would have cheerfully slaughtered a kingdom to obtain so much treasure.

Isla, in contrast, would have cheerfully fired the room to rid Vesselege of Black Argoyne.

Even here, our captor was alone—a small figure immersed in his robes, hunching over his scrolls as though he fed from them. Whatever his needs may have been, for food or drink, for companionship or service, he supplied them by magery. The White Lords and Goris Miniter had made him a pariah to be feared and shunned.

From the back, a nimbus of white hair as fine as silk concealed the edges of his face. And he did not turn toward us. Indeed, he seemed unaware of our arrival. Sacrificing stealth for haste, we had not opened the door quietly, but other concerns held his attention.

As they would have held mine, in his place—

"Asper—" Isla breathed softly.

I ignored her.

Before the Archemage hung an image like the one in which Isla and I had watched the young man's last test. This was far larger, however, filling one end of the hall. And the scene arrayed within it lay at some considerable distance, that was obvious. Argoyne's stone walls—his keep among the peaks of Scarmin—contained no sunlit meadows, rich with wildflowers and grasses, like the one I saw beyond the table.

I knew at once that I gazed upon the ground appointed for the contest of champions. For the blood of the young *shin-te*—or of his opponent. For the resolution of the Mage War.

From the foreground of the image, the young man emerged, striding slowly away from us as if he strolled the meadow at his leisure. At first he was alone among the flowers under a sky defined by plumes and wisps of cloud. Before he had taken ten paces, however, a row of horsemen appeared along the far horizon. Dark with distance, and silent as dreams, they galloped swiftly forward, converging on the *shin-te* as they rode—an ominous throng, fifty or more, most of them soldiers and warriors. Soon I distinguished Goris Miniter by his helm and bearing, and by the crest of Vesselege on his velvet cape. The men on either side of him, clad in flowing robes so pure that they appeared to flame with reflected sunlight, must have represented the White Lords.

Neither Isla nor I advanced. The sight of the young man, isolated among the blooms, facing a force great enough to overwhelm any champion, kept us motionless.

At last the riders drew near enough to encircle him. By some trick of magery, however, they did not obscure our view of him. From horseback, Goris Miniter appeared to address the *shin-te*, but his words made no more sound than the mute hooves and tack of the horses, the silent commands of the soldiers. If the young man answered, we could not hear it. In the image they were all as voiceless as the dead.

Abruptly Argoyne searched among his scrolls, opened another on the table, and set his hand upon it. At once the scene seemed to gain depth as the meadow unveiled its sounds to the hall. A breeze we could not feel soughed gently. Horses stamped their hooves, jangled their reins. Men coughed and caught their breath.

"Goris Miniter," Argoyne muttered, "King of Vesselege, I'm here." By magery his voice carried into the distance until it appeared to resound in the air of the meadow, echoing strangely.

Startled, many of the horsemen searched for the source of the sound. One of the White Lords leaned aside to advise or instruct the King.

Miniter raised his head. His features were plain before us—the iron
will of his mouth, the lines of calculation around his eyes. In Vess he
was known as a clever monarch, a man adept at ruling powers he did not
possess and could not match.

"Join us, Archemage," he commanded the breeze and the sky. "This
war will be decided here. Your absence warns of treachery."

"As does your presence, King of Vesselege," Argoyne answered. His
tone was querulous and unsteady, the voice of an old man, wearied by
his struggles and bitter about death. "I've agreed to this contest in terms
that bind me. If my champion loses, my defenses fail with him. And if I
attempt treachery to help him, my own powers will destroy me.

"Your White Lords are similarly bound. But you are not. You're only
an ally here, not a mage. Not a participant.

"I'll stay where I am," the Archemage concluded, "in case you're
tempted to take matters into your own hands."

Goris Miniter scowled at this response, but did not protest. Instead
he barked, "Then we will begin! The sooner your darkness is brought
to an end, Black Argoyne, the sooner hope and healing will dawn at last
in Vesselege."

With one gloved fist, he made a gesture as if he meant to fling all his
riders against the *shin-te*.

Only one horseman advanced, however. A warrior nudged his mount
a pace or two into the ring. Among so many other men, he had not caught
my eye. But when he left his place in the circle I seemed to know him
instantly by the completeness of his command over his horse, the liquid
flow of his movements as he dismounted, the perfect readiness of his
strides and his poise—and by the palpable force of his *qa*. The might
compressed within his frame was as vivid as a shout.

"Asper," Isla breathed again. "It must be now."

Still I ignored her. Argoyne could not remain deaf to our presence
indefinitely. And when he noticed us, we would be lost. We had no hope
against magery. Yet I could not break the spell cast on me by the sun-
blazed robes of the White Lords, by Goris Miniter's grim attention—and
by the plight of the young man who had fought and died, fought and
died, without knowing why.

The *nerishi-qa* was not a large man, perhaps no more than three fingers taller than the *shin-te*, and of somewhat greater bulk. Among my other apprehensions, this also troubled me. Where skill and *qa* were equal, any contest might be decided by weight of fist. Here was another disadvantage for a young man already hampered by fatigue and sorrow. In contrast, the *nerishi-qa* seemed arrogant and calm, certain of his strength.

His masters had at last accepted the challenge of the *shin-te*. And the fate of a kingdom rested on the outcome.

Respectfully, the young man bowed to his opponent. We could not see his face. Within myself, I prayed that the gaze he fixed on the *nerishi-qa* held anger rather than grief. When it did not sow confusion, anger bred force. Grief nurtured despair. And the harvest of despair was death.

The champion of the White Lords did not bow. His smile held untrammeled disdain as he advanced.

Despite this insult, the *shin-te* withheld attack. From the distance of the keep and the image, I saw no tension in his shoulders, his hips, his *qa*. Standing lightly, he waited in sunlight for the test of the killing stroke.

When it came, Isla also struck. Seemingly borne aloft by his *qa*, the *nerishi-qa* focused both weight and muscle in a flying kick which might have snapped his opponent's spine—and Isla launched herself at the Archemage. While the *shin-te* slipped the kick aside, countering with elbow and palm, she slapped the crook of her arm around Argoyne's throat, clamped her forearm to the base of his skull. Holding him so, she could snap his neck with one quick lift of her shoulders.

Instinctively he clutched at her arm. At once, she swept her leg over the table, wiping the clutter of scrolls beyond his reach.

"Isla—!" I protested.

In her turn, she ignored me.

"Now," she murmured to his ear. "Now you're mine. I hold your death, mage. I'm going to repay my own."

Carried past the *shin-te* by his kick, the *nerishi-qa* rolled in the air to deflect the swift force of the young man's elbow. Then, instead of landing heavily, he seemed to settle into the grass, his poise undisturbed. I could not hear him—the image had lost sound when Argoyne's hands left his scrolls—but he appeared to be laughing.

"Wait," I told Isla urgently. "Wait!"

Hastening to the table, I confronted her past the Archemage. I feared and distrusted him as much as she did. Now that she had grasped his defeat, however, I found that I did not want him slain. Instead I wished to see the outcome of the young man's contest.

I wished to believe that my own deaths had not been wasted.

And I wished to understand this war.

Argoyne the Black had the look of a man who had spent his life among midnights and maggots. His beard was of the same fine white silk as his hair, but beneath it lay the slick, sunless complexion of a fish. And with Isla's arms wrapped about his neck, he gaped like a fish, eyes bulging, scarcely able to breathe. Hints of milk in his eyes obscured his vision.

As she had said, she held his death in her arms. Yet he appeared undaunted. Gasping for breath, he demanded, "What do you think you'll gain by breaking my neck?"

"Our lives," she retorted without hesitation. "Victory for your enemies."

"You won't enjoy it," he warned.

"Won't I?" She tightened her grasp. "You don't know me very well."

I could imagine no appeal which might reach her. Her face held nothing for me, no doubt and no softness. Her scruples lay elsewhere.

I could have killed her there. My skills and my fang were apt for such an action. But my masters would have never forgiven me that dishonor. No *nahia* would have forgiven it.

"And you," Black Argoyne panted in return, "don't understand the tyranny of the pure. You fool, I'm all that remains of hope for this land!"

There I saw my opening. "Hear him, Isla," I urged quickly. "Let him speak. We know nothing of this war. If we will determine its outcome, we must know what we do."

She looked at me. As if involuntarily, her grasp loosened, permitting the mage more air.

"Isn't he the Black Archemage," she challenged me angrily, "devoted to darkness? Hasn't he rained down death on all Vesselege until Goris Miniter himself has been forced to side with the White Lords? How much more do you need to know?"

In the image, the *nerishi-qa* attacked again. His tactics had changed. He no longer attempted to end the contest with one blow. Instead he advanced through a flurry of strikes and feints.

As before, the *shin-te* countered, landing a blow of his own when he could, parrying when he could not. Despite the pressure of his opponent's assault, he moved easily, preserving his strength.

In a sense, the battle had not yet become serious. Both champions still measured each other, probing not so much for victory as for an estimation of their skills and weaknesses.

"You understand honor," Argoyne coughed. Hooking his fingers on Isla's forearm, he strained against her hold. He could not shift her grasp, but he gained space enough to speak more clearly. "Or you should. Every Fatal Art preaches it.

"Why do you think all the White Lords and Goris Miniter have banded together against me? Do you call that honorable? Do you really believe I'm so malign—and so powerful—that they had no choice? I'm just one mage. One man. Would every *mashu-te* in Vesselege go to war against one *nahia*? Or even one *nerishi-qa*?

"This whole struggle," he spat, "is dishonorable."

His assertion surprised me. I had not expected such an argument from a mage. Despite my experience of death, my enmity toward him wavered.

For her part, however, Isla was unmoved. Sneering, she retorted, "And what do *you* have to do with 'honor,' Archemage?"

"Little enough," he admitted. "Everything they say about me is true." His voice held an edge of savagery—of rage prolonged and constricted beyond endurance. Battle after battle, death after death, he had nurtured his fury until it filled him. "I study darkness. The Seven Hells are my domain." He released one hand to indicate the ring of riders in the meadow. "*They* can't bring slaughtered warriors back to life. *I* can. And I *have* rained violence on Vesselege. But not until they forced me to it. Not until they formed their alliance against me.

"Your White Lords—" In his mouth the words were a curse. "They don't just think I'm wrong. They think I should be crushed. Because my magery isn't like theirs. They want to destroy me because I look for power in places they fear. They want to destroy my knowledge. Not because of anything I *did*. Because of what I *am*. And what I know. Until they started this war, I'd committed no crime they could hold against me."

That argument I felt as well, but Isla snorted contemptuously. "They aren't here to defend themselves. Why should I trust anything you tell me?"

My attention was torn between Argoyne and the contest—between Isla's grim hostility and my own uncertain intent. Glancing aside, I saw that the *nerishi-qa* had begun to spin, flinging out kicks and blows as if from the heart of a whirlwind. His balance and the stability of his *qa* on the uneven ground of the meadow seemed unnatural to me, almost inhuman. I could not have done what he did. Even at this distance, I feared to encounter such a master.

The young *shin-te* retreated steadily, dodging from side to side to foil the onslaught, occasionally diving beneath a kick to improve his position. If he discerned any opening in the assault—as I did not—he took no advantage of it.

But the Archemage had not faltered. He pointed at the White Lords before us. "They believe they're in the right," he answered. "*In the right!* As if being in the right has anything to do with knowledge. 'Right' and 'wrong' have to do with how knowledge is used, not with knowledge itself."

Every word he uttered seemed to whet his fury. His tone was as sharp as my fang. I felt its edge against my heart, although Isla held him helpless. My masters might have spoken as he did.

"I tell you on my soul," he rasped bitterly, "if there were fifty mages of my kind in the world, I would not have formed an alliance with them against the White Lords. *I* don't want the White Lords dead. I don't even want them *hurt*." He strained at Isla's grasp to express his ire. "But I *will not* stand by while my knowledge and my life are erased as if they never existed."

She opened her mouth to voice an objection, but he overrode her. "*That* is not a claim your White Lords can make," he insisted. His vehemence seemed to flay at the air. "They *do* wish me dead. They wish my knowledge *destroyed*. Because they believe they're in the right.

"Oh, they're as pure as sunlight," he raged, "and just as cruel. Do you think they care about Vesselege? You delude yourself. They could have ended this war whenever they chose." His voice rose to a shout against the pressure of her arm. "They could have *stopped!* But then I would have been able to keep my life and my power. All the land would have seen that I attacked no one except in my own defense. And *that*," he cried, "they can't tolerate because they are *in the right.*"

Then he subsided to bitterness. "They're so pure that they're prepared to see the whole kingdom laid waste to prove it. As if 'right' and 'wrong' have anything to do with war."

At the edge of my sight, I saw the *shin-te* fall under a vicious wheel of blows. At once, kicks like adzes hacked at him among the grass and flowers. Several he blocked, but one caught him a glancing blow at the point of his hip. As he regained his feet, I saw a small twitch of pain on his cheek. His stance suggested a subtle weakness in that hip—a hurt that slowed and hindered him.

My heart went out to him, alone among his enemies, but I could not help him there. The meadow might have been leagues or days distant. I could do nothing until I found my way through the maze of Argoyne's self-justification and Isla's hate.

Troubled, she looked to me. Apparently she desired some response. She had not been swayed—not as I had—but the Archemage had touched a nerve of uncertainty in her, which she did not know how to relieve.

I took hope from her glance. "Heed him," I urged her softly. "Would the *mashu-te* be enriched if there were no *nahia*? If every master of the *shin-te* were slain? If the *nerishi-qa* ceased to exist? Light must have darkness, Isla. Without contention, the Fatal Arts would have no purpose. Therefore the *shin-te* teach 'acceptance of that which opposes us.'"

When I saw my words strike home in her, I turned toward the mage. Deliberately I toyed with my fang so that he could see it in my hands and know that I, too, might choose to kill him. Studying the blade, I asked, "What is Goris Miniter's place in this?"

Black Argoyne coughed an obscenity. "The tyranny of the pure is easily manipulated. Miniter knows he'll never truly rule this land if he can't rule the mages. And he doesn't have the power to do that directly.

Not without drowning Vesselege in blood. When he was done, he wouldn't have anyone left to rule. So he's playing on the purity of the White Lords. Using it to make them do what he wants. They think he serves them because he knows they're in the right. The truth is, they serve him because he knows how to lie."

Isla tightened her hold. "And you don't?"

He groaned his distress and exasperation. "Of course I know how. But I'm too tired to bother. *I* don't want to rule anybody. Right now the only thing I want is to keep myself and my knowledge alive."

When she eased her pressure, he added, "I'll tell you how you can recognize the truth. If my champion wins"—again he indicated the image before us—"if that poor young man finds some way to defeat the enemy of everything he believes— Those self-righteous fanatics won't stand for it. They'll intervene. They'll strike him down themselves. They'll accept their own ruin to prevent me from surviving."

Darkly, he muttered, "And I still expect treachery from Goris Miniter."

Isla seemed to think that she had found the flaw in his self-justification. As if she were pouncing, she demanded, "'Accept their own ruin'? What good will it do them to strike the *shin-te*, if they're destroyed in the process?"

"Oh, 'destroyed.'" Argoyne made a dismissive gesture. "They won't be destroyed. Fewer than half of them took part in the oath of this contest—the oath which seals them to its outcome. The ones who swore will die. The rest said they would abide the result, but that's only because they think their champion can't lose. If he does, the War will go on as before. They'll say I betrayed the challenge. As long as Miniter stands by them, no one will question their story."

To my surprise, I found that I believed him. I was *nahia*, disinclined by nature and training to trust men and women who predicted the actions of others. But Isla had taught me that those who prized their own scruples did not think as I did.

Belief tempted her as well. That was made plain by the doubt which darkened her gaze, the way her teeth gnawed the inside of her cheek. Where the *nahia* studied habits of mind, the *mashu-te* served convictions.

Was she not prepared to sacrifice her life to gain Argoyne's defeat? Then would the White Lords not do the same? If they were certain of their own purity, as the Archemage insisted?

However, her uncertainty led her to questions which I would not have considered important.

"So that young *shin-te* is your only hope," she snarled in his ear. "If you're telling the truth. You can't betray the oath of this contest, and you won't try, even though you assume your enemies will attempt treachery." Word by word, she tightened her arm on his neck until he again began to gape for air. "So tell me why you've done everything you can to weaken him. Explain why you're trying to make sure he loses."

His eyes bulged wildly. "That's madness," he gasped. "I've done no such—"

She clenched his throat. "You took his memory! You prevented any of us from learning *anything* from all those tests!"

"Isla," I put in sharply, "let him breathe."

The glare she turned toward me had the force of a kick. Still she eased her arms again, granting the Archemage air.

"Do you think it's *easy*," he panted quickly, "bringing people back from death?" With both hands he pulled against her grasp. "Do you think all I have to do is wave my arms and *wish*? You don't know what you're asking.

"If you reanimate a corpse, what you get is a walking corpse. A body without a mind. But restoring the mind— Ah, that's hard. Dreams, memory, reason, layer by layer, you have to bring it all back, or the corpse isn't fully alive. And hardest of all to bring back is the spirit, the"—he muttered a curse—"you don't have words for it. It's *qa*, but it isn't—not the way you think about it." Squirming against Isla's insistence, he tried to explain. "It's the resilience and hunger that makes people want to go on living in the face of death. When you reanimate a corpse, if you restore the memory of death, and don't restore the spirit that refuses to accept it, what you get is a madman.

"I've been fighting a war here." Sorrow mounted in his tone as he spoke. His plight might have been the same as the young *shin-te* master's. "The whole time while I tested you, I've been fighting for my life. And

I've been losing. When I brought you back from death, all of you, I didn't have the time or the power to do everything. So I chose to keep you sane. Instead of making you whole. You're all useless as warriors without *qa*. So I held back memory instead."

I could see—as Argoyne could not—that he baffled her. Her anger could not accommodate his account of himself. Frightened by uncertainty, she demanded, "Then why did you restore our memories when you were done with us? Why did you bother?"

"I hoped," he admitted, "that if you were whole you might find some way to help me. But even if you didn't—even if you hated me too much to try—" He sighed, sagging within his robes. "I couldn't bear to leave you that way. You didn't ask to serve me. And nobody deserves to be crippled like that. To be alive without memory or spirit—" He shrugged weakly. "You'd be better off dead."

At another time, I might have contested this assertion. Whole or crippled, I did not wish for death. I knew it too well, and the knowledge had done me great hurt. For the present, however, I left Argoyne's belief unchallenged. Where Isla suffered confusion, I felt only urgency. I did not know how long the young man could endure his opponent's assault— or how long Goris Miniter would abide the uncertainty of his own fate.

Hampered by the pain in his hip, the *shin-te* was forced to counterattack. He could no longer afford to await openings which he would then ignore. If he failed to drive the *nerishi-qa* back, he was finished.

His weakened stance gave rise to an awkwardness which began to impede his blocks and parries. Blows which he had once deflected with ease now threatened him. His hands seemed to stagger as he warded strike after strike away. Lessened in grace and speed, he appeared helpless to save himself when his ribs were left exposed to a slashing kick. Only the concentration of his *qa* betrayed his intent.

As the kick arrived like the sweep of a mace, he flipped his legs from under him and dived backward below it. The strength of the blow and the momentum of his own fall he used to spear the fingers of one hand into the pit of his opponent's groin. At the same time, he swept his other arm around the *nerishi-qa*'s leg and rolled so that he bore it beneath him to the grass.

Before the White Lords' champion could wrench free, or scissor another kick, the *shin-te* cut with his elbow deep into the nerves at the back of the *nerishi-qa*'s thigh.

When the *nerishi-qa* regained his feet, his jaws were clenched on a pain to match the *shin-te*'s, and his own stance hinted at weakness. A new respect disturbed the arrogance of his gaze.

The time had come. Deliberately I made my choice.

"If Goris Miniter means treachery," I asked the Archemage, "what form will it take?"

Argoyne shrugged. The question did not appear to interest him.

I indicated the image before us. "Are you able to show other scenes? Can you spare the power?"

"As long as my champion is still alive."

Containing my exasperation, I pursued, "Can you reveal our surroundings?" At once, however, a more useful question occurred to me. "Can you detect movement within the keep?"

The mage snorted. "There isn't any. We're alone." His tone suggested that he had been deserted long ago.

"What's the point, Asper?" Isla did not look at me. Disturbed by Argoyne's answers, she kept her gaze on the young *shin-te* while she wrestled with her hate. "The contest is there, not here."

"But if the King means treachery," I retorted, "it will be done *here*." With every passing moment, my urgency grew. "He cannot interfere with the White Lords' champion.

"Can you do it?" I demanded of the Archemage.

He lifted his hands to show that he was helpless without his scrolls.

"Isla," I instructed the woman who had saved me from despair, "release him."

She turned to me hotly. "Have you lost your mind? As soon as you let him touch his scrolls, he'll put us back in that cell." She secured her grip. "He'll turn us to dust. We'll be dead before you can blink."

"No," Argoyne and I said together.

"Do you 'assume,'" she shouted, "that you can trust him?"

"No!" I yelled in return. "I *assume* that the man who troubled to make us whole again after we had failed him has no interest in our deaths!"

She faltered. The simplicity of her loathing for the Archemage did not sustain her. He had challenged too many of her beliefs—as I had as well. "Treachery" was not a threat which the *mashu-te* suffered lightly.

"Asper—" she breathed, warning me.

With an effort of will, she removed her arms from Argoyne's neck.

Instantly his hands plunged among his scrolls, scrambling for the one he sought. When he found it, he slapped it open before him. "Movement?" he croaked as if she had damaged his throat. "Movement?"

Without transition, a new scene—smaller, and apparently more distant—appeared beside the meadow and the contest. The image showed a stone passage, featureless apart from the mage's eternal lamps and the doors on either hand, and entirely empty.

Empty except for the brief flutter of a black robe at the corner of the corridor.

"By the Seven Hells," Argoyne muttered, "you're right. Conniving bastard!" He meant the King of Vesselege. "They're already inside. I can feel"—he paused momentarily, then announced—"six of them."

From his scroll and his power, he produced other scenes, all of passages within the keep, all empty—and all defined by glimpses of stealth.

Somehow the intruders eluded more direct observation.

Ro-uke.

I did not hesitate. I had made my choice. As I left the table, running, I called to Isla, "Guard the door! We must have one of them alive!"

"Alive?" She did not appear to understand me. "Alive?"

"We must have evidence!"

If the *nerishi-qa* did not study honor as well as killing, I did not know how to combat them. I had seen the young *shin-te* slain once. I did not expect him to triumph now.

From the doorway I flung myself into the outer corridor.

Six of them— If they were allowed to reach Argoyne's chamber, they might slay him, regardless of his defenses. Theirs was the Art of Assassination. And their weapons were many.

An hour ago, I would have applauded the Dark Lord's death. But now I did not mean to see the Mage War decided by treachery.

I wished for other weapons myself. My fang's range was limited. But first I required a vantage from which I could watch over the Archemage without hazarding him. I could not seek out the *ro-uke*—I had recognized none of the corridors revealed in Argoyne's images. Therefore I must await his attackers.

A quick circuit of the passage showed only one stair rising to this level from below. That was fortuitous. I might be able to hold one stair against six *ro-uke*—although I doubted it—if they came at me singly, and did not take me by surprise.

Already, however, I had made a false assumption. And assumptions of all kinds were fatal. Because the scenes which Argoyne had opened in the air appeared distant, I had believed that the *ro-uke* were likewise distant.

As I hastened down the stair to select my point of vantage, a trident bit into my shoulder, tearing at my flesh with such force that I was thrown to the wall.

My fall became a tumble on the edged stone. I could not yet feel the pain of my wound, but only the shock of impact and the hard stairs. Later, if I lived, I would chide myself for a fool. Now, while I plunged downward, I reached out with my *qa*, measuring the trident's path toward me, gauging the location of my enemy.

When I struck the floor, he was no more than four paces from me, charging with his *ro-uke* katana upraised to sever the skull from my spine. Masked in black from head to foot, and voluminously robed to both conceal and contain his weapons, he might have been a long scrap of shadow cast by a torch held in an unsteady hand.

But the illumination in Argoyne the Black's keep shone without wavering, as endless and unmoved as stone.

Within two strides, the *ro-uke* folded at the knees and pitched onto his face with my dagger buried in the base of his throat. His sword slithered from his grasp, skidding its steel across the floor.

Now the pain of my shoulder came to me, and I knew at once that the points of the trident carried poison.

How swiftly the toxin would act I could not guess. And there were five more assassins to be considered. I did what I could, however. Retrieving my fang, and snatching up the katana, I ducked behind the foundation of the stair. There I pulled back my torn robe to examine my wound.

Some poisons were swift—others, slow. Some might be endured by a concentration of *qa* and will. To others I was immune. But the nature of this toxin had not yet revealed itself. Gripping my courage, I dug my fang into the wound until my shoulder bled heavily. Perhaps the worst of the poison would be flushed away.

Past its stone foundation, I saw no one approach the stair. No one advanced at my back. No sound carried from above, where—or so I prayed—Isla guarded Argoyne's door. After a moment spent to quiet my heart and my fear, I risked leaving the stair in order to peer beyond the corner of the corridor behind me.

My fang I again secreted within my robe. The sword I bore before me, ready for use.

Although I was cautious at the corner, I was not cautious enough. By ill chance, the *ro-uke* creeping toward me caught my gaze as I met hers. She was some distance from me yet. But now I had neither the advantage nor the disadvantage of surprise.

Rather than attempting to foil her by stealth—which was her Art, not mine—I stepped past the corner to confront her formally. With the katana's point directed toward her heart, I bowed in challenge.

As if by magery, she produced a sword from within her robe. This, too, was her Art, not mine. However, I was not daunted. I was *nahia*, and understood edged weapons. And I had always believed that because the *ro-uke* were proficient with weapons by the score, they were expert with none.

Soundless on the stone, she advanced to assail me.

Her first blow would have cleft me where I stood, but mine was the Art of Circumvention. I slipped her katana away along my blade, then turned my edge against her. She countered fluidly, liquid as a splash of ink.

Point to point, we considered each other.

A low slash followed, and one high. I saw that if I met her blade directly, force against force, I would open myself to her return stroke. However, that was not my nature—or the nature of my training. With each oblique deflection, I disturbed as well the cut which came next.

Again she brought her point to mine and paused.

There I might have died, but the alternation of her *qa* gave me warning. By the standards of the *nahia*, her skills were too thinly spread. She had not the gift of launching an attack without discernible preparation.

Warned, I flinched aside as she flung a shuriken at my face. Her stroke skidded from my blade. Unbalanced by the angle of my deflection, as well as by the force of her throw, she extended more than she had intended.

At once, I stamped a kick into the side of her knee, and felt the tendons tear as she collapsed.

Alive, I had told Isla. *We must have one of them alive!* But a growing numbness had taken hold of my shoulder, and four more assassins still crept the keep. In desperation the *ro-uke* cast another shuriken, but I stepped past it and cut her chest apart.

Dark death spilled and pooled beneath her as though her black attire melted to shadows.

A moment of dizziness swept through me. Fearing for my life, I slashed a strip from her robe and bound it tightly about my shoulder. Its pressure weakened my arm, but might also slow the toxin's progress.

If mine was the Art of Circumvention, clearly I must find some means to circumvent another direct contest. My dizziness receded, but did not pass entirely, and my heart had acquired an unsteadiness which alarmed me. After a moment's deliberation, I compelled myself to cut into the fallen *ro-uke*'s robe and search her until I discovered a rope and grapnel, which a stealthy assassin might use to scale a sheer wall.

Coiling the rope, I returned warily to the stair.

In my absence, any number of intruders might have ascended to the level of Argoyne's chamber. That I could not alter, however. If Isla did not choose to defend him, then the Archemage must defend himself. I could do nothing more than guard the stair.

Among the outer chambers, I found one with its door unlocked. From within the room, with the door nearly closed, I could watch the stair unseen. Failing to imagine an alternative, I accepted the disadvantages of surprise— which had slain my first opponent—and secreted myself to wait.

While I crouched at the slim crack of the door, numbness slowly sank its teeth into the side of my chest. A renewed wave of dizziness bore with it the bitter sensation of despair.

The young *shin-te* still lived, of that I was certain. If he—and Argoyne—had fallen, some sign of it would be felt in the mage's keep. Such powers did not pass lightly from the world. But how long could the *shin-te* endure? How long could I?

Focused and feverish in my confusion, I did not notice the *ro-uke* as he gained the stair. I had seen him approach—and yet he appeared to arrive like an act of magery, without transition.

With my strength ebbing, I waited in silence while the assassin crept upward. I could not challenge him openly, and did not trust my stealth to equal his. Despite the danger that he might ascend beyond my reach—or that another *ro-uke* might come behind him—I did not move until his head had risen into the stairwell, out of sight. Then I eased open the door of my covert and hastened toward him.

By good fortune, he paused where he was, no doubt studying the hazards of the floor above. Whirling the grapnel by its line, I flung it at his legs.

Again by good fortune—for I could not claim skill in my condition—I had cast true. The grapnel caught him securely. At once, I hauled on the rope, heaving him off the stair in a rush.

The snapping sound as he struck the floor told me that he had broken bones. He flopped nervelessly at the impact, then lay still. When I ventured near him, I saw that he was dead. The fall had crushed his skull, or his neck.

Giddy with relief and poison, I stumbled to the foot of the stair, seated myself, and rested my head on my stronger hand.

Three *ro-uke* remained. In a moment, I promised my weakness, I would rise to my feet and consider how I might oppose them. But first I must breathe. So that I could estimate the progress of the toxin, and concentrate my *qa* against it.

"Asper," Isla called softly from the head of the stair. "How many?"

I lifted my head to peer upward. A haze clouded my sight—apparently Argoyne's lamps had begun to smoke—and I could not see her clearly.

"Three," I told the stairwell.

"Then come up." She sounded impatient. "There are three here. One used the stair—I thought you were dead—but the other two must have climbed up the outer wall. They came at me from rooms across the passage.

"Asper, what's wrong?"

I had been foolish. A *ro-uke* must have gained the stair while I fought around the corner.

Vaguely I indicated my shoulder. "Poison."

Like the *ro-uke*, and Argoyne himself, she had lost her need for transitions. I alone still required movement from moment to moment. She appeared at my side, tugged me to my feet. "We don't have much time," she said as she urged me upward. "The *shin-te* is losing. Maybe Argoyne can help you." Rents marked her robe. Blood dripped from a cut in her scalp. Her cheek showed a bruise so deep that it must have covered cracked bones. "I kept one of them alive for you. I stunned her, but she'll recover soon."

Alive— She had succeeded where I had failed.

I could hope again. Gratitude swelled my *qa*, and a measure of stability returned to my limbs. "I am in your debt," I murmured as I amended my pace. "You are a tribute to the *mashu-te*."

"I hope they'll think so," she replied. Apparently her scruples disturbed her yet.

However, they no longer troubled me.

In the chamber of the Archemage, I saw at once that Isla had spoken truly. Argoyne's young champion stood near defeat. The resilience was gone from his movements, his eyes were empty of purpose, and his *qa* seemed to flutter within him like a torn rag. He still kept his feet, still blocked and countered. And he had exacted a price from his opponent. The *nerishi-qa* fought with one eye swollen shut, two broken fingers, and a falter in all his steps. The arrogance was gone from his gaze. Yet it was plain that the *shin-te* would be the first to fall. If I had not felt the proximity of his death like an emanation from Argoyne's image, or read it in the vehemence of his opponent's *qa*, I would have seen it on the faces of the White Lords, and of Goris Miniter. Anticipations of triumph defined the sunlight in their eyes. The young master had received blows which his flesh could not withstand.

The remaining *ro-uke* had recovered consciousness. Isla and I kept the woman between us, pretending to hold her captive. Perhaps Isla did so. For my part, however, I clung to her for support. Unsteadiness surged and receded in my head, and I could not trust my legs to sustain me. Like Argoyne's champion, I would soon fall.

Without delay, Isla informed the mage, "Asper needs help."

Reluctantly Argoyne turned from the meadow to consider my plight. His obscured vision regarded me as though I had lost my place in his attention.

"No," I said at once. "His need is greater." I indicated the *shin-te*. "Send us there. While you still can. We must go now."

The Archemage appeared to understand me. "They won't listen to you," he warned.

I sighed. "Then we will not speak to them."

Isla glared a question at me, but I had neither the heart nor the will to answer her. The outcome of the Mage War lay between warriors now, *shin-te* and *nerishi-qa*. Goris Miniter and the White Lords no longer had any part to play.

Argoyne nodded, reaching among his scrolls. "After all," he muttered as he found the one he sought and opened it, "I have nothing more to lose. If you wanted me dead, all you had to do is wait for it. And it's always easy to trust warriors. That's why," he finished cryptically, "they're called 'the Fatal Arts.'"

I could not have asked him what he meant if I had wished to. He and his chamber and the stone keep were gone.

Washed by morning sunlight, we stood in the meadow, surrounded by Miniter's horsemen. Isla still held the *ro-uke* by one arm, and I clung to the other, concealing my weakness as well as I was able. Five paces from us, both the young *shin-te* and his opponent had paused to stare in confusion and mistrust at our sudden interruption.

Around us, horses flinched and reared, snorting their alarm. Several of the riders prepared to charge against us until the King called them back to their places. The White Lords made warding gestures in our direction, but sent no magery to harm us.

Again haze dimmed my sight, as though the smoke of some vast and fatal bonfire had clouded the meadow. Yet I could see well enough to determine where we were. The meadow lay in a broad valley among the abrupt foothills of the Scarmin. Beyond them, crags and mountains shrouded by distance towered into the sky. And there, distinct against the high cliffs, stood Argoyne's keep.

This struggle for the fate of Vesselege took place at the boundary between the domains of magery, separated by height and stone—the borderland between the White Lords and the Dark.

Before Goris Miniter could raise his voice to demand an explanation, Isla and I bowed to him formally. Coerced to do so, the *ro-uke* followed our example.

"King of Vesselege," Isla said at once, "this test of champions has been dishonored. We've brought proof of treachery."

At her words, quick consternation echoed around the ring. Horsemen muttered and cursed. If she had announced to him that all his pain and effort had been wasted, the young *shin-te* could not have looked more bereft. Bowing his head, he slumped in sorrow or despair. However, the *nerishi-qa* reacted otherwise. He advanced a step or two angrily, as though he meant to challenge us. His *qa* was a furnace, feeding him where a lesser man such as I would have been consumed.

Once more Miniter stilled his riders. At his sides, the White Lords considered the peaks of Scarmin like men striving to bridge the distance in order to see Argoyne's thoughts.

Despite the haze which troubled my eyes, I could not mistake the King's calculation as he asked in tones of iron, "What has the Archemage done?"

"King of Vesselege," I answered, "the treachery is not his." Although

I spoke weakly, my voice carried across the meadow. "The dishonor belongs elsewhere."

The White Lords' champion approached another step, outrage burning in his open eye.

"Inside the keep of the Archemage," Isla explained for me, "this *nahia* and I met and defeated six of the *ro-uke*. They are assassins, King of Vesselege. I think it's safe to *assume*"—she gave the word a sneering force—"Argoyne didn't send them against himself."

"Then who?" the King countered harshly. "And for what purpose? If you 'assume' so much, do you also 'assume' you know why they were there? The *ro-uke* have as much honor as the *mashu-te*. Their presence is not 'proof of treachery.'"

Turning to the captive woman, I shifted my grasp on her arm so that my mouth reached her ear.

"Speak," I told her softly. "The truth. On the honor of your Art." Within her robes, my fang drew blood from the skin along her spine. "I do not hold you accountable for the service you were asked to perform. But your life and all Vesselege are forfeit if you lie."

Bitter as a blade, Miniter continued, "And you ask us to believe that you and one *nahia* alone defeated *six* of the *ro-uke*? That is hard to credit. If there is treachery here, perhaps it is yours."

The assassin cleared her throat, lifting her head to the young *shin-te* and his opponent rather than to Goris Miniter and the White Lords. "No," she pronounced. She, too, recognized the nature of this battle. And, as Goris Miniter had said, the *ro-uke* understood honor. "The King of Vesselege sent us to rid his land of Black Argoyne, the last of the Dark Lords. He wished the Archemage slain during your contest."

A hush fell over the meadow—the silence of shock and dismay. The sky itself seemed to carry an echo of chagrin like a suggestion of distant thunder. Although his glare spoke of murder, Goris Miniter held his tongue. It may have been that his soldiers and adherents were more disturbed to hear the words spoken than they were by what the words meant. The White Lords revealed no surprise. But there were warriors among the horsemen, students and masters of the Fatal Arts, and their distress was plain.

To the *nerishi-qa*, I said, "There is no honor for you here. No victory. The contest is meaningless. Let it go."

"No!" one of the White Lords returned sharply. "The challenge was made and accepted in good faith. The contest is between mages, and we are bound by it. We stand or fall by the deeds of our champions, not by the honor or falsehood of kings and assassins. Goris Miniter's actions are his own, irrelevant. The contest must be resolved."

Although the mage's lips moved, his voice did not appear to issue from his mouth, but rather from some source as distant as Argoyne's keep.

The *nerishi-qa* withheld reply. He studied me narrowly for a moment, considering my wound and my weakness—gazed briefly at the young *shin-te*—then strode from the center of the ring toward Goris Miniter. Raising his head and his *qa*, he confronted the mounted King as though he were accustomed to passing judgment on the actions of sovereigns.

"Is this true?" he inquired softly.

Goris Miniter's calculation was written on his face, plain to all who chose to see it. His eyes sifted lies and half-truths, deflections, while under his beard his jaws chewed the consequences of whatever he might say. In the end, however, the man before him was a *nerishi-qa* master, able to distinguish truth from falsehood, and he did not hazard prevarication.

"In case you failed," he answered. "The Dark Lords are an abomination. Vesselege will never be whole while one of them endures."

"Vesselege," the champion of the White Lords retorted, still softly, "will never be whole while the King is treacherous."

So suddenly that his action startled the wildflowers, the *nerishi-qa* braced a hand on the neck of the King's horse and vaulted upward, sweeping a kick which struck Goris Miniter upon the helm and dropped him like a stone to the meadow.

Among the grasses the King of Vesselege lay still, with blood drooling from his mouth, and his skull crushed.

The young *shin-te* watched in bafflement and rue, as though he grasped nothing.

On all sides, soldiers and adherents shouted their fury and fear. They might have goaded their mounts to charge at the *nerishi-qa*, but the warriors around the ring were quicker. *Ro-uke* and *mashu-te*, they hastened their horses forward to block the soldiers. Doubtless they felt as the King's adherents did. For one reason or another, they had pledged their service to Goris Miniter. Yet they understood that a contest of champions had been dishonored.

And without honor the Fatal Arts would fall to dust.

In relief, I sagged against the support of the captured assassin. The toxin in my shoulder had become stronger than my resistance, and I believed that I had accomplished my end. The *nerishi-qa* had acknowledged the contest dishonored. Now he and his opponent could withdraw without loss on either side. Without more death. Argoyne would live to defend his knowledge a while longer. And my life, and Isla's, and the young *shin-te*'s, would not be forfeit for our service to the Black Archemage.

Haze gathered over the meadow. Helpless to do otherwise, I trusted that the *ro-uke* would uphold me.

I could only stare in dismay as the White Lords announced together, "The King's treachery has been repaid." Their voices tolled thunder. "The honor of this contest is restored. It will continue."

Isla groaned. She may not have felt my qualms about sacrificing her own life, but she could see that our young comrade was already beaten. Only a few blows were needed to complete his death.

The *nerishi-qa* appeared to ignore the White Lords. Turning his back on them, as well as on Miniter's corpse, he advanced again into the trampled circle of the contest. When he was within five paces of his opponent, he stopped.

He spoke quietly, but the thunder which the White Lords invoked was not more clear.

"I care nothing for mages," he informed the *shin-te*. "If they are bound here—White Lords or Dark—the oath is theirs, not mine. This test lies between *nerishi-qa* and *shin-te*.

"For years we have refused your challenge, believing you fools. But you have become offensive to us. You have named *nerishi-qa* a false Art. I was sent by my masters to repay your folly, and to teach you that the falseness you repudiate is your own."

Although he had been injured, his readiness for combat betrayed no flaw. The resilience compressed in the muscles of his legs matched the hard force of his *qa*. Relaxed and quick, his hands seemed to hold every blow which had ever been struck.

"Now," he concluded, "our contest has meaning."

From the edge of the ring, the White Lords nodded their approval.

A low moan escaped the young man's lips. Yet he did not withdraw. Wavering on his feet, he answered, "Then I must accept. This test lies between us." A maimed formality dignified his words, despite the frailty of his flesh. "Yours is the Art of the Killing Stroke. I will show you that it is false."

His knee buckled as he assumed his stance, and he nearly fell. Staggering, he drew himself upright again. The loss in his eyes was terrible to behold.

He had met despair. Already it proved itself against him.

Had I been less weak, I might have wept for him. My own death crouched near me on the meadow, but it did not trouble me as much as his. Poison filled my thoughts, and I could not imagine any help which might save him. His spirit and his *qa* had not failed him. Still he was too young for the burden Argoyne had given him to bear.

Unsteadily he braced himself to meet his opponent's last attack.

Within me, the toxin seemed to clench its jaws. The *nerishi-qa* had not yet moved. However, I could see his assault in the haze before me, precise and fatal. When he struck—

"*Shin-te*," Isla called out suddenly, "remember your Art!"

As if involuntarily, the young master turned his bereavement toward her.

"There is no killing stroke," she reminded him. Her voice rang with certainty. "There is only choice. Or despair."

I feared that she had lost her mind. Had she not contested his beliefs herself? Yet in the end it was plain that she understood him better than I did. Or that he understood her—

Empowered by the magery of her words, his limbs regained a measure of their strength, and the sorrow receded from his eyes. Years of pain shed themselves from his shoulders. As he rose out of his stance to face his opponent again, he conveyed the impression that he was being lifted beyond himself.

Surprised by the young man's movement, the *nerishi-qa* paused, easing his own stance.

Deliberately the *shin-te* bowed to his opponent. When he straightened his back, his arms hung defenselessly at his sides. Yet he appeared taller in some way, as if his own words in Isla's mouth had given him stature.

"Your skill surpasses me," he told the *nerishi-qa*, echoing her certainty. "But your will does not. No man's choice exceeds another's. You cannot make me other than I am."

Slowly he spread his arms wide, closing his eyes as he did so.

"Here I stand," he said, "unguarded. Strike me, if that is your wish. Your blow is mine. The victory is mine. If I have chosen to die, you cannot kill me. Any blow of yours can only carry out my will.

"How, then," he finished softly, "will you teach the *shin-te* that they are fools?"

The *nerishi-qa* frowned, studying his opponent's displayed form as though to determine the best target for a killing stroke.

"Strike," one of the White Lords commanded urgently. "His choices have no significance. The contest does not rest on them. Only the blow matters. Only his death matters. The Dark Lord will be destroyed when his champion falls."

Clinging to the *ro-uke*, I fought to clear my sight.

Without warning, the *nerishi-qa* struck—a blow so fierce that it seemed to stun my own heart. His fist flashed forward with all his *qa* behind it. Under its force, the cloth of the young man's robe sprang to tatters across his chest, torn thread from thread.

And yet the *shin-te* did not flinch. His skin had not been touched.

His arms remained wide in sacrifice.

With great care, as though he had found himself on the edge of a precipice, the *nerishi-qa* stepped back, rising from his stance. After a moment, he snorted under his breath.

"Look at me," he instructed his opponent.

Obediently the young master opened his eyes.

"You are indeed willing to die," the White Lords' champion observed between his teeth.

Lowering his arms, the *shin-te* shrugged. "Your skill surpasses mine," he repeated. "Yet my life is my own."

The *nerishi-qa* snorted again. "The *shin-te* are fools to challenge us."

For the first time in my experience of him, the young master smiled. "So I believe." Years lifted from his face in an instant. Without transition, he resembled a boy, innocent and unbereaved. "We learn nothing from each other."

As if at a great distance, I heard Isla sigh, "Well said. Well done."

The *nerishi-qa* did not smile in turn. Scowling around his swollen eye, he left the center of the ring to stand before the White Lords on their mounts.

"The contest is ended," he informed them. The authority of his tone allowed no contradiction. "The *shin-te* has proven himself against me. I am forced to acknowledge defeat."

Hearing him, I buried my face against the shoulder of the *ro-uke* to conceal my tears. The *nerishi-qa* had studied honor in such depth that I was humbled by it.

Yet I looked up again at once, for the White Lords had raised their voices in a cry as cruel as the clamor of a storm. From within their bright robes, they summoned their power, and thunderclaps answered, rolling among the foothills and over the meadow, gathering fire. Called from the clear sky, lightning hammered downward. Isla, the *ro-uke*, and I were knocked from our feet, horses were scattered, soldiers and warriors were tossed to the ground.

In the center of the ring, the blast scorched wildflowers and grasses to char—and the young master with them.

But his death was not defeat. The White Lords who struck him down had already ceased to exist.

We did not, however. Instead we stood in the chamber where we had left Argoyne, the three of us, *shin-te*, *mashu-te*, and *nahia*. The Black Archmage was not present. In his place we found three goblets brimming with wine, enough food to satisfy us twice over, and the rich silence of peace.

Like our struggles in the meadow, the Mage War had ended.

My shoulder had been healed, although it still held the low ache of remembered poison. Isla's lesser hurts had been made whole. And the young master stood intact before us, restored by a Dark Lord's magery. He had shed his sorrow in fire, and his eyes smiled when his mouth did not.

His memory also had been restored, but he neglected to tell us his name. Perhaps he thought that we already knew it.

Smiling, he raised his goblet to thank us for the part we had played in his victory. "While I live," he told us with the earnest sincerity of youth, "I am in your debt."

I bowed to answer him. "As we are in yours." I was foolishly pleased with myself, and cared not what I said.

Isla also bowed. She smiled as well. Yet the expression in her eyes revealed the trouble in her heart. After a moment, she protested, "But we didn't do anything."

The young man laughed—a happy sound which suited him well. "I also did nothing," he assured her.

Perhaps for that reason *shin-te* was called the Art of Acceptance.

But her concern was not relieved. With some severity, she observed, "You took a great risk. That blow—" She shuddered, despite her training. "Your heart would have burst."

He nodded gravely. "I believed that I would die." Then he added, "But that was a small matter. I was already beaten. Yet when you spoke my own words to me—one of the *mashu-te*—a student of the Direct Fist—I heard them in a new way. They became"—he rolled his smiling gaze at the ceiling—"how shall I say it? They became simple. Despair is the killing stroke. There is no other." Lightly he shrugged. "My hazard was no greater than yours."

That was true. If their champion had killed the *shin-te*, the White Lords would no doubt have slain both Isla and me, for the help we had given Argoyne.

We lived only because the young man had stepped beyond the circle of his own comprehension.

Still Isla had not named what was in her heart. Instead she asked, "What will become of Vesselege now?"

The wine seemed quick to intoxicate me. I, too, laughed. "Argoyne and the White Lords will endure each other until the contest between them takes another form. Then they will resume their struggle. As for the rule of Vesselege— Sovereigns are easily replaced. Perhaps the new King will profit from Goris Miniter's example." I drank more wine so that I would not laugh again. "I would advise him to make peace with both the White Lords and the Dark while he can."

"And what will you do?" Isla inquired of the *shin-te*.

He did not hesitate. "I have learned a precious truth. I must teach it."

She looked to me. "And you, Asper?"

I met her gaze across the rim of my goblet, concealing my mirth. "First I will drink. Then I will sleep. And when I have recovered, I will dedicate myself to the study of dangerous assumptions. There is power in them, which the *nahia* have neglected."

She fell silent, frowning to herself.

Seeing her unease, I returned her question to her. "What are your intentions, Isla? The wine is excellent, we are whole, and the sun shines on Vesselege. What disturbs you?"

With an effort, she revealed her thoughts. "I've come to doubt the teaching of the *mashu-te*," she admitted unhappily. "If *nerishi-qa* is a false Art, then so are the others. I'll have to leave my home to study among the *shin-te*."

I stared at her. The idea of turning away from the *nahia* had never occurred to me. Her scruples—her need for the purity of her beliefs— surpassed me.

"Do not," the young master urged at once. "The *shin-te* are indeed fools to challenge the *nerishi-qa*. My Art is as false as any."

"And as true," I murmured.

That challenge had been rightly spurned by the *nerishi-qa*. It resembled the hostility of the White Lords toward Black Argoyne. In the meadow surrounded by enemies, however, the young *shin-te* had learned his own wisdom.

After a time, Isla nodded.

When she had let her concern go, I sighed my relief, and drank again. In all my life, I had never been farther from despair.

What we were could not endure without honor. And the price of honor was death, in one form or another. I thought of the young man's acceptance of death—of Isla's willingness to sacrifice her life—of the *nerishi-qa*'s surrender to defeat. I thought of the hazards I had faced.

Argoyne had said, *It's always easy to trust warriors. That's why they're called "the Fatal Arts."* I believed now that I had begun to understand him.

The Kings of Tarshish Shall Bring Gifts

People who dream when they sleep at night know of a special kind of happiness which the world of the day holds not, a placid ecstasy, and ease of heart, that are like honey on the tongue. They also know that the real glory of dreams lies in their atmosphere of unlimited freedom. It is not the freedom of the dictator, who enforces his own will on the world, but the freedom of the artist, who has no will, who is free of will. The pleasure of the true dreamer does not lie in the substance of the dream, but in this: that there things happen without any interference from his side, and altogether outside his control.

[The dreamer is] the privileged person to whom everything is taken. The Kings of Tarshish shall bring gifts.

—ISAK DINESEN, *OUT OF AFRICA*

I have often wondered why there are tyrants, and I have come to the conclusion it is because some men remember their dreams. For what do we know of dreams? What is the truest thing to be said of them? Surely it is that we forget them. And therefore it is also sure that this forgetting must have a purpose. Hungers are conceived in dreams in order to be forgotten, so that the dreamer and his life may go on without them. That is why most men remember nothing—except the sensation of having dreamed.

But men who do not forget are doomed.

Such a man was Prince Akhmet, the only son of the Caliph of Arbin, His Serene Goodness Abdul dar-El Haj.

After a reign enviable in every respect except the birth of male off-spring, in his declining years His Serene Goodness at last produced an heir. This, as may be imagined, was a great relief to the Caliph's wives, as well as a great joy to the Caliph himself. Thus it is easily understood that from the first young Akhmet was coddled and pampered and indulged as though he came among us directly from the gods. In later years, during the Prince's own brief reign, men looked to his childhood as an explanation for his tyrannies. After all, Arbin had no tradition of tyranny. His Serene Goodness Abdul dar-El Haj, like his father before him, and his father's father, was a man in whom strength exercised itself in the service of benevolence. Some explanation was needed to account for Prince Akhmet's failure to follow the path of his sires.

But I do not believe that a childhood of indulgence and gratification suffices to explain the Prince. For with his pampering and coddling young Akhmet also received example. The Caliph was demonstrably benign in all his dealings. Therefore he was much beloved. And the Prince's mother was the sweetest of all the Caliph's sweet young wives. Surely Akhmet tasted no gall at her breast, felt none at his father's hand.

His Serene Goodness Abdul dar-El Haj, however, remembered none of his dreams. His son, on the other hand—

Ah, Prince Akhmet remembered everything.

This was not, of course, a salient feature of his childhood. For him, in fact, childhood was what dreams are for other men—something to be forgotten. But his ability to remember his dreams was first remarked soon after the first down appeared on his cheeks, and he began to make his first experiments among the odalisques in his father's harem.

That is always an exciting time for young men, a time of sweat at night and fever in daylight, a time when many things are desired and few of them are clearly understood. It is, however, a strangely safe time—a time when attention to the appetites of the loins consumes or blinds or transmutes all other passions. Men of that age must think about matters of the flesh, and if the flesh is not satisfied they are rarely able to think about anything else. So it was only after he had more than once awakened in the bed of a beautiful girl about whom he had believed he dreamed, thus at once deflating and familiarizing such visions, that his true dreams began their rise to his notice, like the red carp rising among the lilies to bread crumbs on the surface of his father's ornamental pools.

"I had the most wonderful dream," he announced to the girl with whom he had slept. "The most wonderful dream."

"Tell me about it, my lord," she replied, not because she had a particular interest in dreams, but because his pleasure was her fortune. In truth, she already knew how to be enjoyed in ways which had astonished him. But she was also prepared to give him the simple satisfaction of being listened to.

He sat up in her bed, the sheets falling from the graceful beauty of his young limbs. His features were still pale with sleep, but his eyes shone, and they did not regard his companion.

"I can see it now," he murmured distantly. "I can see it all. It was of a place where there are no men."

"No men?" the girl asked with a smile, "or no people?" Her fingertips traced his thigh to the place where her notion of manhood resided.

The Prince heard her question, but he did not appear to feel her touch. "No people," he answered. "A place where there are no people, but only things of beauty."

The girl might have said again, "No people?" with a pout, thinking herself a thing of beauty. But perhaps she knew that if she had done so he would not have heeded her. All his attention was upon his dream.

"The place was a low valley," he said, showing the angle of the slopes with his hands, "its sides covered by rich greensward on which the early dew glistened, as bright in the sunshine as a sweep of stars. Down the vale-bottom ran a stream of water so clean and crystal that it appeared as liquid light, dancing and swirling over its black rocks and white sand. Above the greensward stood fruit trees, apple and peach and cherry, all in blossom, with their flowers like music in the sun, and their trunks wrapped in sweet shade. The air was luminous and utterly deep, transformed from the unfathomable purple of night by the warmth of the sun.

"The peace of the place was complete," murmured young Akhmet, "and I would have been content with it as it was, happy to gaze upon it while the dream remained in my mind. But it was not done. For when I gazed upon the running trance of the stream, I saw that the dance of the light was full of the dance of small fish, and as my eyes fell upon the fish I saw that while they danced they became flowers, flowers more lovely than lilies, brighter than japonica, and the flowers floated in profusion away along the water.

"Then I gazed from those blooms to the flowers of the trees, and they, too, changed. Upon the trees, the flowers appeared to be music, but in moments they became birds, and the birds were music indeed, their flights like arcs of melody, their bodies formed to the shape of their song. And the shade among the tree trunks also changed. From the sweet dark emerged rare beasts, lions and jacols, nilgai deer with fawns among them, oryx, fabled mandrill. And the peace of the beasts, too, was complete, so that they brought no fear with them. Instead, they gleamed as the greensward and the stream gleamed, and when the lions shook their manes they scattered droplets of water, which became chrysoprase and diamonds among the grass. The fawns of the nilgai wore a sheen of finest silver, and from their mouths the mandrill let fall rubies of enough purity to ransom a world.

"I remember it all." A sadness came over the Prince, a sadness which both touched and pleased the girl. "I would have been content if the dream had never ended.

"Why are there no such places in the world?"

His sadness brought him back to her. "Because we do not need them," she replied softly. "We have our own joys and contentments." Then she drew him to her. She was, after all, only a girl, ignorant of many things. She took pleasure in the new urgency with which he renewed his acquaintance with her flesh, and saw no peril in it.

But I must not judge her harshly. No one saw any peril in it. I saw none in it myself, and I see peril everywhere. When he came later into the cushion-bestrewn chamber of his father's court, interrupting the business of Arbin with a young and indulged man's heedlessness in order to describe his dream again for the benefit of the Caliph and his advisers, none of those old men took it amiss.

His Serene Goodness, of course, took nothing that his beloved son did amiss. The sun shone for his son alone, and all that his son did was good. And he was entranced by the Prince's dream, full as it was with things which he had himself experienced, but could not remember. The truth was that the Caliph was not an especially imaginative ruler. Common sense and common sympathy were his province. For new ideas, unexpected solutions, unforeseen possibilities, he relied upon his advisers. Therefore he listened to young Akhmet's recitation as if in telling his dream the Prince accomplished something wondrous. And he cozied the sadness which followed the telling as if Akhmet had indeed suffered a loss.

With the Caliph's example before them, Abdul dar-El Haj's advisers could hardly have responded otherwise themselves. Each in his own way, all of us valued our suzerain. In addition, we were accustomed to the indulgence which surrounded the Prince. And lastly we enjoyed the dream itself—at least in the telling.

We listened to it reclining, as was the custom in Abdul dar-El Haj's court. His Serene Goodness was nothing if not corpulent, and liked his ease. He faced all the duties of Arbin recumbent among his cushions. And because none of his advisers could lay even a distant claim to youth, he required us all to do as he did. We were stretched at Prince Akhmet's feet like admirers while the young man spoke.

When the telling was done, and His Serene Goodness had comforted his son, the Vizier of Arbin, Moshim Mosha Va, stroked his thin gray beard and pronounced, "You are a poet, my lord Prince. Your words give life to beauty."

This was not a proposition to which the High Priest of the Mosque, the Most Holy Khartim a-Kul, would have assented on theological grounds. Beauty was, after all, a creation of the gods, not of men. As a practical matter, however, the High Priest nodded, shook the fringe around his cap, and rumbled, "Indeed."

For myself, I primarily wondered whether it was the recitation itself which enabled Akhmet to remember his dream so vividly. Nevertheless I expressed my approval with the others, unwilling to launch a large debate on so small a subject.

But the Prince was not complimented. "No," he protested, at once petulant and somewhat defensive. "Words have nothing to do with it. It was the dream. The beauty was in the dream."

"Ah, but the dream was yours, my lord Prince, not ours." The Vizier was disputatious by nature, sometimes to his own cost. "We would not have been able to know of its beauty, if you had not described it so well."

"No!" young Akhmet repeated. He was still close enough to his childhood to stamp his foot in vexation. "It was the dream. It has nothing to do with me."

"Of course," His Serene Goodness put in soothingly. He liked nothing which vexed his son. "But Moshim Mosha Va is quite correct. He only means to say that your words are the only way in which we can share the beauty of what you have seen. Perhaps there are two beauties here— the beauty of your dream, and the beauty of your description."

For some reason, however, this eminently reasonable suggestion vexed the Prince further. His dream had made him sad. It had also made him fierce. "You do not understand!" he cried with an embarrassing crack in his young voice. "I remember it all!" Then he fled the court.

In puzzlement, the Caliph turned to his advisers after his son had gone and asked plaintively, "What is it that I have failed to understand?"

The Vizier tangled his fingers among his whiskers and pulled them to keep himself still, a rare effort of self-restraint. Perhaps he knew better than to venture the opinion that Prince Akhmet behaved like a spoiled brat.

"My lord Prince is young," commented the Most Holy Khartim a-Kul in his religious rumble. "It may be that his ideas are still too big for his ability to express them. It may be that his dream came to him from the gods, and he rightly considers it false worship to compliment the priest when praise belongs only to Heaven."

This notion "rightly" made His Serene Goodness uneasy. A son whose dreams came to him from the gods would make an uncomfortable heir to the rule of Arbin. The Caliph's eyes shifted away from his advisers, and he resumed the business of the court without much clarity of thought.

As for the Prince, when he returned to his apartments he kicked his dog, a hopeless mongrel on which he had doted for most of his boyhood.

At the time, no one except the dog expressed any further opinions on the subject.

But of course it was inevitable that the Prince would dream again.

Not at once, naturally. In him, the carp had only begun to rise. The bread crumbs on the surface were few, or the fish did not see them. He was in a sour humor, and his attention was fixed, not on the hope of new dreams, but on the failure of other people to understand the significance of the first one. For a time, he lost interest in women—at least to the extent that any young man can be said to have lost interest in women. At the same time, he experienced an increased enthusiasm for the manly arts of Arbin, especially for hunting, and most especially for the hunting of beasts of prey, creatures of disquiet, feasters on blood. Arbin is a civilized country. Nevertheless the great forests do not lack for leopard and wild pig, with tusks which can gut a horse with one toss of the head, and packs of hungry langur often harry the flocks on the plains. By the standards accepted for a young lord of the realm and his father's son, Akhmet expended a not-unreasonable amount of time upon matters of bloodshed. Until he dreamed again.

He and his companions, several young men of the court and a commensurate number of trusted retainers and hunters, had spent the night camped among the thick trunks and overarching limbs of a nearby forest. In this forest was said to live a great ape which had learned a taste for human flesh—a small matter as the affairs of the world are considered, but by no means trivial to the villagers whose huts bordered the trees—and for three days Prince Akhmet with his entourage had been hunting the beast under conditions which can best be described as gracious hardship. Apparently, fatigue enabled him to sleep especially well. On the morning of the fourth day, he sprang from his bedding like a dust devil, chasing in all directions and shouting incoherently for his horse. When his companions inquired as to the meaning of his urgency, he replied that he had had another dream. His father must know of it immediately.

Clattering like madmen in their haste—a haste which no one but the Prince himself actually comprehended—Akhmet and his entourage raced homeward.

Now when he burst among us, hot and flurried from his ride, with stubble upon his cheeks and a feverish glare in his eyes, and announced, "I have dreamed again. I remember it all," I felt a serious skepticism. To remember one dream is merely remarkable, not ultimately significant. To remember a second, however, so soon after the first—if a few weeks may be called soon—as well as after the confusion of a hard ride, and without the exercise of relating the dream to anyone else—

Well, in all honesty, I doubted young Akhmet. I watched him closely for signs of stumbling or invention, which would call the accuracy of his memory into question.

In contrast, His Serene Goodness appeared to feel no skepticism at all. Perhaps he was simply delighted to see his son after an absence of a few days. Perhaps he was delighted by the idea of dreams. Or perhaps he saw in Akhmet's eyes that the Prince would brook no opposition. Unlike his advisers, who exchanged uneasy glances as unobtrusively as possible, the Caliph only beamed pleasure at his son and said, "Another dream! Tell us at once. Was it also wonderful?"

"It was," the Prince pronounced, "wonderful beyond compare."

Steadying himself as well as his excitement allowed, he said, "I stood upon a great height, and below me lay the city of Arbin at night, unscrolled with all its lights as legible as any text, so that the movements of the least streetsweeper as well as the activities of the mightiest house were plain to be read. Indeed, the city itself was also alive, breathing its own air, flexing its own limbs, adding its own superscript to the writing of the lights. I knew that the truth and goodness and folly of all our people were written there for me to read.

"Yet as I began to read, the height on which I stood grew even greater, and the city itself expanded, and I shrank to a mote among them—a mote without loss or grief, however, but rather a part at once of the lights and of the darkness between the lights, much as a particle of blood partakes of all blood while it surges through the veins." The Prince spoke with a thrill in his voice which answered my skepticism, a blaze in his eyes which bore me with him. "Thus at the same time I rose and shrank, losing myself within a greatness that transformed and illumined me. I rose and shrank, and the city grew, and the lights became stars and suns and glories, lifting every living heart to heights which we have never known. And the darkness between the lights was the solace in which every living heart rests from wonder.

"While I dreamed, I was among the heavens and the gods."

There he stopped. His chest rose and fell with the strength of his breathing, and the fever in his eyes abated slowly.

"This is truly a wonder," said His Serene Goodness when he had collected his thoughts, "a wonder and wonderful." Like his advisers, he had no intention of repeating the mistake of the previous occasion. "Is this not so, Vizier?"

"It is, my lord," replied Moshim Mosha Va sagely. He tugged at his beard for a moment, then ventured to add, "Perhaps it is also something more."

"More?" The Prince and his father spoke at once, but in differing tones. Abdul dar-El Haj was naturally delighted by anything which would enable him to think even better of his son. Young Akhmet, however, appeared strangely suspicious.

"To remember one dream, my lord," said the Vizier, echoing my earlier ruminations, "is pleasant and desirable. More so when the dream itself is peaceful and lovely. But to remember two—two such dreams in so short a time—is unusual. It may be that Prince Akhmet has been given a gift. It may be that he has been touched by wisdom or prophecy. In that case, his dreams may have meaning which it would be folly to ignore.

"Perhaps we would do well, my lord, to seek interpretation for his dreams."

Both the Caliph and his son were startled by this suggestion, and now their expressions were nearly identical. His Serene Goodness had too much common sense—and too little imagination—to believe that a gift of wisdom or prophecy would be a good thing in an heir. And the Prince seemed to dislike any deflection of attention from the dream itself. Nevertheless he held his peace, and his father turned to the Most Holy Khartim a-Kul.

"Do you concur, High Priest?"

Khartim a-Kul waggled the fringe on his hat to conceal his squirming. Wisdom and prophecy were matters of religion, and did not belong to spoiled young princes. Yet he could not ignore his responsibility to His Serene Goodness, or to Arbin.

"Two dreams are only two dreams, my lord," he murmured judiciously. "It is, however, better to search for meaning where meaning is absent, than to ignore it where it is present."

Sadly, Abdul dar-El Haj was not judicious where his son was concerned, and so did not enjoy judiciousness in others. Somewhat sourly, he demanded, "Then interpret this dream for us, High Priest. Give us the insight of the gods."

The Most Holy Khartim a-Kul rumbled inchoately past the dangles of his hat. He did not enjoy being made to squirm. Neither did he like to fail either his religion or his ruler. After a moment, he said, "The language of dreams, my lord, is private, and requires study. There are interpreters who make a specialty of such matters." Seeing the Caliph's mounting vexation, however, he hastened to add, "Yet I might hazard to say, my lord, that this dream speaks of Prince Akhmet's future. At that forever-to-be-lamented day when your Serene Goodness ceases to be Caliph in Arbin, and Prince Akhmet ascends to his inheritance, he will be one in spirit as well as in body with all his people—'much as a particle of blood partakes of all blood.' He will see the good of the whole as well as the good of each individual, and will rule with the same selfless benevolence which has made Abdul dar-El Haj beloved throughout this land."

Thus the High Priest of the Mosque extricated himself from his lord's displeasure.

While I, who see peril everywhere, saw peril not in Khartim a-Kul's interpretation, but in young Akhmet's reaction.

So vehemently that spittle sprang from his lips, he snapped, "Nonsense, Priest. You rave. Dreams have no meaning. Only the memory of them has meaning."

In fury, he withdrew himself from the court.

The Caliph was shocked. "*Now* what have we done amiss?" he inquired plaintively.

None of his advisers answered. Apparently we had once again misunderstood Prince Akhmet's reasons for relating his dream.

Later, we learned that the Prince had gone straight to his father's harem, where he had covered one of his favorite women savagely, leaving the marks of his teeth on her breasts—marks which took weeks to heal.

So the seeds of concern were planted.

Those seeds did not sprout, however, until the Prince dreamed again, despite the fact that during the interval he tended them in a desultory fashion, giving them occasional water and fertilizer. In a time of unusual application to the study of weapons, he presumed upon his favored station to do one of his instructors an injury. He became increasingly rough in his treatment of women. His commands to his servants were sometimes far-fetched—and sometimes his anger was extreme when those commands were not carried out to his satisfaction. Such signs, however, such bubbles rising from the depths of the pool, were generally ignored. We are taught to be indulgent of the behavior of princes. And he was still young. In the words of one of his grooms, he had conceived an itch which he did not know how to scratch. Therefore he was irritable. And he had not yet learned the benefits of self-restraint.

Finally, Akhmet's actions passed unheeded because our fears were focused elsewhere. After many years of health, His Serene Goodness Abdul dar-El Haj began to fail. A cough which the physicians could not ease brought blood to his lips in flecks. His appetite left him, and his flesh began to sag from his bones. His wives lost the capacity to comfort him. Often he needed assistance to rise from his cushions. Because he was so much beloved, the sight of his decline filled his advisers and all his people with grief. We had little heart to spare for the vagaries of the young Prince.

So he committed small hurts without reprimand, performed small acts of unreason without restraint, caused petty vexations throughout the court, and was ignored. Too little notice was taken of him until he dreamed again.

This time, his dream brought him out of sleep in the lonely hours of the night. Such was the power he remembered that he could not contain himself until morning. He must relate what he had seen. Regardless of the Caliph's weakness, Prince Akhmet hurried at once to his father's chamber, where physicians stood watch at his father's bedside, and maidens dabbed away the blood as it came to his father's lips.

"I have dreamed again," he announced peremptorily, ignoring his father's weakness, his father's uneasy sleep, "the most wonderful dream."

With difficulty, His Serene Goodness opened his eyes. Perhaps because he was still partly in sleep, or perhaps because his pain ruled him, or perhaps because he could not be blind to his son's inconsideration, he replied in a weary tone, "I, too, have had a dream. I dreamed that I had a son who loved me."

At this time, young Akhmet was still within reach of chagrin. He seemed to see his father's illness for the first time, and all his demand left him. Falling to his knees at the bedside, he cried, "Father, forgive me. You are ill, and I have been heedless, heartless. What can I do to comfort you? Why do these physicians not heal you? Why do you tolerate them, if they have no power to heal you? I will do everything I can."

This at once dispelled whatever anger the Caliph may have felt toward his son. Stroking the youth's beautiful head, he said, "You will give me ease if you tell me of your dream. Only be still while my advisers are summoned, so that they may hear you also. And permit the High Priest to bring his interpreters, so that the truth of your wonderful dream may be understood."

Prince Akhmet bit his lips, plainly distraught. Yet he acceded to his father's wishes.

And so the advisers of the court were summoned to Abdul dar-El Haj's chamber, along with interpreters roused and admonished by the Most Holy Khartim a-Kul himself.

In the corridors of the palace, upon the way to the Caliph's sickchamber, I encountered Moshim Mosha Va. The High Priest of the Mosque strode some paces ahead of us with his interpreters. We were able to speak quietly.

"This is unseemly," said the Vizier, with disgust hidden under his beard. "I am old. I need more sleep."

"You are old," I replied, "and need less sleep, not more. You have no more use for dreams."

He snorted to me. "You are glib, wizard. I know of no other reason why the Most Pompous Khartim a-Kul has not branded you a heretic. But glibness will not save you when that little shit becomes Caliph. For myself, I believe I will put an end to my life. I do not wish to spend my waning years tormented by his fancies."

I smiled at the thought that the disputatious Vizier would ever consent to death. Pleasantly, I answered, "That is because you do not understand him."

He paused to peer closely into my face. "Do you?"

"No," I admitted. "But I will." I must. Have I not said that I see peril everywhere?

Together, we followed the High Priest into the sickchamber of His Serene Goodness Abdul dar-El Haj.

The young Prince still knelt at his father's side. The Caliph's fingers stroked his son's fine hair. In that pose, the lord appeared to be passing his blessing to his heir.

"Come and hear what my son has dreamed," said His Serene Goodness when we had gathered around him. "This is the third dream, and
must have meaning." It seemed that the Caliph had reconciled himself
to the idea of a gods-gifted scion. Or perhaps he realized, in his unimaginative way, that Prince Akhmet must be reconciled to himself in order
to become a fit lord for Arbin. "High Priest, are these men the interpreters
of dreams?"

"They are, my lord," answered the Most Holy Khartim a-Kul, sound-
ing more than ever like a subterranean mishap. "We have prayed over the
young Prince and consulted the stars."

I knew for a fact that this was pious falsehood. Khartim a-Kul had
had no attention to spare for Akhmet. All his hours had been spent in
preparation for the rites and ceremonies of the Caliph's passing, and of
the installation of a new lord. I kept this knowledge to myself, however.

"We are ready," the High Priest concluded, "to bring you our best
insight."

"Very well," said His Serene Goodness as though his breath were
fading. "Let my son speak his dream."

At the Caliph's bedside, Prince Akhmet rose to his feet and told us
what he had dreamed.

"In my dream, I saw a mighty suzerain, a nameless caliph in a land I
have never known. He was in the time of his best youth, and though I
did not know him and could not name him, his features were the features
of the Caliph of Arbin, His Serene Goodness Abdul dar-El Haj, my
father."

Had the Prince been more of a politician, I would have believed this
beginning false. But it was impossible to mistake the ardor of his stance,
or the growing hunger in his gaze.

"His head was crowned with light," said young Akhmet, "and love
lived in his eyes, and his limbs were of such beauty that all hearts were
drawn to him. He was the center of the storm, where peace lives untouched
by pain. He was the pause between the beats of the pulse, the rest between
respirations, and his gift to all who knew him was balm.

"Yet he was more than this. Indeed, when he spread out his hands,
the world was shaped by his gestures, so that nature itself took on the

form of his will. He stretched his fingers, and plains were made. He shrugged his shoulders, and mountains grew. Where he pointed, there were rivers. The seed of his loins gave birth to new peoples, and his caress left all women faint with pleasure."

While he spoke, I observed, as I should have observed weeks ago, that he had changed. His lips had grown pinched like a simoniac's, and his cheeks hinted at hollowness, and his form was as gaunt as his youth and beauty permitted. Regret is useless, but still I regretted that I had not turned my attention to him earlier.

"And in my dream," he continued, "the storm of pain which drives all men, but which could only run in circles of folly around the nameless caliph, took notice of him and grew wrathful, for it is not given to men that they should be free of pain, or that they should free others, or that the world should shape itself to their will. Therefore the storm moved against him. Great was its wrath, and terrible, and whole lands and peoples were bereaved by its power. The reach of his beneficence was constricted as pain bore peace away and his place in the center of the storm shrank.

"Then there was grief everywhere, for all men were hurt, and so all men believed that the nameless caliph could not endure against pain.

"At last the storm withdrew, thinking itself victorious.

"And yet the caliph stood as he had stood before, with light upon his brow and beauty in his limbs. Nothing about him was changed, except his eyes. There love still shone, love for all peoples and all lands, love which healed all it saw. But with the love was also knowledge of pain, understanding for the injuries and losses which drive men to do ill, forgiveness for frailty. He had accepted pain into his being and searched it to its heart and taken no hurt.

"That was my dream," concluded the Prince. For a moment, he seemed overcome by sorrow. Then, however, he lifted his head, and in his eyes was a look which might have signified both love and the knowledge of pain. Or perhaps it was only madness. Softly, he added, "It was wonderful. It lives with me still, and will live always. I will forget nothing."

His Serene Goodness did not reply. But his eyes also shone, and there were tears upon his cheeks, and his hand clung to his son's until it trembled.

"Such dreams must be valued," murmured the Most Holy Khartim a-Kul. He may conceivably have been sincere. "To have such dreams is surely a gift from Heaven. We are blessed to be in your presence, my lord."

During the pause between one heartbeat and the next, Prince Akhmet's face lost its look of love and knowledge. At once, it became as tight and miserable as a miser's.

"Wonderful," breathed the Caliph past the blood on his lips. "Wonderful. Oh, my son."

"High Priest." A fit of coughing gripped him. When it passed, it left fresh red upon his chin. Nearly gasping, he asked, "How is this dream to be interpreted?"

Khartim a-Kul was nothing if not a politician. Graciously, he deferred to his chief interpreter, not because he doubted what to say, but because he knew the words would carry more weight if they came from a professed student of dreams.

The chief interpreter was a plump individual with more oil in his manner than most men can comfortably digest. "My lord Caliph," he began, "I pray devoutly that you will live forever. The reading of dreams is at once a mystery and a science. This is because the language of dreams is a language not of words but of images, and images do not speak. They only show themselves and leave their meaning to the insight of the observer. And yet they *are* a language, and all languages must be coherent. Their meaning can be learned, much as other men learn to speak foreign tongues."

This disquisition left the Prince shifting his weight from one foot to the other like a man restraining outrage. For his father's sake, however, he did not speak.

"Usually, my lord Caliph," the chief interpreter went on, "we do not presume to explain dreams until we have studied them, until we have had time to learn the language of their images." Nevertheless even he could see that His Serene Goodness was losing patience. He hastened to say, "But the present case is exceptional. Prince Akhmet's dream is so precise that its import is unmistakable.

"My lord Caliph, your son has been given a vision of the journey of man from life to paradise. The nameless suzerain of the dream bore your face as a symbol of goodness, of the virtue and value which the gods intend for all men. If all men were ruled by goodness, the world would be remade into a place of joy. Thus the nameless suzerain has the power to shape the world. He is opposed, however, by the storm of pain, the storm of death, by the conflicting and petty intentions which assail goodness out of fear. And against this storm goodness cannot prevail because it is mortal and must die.

"But when goodness has faced death and understood it, when goodness has learned the true compassion of experience for all fear, all pain, then goodness itself becomes paradise, the perfect and healing home of the soul. Pettiness and hurt are made whole, conflicts are swept away, and joy becomes the heart's demesne."

As the chief interpreter spoke, the impatience faded from His Serene Goodness' face. The strain of his illness also seemed to fade, and peace filled his eyes. He was pleased by what he heard. Who would not have been pleased? Watching him, however, I believed that he would have been pleased by any interpretation which did not falsify the tone of the dream. For a moment, I was fascinated by the contrast between the two lords, father and son. The father thought of reasons to go to his death unafraid. The son could barely contain his fury. At the sight, I was struck by the odd notion that the true benefit of dreams comes, not to those who have them, but rather to those who hear about them.

Then the Most Holy Khartim a-Kul began to intone a prayer, and the notion was forgotten.

But Prince Akhmet had come to the end of his restraint. Despite the prayer—despite the necessity of reverence for the High Priest, or of respect for his father's pain and contentment—he left the Caliph's bedside and swept across the chamber to confront the chief interpreter. Knotting his fists in the plump man's robes, he hissed so that his father would not hear him, "You are a fool! You are all *fools*. You will not demean my dreams with your unctuous pieties. Do you hear me? When I am Caliph, I will have you *beheaded*."

The Vizier Moshim Mosha Va cast me a look which said, I mean what I say. When this little shit becomes Caliph, I will put an end to my life.

Standing much closer to the chief interpreter than to the bedside, Khartim a-Kul heard the Prince's words. He was shocked, of course, and outraged. But he could not stop his prayer without drawing the Caliph's attention to the fact that something was amiss. Grinding his teeth, he continued his unheeded appeal to the gods to its end.

By that time, young Akhmet had left the sickchamber.

He kept his word. As soon as his father's corpse began to blacken and shrivel on the pyre, he commanded the beheading of the chief interpreter. The man was dead before sundown.

Abdul dar-El Haj's death was still some days away, however. His son's dream seemed to give him respite in his illness. He rested well that night, and for a day or two he grew stronger. And when his decline resumed, drawing him steadily toward his death, he remained contented, blessed with peace. He, too, believed the Prince's dream.

During those days, Akhmet had a number of dreams.

He remembered them all and told them to whoever would listen. The only restraint he exercised was that he did not trouble his father again— and did not permit his dreams to be interpreted in his presence. Yet his look of simony worsened. More and more, I came to think that he was paying the price for his father's ease.

And at last His Serene Goodness Abdul dar-El Haj died.

At once, all Arbin was plunged into a veritable apotheosis of mourning. That is to say, the entire land was seized by such a frenzy of religious prostration, ceremonial grief, and ritualized emotional flagellation that it became nearly impossible for men like the Vizier and myself to remember that the love underlying the Mosque's extravagances was genuine. The advisers of suzerains become cynics of necessity, and the Most Holy Khartim a-Kul was surely the most cynical among us. Therefore Moshim Mosha Va and I were hard-pressed to perceive the relationship between show and substance, between the public display of grief and its private truth. But we were grieved ourselves, perhaps not at our best. And, like the High Priest, we had reason to wonder what would become of us with the loss of our lord—but, unlike the High Priest, we had no outlet for our uncertainty.

We were not made less uncertain by the beheading of Khartim a-Kul's chief interpreter. For that act of tyranny, however, we had been forewarned. We had had time to accustom ourselves to the concept, if not to the actuality. As a consequence, we were more deeply disturbed by young Akhmet's other contribution to his father's funerary commemorations.

In tribute to His Serene Goodness, Khartim a-Kul revived a number of extreme liturgies and worships which had not been used for several generations—had not been used, in fact, precisely because they were so extreme. Like several of his fathers before him, Abdul dar-El Haj had become Caliph not as a youth, but as a man, and as a man, with the common sense of his forebears, he had forbidden the exercise of any liturgies or worships which he considered excessive.

Doubtless the Most Holy Khartim a-Kul deserved blame for his breach of recent custom, even though his decisions were made understandable by his fear of his new lord. But he could not have been blamed for the use young Akhmet made of his example.

Entirely to the High Priest's surprise, the new Caliph revived the old custom of suttee.

As an idea, suttee was alive among the people of Arbin. Upon the death of a caliph, all the ruler's wives and odalisques were expected to join his corpse in cremation. And this harsh practice was not utterly unjustified. It preserved the succession of rule from the confusion which could result if one of those women bore a son after her lord's death. For several generations, however, no wife or odalisque had actually been required to commit suttee. Each new caliph of Arbin had spared his father's women by the simple expedient of claiming them for himself, thus at once establishing his own reputation for benevolence and resolving any questions of legitimacy in his father's offspring.

The consternation among Abdul dar-El Haj's harem must have been profound when young Akhmet announced that he would not follow the path of his predecessors. Specifically, he refused to claim or exempt any woman with whom he had shared carnal pleasure. He wished, he said, to begin his rule in Arbin pure. As a demonstration, he said, of his devotion to virtue and the Mosque.

The Most Holy Khartim a-Kul looked as ill as a fish as his priests led the beautiful and innocent women whom Akhmet had loved up onto Abdul dar-El Haj's pyre. The High Priest was only cynical, not heartless. Primarily to contain his own anger, the Vizier Moshim Mosha Va insisted that the High Priest deserved his distress. I found, however, that I had lost my taste for things which distressed Khartim a-Kul.

When the funerary rites and ceremonies were concluded, the new Caliph disposed of the rest of his father's wives by divorce. Doubtless he had no interest in hearing what his mother or the other older women might say about his purity or virtue.

The question in Arbin was not, What manner of caliph will Akhmet become? It was, Whom will he kill next?

The necessity of understanding him had become imperative.

"How long will it take, do you think?" asked the Vizier when we were alone. "You are a wizard. You have strange arts." His tone was bitter, although I knew he meant me no harm. "Read the signs. How long will it take before he has one of us beheaded? How long will it take before he has *me* beheaded?

"*Suttee*, by my beard! We are all disgraced. No civilized people will have dealings with us again for a hundred years."

Well, I am no prophet. I do not see the future. In the case of young Akhmet, I could hardly see my hand before my face. Nevertheless I had seen Arbin flourish under a line of benevolent rulers. I had watched Arbin's people grow in tolerance, as well as in religion and wealth. And I had loved His Serene Goodness as much as any man.

"Moshim Mosha Va," I said formally, so that the Vizier would heed me, "your death is already written—but it is written in the heart of the rock, where I cannot read it. Yet you are the Vizier of Arbin. Safe or doomed, you must uphold your duty."

"Oh, truly?" he snapped at me. "And must I uphold *suttee*? Must I uphold the murder of interpreters? Must I uphold the whims of a spoiled whelp who remembers his dreams?"

"No," I snapped back, pretending to lose patience with him simply to conceal my own fear. "You must uphold the succession in Arbin. You must uphold the integrity of the realm. Leave this new Caliph to me."

The Vizier Moshim Mosha Va studied me until I dropped my gaze. Then he breathed softly, "Yes. Wizardry and dreams. I will leave this new Caliph to you. And may the gods pity your soul."

"If you will prevent the Most Holy Khartim a-Kul from interfering with me," I replied, speaking half in jest to dispel the seriousness of the moment, "my soul will venture to fend for itself."

Moshim Mosha Va nodded without hesitation. Still studying me, he asked for the second time, "Wizard, do you understand our lord?"

"No," I answered for the second time. "But I will."

The truth was that I did not need understanding to know that Caliph Akhmet would come to me when he had dreamed again. He had already rejected the interpretation and counsel of the Mosque. And he surely had little use for the Vizier's manner of wisdom. Where else would he turn?

He did not dream again for some weeks. During the same period, he did nothing outrageously cruel. Apparently, the beheading of the chief interpreter and the burning of all his lovers had sated him in some way. The state and luxury of his new position he enjoyed. The responsibilities he ignored, except as they gave him opportunity to demonstrate new powers or obtain new satisfactions. For the most part, his time was spent replenishing his harem, and there his instinct for tyranny showed itself most plainly, for he seemed to choose his women, not because they were ripe for love, but because they were apt for humiliation. Nevertheless in the eyes of Arbin women were only women. Unthinking people began to believe that perhaps Caliph Akhmet's rule would not prove intolerable.

I did not make that mistake. I readied my arts and waited.

At last, in the small hours of the night, when even such men as I am must sleep, I was summoned to the Caliph's chambers.

I arrived to find him busy atop one of his women, and it was clear from the sound of her moans and whimpers that she did not relish the nature of his attentions. I would have withdrawn, of course, but I was commanded to attend and watch.

Had I been Moshim Mosha Va, I might have withdrawn regardless and accepted the consequences. Sadly, I lack the Vizier's pragmatic soul. Therefore I stood where I was until the Caliph had achieved his satisfaction. Then I risked saying, "It appears that I have misunderstood your summons, my lord. I believed you wished to discuss the matter of dreams. If I had known you wished me to comment on your performance, I would have prepared myself differently."

"Wizard," Caliph Akhmet replied as if I had not spoken, "my advisers are fatuous in all things, but especially where the wonder of my dreams is concerned. Pious Khartim attempts to interpret what I dream. Sour Moshim attempts to interpret the fact that I dream—and remember. Only you have not made a fool of yourself on this subject. Why is that?"

"Two reasons, my lord," I said at once. "First, I am a wise man. I understand that there are powers which lie beyond mortal interpretation. There the Vizier makes his mistake. He sees nothing which surpasses his own mind. Second, I am a wizard. I know that those powers will not allow themselves to be limited or controlled. There the High Priest makes his mistake. He fails to grasp that religion is not an explanation or a control for that which transcends us, but is rather an explanation or a control for how we must live in the face of powers which will not be defined or interpreted."

"Very good," said the Caliph, and his eyes glittered with the confused penetration of the simoniac, at once insightful and blind. "I see that you want to live. Now you will earn your life.

"I have dreamed the most wonderful dream. I remember it all. Every detail lives in my soul, shining and immaculate, never to be lost. No man has ever remembered such things as I remember them.

"Wizard, I will tell you what I have dreamed. Then you will tell me what to do."

I bowed my acquiescence calmly, although my mouth was dry with fear, and my heart trembled. I had not come to this crisis adequately prepared. I still did not understand.

"I dreamed of wine," said the Caliph, his gaze already turning inward to regard his dream, "of strange wine and music. There were colors in the wine which I have seen in no wine before, hints of black with the most ruby incarnadine, true gold and yellow among straw, regal purple swirling to azure in my cup. There were depths to the liquid which my eyes could not pierce. Its taste was at once poppy and grape, at once fermented and fresh, and all its colors entered my body through my tongue, so that my limbs lived and burned and grew livid because of what was in my mouth. My member became engorged with such heat that no mere female flesh could cool it.

"And while my nerves sang with ruby and gold and cerulean, the music about me also sang. At first it was the music of lyre and tambour, plucked and beating. But as the colors of the wine filled my ears, the music became melody, as if strings and drum had voices full of loveliness, sweet as nectar, rich as satin. Those voices had no words for their song and needed none, for the song itself was as clean as air, as true as rock, as fertile as earth. And the music entered my body as the wine had entered it, came through my ears to live and throb in every muscle and sinew, transporting all my flesh to song. It was promise and fulfillment, carrying comfort to the core of my heart.

"Then the heat of my member grew until it became all heat, all passion, and my whole body in its turn became a part of my member, engorged with the same desire, aching with the same joy. And because of the wine and the music, that desire, that joy, were more precious to me than any release. I knew then that if my member were to spend its heat, all my flesh would experience the climax as part of my member, and the sense of ecstasy and release which would flood my being would be glorious and exquisite beyond any climax known to men—and yet that ecstasy and release, despite their greatness, would be only dross compared to the infinite value of the engorged desire, the aching joy.

"Therefore I was not compelled to seek release, as men are compelled by the lesser passions of wakefulness. Transformed by wine and music, I hung suspended in that place of color and glory and song until the dream ended and left me weeping."

The Caliph was weeping now as he remembered his dream, and his voice was husky with sadness when he again addressed me.

"Wizard, tell me what to do."

He might have been a small boy speaking to his father. Yet his need was not for me, but for a father wiser than I or all the old men of Arbin.

It is conceivable that I could have helped him then. But still I did not understand. I had lived too long in the world, away from dreams.

"My lord," I said, "you are the Caliph. You will do what you wish."

He strove to master his emotion, without success. "And what is it that I wish?"

There I failed him. As if I were wise and sure, I replied, "You wish to make your dreams live. That is why you have summoned me."

He stared at me while the tears dried in his eyes, and his mouth drew down into lines of simony, and I knew then that I had failed him. "Explain yourself, wizard," he said in the tone of a man who hurt women for pleasure.

Now, unfortunately, I could not stop or recant. "My lord," I answered as well as I could, "dreams and wizardry have much in common."

From within my robes, I produced a bouquet of rich flowers.

"Both are composed of illusion and freedom."

When I spread my hands, the flowers became butterflies and scattered themselves about the chamber.

"Yet the freedom and illusion of dreams are internal and may only be reached in sleep, without volition."

Again I spread my hands, and now music could be heard in the air, soft voices whispering melodiously of magic and love.

"The freedom and illusion of wizardry are external, matters of choice."

A third time I spread my hands, and this time flame bloomed in my palms, rising toward the ceiling as I spoke.

"You wish the power of wizardry to make the wonder and glory of your dreams accessible to your waking mind, to make wonder and glory matters of choice."

When I lifted my arms, the flame enveloped me entirely, causing me to disappear from his sight. Only a pillar of fire remained before him, burning the air, consuming nothing. From out of the flame, like the voice of the music, I said, "Wizardry is the path you must follow to pursue your dreams. You must turn away from cruelty and become my disciple. You will find no true happiness in the pain of helpless girls."

Then I stepped from the flame and let the fire go.

"My lord," I said, speaking quietly to contain my fervor, "allow me to serve you. I have knowledge which will enable you to make your dreams live."

That was my best effort, yet I had already lost him. He held a harsh bit clenched between his teeth, and his eyes were as wild as an overdriven mount's.

"So you are a fool after all, wizard," he snarled. "You do not understand. For all your *knowledge*, you cannot comprehend the worth of my dreams."

The truth must be told. Behind my aged composure, I was near to panic. Nevertheless fright has its uses. It gave me the courage to say, "You are mistaken, my lord. I comprehend very well. Dreams have no worth in themselves. Their only value is the value we find in them, the value we bring to them with our waking eyes and hearts. Because they stir us or move us or teach us, they are precious. Otherwise they are nothing."

The Caliph regarded me, a twist of loathing on his lips. "Do you believe that?"

I made some effort to hold up my head. "I do, my lord."

"Then, wizard," he said grimly, "you will have the satisfaction of dying for your beliefs. They are a fool's beliefs, and they become you."

I could think of no way to appeal to him as his guards dragged me from the chamber.

For reasons which I did not grasp at the time, however, he let me keep both my head and my life. Instead of sending me to the block—or to the lion pits, or to any other more imaginative or painful death—he sealed me in my workrooms, with little food and water, less light, and no companionship. Indeed, the only contact I had with the court or Arbin came daily at noon, when for a brief time the Vizier Moshim Mosha Va was permitted to stand outside my door and report on the state of Caliph Akhmet's rule.

At first, of course, I believed that I was simply being held in my rooms until a suitable torture and death could be devised. By the second day, however, I began to think that young Akhmet had other intentions. When the Vizier came to my door, I asked him, "Why am I not dead? Does the Caliph imagine I fear death so extremely that I will go mad here among my arts and tools?"

In a sour tone, Moshim Mosha Va replied, "He is not done with you, wizard."

"What remains?" I inquired, daring to hope that I would be given one more chance.

"Who can say?" The Vizier's words were deferential, but his manner of speaking was savage. "Our illustrious lord surpasses us all. There are signs, however, which perhaps you will read better than I can. This morning he commanded one of his wives to be stretched upon the rack. And while her limbs strained with agony, he mounted her. His thrusts caused her to bleat like a sheep."

"Indeed," I muttered to myself. "How quaint." Then I asked, "And what pleasure did the Caliph take in this action?"

"He appeared blissful," retorted the Vizier, "if such fierceness may be called bliss, until he had spent himself. But then his joy curdled. He ordered the torturer racked until he died, as though the fault lay in the instrument of his will. I think, however, that he meant the man no harm. He was merely vexed."

Perhaps that was the point at which I began to understand Caliph Akhmet and his distress.

"Indeed," I said again. "You have become sagacious since the passing of His Serene Goodness, Vizier. You have grasped an important truth. He means harm to none of us. He is merely vexed."

Moshim Mosha Va made a noise which would have been a curse if the Caliph's guards had not stood beside him, listening. After a moment, he resumed, "Nevertheless the hand of our good lord's vexation is heavy. Why do you not free yourself, wizard? Surely wizardry is good for that, if not for Arbin."

It may have been possible for me to do as he suggested. I could have conjured an affrit to appear before the guards and command them to unlock my prison. Perhaps they would have obeyed instead of fleeing. Freedom lay no farther away than the other side of the heavy door. Yet the distance was too great for me. I had loved Abdul dar-El Haj. I loved Arbin. And I had begun to hope again.

"Wizardry is illusion," I replied to the Vizier. "It is not power. And it is assuredly not freedom. I will await my Caliph's pleasure."

Then, whispering to reduce the hazard that the guards would overhear me, I added, "In the meantime, you must provide for the succession."

The Vizier snorted in disgust and went away.

For a number of days subsequently, he came at noon as he was permitted, bringing me the news of Arbin, which was essentially the news of Caliph Akhmet's attempts to achieve the sensation of his dreams through the exercise of power. He caused considerable pain and occasional death, striving to grasp a knowledge of mortal hurt. At unexpected intervals, he was generous, even benign, so that he could see gratitude on the faces of his subjects and compare it to the look of their distress. Well, he was young, and the young are foolish. He had had too few years in which to learn that power binds rather than releases. It was little wonder that he was vexed.

Therefore I readied myself for the time when he would summon me again.

He did not summon me again, however. Instead, covered by a bright blaze of daylight and torches, he came to see me in my workrooms. The door was flung open, allowing me light for the first time during my captivity. Among guards armed with lamps, Caliph Akhmet strode forward to confront me.

I endeavored to hold up my head, but failed. My old eyes could not bear the brightness. As if I were weeping and ashamed, I bowed and hid my face before my lord.

"Wizard."

I was unable to see him. I could only hear the strain in his voice, the struggle against frailty and grief.

"I need you."

"My lord," I mumbled as if I had become decrepit, "I will serve you."

"Tell me what to do."

"You are the Caliph. You will do what you wish."

"I do not know what I wish."

Indeed. This I had already grasped. Softly, I said, "Tell me what troubles you, my lord."

Out of the light blurred by my tears, young Akhmet answered, "Wizard, I am only myself."

There at last I became sure that I had gleaned the truth. "The same may be said of all men, my lord," I responded gently.

"But all men do not remember their dreams!" If a tyrant can suffer anguish—if such pain can be ascribed to a man who causes so much pain in others—then the Caliph deserved pity. "They are the most wonderful dreams! And I remember them all. Every touch, every color, every joy. Nothing is lost. I have with me now the first dream as clearly as the last, and both are desirable beyond bearing.

"But when I have dreamed, I awake, and I am only myself.

"Help me, wizard."

"I will, my lord." My voice shook, and I cursed the blindness of so much light, but I did not falter. "You wish to live your dreams. You desire to be possessed by dreaming, to give yourself to that glory and freedom always. You wish to cease to be yourself. Therefore you resent anything that takes you from your dreams, any interpretation, any distraction, any release which restores you to your mortality. Waking, you strive for joy and accomplish only dross.

"My lord, I can make you dream always, waking or sleeping. I can enable you to be entirely the dreamer who remembers, beyond interpretation or distraction or release."

I felt his hands clutch at my robes, felt his fingers grip my shoulders to implore. "Then do so. Do so. Do it now."

"Very well, my lord. Give me a moment in which to prepare myself."

In order to gather my strength, as well as to draw the attention of the guards to me, I stepped back from Caliph Akhmet.

Rising to my full height, although I was still effectively blind, I said in the resonant voice of wizards, "Let all witness that what I do now, I do at my lord's express command. He has made his wishes known. I seek only to fulfill them. By my arts he will become his dreams, become dreaming incarnate."

Before the guards could ask whether it lay within their duty to permit this to happen to their lord, I spread my arms and filled the room with fires I could not see.

I did not need to see them, of course. I knew them well. Their suddenness made them seem hotter than they were, and they blazed among my tables and periapts and apparatus as if Caliph and wizard and guards were about to be consumed in conflagration. They did no hurt, however. Instead, as they leaped, roaring silently toward the ceiling, they began to spew out the known stuff of young Akhmet's dreams. Mandrill leaped and snarled, spitting rubies and blood. Nilgai chased silver fear among the flames. City lights unfolded maps of tyranny across darknesses implied by the cruel gaps between the fires. His Serene Goodness Abdul dar-El Haj stretched his mouth to let out a cry of love or pain. Akhmet's swollen member ached for the most glorious and rending ejaculation. To all appearances, my workroom had been filled with dreams come to madness and destruction.

Caliph Akhmet saw those fires no more than I did. They were intended for the edification and appeasement of his entourage. He saw, rather, that I reached among my vials and flasks, uncorked a dusty potion, and poured a liberal draught into a goblet ready with arrak.

"Drink this, my lord," I said as my arts distracted the spectators. "It will enable you to live your dreams even while you are awake."

Young Akhmet had not been a tyrant long enough to learn the fear which corrupts and paralyzes hurtful men. He took the goblet and drank. I could not see the expression on his face.

———

Several days later, after Akhmet had died, and I had outfaced the accusation that I had killed him, and a previously forgotten relation of His Serene Goodness Abdul dar-El Haj, discovered and prepared by the Vizier, had been installed as the new Caliph in Arbin, Moshim Mosha Va took me aside and challenged me.

"The truth, wizard," he demanded. "You killed that little shit, did you not?"

"I did not," I replied in feigned indignation. "Did not the guards declare that I gave our lamented lord no draught or potion, but only a vision of his dreams? Did not the best physicians in Arbin proclaim that our lamented lord showed no evidence of poison? This truth is plain, Vizier. Caliph Akhmet brought about his own death by refusing to eat or drink. He died of thirst, I believe, before he could have died of hunger. Can I be blamed for this?"

"Apparently not," growled the vexed Vizier. "Yet I will continue to blame you until you answer me. By what miracle have we been freed of him? What wizardry did you use? What power do you have, that you do not reveal?"

"Moshim Mosha Va," I responded piously, "I gave our lamented lord exactly what he desired. I gave him the capacity to dream his wonderful dreams while he remained awake. Sadly, his dreams so entranced him that he neglected to live."

The Vizier treated this answer with disdain. He could not obtain a better, however, and in time he grew to be content with it.

Wizardry is illusion. I put the potion which had drugged Caliph Akhmet away in my workroom and made no use of it again. I am a man, and all men dream. But I have forgotten my dreams. I have no wish to become a tyrant.

Penance

The previous evening, I had restored the Duke's son and heir, the Lord Ermine, bringing him back from the deep mortality of his wounds. For safety's sake, I had given of my life in the strict privacy of the Duke's chambers. Indeed, I was attended only by Duke Obal himself, so that no lord of the Duchy, no official of the court, no commander from the field, and no servant in the palace would witness what I did. And when I had infused the young man with my vitality, his death had withdrawn from him, allowing him to rest and grow strong again. Then, depleted and grieving, I had crept quietly from the palace, observed by none except those whom the Duke had commanded to protect me.

Now, in the dusk of the battlefield, I scavenged to restore myself.

All day, Duke Obal's forces had labored against the High Cardinal's siege. Sorties had ridden forth from the walls of Mullior, probing for weakness in the Cardinal's holy persecution. Feints and forays had spent their lives and their horse to protect the Duke's fervent efforts to shore up his defenses, as well as his attempts to ensnare or sabotage the Cardinal's siege engines. Arrows of flame had flown the sky among heavy stones arching from the trebuchet, their flights punctuated by the blaring of the Duke's few cannon, the flatter shouts of his fusils, and the more brazen replies of the Cardinal's harquebus. Now gunpowder added its reek to the stench of charred flesh and garments, the odor of opened bowels, the stink of sweat and pain. On such days, death and bodies seemed to fall like rain, although they fed no harvest on the churned ground. The only crop of so much killing was blood.

Yet it suited me, in its way. To my cost, I gained sustenance from it, and grew strong again. Giving my life to the Duke's son had left me famished and forlorn—so near collapse that my daily resolve to wait until dusk nearly drove me mad.

I had vowed that I would feed from no man or woman except those to whom God had already given death. And in daylight the battlefield was too hazardous for me. I could be hacked apart as easily as any other man, or killed by shot, or burned to death. Nothing warded me except the brief strength which I had already spent in Duke Obal's name. Until I fed, I was as frail as I appeared—and no less contemptible. Indeed, daylight itself threatened me. It encouraged witnesses and denunciation. Therefore I awaited the sun's decline, although my hunger and weakness were anguish.

When the sun at last dipped from the heavens, however, drawing daylight westward off the plain of battle, I presented myself to the secret portal in Mullior's outer wall. There the guards had been commanded to let me pass—and to admit me again when I was done. This, too, was hazardous. If ever the guards had refused my reentry, I would surely have fallen prey to the High Cardinal's retribution. But they were ignorant of what I was, and had never scrupled to fulfill their lord's instructions. Piously they gave me Godspeed when I departed, and welcomed me when I returned. Doubtless they considered me a spy, charged with some small, regular mission for the Duke, and for that reason they wished me well. Duke Obal was well loved in Mullior, as in the Duchy at large.

My own love resembled theirs, although I did not demean the Duke by speaking of it. Even in Mullior, my esteem would have brought him execration, if I were known.

Concealed by twilight and battle fume, I emerged from the portal and followed failing light across the human wreckage of the siege.

Crouching as I went, I scurried among the corpses and the dying—as timorous as the vermin which now thronged the field, and as ravenous.

It was commonly said of my kind that we drank blood. The High Cardinal himself had pronounced anathema upon me in those terms, calling me "blood-beast" and "spawn of Satan." We were misunderstood, however. I did not drink blood. I did not consume blood at all. I drew life from blood—and I drew it by touch. The vitality in the blood of any man or woman who still lived could sustain me.

It was a fact of my nature that I absorbed nourishment and strength more quickly and easily, and with more pleasure, through the touch of my tongue than of my fingers. But at need any portion of my flesh would suffice. Life passed by blood from the one who bled to me, and I was made whole.

As for those who bled— Their lives became mine, and so they died.

For that reason, I fed only from the doomed.

Because their vitality was diminished, tainted with death and therefore noxious, they sustained me ill. I was forced to range widely to preserve myself, groaning with the nausea of my kind.

Nevertheless I was scrupulous, careful of my vow, although it was commonly believed that my kind had no souls and no conscience, and existed beyond the reach of God's redemption. I had joined my heart to Mother Church, and to the sweet maid Irradia, for whom I still wept, and what I had sworn to do I did. I took no life which had not already been claimed by God. Any of the fallen for whom the faintest hope of rescue or healing still breathed, I passed by.

However, Mullior was at war with Mother Church, in the person of the High Cardinal, His Reverence Straylish Beatified. And each day of the contest harvested enough soldiers and commanders, camp followers and lords, to sate me several times over. I did not lack for sustenance, despite my scruples.

Yet I may indeed have lacked a soul, or the impulse for redemption. I kept my vow—and all this carnage did not content me. Touching my hand to a torn side here, my tongue to a gutted chest or a ripped throat there, I skulked among the bodies and the charnel stench, feeding abundantly—and still I desired more. Nausea hindered my satisfaction.

This night, trouble found me in spite of my caution. My foraging had drawn me nearer than I realized to one of the Cardinal's encircling camps, and their tents and fires stood no more than an arrow's shot distant. I heard the unsteady crunch of boots among bones and mud as a heavy tread approached me, but the warning came too late. I could not slip away among the shadows and corpses before I was observed.

The man's presence was dangerous enough. More fatal to me, however, was the lantern in his fist. He had shielded its light so that it would not expose him to hostile eyes, but when he turned its radiance directly toward me he could not fail to see the blood upon my hands and lips— the stigmata of my unalterable damnation.

Hunching among the fallen, I stared up at him, unblinking, transfixed by the cruelty of illumination.

"Ho, carrion-crow," he snorted as he regarded me. "Eater of the dead." His tone held no fear. Rather it suggested the amiable malice of a soldier who took pleasure in killing and meant well by it. His grin showed teeth the color of stones. "Straylish told us Mullior's foul Duke harbored such as you, but I doubted him. I doubted such fiends existed. Now I see the virtue of this war more clearly."

I made to rise, so that I might better defend myself. At once, the soldier snatched at his falchion. In the light of the lantern, its notched and ragged edge leered toward me, eager for butchery.

"Stay where you are, hellspawn," the man warned. "There will be promotion in it when I deliver you to the High Cardinal. He will be pleased if you are presented to him alive—but he will find no fault with me if you are dead."

And Straylish the High Cardinal would certainly recognize me. This war attested daily to the enmity between us.

The soldier's grin sharpened as I sank back. His lantern reflected sparks of greed in his gaze—for advancement, for pain. Directing his falchion at my neck, and confident of his authority, he shouted over his shoulder toward his camp, "Ho, you louts! Here! On the run!"

While his head was turned, I rose.

Here was one of the High Cardinal's captains, brutal and righteous— and rich with life. I had fed enough, and could overmatch him, striking a blow against my accuser in the person of his servant. Within my stained robes, behind my tattered beard and shrouded eyes, I was no longer the frail figure who skulked the shadows of Mullior, or crept tottering in prostration from the Duke's chambers. I had become strong again. This man's blood would exalt me.

Yet I had forsworn such measures. In my heart, I had accepted the accusation.

Instead I leaped upon him, sweeping his sword aside as I sprang. My unexpected bulk staggered him, hampered his reactions. In that instant of advantage, I struck him senseless to the ground.

Shouts carried across the field, answering his call. His men had heard him, and hastened to respond. But they would not catch me now. With nourishment I had grown fleet as well as strong, and the dark was my ally in all its guises.

Before I could flee, however, I saw that the captain's lantern had fallen with him, spilling its oil over him as it broke. Already flames licked at his side. In another instant he would begin to burn.

His men might save him. Or they might reach him too late.

And I had sworn that I would take no life not first claimed by God. Uncertain of my own soul, I had sworn it on the maid Irradia's, in the name of Mother Church.

The soldiers of the Cardinal charged toward me, yelling. Their weapons caught the unsteady light of the campfires and shed it in slivers of ruin. Although I was frantic for my life, I spent a precious moment stamping out the flames. Then I turned and ran.

The captain had named me "carrion-crow," and so I was. Threadbare, my robe fluttered and snapped about me like wings as I raced among the dead. I stooped and turned like a raven assailed by hawks. My only haven was Duke Obal's secret portal, distant before me, but I did not aim for it. I feared betraying its existence to the High Cardinal's forces. Instead I directed my flight elsewhere.

Blood I encountered aplenty as I ran. My senses discerned it acutely, despite my haste through the enfolding darkness. I knew it by its aroma, and its luminescence, and its aura of life. Its sweetness clad the fallen wherever they lay. Yet I did not pause to feed.

There was purpose to my path—and hope. Although the soldiers pursued me perilously, I trusted the Duke's defenses, and bent my flight ever nearer to his walls. Like their captain, the men on my heels carried lanterns, as revealing as corpse-light, else they would have lost me at once. And those shielded flames were apparent from the walls. Soon I heard shouts from the city, a quick fusillade, cries at my back.

Several of the soldiers dropped, shot-struck. Cursing, the rest fell back and let me go.

Those who had been mortally wounded died at my hands. Cardinal Straylish was my enemy, and when my vows permitted it I did him what harm I could. By choice, I accepted the taint of Hell with each flicker of life I consumed from the dying.

Once I had fed deeply, I turned away.

Ashamed of the carelessness which had led me into difficulty, and haunted by the ceaseless fear of my kind—the alarm that I had not fed enough to sustain me until I could feed again—I returned to my portal and signaled for admittance.

Had I possessed a soul, its sickness might have driven me to madness or suicide. I had embraced the teachings of Mother Church, and knew my own evil. From Irradia's sweet love I had learned to yearn for Heaven. With the eye of my heart, I saw clearly the baffled distress and— perhaps—revulsion she would have felt at my actions since her tormented death. Although I had not caused this war, I used it to serve me. Duke Obal and all Mullior unwittingly carried out my contest with the High Cardinal. Grieving, Irradia might have begged me to surrender, as she would have surrendered in my place.

I, too, grieved. I had no hope for the redemption which had surely enfolded her in God's grace. But I had chosen another road, and did not turn aside from it.

Because I grieved, however, I resolved to spend this night in the hospital where the Duke's surgeons tended those who had been injured in battle—both Mullior's men and the soldiers of High Cardinal Straylish. There I could repay in some small measure the life I had stolen from the battlefield. I was familiar to the surgeons and nurses, although they knew nothing of my nature. I had moved among them often, when Duke Obal did not require my service. Where the portal guards considered me a minor spy, the hospital's attendants believed me a holy man of an obscure sect, visiting the injured and dying in expiation for my sins—a man whose piety and prayers gave rest to pain, healing for fevers, and relief from infections. I was subtle and circumspect, so that no one grasped what I did. The small restorations which helped the victims of this war survive their hurts passed unremarked.

I felt the need for expiation. My carelessness had led to deaths which might not have occurred otherwise, and that burden I did not bear easily.

But at the portal a new trouble awaited me, more ominous than my encounter with the Cardinal's captain. The guards informed me that Duke Obal required my presence. I was instructed to obey swiftly.

That he saw fit to risk my aid two nights running was highly unusual. It was also profoundly unwise. The "miracles of healing" which I performed in his service endangered us both. They attracted notice. Members of the Duke's court, as well as of his army, could hardly fail to observe that men such as Lord Ermine—or one of the field commanders—or indeed the Duke himself—were borne, dying, from the day's carnage, only to return entirely whole. In sooth their recovery was so remarkable that even the opposing forces noted it. No ordinary surgeon or priest could account for the new health of those men, except by miracle—or by Satanic intervention. And Straylish preached that God's judgment would permit no miracles in the name of an excommunicate like Mullior's Duke. Thus were spread the rumors that fiends and hellspawn served Duke Obal, empowering his resistance to the righteous authority of Mother Church in the person of the High Cardinal.

This notion was so fearsome to the devout of the Duchy that it undermined Obal's position and strength, despite the fact that his people loved him. To all appearances, I alone bore the cost of the arduous restorations which I wrought on the Duke's behalf. I passed stored vitality to those of his most precious adherents who had been sorely wounded—a transaction fraught with pain for me, as well as with the weakness of deep loss, all compounded by the unannealed visceral terror of giving away my own life. While it drew its recipients back from death, the infusion left me drained and frail, scarcely able to provide for my own continuance. Thus the core of the Duke's support in Mullior was preserved. All the suffering of the stricken became mine.

Nevertheless Duke Obal also paid a price for my aid. It may have been more subtle than that which I endured, but it was no less grievous.

The High Cardinal and others of his ilk argued that I was the whole cause of the war which had set the Duke against Mullior's more pious neighbors. Priests damned me with their prayers even when they supported Duke Obal. Religious families shuddered at the thought of Satan in their midst. And ambitious men, men who might perhaps have made their fortunes and their futures by replacing those whom the Duke trusted, advancing to positions of power from which they could conceivably have delivered Mullior and all its riches to the Cardinal—ah, such men loathed me where I stood.

It was more than unwise for Duke Obal to call upon my service too often or too frequently. It was foolish and fatal.

I considered refusal. I sensed a crisis in Mullior which might prove lethal to me. And at all times I lived in fear that the Duke might be persuaded by his advisers, or by his people's need for peace, to turn against me—to deliver me to Cardinal Straylish so that the siege might be lifted. I had saved his life twice—that of his beloved son, thrice—his dearest and staunchest friends half a score of times. For all men, however—and even more for Dukes and Cardinals—necessity was the mother of cruelty. I could too easily imagine that the Duke might decide my life, like his own most prized convictions, was too expensive to merit so much death.

Perhaps I had expended my last hope, and only flight remained to me.

Yet I knew I could not deny Duke Obal's summons. He had earned my unflagging service by the simple expedient of accepting it from me. I had seen the maid Irradia tortured, and heard the High Cardinal pronounce anathema upon me. How could I not love a man who opposed such evils?— a man who did not fear my nature because he trusted my honor?

Escorted as much for my own protection as to ensure my haste, I left the portal and found my way to the Duke's low-lying palace in the heart of Mullior.

There another surprise deepened my dread. Necessarily cautious, I turned my steps toward the private gate and the unfrequented corridors through which I customarily approached my lord. But my escort redirected me. A guard at either shoulder led me to the ornate portico which gave formal entrance to the hereditary domicile and seat of Mullior's rulers. Before I was announced to the fusiliers at the polished and engraved doors, I grasped the significance of this development.

Despite the peril to us both, Duke Obal had commanded me to a public audience.

Holding my breath to contain my fear, I listened narrowly to the terms in which my escort had been instructed to announce me. I understood that the Duke had chosen to place my damned head on the executioner's block of his court's opprobrium. Apart from the danger, this violated the unspoken terms of my service. Only the form of my announcement offered any hint as to whether or not I could hope to survive the night.

The leader of my escort clearly found the occasion tedious. If I was doomed, he did not know it. In a tone of bluff boredom, he stated, "Here is Duke Obal's faithful handservant Scriven. By the Duke's express wish, he presents himself to attend upon his lord."

The reaction of the palace fusiliers was more ominous. As if involuntarily, they flinched and crossed themselves. One of them muttered, "Carrion-eater." Others breathed fervent oaths.

This caused my escort to look at me askance. Unlike the fusiliers, however, they were familiar with me, comfortably convinced that I was a minor spy serving their lord. They were veterans of the siege, hardened to it, and reserved their fear for the enemy. Surprised at my reception, they did not step back from my shoulders.

"'Carrion-eater'?" one of them demanded. "Where?"

The fusiliers did not reply. Their captain silenced them. Stiff with disapproval and alarm, he spoke a prepared welcome. "The lord of Mullior welcomes all who serve him faithfully." Between his teeth, he added, "I am to say that the Duke himself awaits his handservant Scriven's arrival."

His obedience did not comfort me. "Scriven" was not my name. Straylish Beatified knew me otherwise. However, it was the name I had chosen for the Duke's use. While I lived, I bore Irradia's fate written on my soul.

Covering my unsteadiness, I required myself to draw breath. My danger was as great as I had feared. Already rumor had run ahead of the Duke's intent, hinting at worse within.

At the captain's word, my escort bowed themselves haphazardly away. Eager to be rid of me, the captain detached a fusilier to accompany me into the palace, presumably so that I would not wander astray. I was hastened forward. For the first time, I stood accursed and dismayed in the formal entry hall of Duke Obal's home.

It was not the opulence of the space which daunted me. I had little use for wealth myself, and saw no value in the devout tapestries, woven of gilt and verdigris, which behung the walls, the sheened marble of the floor, the lamps burning scented holy oils in their stands of gold and mahogany, the sculpted and pious busts of Mullior's lords. Rather, I was chagrined by the fact that such luxuriance existed. An effort I could not conceive had gone into the creation of Duke Obal's ornaments—and the work had not been done by men or women of my kind. Our lives were fixed on survival, and from day to day we had neither leisure nor inclination for embellishment. The palace's wealth daunted me because it reminded me that I was vastly outnumbered by souls accepted by God and Mother Church, souls who could hope for Heaven—and who could afford to spend their existence on decoration.

Each step I took in such a place increased my peril. I did not belong there. I belonged in servants' entrances and private passages, small rooms secreted from scrutiny, lofts and stables and mud. The farther I intruded here, the greater grew the certainty that my nature would be discovered. And each bust and weaving seemed to mock the idea that I would ever be free to depart.

Clutching to my breast the faith which Irradia had taught me—the faith that some among humankind understood loyalty and honor as well as they grasped war and anathema—I followed my fusilier toward the Duke.

Chamber succeeded chamber, some high and stately, others smaller and more discreet. Servants tended a few, but most were vacant, and their emptiness troubled me. It suggested that their usual occupants and attendants had been called elsewhere. Therefore I feared that Duke Obal meant to make me known to the entire palace.

Instinctively I yearned to cower and skulk forward as though I had come to haunt a battlefield. The strain of walking erect tested me sorely. Only the wisdom of my kind restrained me from creeping—the given knowledge that the more I showed my fear the more I would empower my enemies to act on their own.

Before me loomed a set of doors as high as those which guarded the portico, but at once less massive and more ornate. There the fusilier led me. Anxiously bidding me to wait, he tapped his knuckles on the wood, then stepped back to compose himself.

At once, the doors were jerked partly aside, and a man slipped between them to confront us, closing them swiftly behind him so that we might not see inward or enter.

He wore the rich braid and tooled leather of Duke Obal's livery, although his costume was more elaborate than those I knew by sight. A pectoral cross hung by a chain of heavy gold from his neck, and a short satin cloak of midnight purple with the Rose of Obal picked out in crimson thread draped one shoulder. In his hand he held a slender staff surmounted by Mullior's Eagle in silver and gems. This rod proclaimed him the Duke's majordomo.

He did not look at me. Indeed, he seemed determined to avoid sight of me. Vexed by trepidation, he snapped waspishly at the fusilier, "Who is this?"

Too loudly, the fusilier replied, "By your grace, this is Duke Obal's handservant Scriven." Sweat stood on his brow, although the night was cool. "His presence has been commanded."

At last the majordomo flicked a frightened glance at me, then swore in a whisper. "I know that, fool. You would have done the Duke and all Mullior a service if you had failed to find him, no matter how strenuously his presence was commanded."

The fusilier retreated a step from the majordomo's anger. "I'm sorry," he murmured uncertainly. "We didn't know—"

The majordomo swore again. "Return to your duties. Say nothing." Flapping his hand, he dismissed my escort. Then he demanded of me, "You are Scriven? You and no other?" Again his eyes evaded my face.

Alarm closed my throat. Unable to speak, I nodded awkwardly. His manner foretold that I was doomed as well as damned.

Staring past my shoulder, he breathed, "On my soul, and for the sake of this House, I pray that the horrors rumored of you are false."

Before I could attempt a reply, he returned to the doors. "Enter," he commanded as he drew them aside. "The Duke awaits you."

I could not believe that I would have been greeted in this fashion, hostile though it was, if the Duke openly meant to harm me. He could have easily had me brought before him in irons, disavowing me without subterfuge. Yet any direct rejection would have called into question the acceptance which had preceded it. Therefore, my terror suggested, I would be asked to betray myself. If I did so, I would spare Duke Obal the censure of Mother Church and his own lords for his former acquiescence in my designs.

Even then I might have changed my mind and fled. I was strong enough. I could have run like the wind—overpowered most ordinary opposition— broken from the palace and dashed into the dark streets and alleys of Mullior, outdistancing immediate pursuit. And if I set my scruples aside so that I remained strong, I might prolong my life for days. On the brink of the fate Duke Obal had prepared for me, I nearly turned aside.

But I did not. I had sworn my vows to myself and to God, and to Irradia's memory, and they held me.

Duke Obal opposed the High Cardinal. In the Cardinal's person, he opposed the worldly might of Mother Church. And he did not do so because that course was convenient for him, or expedient, or free of peril. Already he had been excommunicated. Worse would befall him if Mullior fell. Therefore I would trust him, and remain true to the service I had chosen to give him.

Hunching within my robes, I stepped between the doors and joined the majordomo in the hall beyond.

Although my eyes had grown accustomed to the profuse illumination within the palace, I was not prepared for the brilliance of the Duke's ceremonial chamber. Intricate chandeliers depended thickly from the ceiling. Candelabra without number lined the walls. And they were enhanced at intervals by braziers and glittering lamps. In two high hearths blazing logs cast back the evening's chill. From end to end, light searched the space, seeking fears and effacing concealment. By preference and necessity, I was a creature of the night, inclined to coverts and darkness—

dismayed by so much flame-shine. I quailed at the majordomo's side, despite my resolve to show no fright.

That the hall was crowded with people only augmented my alarm.

Here apparently were gathered all the highborn and significant citizens of Mullior. Among the Duke's servants and fusiliers, I saw folk that I knew—lords and ladies, captains and commanders, priests and officials, merchants and moneylenders—and at least twoscore men and women that I did not. Some wore the garb of their duties and rank. Others displayed their finery, their wealth, or their charms, as those who courted suzerains were inclined to do at any provocation, claiming their stature by right of ostentation or appearance.

As palpable to me as the vitality of blood, their tension gave flesh to my apprehensions.

It was a singular assembly—and not a disinterested one. All Mullior stood excommunicate. Highborn and low, lords and streetsweepers, ladies and whores—all Mullior's inhabitants faced anathema from the High Cardinal's indignation and ruin for their immortal souls. Here were gathered, however, those whose riches and power—as well as salvation—were either threatened or enhanced by the siege of Mother Church. According to their factions and loyalties, to the sources of their wealth and standing, these men and women had tangible, worldly reasons to support resistance, or to encourage surrender. They might speak of evil and redemption— some of them sincerely—but they had other concerns as well.

As did I. I did not think ill of them for their personal considerations. I had no right—and no soul to give my judgments worth. But I also did not trust them. None of their concerns were mine.

They would not hesitate to sacrifice me.

After a moment I caught sight of Duke Obal, some distance from me. He stood in a cluster of his supporters and adherents, among them Lord Ermine, heir to the Duchy, Lord Vill, who commanded the Duke's forces in the field when the Duke himself was absent, Lord Rawn, Master of Mullior's Purse, and several captains noteworthy for their daring in battle. Another observer might not have remarked the particular company surrounding the Duke, but I was struck by it.

They were all men whom I had restored, in the name of my vow.

The rest of the assembly appeared less deliberately composed—grouped more by family or rank than by faction—although the Bishop of Mullior, His Reverence Heraldic, kept the company of his priests and confessors close about him. Yet the general flow and eddy of social intercourse preserved a discreet space around those who stood with the Duke. I judged that these folk were discomfited by the occasion, chary of seeming uncritically allied to the House of Obal. Perhaps under the troubled gaze of the Bishop they did not wish to appear impious by too obviously supporting a man accused of sacrilege and threatened with anathema.

A low murmur of taut conversation and uneasy riposte filled the hall, softened by the rugs which overlay much of the marble floor. The majordomo had ushered me inward quietly. At first we attracted no notice. But clearly my escort had been given instructions which defied his preferences. With his head turned from me and his shoulders clenched in distaste, he struck his staff against the floor. By some trick of the light, Mullior's Eagle appeared to flap its wings, barking for attention. Almost instantly, every voice in the hall was stilled, and every eye swung toward us, some with interest, others in trepidation.

The impulse to cower multiplied within me. If I had not fed so recently, I would not have been strong enough to refuse it.

Clearing his throat, the majordomo declaimed unsteadily, "My lords and ladies, here is Duke Obal's faithful handservant Scriven." The decreed litany of my peril had already grown ominously familiar. "By the Duke's express wish, he presents himself to attend upon his lord."

The growl of opprobrium which at once greeted this announcement shriveled my heart in my chest. I heard "carrion-crow" muttered and "blood-beast" moaned. Priests and devout ladies crossed themselves or clutched their beads, their lips busy with prayer. Fusiliers gripped their guns or their falchions. Lords closed their hands on their sabers. Every man and woman near me drew back, looking to each other for protection.

Somehow my nature had become known—or suspected—despite all my caution. I was now a threat to the Duke. He had called me here to resolve the matter.

All that remained was to discover what form my doom would take.

I told myself that I was merely suspected, not known. Otherwise some righteous soul would have struck me where I stood, compelled by his devotion to Mother Church. But that was cold comfort, and tenuous. I could not long endure the scrutiny of so much light.

From the cluster amid which he stood, Duke Obal turned his head. Blinded by the illumination, I could not descry his features, or his expression. When he spoke, his tone was neutral, rigidly controlled.

"Ah, Scriven." He did not seem to raise his voice. Yet nature had made him potent, despite his years. And he was no longer the wracked invalid to whom I had first offered my service. Both disease and injury had been lifted from him. His voice carried easily. "You are welcome here. My thanks for your promptness.

"Approach me." He beckoned firmly. "You are needed."

His self-command was evident. Still his words did not suggest that he meant me ill.

Before I could comply, however, Bishop Heraldic intervened. A hush fell over the hall as he stepped forward.

He was a fleshy individual, disinclined to asceticism. That may have explained his acquiescence to the moral ambiguity of serving Mother Church without supporting the High Cardinal's siege. Any serious effort to denounce the Duke would have cost him considerable comfort. Nevertheless he made an imposing presence, resplendent in his vestments and miter, the gold of their stitching, and of his heavy pectoral cross, agleam with reflected lampshine. His protuberant eyes glowered, and his pendulous jowls quivered, giving the indignant authority of his office corporeal form. It seemed that his conscience had reached its limits.

Disdaining to glance at me, he confronted Duke Obal across an interval of rugs and marble.

"No, my lord," he proclaimed, sententious with virtue. "I must protest. By my cloth, and in the name of Mother Church, I forbid this sacrilege. Fiends and demons give no service to Heaven, whatever they pretend. A life is a small price to pay for the sanctity of an immortal soul."

The Duke raised his chin. "So you have said, my lord Bishop." Although he owed deference to Mother Church and all Her representatives, he permitted himself an acerbic reply. "I have heard you. I have *understood* you. But I am the Duke of Mullior, and within these walls my will rules. I will address your concerns—later.

"Approach me, Scriven," he repeated. Again he beckoned, but with more force. "I am impatient of delay. There is much at issue between us."

Murmuring, "Yes, my lord," I left the majordomo's side and ventured into the expanse of the hall.

Whispers of renewed execration followed me as I moved—a miasma of revulsion and alarm. Ladies and their lords retreated to avoid my proximity. Half the assembly glared at me as though I had arrived in an eruption of brimstone and flame. The rest watched His Reverence Heraldic, hoping—or perhaps fearing—that he would call upon their righteousness to join him in protest or revolt.

For his part, the Bishop withdrew to await events. What he hoped to gain, I did not know. I could not conceive how Duke Obal meant to resolve the dilemma of my presence in Mullior.

Approaching the Duke, I crossed luxurious rugs over a floor of burnished marble, but they had no value to me. I would have preferred to walk in mud.

My lord wore the full regalia of his station—the ornamental hauberk chased with silver, the sash gathered in a rosette at his waist, the tooled greaves and boots, the saber on his hip, and beneath it all a blouse and hose of blackest silk. Rings studded his fingers. The gems of a circlet glittered in his hair. Clearly he intended a commanding display, so that he would be difficult to contradict.

In that he succeeded, for his demeanor and visage conveyed as much authority as his attire. An iron beard shot with gray sculpted the line of his jaw, and the sun-hued planes of his face might have been cast in bronze. When I had first offered him my service, he had been a mere husk of himself, drained by consumption and time, as well as by half a dozen wounds. And even then, he had sustained the High Cardinal's siege and held the loyalty of Mullior by the unbroken force of his will. Now, however, he was whole and well, and his spirit shone with renewed vitality. He appeared as merciless as his blade.

Only the gentle intelligence of his gaze—the troubled, accessible color of his eyes—revealed the man who was loved more than feared in his

Duchy, the man who could defy the edicts of Cardinal Straylish and still trust the hearts of his people. The man whose easy justice and open concern had taught me that not all rulers and powers were cast in the High Cardinal's mold.

As I neared him, his companions stepped apart, making way for me, and I received a new surprise, a blow so sudden and unexpected that it nearly halted the labor of my heart. For the first time I glimpsed the nature of Duke Obal's purpose. With his lords and captains, and his son, he had placed himself to conceal a cot on which lay a man of middle years, plainly dying.

I did not recognize him. And he was not identified by attire, for he wore only a cloth wrapped about his loins. Yet I saw his death beyond mistake in the waxen hue of his flesh, the sheen of sweat strained from the pores of his brow, the flecks of blood on his ashy lips. It was my nature to feed on life, and I knew its passing with an intimacy which other men reserved for their lovers, or for God. His soul would achieve its culmination before dawn, and then he would know only bliss or torment forevermore.

And Duke Obal meant— He wished—

The brightness of the hall seemed to gather about me, multiplying on the pale flesh of the dying man, so that my vision blurred, and my mind with it. Here before scores of witnesses rife with censorious piety, Duke Obal intended—

Hardly conscious of what I did, I stumbled in my alarm, and would have fallen if Lord Ermine had not caught my arm.

"Calm your fear, Scriven," he breathed in my ear. Born late, he little resembled his father. His features did not yet bear the stamp of his character. He had the Duke's eyes, however, and had recovered his life at my hand. "This is necessary. You have not been abandoned."

His reassurance was kindly meant. I did not believe him—I was wise enough to fear dukes and lords when they spoke of what was "necessary"—but I drew courage from his words and his grasp, and regained my legs.

Beckoning yet again, the Duke urged me to the side of the cot.

I had expected denunciations and curses—at the worst, I had expected a doomed battle to preserve my life—but in my gravest terrors I had never dreamed that I would be asked to betray my nature before all the powerful of Mullior. The prospect appalled me. But it also shamed me. Mother Church taught that my kind had no souls, and could never win release from anguish. Now I was asked to demonstrate the lack. I would not have been more distressed if Duke Obal had commanded me to rape a child in the hall.

The Duke's Commander joined Lord Ermine beside me. He, too, whispered for no ears but mine. "Come, Scriven. We cannot endure delay. Mullior is a powder keg this night, and every moment the fuse burns shorter."

I turned toward him in my weakness. "My lord Vill," I murmured, "I have not deserved this from you."

Impatiently Lord Rawn, the Master of Mullior's Purse, snapped his fingers. "What you deserve," he hissed softly, "is not at issue. Duke Obal's rule *is*. He will stand or fall here, and your hesitancy weakens the ground under him. Step forward, or recant your service, as you wish—but do it *now*."

At once, however, the Duke intervened, sparing me an immediate response. "You are mistaken, my lord Rawn." His tone was mild despite its tension. "We can afford a few moments."

Turning from the men at my sides, I concentrated my attention on the lord to whom I had sworn my service against Cardinal Straylish.

"Scriven," he informed me softly, "you have become known. I cannot explain it. I will not believe that you have been betrayed here." He meant within his palace. "Those who serve me have earned my trust. But rumor is a powerful foe. And I doubt not that the High Cardinal's spies are among us"—a sneer curled his lip—"spreading any tale Straylish desires.

"The charge that I countenance a scion of Hell is one I must confront." The set of his jaw bespoke anger and restraint. "If I fail, I will fall, as Lord Rawn suggests. Until now, as you know, Bishop Heraldic has withheld the condemnation of Mother Church from my actions, preaching that it is not the duty of God's servants to judge worldly princes. If he turns against me—if he persuades Mullior's more devout lords to make cause with the Cardinal—I am done."

I considered it significant that Bishop Heraldic did not preach—as

Irradia had taught me—that Scripture urged all souls to embrace love and meekness rather than to practice execration or crave power. In my heart, I deemed him no better than the High Cardinal. He was merely more indolent.

"Scriven," Duke Obal concluded urgently, "you have trusted me until now. Trust me still, and we will do what we can to defuse this powder keg."

I could hardly refuse him. He had set my head on the block, and no one else could deflect the executioner's stroke. Bowing weakly, I replied, "How may I serve you, my lord?" although I knew the answer all too well.

The cast of his features suggested gratitude, but he did not express it. Instead he indicated the man recumbent before us.

"This is Lord Numis. He is Bishop Heraldic's chancellor—the Bishop's adviser and agent in all things which pertain to the legal affairs of Mother Church in Mullior. As you see, he is dying. Surgeons and physicians without number have failed to relieve his illness." The Duke's gaze held mine. "I ask you to restore him."

He confirmed my gravest dread. Doubtless his actions were necessary, as I had been told. Still I hesitated, fearing the outcome of any public declaration of my nature.

While I faltered, Lord Rawn offered sourly, "It may interest you that among Bishop Heraldic's advisers, Lord Numis is the High Cardinal's most vigorous and vehement supporter."

Frozen by apprehension, I temporized. "My lord," I murmured, "I do not understand. He is my enemy—and yours."

In fact, I understood perfectly. Terror rendered me acute. But I wished to hear Duke Obal's reply.

He spread his hands as though to reveal their openness—their honesty. "Scriven," he admitted, "I cannot defeat these rumors by pretending that they are false. With contradiction, they will swell until they burst, and their putrefaction overwhelms me." He shrugged. "Yet if I acknowledge that they are true, I must also name myself damned. Accepting the service of Satan's minions, I cannot escape the conclusion that I number among them."

He paused as though to consult his conscience, then continued, "This conundrum offers only two outlets. I might denounce you now, swearing that I lacked prior knowledge of your nature. By joining Mother Church in your condemnation, I might save myself.

"This course has been urged to me." Duke Obal did not glance at anyone present. "But I will not do it." Anger roughened his tone. "It is cowardly and dishonorable. I have promised otherwise. In addition, however, it is impolitic. It would undermine my plain opposition to the High Cardinal."

Then with an effort he seemed to set his ire aside. More gently, he said, "The other outlet is more difficult. We must demonstrate to this gathering that whatever your nature may be, you are not in truth a scion of Hell. If you are seen to heal, these folk will be hard-pressed to name you a killer. And any demonstration will convey more conviction if it benefits your enemies, rather than those who condone your presence." A nod indicated Lord Numis. "The healing of the Bishop's chancellor will not be marred by any appearance of self-interest."

Sore of heart, I noted that he did not advance an argument which might have touched me more deeply—the maid Irradia's belief that in God's name we were commanded to cherish those who reviled and persecuted us. If her sufferings had permitted it, she would have prayed for the Cardinal's soul while she died—

Still the fact remained that I had no choice. I could not hope to survive by flight or struggle, despite my strength. And until this night Duke Obal had given me no cause to doubt his given word. Bowing my head, I acquiesced.

"I will do what I can, my lord."

Again his expression suggested gratitude, but he did not voice it. Firmly he gestured me toward the chancellor's cot.

Dry of mouth, and trembling in all my joints, I approached the invalid. Lord Ermine and Lord Vill remained protectively at my sides. All others stepped back.

At the cot's edge, I knelt. The assembly might think that I prayed—or that I feigned prayer to disguise my malice—but in truth I lacked the will to stand. Fear loosened my joints. And I was also, suddenly, filled by the hunger of my kind, avid and ceaseless. Despite my strength, I desired more sustenance. And here lay a life apt to be consumed—a life already claimed by God—nourishment my vows permitted.

Further, Lord Numis was my enemy. Although his ribs started from his chest, and his flesh held the waxen pallor of death, I detected the heartless exigencies of the law in the shape of his mouth, and under his grizzled beard his jaw had a fanatic's strict cruelty. Hating such men, I burned to hasten his passage to Heaven or Hell.

Then, however, he turned a gaze dull with fever toward me. Despite his illness, he seemed to know himself and where he was—he seemed to know me—for he moistened his lips with blood in order to murmur hoarsely, "Stay back, fiend. Taint me not. Touch me not. I die because I must." He coughed thinly. "I will not go to God with your foulness upon me."

After he had spoken so, I could no more have taken his life than I could have turned my back on Irradia's memory. I had no soul, and knew myself damned. Nevertheless I had sworn vows I meant to keep.

Above my head, Duke Obal addressed the gathering. His voice grew in force and conviction, yet I hardly heard him. References were made to "tests" and "healing" and "Heaven," but I did not regard them. Shamed by my unrepentant appetites—and grieving at my own cruelty—I made a show of what I did, so that my actions would be visible to the whole gathering.

From within my robe, I drew out an inquisitor's dirk, a blade as keen and well pointed as necessity and a whetstone could make it. For a moment I brandished it above my head as though I might plunge it into the chancellor's breast, or my own. Then, swiftly, I drew a thin cut across the pad of my middle finger—one new cut among the lattice of scars I had acquired in Duke Obal's service.

Bright and precious in the intense illumination, a drop of rich ruby swelled from my wound.

By blood I devoured life—and restored it. Just as I consumed a man's vitality through the touch of his vein's fluid, so I returned it with the touch of my own. Lord Numis moved his lips in supplication, but I did not heed him. A last moment I hesitated, gazing at the gem of blood upon my finger—a bead of purest ruin—and dreading what was to come. Then I set all pity aside. Deliberately I slid my finger between the chancellor's jaws and stroked his tongue with my strength.

Whatever the reaction behind me may have been, I did not witness it. The instant Lord Numis tasted my blood, I felt the life pour from me like oil from a broken amphora, to be replaced by weakness and despair—and by a near-murderous hunger. My substance withered within my robes, the pliancy fled my muscles, and hope dwindled in my veins. Between one heartbeat and the next, I passed from vitality to utter sorrow. Now a child might have slain me—if I did not first contrive to snatch a touch of his blood. I had become no more than the sum of what I had lost.

For a brief time, I failed of consciousness. Fainting, I slumped into the depths of the Duke's rugs.

Yet the very richness of my bed seemed to spurn me. Stricken by panic and inanition, I heaved up my head and clawed my limbs under me, thinking to see swords high in the harsh light, men rabid with execration, guards and lords armed for slaughter—

Apparently, however, the interval of my stupefaction had been too brief for so much motion. Indeed, no one present had lifted a hand. Caught in a hush of mortal trepidation, none spoke or breathed. Duke Obal and his adherents remained poised like inquisitors about me. Lord Numis had not shifted on his cot.

Then the chancellor raised his head—and a hoarse sigh spread across the assembly.

Frowning bitterly, he considered his circumstances. His eyes held an unappeased glitter, which showed that his fever had left him. In its place, disgust twisted his lips, and his jaws seemed to chew the fouled meat of his restoration as though its rank savor pleased him obscurely.

When his abhorrence had collected all the force of my gift—my spent life—he swung his legs from the cot's edge and stood, trembling and strict, clad only in his loincloth and his righteousness.

At once Lord Ermine swept a cloak from his own shoulders and wrapped it about the rigid chancellor. But Lord Numis shrugged it aside as though he craved the humiliation of his nakedness—as though he wished all the gathering to see how he had been abased.

"Abomination," he croaked. "Abomination and sin."

Clearly he meant to shout, but at first his disused voice betrayed him. He did not falter, however. Swallowing the residue of fever from his throat, he began again, more strongly.

"Abomination, I say!" he declared, claiming the right to dispense Heaven's judgment. "Abomination and *sin*!"

"My lord, you forget yourself," put in Lord Rawn quickly. At a sign from the Duke, he and Lord Vill moved to interpose themselves between Lord Numis and the assembly. "You have been most gravely ill. You do not grasp the wonder of your recovery."

But the chancellor thrust them away. Fired by the force I had given him, he confronted his shocked audience.

"I have been most foully harmed!" he cried. "This vile minion of Satan has placed his taint upon my soul!" With one grim arm he aimed his accusation at my bowed head. "My God whom I have served with my life called me to the bliss of my just reward, and I answered gladly. But this blood-beast, this *hellspawn*, this eater of *death*, has snatched me back from Heaven! With the Duke's knowledge and consent, he has practiced his evil upon me, and I am prevented from peace."

I made an attempt to rise, and found that I could not. My weakness outweighed me. No other voice was raised, yet the atmosphere in the hall fairly crackled with apprehension, as furious and frantic as a fusillade. I had heard similar denunciations before. They carried the pang of sweet Irradia's death, and of my helplessness to save her, and in my despair I was filled by such a fury of weeping that I could scarcely suppress it.

Lord Numis swung toward me. His ire blazed from him in the excruciating light. "Carrion-crow," he ranted over my kneeling form, "*slave of evil*. I will know no rest until I have seen you *slain!*" Then he turned to the assembly again. "My lord Bishop, for my soul I beg you. I implore. Command his death. Instruct all Mullior on peril of damnation to hack him limb from limb and heart where he kneels. Anele me of this corruption before my soul is consumed by it."

Under the lash of his fanaticism, the highborn of the Duchy stirred and fretted. Some glanced uncertainly at their comrades, perhaps perturbed to hear such violence urged in the wake of unexpected healing. A number of them, I believed—those most sincere in their love for the Duke—disliked and distrusted Lord Numis. But others began to mutter encouragement for the chancellor's demand. Clergymen crossed themselves, and ladies prayed. Guards and fusiliers clutched at their weapons.

Merchants and officials drew back in dread, or edged forward angrily. My kind was easily feared. And the strictures of Mother Church, harsh in the name of God's love, multiplied that alarm. Men and women who would have risked their own souls without hesitation to postpone death assented eagerly to the legalist's righteous umbrage.

They had never known my weakness, and could not conceive how my kind treasured life.

For a moment every eye was fixed on His Reverence Heraldic. Every heart awaited his response.

I would not have called the Bishop courageous. However, he was not a man who shirked precedence and power when they were offered without apparent cost—or apparent hazard. He put himself forward a step or two, announcing his authority. With both hands, he held high the wealth of his pectoral cross so that it shone like a beacon in the acute illumination.

"Guards," he called—and more loudly, "servants of Mother Church!" In stentorian tones, he proclaimed, "I name this Scriven damned. He is an eater of death, vile in the sight of the Almighty, and must be destroyed. The gifts of fiends are corrupt, and the more precious they appear the greater their corruption must be. Acceptance leads to damnation. The will of Heaven is plain. He must be destroyed now."

Irradia would have asked Heaven to forgive him. I did not.

Half the assembly shouted an acclamation at once, eager to see the source of their fear exterminated. Released from their tension, guards and lords surged to assail me, drawing their swords as they advanced.

I strove anew to gain my feet. "Do it yourself, my lord Bishop," I panted as I rose. "If you dare." But my defiance was so frail that even those near me did not hear it.

Instead Duke Obal compelled their attention. With a feral stride, he moved to confront those who meant my death. Closing one hard fist on the back of the chancellor's neck, he drove Lord Numis forcibly to his knees. The other he raised in threat.

"Hold!" he commanded, his voice ringing off the walls. "Stop where you stand!" The fury and force which made him dreadful in battle emanated palpably from him. "I have promised Scriven safety. He serves me, and is under my protection. Any man who lifts a hand against him will answer for it with *blood*."

Lord Ermine closed with his father, as did Lord Vill and the Duke's captains, forming a barrier to shield me. Accustomed to obey their lord, the hostile throng paused. While a few judicious voices called for restraint, men in the grip of righteous fervor looked uncertainly toward the Bishop, seeking his support.

To this Lord Numis croaked a protest. But the Duke's hard grasp on his neck prevented him from speaking clearly.

At another time, His Reverence might have regretted his hasty opposition. However, the chancellor's outrage had touched on the most sensitive part of Bishop Heraldic's posture of accommodation toward Duke Obal's apostasy. On other points, the Bishop could argue that he sought to prevent a rift between Mother Church and the people of Mullior. On *this* point, however, on the subject of tolerance for the creatures of Satan—

"*No*, my lord Duke," he retorted with apparent courage. "I know my duty to Mother Church, and to God. This Scriven is an abomination! We have witnessed his vile power, and must not endure it. In the name of Heaven, he must—"

Harshly the Duke interrupted His Reverence. "Have I not made myself plain?" he blared. "*Scriven has my protection.* If any hand rises against him, I will *lop it off*! Even yours, my lord Bishop.

"Have you forgotten where you are? This is the ducal palace of Mullior. *I rule here.*"

To my amazement and chagrin, and to my vast sorrow, Duke Obal bound his fate to mine inextricably. He had spoken words which could not be recalled. If Mullior accepted Bishop Heraldic's denunciation now, the lord I served would share my doom.

And he was not done. "Perhaps it has escaped your notice," he continued acidly, "that this 'abomination' has saved a life. In fact"—here he jerked Lord Numis upright, so that the energy of the legalist's struggle was displayed for all to see—"he has saved the life of a man dedicated to Mother Church." Then he released Lord Numis so that the chancellor staggered away toward Bishop Heraldic and the shelter of the Bishop's retinue.

"I was taught by clergymen," stated the Duke, "that those who heal do God's work. I am no theologian, but I will venture to assert that the condition of my lord Chancellor's soul is not determined by the illness or health of his flesh."

The assembly stirred in confusion and thwarted ire. Fearful of their own temerity, and of their lord's wrath, the guards retreated to their duties. Bishop Heraldic did not fall back, however. Supported by some score of Mullior's most devout folk, he bore the withering force of Duke Obal's scorn.

Nevertheless he moderated his manner. "My lord," he answered carefully, "you cannot so lightly set aside Heaven's revulsion. Yes, Mother Church teaches that healing is God's work. But She also teaches that the stalking fiends of night, all werebeasts and succubi, vampyrs and ghouls, are scions of Hell. Merely to encounter them is to hazard damnation. To treat with them—to accept their service—to cover them with your protection—"

Piously rueful, His Reverence shook his head. "Perhaps you believe you have the strength to endure such evil, my lord. But you do not. It is not given to men to be greater than evil. Only by God's grace, and by the strict intervention of Mother Church, do we withstand Satan's depredations."

I had gained my feet, but I retained scarcely enough vitality to keep them. The blaze of the illumination seemed to bear down upon me as though I were a blot to be effaced from the hall. Nevertheless in my frailty and grief I sought for words potent enough to fend off Duke Obal's doom.

"My lord," I might have urged him, "withdraw your protection. My service will cost you more than it merits. If you turn against me now, you may yet retain the countenance of Mother Church in this siege. Without it, you must fall, and the Cardinal's triumph will be inevitable."

I could conceive no other salvation for him.

Yet I remained mute. My vows precluded surrender. And I had not yet been granted opportunity for supplication or defiance. Duke Obal did not hesitate to answer His Reverence.

"My lord Bishop, I am not a fool." He spoke as though to the emissary of a mortal enemy. "And I am a good son of Mother Church, whatever the High Cardinal may preach, or you may think. I am not careless of my soul's sanctity, or of my hope of Heaven. If I have accepted Scriven's service, with all its perils—*I, Obal, Duke of Mullior*"—vehemence flew like spittle from his lips—"then you must bow to the knowledge that *I have good reason!*"

At first His Reverence appeared shaken by this rejoinder. He could not reiterate his demands without insulting Duke Obal—and that would have been gravest folly at any time. While the Bishop searched his uncertainty for a reply, however, Lord Numis called fiercely, "Name them, my lord! Name your reasons."

The Duke gave a bark of harsh laughter. "Thank you, my lord Numis," he returned, his tone trenchant. "That is precisely why I have called my handservant Scriven to this assembly. I have had enough of rumor and innuendo and baseless defamation. Mullior has been sickened by them, and they must cease. Tonight their place will be taken by plain speech—and plain truth."

Felled by the import of what I heard, I found myself on my hands and knees. The senseless intricacy of the rug confronted me blindly. If the Duke desired "plain speech," "plain truth," he could ask it of but one man here—and that burden was greater than I could bear.

From the hour when I had first entered Mullior, I had told my tale to no living soul. Duke Obal himself had no knowledge of it. He had inquired into it, of course. He had inquired often. But I had answered him with evasions—evasions which he had accepted because my service to him was precious.

He did not know what I might say if he searched me now. In my worst nightmares, I had not dreamed that he might place us both in a danger so extreme.

And I had given up my strength to Lord Numis. I could not survive by flight or struggle. Scant moments ago, I had tried to envision how I might save Duke Obal. Now I could grasp no salvation for myself.

Despite my despair, however, I was forced to acknowledge the Duke a man of honor, worthy of service. With all Mullior at stake, he meant to place himself in my hands. If I told the truth and was damned for it, he would be damned as well.

When the gathering had fallen silent, he turned to me. At the sight of my huddled posture, he scowled. Glancing toward his son, he breathed, "Help him. He must stand. He must answer."

Joined by Lord Rawn, Lord Ermine hastened to my side. Together they supported me upright, their concern evident on their faces. Upon occasion they had witnessed my weakness, just as they had benefited from my strength, but they had never seen me so profoundly drained. In me sorrow and dread altogether surpassed my kind's more ordinary fear of hunger and frailty.

"Hold up your heart," Lord Ermine urged me. "We will prevail some-how. My father is unaccustomed to failure. And we believe that he has rightly judged Mullior's mood—and Mullior's needs."

He sought to fortify me, but I was unable to hear him. The light seemed to leave me deaf as well as blind. I could not blink my sight clear, or lift my heart.

"My lord," the Master of Mullior's Purse whispered to the Duke, "he is too weak for this. Look." Lord Rawn shook me so I staggered, although his grasp was gentle. "He is prostrate where he stands. If he does not feed, he will collapse before us, and then we are lost."

"That," stated Lord Vill through his teeth, "is impossible. If he feeds, someone must die for it. We cannot countenance such an act in front of these pious cowards. They will rise against us. We will be garroted before we can gain the doors."

That, too, was plain truth. In the name of my vows, and of my debt to Irradia, I summoned the resolve to raise my head. Although I failed to drive the blur of tears from my gaze, I faced Duke Obal and said for the second time, "I will do what I can, my lord."

He appeared to nod. "Good," he remarked privately. "I ask only the truth. Grant that, and I will abide the outcome."

Then he continued more strongly, so that the hall could hear him. "Speak openly, and fear nothing, Scriven. I have named you my hand-servant. As you restored Lord Numis, so you have also renewed my own life, and that of my son, as well as many others. For yourself, you have drawn sustenance solely from the fallen of this cruel siege. My lord Bishop calls you an abomination, but I have seen no sign of evil in you. I have felt no harm at your touch.

"The time has come for an accounting between us. Scriven, why do you serve me?"

I had said that I would do what I could, but dismay mocked my given word. The compulsion to dodge and feint in the face of peril ruled me. Rather than answering honestly, I countered, "My lord, why do you oppose the High Cardinal?"

The Duke's eyes narrowed, and a glower darkened his visage. I felt impatience through his urgency. He had not brought me to this hall in front of these witnesses in order to watch me scurry aside. Yet his self-mastery was greater than mine. Despite his vexation, he responded as I had asked.

"All Mullior knows my reasons. You know them yourself, Scriven. I oppose High Cardinal Straylish on both worldly and spiritual grounds."

In a formal voice, Duke Obal declared, "His Reverence Beatified has made plain that he considers it the province of Mother Church to dictate both law and policy to such states as Mullior. I do not." Each word he articulated with the force of a decree. "Where the duties of my station and my birth are concerned, I will be no man's puppet. The soul and its salvation are the proper care of Mother Church. Worldly circumstances are not. It is not the place of Mother Church to judge or control the actions of suzerains. Such matters as whether I form an alliance with one neighbor, or welcome refugees from another, are not resolved by theological debate. And I take it as a transgression—as a personal affront—when Cardinal Straylish commands me to enact laws which restrict or punish those citizens of Mullior who have not entrusted their souls to Mother Church. I grieve when my people do not recognize the light of Heaven, but I will not in any fashion deny them the freedom of such determinations."

Lord Vill and Lord Rawn nodded their approval, but no one in the hall spoke. All Mullior's highborn had often heard Duke Obal assert his convictions. They waited restively for the outcome of his peroration.

"These are worldly questions," the Duke continued. "On spiritual issues also I am not persuaded by the service His Reverence Beatified gives to God. Its tenor disturbs me.

"I was taught by the clergy of Mullior, Bishop Heraldic among them"—subtly he undermined the Bishop's censorious disapproval—"that God is a God of love, that Heaven is a place of joy, and that the task of Mother Church is to teach us to open our hearts to such benefi- cence. Therefore I believe that the true sign of those who serve Mother Church is that their hearts *are* open. Filled with God, they are neither condemnatory nor cruel.

"Yet the High Cardinal has closed his heart to all who do not honor his dominion. He *persecutes* any and all who do not share his beliefs, or his nature. He does not ask if they are *accessible* to salvation. Rather, he *coerces* them to it. And if he deems them beyond coercion, he seeks their destruction."

Duke Obal made no effort to disguise his bitterness. "In this His Reverence Beatified does not count the cost. Because he loathes evil, he prefers to torment and maim, to make war, to spill the blood of the harmless like water, and to impose his will by terror, rather than to suffer the existence of hellspawn. Better, he believes, to excruciate and murder an innocent—or a thousand innocents—than to risk letting one blood- beast escape him.

"I disagree," the Duke pronounced harshly. "I do not believe that coercion and torture are the proper instruments of love and joy. While I live, I will oppose them. If I am wrong, I will answer for it before Heaven. But I will not answer to His Reverence Straylish Beatified."

There he stopped. He had said enough to demean my evasion, and I was ashamed of it. Yet I strove to conceal myself still. Across the expec- tant silence of the assembly, I answered softly, "And does that not suffice to account for my service, my lord?"

He shook his head. "It does not."

And Bishop Heraldic echoed behind him, "It does not."

Their eyes held me. Every gaze in the hall was fixed toward me. Although I could not stanch my grief enough to see clearly, I felt horror and fascination from my witnesses—revulsion accentuated by the secret excitement of proximity to forbidden things.

"Very well," I sighed. "If I must."

And still I temporized. Of the Duke's son I inquired, "May I have wine, my lord? It will not restore me, but it will ease my throat."

I meant that I hoped it would ease my abasement.

"Certainly," answered Lord Ermine. He left my side. I heard murmuring, and a low voice asked, "Where is the wine which the Duke requires?" For a reason that eluded me, Lord Ermine was answered by a priest of the Duke's retinue—he may have been the Duke's personal confessor. The tension of the gathering grew sharper still. But I gave no heed. I cared only that when Lord Ermine returned he placed in my hands a goblet brimming with the sacred color of deep rubies and blood.

I preferred water, but I drank the wine, praying that it might have an effect upon one of my kind—that it might serve to blunt the edge of my distress, as it did for other men. And if it did not lift my weakness, or soften my woe, perhaps it would sanctify my penance.

With what strength I had, I declared, "I serve you, my lord, because His Reverence Straylish Beatified instructed me to do so."

My audience reacted with disbelief and indignation, and also with a kind of febrile mirth, heated by alarm. Bursts of harsh laughter punctuated shocked expressions of virtue and rejection. I was accused of "sacrilege," "Satanic cunning," and—more kindly—"madness." However, Duke Obal dominated the response.

"Explain yourself, Scriven," he demanded. "Are you a spy?"

I shook my head. "No, my lord. You will understand—"

As best I could, I hardened my heart.

Directing my gaze into the red depths of the goblet, I told my tale for the first and only time.

"Like others of my kind," I explained, "I am commonly homeless. We cannot nourish each other, and none sustain us willingly. We are cursed to isolation. Therefore we wander.

"Perhaps a year ago, my roaming took me to Sestle"—the birthplace of the Cardinal, and the seat of his power. "There I settled to fend for survival as unobtrusively as I could.

"I cannot tell how others of my kind make their way. I suspect that we are diverse as ordinary men, and that some of us cut as wide a swath as they may, while others covet more timid existence. For myself, I had learned as I roved that places of worship provided congenial feeding grounds. In such places men are plentiful—and careless of their safety, thinking themselves protected by their gods. For the same reason, when a community comes to fear one of my kind, it seldom searches its sanctuaries and chapels. In lands to the east and south of Sestle"—lands which had not been enfolded by Mother Church—"I had lived well and long by secreting myself and selecting my prey within places of worship.

"That was my intention in Sestle. Avoiding the great cathedrals, I chose a decrepit chapel immured among the city's multitudinous poor, in a region named Leeside, where the worshipers were at once devout and defenseless, and where any number of unexplained deaths might pass unremarked. At first I made my home among the nameless graves in the chapel basement. Later, however, I learned that the chapel's builders, dreaming of grander sanctuaries, had given the edifice lofts and attics among the high rafters, and there I eventually took up residence. From above I could watch and hear what transpired below me, among the worshipers. This greatly improved the efficacy of my position.

"I believed that I had found a place where I might live for many years and be secure.

"However, its effect was not what I had imagined. From my lofty perch, I watched and heard—too much.

"The congregation I observed comprised little more than human refuse, more ruined than their house of worship, reduced by poverty and near-starvation to the semblance of vermin. And yet the devotion on their faces, the simplicity revealed through their grime and pain, the untrammeled trust of their hymns and prayers—these things touched me as I had never been touched before.

"Must I speak the truth, my lords? Then I will acknowledge that I saw myself in them. My homelessness and wandering, and my ceaseless isolation, had taught me to understand their deprivation. And my kind is always hungry.

"As I watched my intended prey, there reawakened in me a yearning which I had ignored for so long that it seemed to have no name, a longing of the heart to stand among other men, other folk, and call them mine."

Hearing whispered opprobrium and doubt, I admitted, "I am well aware that I revolt you, my lords. Throughout my life I have known only revulsion. It is the fact around which my existence revolves. Yet the truth remains. In that chapel I ached to join the congregation, and give myself up to be healed."

Then I resumed.

"As I say, I saw too much when I watched. And when I listened I heard too much. For the first time, I attended to the conduct and attitudes of my prey. Their priest—an old man called Father Domsen—was no less ruined than they, no less tattered and besmirched, no less stricken by want. But he was also no less devout, and his love of Heaven seemed to shine like a beacon in the dim sanctuary. Again and again, day after day, he spoke of love and acceptance and peace, and of an immortal joy beyond the smallest taint of earthly suffering, and in his faith I heard intimations of an ineffable glory. I was persuaded by it, my lords, when I had not known that I could be moved at all.

"The alteration in me was gradual, but it brooked no resistance. At first I was hardly conscious of the change. Then I found that I had grown loath to prey on those who worshiped in my chosen home. This required me to search more widely for sustenance, and to accept more hazard. Nevertheless I gained a comfort I could not explain from the knowledge that the chapel's congregation was in no peril. And for a time that contented me.

"As I listened to the priest's kind homilies, however, and to his gentle orisons, and heard the heartfelt goodwill of his blessings, I came to desire a deeper solace. I wished for the more profound balm of standing shoulder to shoulder with men and women who did not abhor me, and of sharing their simplicity.

"So it was that perhaps three months after I had arrived in Sestle I left my high covert in order to join the congregation when it gathered to worship.

"That was difficult for me, my lords. As I say, I had known only revulsion from ordinary men—only hatred, and a lust to see me exterminated. To mingle with folk who would avidly rend me limb from limb under other circumstances cost me severely. My pulses burned with fear, and at intervals my hunger swelled with feverish urgency. Yet I endured. Having entered among the congregation, I could not withdraw without drawing notice. At all times, notice threatens me. And in that gathering to be noticed would block any relief from the yearning which had driven me there.

"I did not know the prayers or the hymns, and the liturgy itself was new to me. But I mimicked those around me until I had secured a rote knowledge of their service. So I avoided the notice I dreaded. Men granted me the same vague nods they gave their fellows, children laughed or squalled in my presence, women and maids curtsied to me without recognition or concern. By small increments I began to feel that I was accepted."

I gripped my goblet weakly. "This was an illusion. I understood its ephemeral nature. The folk around me did not know what I was.

"Yet there was truth in it also. The poor of Sestle feared no one who was not better born, or wealthier, or more predatory than they. Within its plain limits, their acceptance of me was sincere.

"And I valued it for what it was. Soon I learned to treasure it.

"Determined to pose no danger in Leeside, I hunted ever more widely for sustenance. Consequently disturbances and rumors began to circulate in the neighborhoods of the rich and the wellborn, causing guards and watchmen to increase their vigilance—and my difficulties. Yet I regretted nothing that I did. The illusion of acceptance eased and nurtured me. I would willingly have incurred far greater hazards to preserve it.

"Still it *was* illusion. It taught me to crave more substantial consolations.

"However, I found that I could not glean what I sought by rote and mimicry. The forms of the chapel's worship were potent in my heart, but their content—I could not comprehend it. Apparently my life and my nature had precluded essential insights or assumptions which the devout of Mother Church shared with their priest, but which conveyed nothing to me. What was 'God'—or 'Heaven'—or 'soul'? I had no experience of their import. I knew only life and death. And death terrified me because it was not life. When the priest spoke of 'sin' and 'forgiveness' and 'salvation,' I could not imagine his meaning. I could only mouth the hymns and the prayers, and feel true acceptance slipping from my grasp.

"Eventually my desire to stand among those worshipers in their sanctuary might have curdled to darkness. My yearning had been reawakened, and its frustration could well have driven me to other extremes. However, I was spared that loss.

"Men say that my kind have no souls, and it may be true. But if we do not, I am unable to explain why God deigned to lift the burden of my isolation before it grew too cumbersome for me to bear."

Sighing, I drank from my goblet. In some measure, the wine did ease me. It cleared my throat for speech. But it did little to disperse the thunderheads of weeping and fury which threatened to overwhelm my fragile composure with storms. I had never told my tale because it gave me too much pain.

Nevertheless I did not stop. I hungered for expiation, despite its cost.

In the silence of the assembly, I continued my litany of woe.

"Like 'Heaven' and 'sin,' 'love' was a word I did not comprehend. I had no experience of it. I could not have explained 'kindness' to a passing cur. How then could I grasp the higher concerns of the spirit? But I was taught—

"One day as I entered the sanctuary among the worshipers, a maid curtsied to me. I hardly regarded her, except that I feared all notice, and so I replied with a bow, not wishing to call down attention by rudeness. Then I passed her by.

"However, she found a place near mine in the sanctuary. The hood of her threadbare cloak covered her hair, but did not conceal her face from me. During the first hymns, she met my gaze and smiled whenever I chanced to glance toward her.

"Instantly I feared her. How had I drawn her notice? And how could I deflect it elsewhere? Attention led to death, as I knew too well. Yet I was also intrigued by her. I saw no revulsion in her soft eyes—and no malice. No cunning. No knowledge of what I was. Rather, I seemed to detect a shy pleasure in my confusion, my muffled alarm. Although I knew nothing of such matters, I received the impression that she wished me to repay her notice.

"Covertly, I studied her during the prayers and readings. To me, she was comely—smooth of cheek and full of lip, alive with the vitality of youth, yet demure and pious in her demeanor. Her poverty was plain in the wear and patching of her attire, but if she understood want—as did all Sestle's poor—she had not been dulled by it. No taint of bitterness or envy diminished her radiance. In the depth and luster of her gentle gaze, I caught my first glimpse of what Father Domsen meant when he spoke of 'the soul,' for her eyes seemed to hold more life than mere flesh could contain.

"Her smiles teased me in ways which disturbed me to the heart."

Within myself I wailed at the memory. But I did not voice my sorrow.

"The priest delivered his sermon earnestly, but I did not heed him. I could not. I felt a mounting consternation which closed my ears. I wished only to flee the maid's nearness—and dared not, fearing to attract still more notice. Through the final hymns and prayers, and the priest's distant benediction, I stumbled. Then I sought my departure with as much speed as I could afford.

"To my chagrin, she accosted me in the aisle before the doors. Avoidance was impossible. Curtsying again, she stepped near and laughed to me softly, 'Sir, you sing very badly.'

"To my chagrin, I say—and yet I felt a far greater dismay when I found myself unable to turn away from her jest. She meant no harm by it, that was plain. No insult sullied her mirth. She simply wished to speak with me. And the impulse gave her pleasure.

"By that soft enchantment she held me, despite my knowledge of death, and my fear. I might safely have stepped past her there, urged ahead by the moving throng, but I did not. Instead I bowed to conceal my face, murmuring, 'The melodies are new to me.'

"While I spoke, I cursed myself because I did not flee. But I cursed myself more because I could not match her smile. The pain of my loneliness had become greater than I knew.

"'You are a stranger then,' she remarked.

"'I am,' I told her. Because my discomfort seemed rude to me, I added, 'My lady.'

"She laughed again. '"My lady"? You are truly a stranger. No native of Sestle would attempt such excessive courtesy here. I am not so well-born, sir.

"'I am called Irradia. Those who desire more formality name me "Irradia-of-the-Lees," for I was discovered as an infant among the dredgings of the river, and raised by the good folk of Leeside. This chapel is my home.' She glanced fondly about the edifice.

"Her enchantment did not release me. Awkward with difficulty, I strove to answer her. 'You honor me,' I said gruffly. 'As for me, I am so far from my birthplace that I have no name. But you will honor me further if you call me Aposter.'"

Unable to face my audience, I gazed into the darkness of my goblet. "My lords, that is not my name," I told the last of my wine. "Nor is Scriven. But it is the name I chose to give her. And it is the name by which I am known to His Reverence Straylish Beatified."

Hardening my sorrow, I resumed.

"She accepted it without demur. How could she have known that it was false? That I was false myself?" Or that she would die in anguish because she could name me? "So commenced my true conversion to the teachings of Mother Church. Until that day, I had stood among the worshipers, singing and praying attentively, but I had only aped their devotion, not shared it. I desired it, but could not grasp its import. From that moment forward, however, the maid Irradia became my teacher, and I began to learn.

"At first, of course, she did not know that she taught me. She did not know what I was—and I gave her no glimpse of my ignorance. She merely offered me her friendliness and courtesy. Perhaps she did so because she could see that I was lost in loneliness despite my mimicry. Perhaps she was guided to me by the hand of Heaven. Or perhaps the flawless bounty of her heart surpassed the ordinary bounds of flesh and blood. I could not account for her actions then, and cannot explain them now. But in the days which followed she showed me what friendship and kindness were. By example she gave me my first instruction in righteousness.

"And with every taste of her companionship, I found that my hunger for it swelled. I grew eager for her smiles and mirth. I gave her occasion to tease me because her jests brought me pleasure. I accompanied her on the rounds of charity, the innumerable generosities, which filled her days as an adopted daughter of the chapel, and my small part in them warmed my heart. And when we were apart—as naturally we were more than we were together—I craved the sight of her as I craved survival. Her presence was like the vitality I drew from my victims. It elevated me, it made me strong and whole, it added a sparkle to the light of day and a glow to the depth of night—but it did not satisfy me. I desired more. I had been lonely too long. Her company became as necessary to me as blood, and I grew insatiable for it.

"So I began to reveal myself to her, hoping to strengthen the bonds between us—bonds which I had never felt before, and had no wish to break. I did not tell her what I was. But when I had known her for a month or more, I unfolded my ignorance to her. Embarrassed and cunning, I described the yearning which caused me to stand among the congregation and sing—badly—although I lacked all comprehension of what my worship signified.

"My ploy succeeded better than I could have dreamed. It drew Irradia to me, for she was pure in her faith, and the thought of healing the breach which separated me from Heaven enchanted her. At the same time, however, it increased my own attraction to the teachings of Mother Church. As my companion exemplified them, they seemed entirely lovely to me, worthy of all devotion. The idea that my long experience of revulsion might be redeemed transported me. Hopes and desires beyond imagination took root in my once-barren heart, and sprouted richly.

"The more I knew of Irradia, the more I longed for her. And the more I learned from her, the more I desired the solace and acceptance of Mother Church."

The assembly stirred, restive with distress—indignant tinder smoldering toward outrage. They had seen that I was fearsome, a creature of powers miraculous to them, and therefore cruel. That I now laid claim to the teachings of Mother Church, which they held as their own, affronted them mortally. The Duke himself appeared disturbed, and his supporters with him. I heard whispers of "blasphemy" and "carnal evil." No doubt the gathering thought that I expressed a wish for Heaven in order to disguise my lust.

But Duke Obal had cornered me in his bright hall. I was as ready to give battle as any trapped beast. And the pain of Irradia's loss—and of my part in her torment—gave me a kind of strength. Briefly I could raise my voice.

"Do you question my *sincerity*, my lords?" In sudden fury I flung my goblet so that it bounded, soundless and empty, across the rugs. "Do you believe that I *dissemble*?"

My vehemence shocked the whispers to silence.

"It may be that I have no soul," I cried. *"But I have a heart."* There my flare of force consumed itself, and died. Ash and regret seemed to fill my mouth as I repeated, "I have a heart. I wish daily that I did not."

Then I rallied against my weakness. "But I do not ask God to take it from me. It is *mine*. My life is only my life. Doubtless you will slay me, when I am done with my tale. But you cannot erase my pain, or stifle my yearning—or avoid the cost."

The Duke covered his eyes. Perhaps he lacked the courage to regard me directly. "Continue, Scriven," he murmured as though he had been moved. "Fear nothing. I am as mortal as any man, and as flawed. But I am not so easily turned aside from my promises."

He could not truly believe that I would "fear nothing" at his command. He was not such a fool. But I had set my feet to this path, and did not mean to step back now. Bowing my head, I answered, "As you wish, my lord."

All the influential of Mullior watched me as they would a serpent. Under the bale of their fascination, I pursued my tale.

"As I have said, the maid Irradia gave me instruction, binding me to her with every lesson—and her to me. Indeed, the growing warmth of her regard taught me the truth of her words, for it demonstrated God's forgiveness. In the name of Mother Church, she offered me a life which was not defined and circumscribed by revulsion.

"And when she believed that I had understood her, she took me to Father Domsen, so that he might further my edification."

Bishop Heraldic and his confessors crossed themselves in self-protection, warding away heresy, but I paid them no heed.

"That good man welcomed me," I said without scorn, as though I had seen no reaction. "He taught me gladly. He was Irradia's father—in a manner of speaking—both temporally and spiritually, and at first I thought that he extended his kindness to me for her sake. Later, however, I understood him better. His love for her enriched but did not determine his acceptance. The simplicity of his faith, and the embrace of his heart, were wide enough to enfold all who worshiped with him.

"Sooner than I would have thought possible"—and altogether too soon for my dismayed auditors—"he and Irradia began to speak of my baptism—of my union by water and sacrament with Mother Church."

Despite the moisture in my gaze, I held up my head as though I meant to stare down the assembly. But I needed more valor to confront my memories than to outface my enemies. Word after word, my tale gathered its anguish.

"My lords, I know now that I should have feared baptism. Belatedly I have heard that holy water is agony to my kind, scalding us with Heaven's rejection. At the time, however, I had no such concern. Irradia and Father Domsen had taught me to trust God's utter benison. Having no soul, I was unaware that I was damned.

"Yet I was troubled in my mind—and in my heart, if I have no soul. Throughout my life, I had known only abhorrence. And from abhorrence I had learned shame, although I did not realize it until I had recognized my loneliness. I am what I am, and life is life, and I had not ceased to feed. No creature of flesh endures without its proper sustenance. I studied the will of Heaven openly, desiring it as I desired Irradia's love. Yet still I preyed widely in Sestle so that I would not perish.

"Ashamed, I feared that Irradia—and Mother Church—would repulse me if they learned the truth.

"Further, I knew that I had been careless, although I had not yet imagined the consequences. Blinded by yearning, I had fed too often upon the fat and the wellborn, the wealthy and the publicly devout. And in so doing I had drawn notice.

"A child might have foreseen this, yet I did not. Ignoring the hazard of my actions, I had brought myself unwittingly to the awareness of His Reverence Straylish Beatified."

And the High Cardinal had completed my instruction. I abided by his precepts still.

"From his spies and informants," I explained, "as well as from more common sources, he heard tales of unexplained deaths, sudden passings. And some of the lost were his supporters, vital to his stature in the affairs of Sestle. Inspired by righteousness, he guessed the truth.

"So he searched for me." Relentless as a deathwatch, my tale progressed toward its doom. "With every resource at his command, he hunted the byways and coverts, the dens and hovels, the inns and stables, the markets and middens, seeking some sign of my presence. As yet he did not know who I was, or where I resided, or how I selected my victims. But he knew *what* I was, and he bent the annealed iron of his loathing toward me."

I sighed so that I would not groan aloud. "Yet I was oblivious, immersed in my hunger for salvation. Only the sanctuary of my loft protected me, for I had lost the true habit of self-regard. While Cardinal Straylish stalked me with all his priests and allies, I concentrated on the impending crisis of my baptism.

"As I have said, I was ashamed. I saw my nature as an obstacle to my baptism—a bar to my union with Mother Church, and to Irradia's love, and to all good. Yet for that same reason I was loath to speak of my dilemma. The rejection of the congregation I might survive. I had endured for many long years without a place among ordinary men, and might do so again. But the thought that Irradia might hear my revelation with horror—that her outpouring love might curdle against me—caused such pain that I did not think I could bear it.

"At last, however, I accepted the risk. How could I ask for love if I did not honor truth? Irradia and Father Domsen preached that the welcome of Heaven knew no end or limit—that all life was of Divine creation, born of God to seek God's glory through Mother Church. How then could anyone who saw the worth of that worship be refused?

"On the eve of the day appointed for my baptism, I told Irradia what I was."

Inwardly I flinched at the memory. Yet I suffered it alone. Only the ceaseless blurring of my sight and the quavering of my voice betrayed my distress to the assembly.

"At first her response was all I had dreaded. Her dear features paled, and she shrank from me as though I had become loathsome to her. She trembled, feverish with alarm. And she avoided the supplication of my touch, hid her face from my gaze. Weeping threatened to overtake her.

"The blow was a devastation to me, my lords. My life in Sestle, and my heart, cracked wide at the impact. In another moment, I would have begun to tear my garments and wail in despair. And when that was done, I might have turned my thoughts to ruin. She was the foundation upon which my dream of love and Heaven rested, and she could not stand.

"However, she rallied. Groaning my name, she turned toward me. Pain in runnels streaked her face. 'Have you lied to me all this time?' she cried out. 'Are this chapel and this congregation no more than a trough at which you mean to feed? Am I nothing more to you than meat and drink?'

"I knew not how to answer her. I cannot prove my sincerity to you, my lords, and could not to her. But at last I said, 'All my days, Irradia, I have spent alone. I have known only fear and abhorrence. Your regard, your gentleness, Father Domsen, this congregation, the teachings of Mother Church—they are sacred to me. Ask me to sacrifice myself for your preservation, and I will do it.' My desire for life had never been greater, yet I spoke truly. 'Death would be kinder to me than the loss of Heaven's blessing, which I have tasted only from you.'

"Gradually she calmed. Her innocent heart and her faith defended me when her mind quailed. Doubt still held her, but her revulsion had passed. When she had composed herself, she sighed, 'Oh, Aposter. This matter is too grave for me. A darkness has fallen over me, and I cannot see. I must speak to Father Domsen.' She studied me sidelong. 'Will you accompany me?' In that way she tested my protestations. 'Will you tell him what you are?'

"I felt the burden of her request. It weighed heavily upon my scant courage, my slight hopes. I esteemed the priest highly—but I trusted only her. However, I did not hesitate. 'I will,' I told her shortly. 'I will abide his judgment.'

"'Then I will believe you, while I may,' she replied with a wan smile.

'You have given me no cause to fear you. I have met no harm in you, and no malice.' Then she added, 'I, too, will abide his judgment.

"'Come.'

"I complied. Together we sought out the good Father."

Shading my eyes to ease the sting of the light, I walked that path again in my mind, dreading what followed.

"The hour was late, and he had retired, for he was old. When her knock summoned him to the door, however, he welcomed us into his dwelling.

"His quarters had been erected against the side of the chapel as an afterthought, and they were draughty, ill lit, and damp. Still his congregation had given what they could for his comfort. A fire burned in the hearth of his small study, warming the moist stones. At his invitation, we seated ourselves on hard lath chairs softened by pillows.

"He asked Irradia to speak of her plain distress, but I forestalled her. Seeking to spare her as much as I could, I blurted without grace or apology, 'Father, I have concealed what I am. I am not of your flesh—not an ordinary man, as I seem. Because I hunger to be united with Mother Church, and to earn Irradia's esteem, I feared to reveal myself.'

"He regarded me in confusion. Quailing within myself, I continued weakly, 'Yet I must speak the truth, or set aside my hope of Heaven.'"

Remembering that moment, I uncovered my eyes again so that the Duke's assembly might see my pain.

"'Father,' I told him, 'I am called "vampyr" and "death-eater."'" Among much harsher names. 'I do not feed on beasts or growing things that have no souls. I sustain myself on the lives of men and women formed in God's image.'

"At my words, he fell back in his seat, overtaken by clear shock and apparent horror. Watching him, I felt my hopes shift from under me, as though they rested on sand. How had I so entirely misconstrued his instruction? Had God created me and my kind solely so that innocent maids and gentle priests could name us evil?

"His hands clasped each other around his crucifix. For a moment it seemed that he would not speak—that he could find no words sufficient to denounce me. But then he asked, whispering terribly, 'Do these men and women die to feed you? Do you slay them?'

"I wished to cry out against his revulsion. But I did not. Irradia's need for his guidance was vivid in her gaze, and it restrained me. Instead I answered, 'I do not slay them in order to feed. Yet they are slain. They die at my hand. Their life becomes mine as they nourish me, and they fall.'

"His voice trembled. 'Then how can it be that you desire baptism?—that you seek the embrace of Mother Church?'

"There he saved me, although he did not know it. Despite my distress, and his, I heard his bafflement—and his sincerity. I had misread him. He had been profoundly disturbed, shaken to the core, but not by abhorrence. His nature may have lacked that capacity. He had asked an honest question. His dilemma was one of incomprehension.

"And Irradia clung to his every word, as though it issued from the mouth of Heaven.

"I replied as well as I could, like a man who had been snatched back from the rim of perdition. 'I did not cause what I am. I cannot alter it. But I have met kindness from you, and from Irradia. I have learned to know love. And I ache for the teachings of Mother Church. If the grace of Heaven is without end or limit,' I pleaded softly, 'surely it holds a place for such as me?'

"At first he did not answer my gaze. Raising his hands, he fixed his eyes upon the crucifix. Prayers I could not distinguish murmured from his lips. Unsteady light from the hearth colored his features, and Irradia's. Together they appeared to contemplate the flames of everlasting torment.

"When he had finished his prayer, however, he turned toward me. Tears reflected in the lines of his face, but he did not waver.

"'Then, my son,' he avowed, 'I will baptize you tomorrow.'

"I heard him without moving, without breath. Trained to apprehension, I feared that if I stirred his promise would be snatched away.

"'Father—' protested Irradia. Perhaps he had answered his own uncertainty, but he had not yet relieved hers. 'If he is a vampyr—'

"He silenced her gently. 'Whatever he is, my daughter, he has been created by God, for God's own reasons. It is not our place to judge what the Almighty has made. In baptism Heaven will accept or reject him, whatever we do. But if for the sake of our own fears and ignorance we refuse that which Heaven welcomes, our sin will be severe. Mother Church does not empower us to withhold the hope of redemption.

"'If he is accepted, the flock we serve will see it. That will do much to ease his way among us.' His tone darkened. 'And if he is rejected, they will be forewarned.

"'But there is a condition, my son,' he told me before I could speak. 'You must cease from slaying.'

"My hopes had blazed up brightly. Now they dwindled again, doused by Father Domsen's words. 'Then I will die,' I retorted bitterly. 'Does Heaven honor self-murder?'

"He shook his head. 'It does not. Yet you must cease,' he persisted. 'Since you require sustenance, as do all things living, seek it from those whose lives have already been claimed by God. Nourish yourself among the dying. It will—' He faltered momentarily, and I saw a new sorrow in his gaze. Yet he did not relent. 'I fear it will not be pleasant,' he continued more harshly. 'But I cannot condone any other course for you. To take lives which have not yet been called by Heaven is more than murder. It is blasphemy. It offends the sacredness of God's creation.'

"At once a great relief washed through me. The restriction he required would *not* be pleasant. In that he spoke more truly than he knew. Yet its difficulties were within my compass. In Heaven's name, I could bear them gladly.

"'Father,' I vowed, 'I will do as you say.'

"Irradia stared at me with wonder, as though she hardly dared to believe that her doubts had been lifted.

"Father Domsen showed no relief, however. He accepted my oath without question, but it did not ease him. Wincing, he bowed his head and slowly slumped into his seat. Perhaps he had seen visions in the firelight, and Irradia's face, and mine—sights which wracked him.

"'Leave me now, my children,' he breathed thinly. 'I must pray.' His sorrow did not abate. 'I must pray for us all. Tomorrow the will of Heaven will be made plain.'

"I heard his grief well enough. Yet I did not understand it. He had glimpsed a future which lay beyond my comprehension. And," I admitted ruefully, knowing the aftermath—knowing my failure, and its cost—"I made no attempt to grasp it. As Irradia and I departed, my heart arose, and an unwonted joy seemed to chirp and warble in my blood's vitality. My deepest dreams had become real to me again, brought back from transience and illusion by the good Father's willingness to hazard my baptism. His restriction I welcomed, for it provided a reply to my shame. And—most joyous of all things—I saw hope in Irradia's gaze again. He had restored her dreams also. She clasped my arm as we made our way from the chapel, and her smile held a hint of its familiar pleasure.

"Before our ways parted, she addressed me gravely.

"'Aposter, I said that I would abide Father Domsen's judgment. Now I say that I will stand with you when you are baptized.' Her tone was firm, and clarity shone from her eyes. 'I do not believe that God's face will be turned away. If my trust has worth in Heaven—as it must, for God is good—it will weigh on your behalf.'

"Laughing, she kissed my cheek to forestall any return for her generosity. Then she was gone.

"As I returned to my loft, I sang her name as I would the most sacred of the hymns. Before Heaven she had taken a vow of her own, and I cherished it. After all my fears, I was avid for the morrow, and for my sacramental union with Mother Church, and for her."

My own grief welled up in me. I had come to understand Father Domsen's sorrow. I did not think that he had foreseen his own weakness. Rather, I conceived that he knew the public life of Sestle, and the worldly affairs of Mother Church, better than his innocence could tolerate. For that reason, he had sequestered himself in Leeside chapel, hoping that broader, more hurtful concerns would pass him by.

Past my pain, I sighed, "But the time appointed for my baptism never came."

Involuntarily I paused, striving to master myself.

"It did not," interjected Bishop Heraldic suddenly, "because Heaven spoke to your priest—your Father Domsen—and gave him better wisdom."

No doubt His Reverence believed that he had been silent too long. Fearing the effect of my tale, he wished to assert himself in the hall. But I had no patience for him.

"No," I retorted harshly. "It did not because Cardinal Straylish found me."

When my ire had stifled the Bishop's interruption, I added, "Or I should say that he found Irradia."

Of all my victims, my prey, she was the most blameless—and the most dear.

"Later," I told Mullior's assembled lords and authorities, "I learned of the wide net which he had cast over the city, searching for me. I heard how he had become suspicious of Leeside, for that region seemed exempt from my activities. And I was informed that rumors of a stranger had at last reached the ears of his agents—a stranger who seemed to have no dwelling place, but who had been befriended by the maid Irradia, the chapel's adopted daughter.

"On the morn of my intended baptism, however, I knew none of this. Ignorant of the ruin prepared for me, I readied myself gladly, singing her name, and remembering all the words I must say in the liturgy of the sacrament. When the time came, I crept from my loft so that I could join the worshipers gathering before the doors of the chapel, as was my custom.

"Entranced by excitement, and by the prospect of Irradia, I was slow to notice my peril.

"The doors remained shut, although the time of worship was near. That in itself was strange, and should have alerted me. But there were other signs also. Men on horseback crowded the approaches to the chapel. Ruffians unlike the Leeside congregation in both aspect and comportment shifted among more familiar men and women, attentive as hounds. And Father Domsen stood at the doors as though he meant to address his flock in the street. His old eyes hunted the growing throng anxiously.

"When he saw me, he beckoned. The gesture appeared to cause him pain.

"I approached to discover what he wished of me. As I drew near, I heard him speak the name I had given myself. 'Aposter. There he is.'

"Finally I grasped that there was something amiss. Events had gone awry in Sestle. Perhaps I should have fled. But I did not conceive that I was in peril. I could not. At that moment I feared only for Irradia, and for the priest.

"Pointing toward me, he repeated, 'There he is.' I saw now that weeping filled his face.

"Then some blow or bludgeon seemed to take away the back of my head, and I stumbled into darkness."

There I paused. I had reached the crux of what I must relate, and I faltered. "My lord Duke," I inquired hoarsely, "may I have more wine? I thirst." After a moment, I added, "And I am afraid."

Duke Obal flicked his fingers, a brusque command. His strained gaze did not leave my face.

At once a fresh goblet was given to Lord Ermine at my side. He offered it to me, frowning in solicitude. I accepted it and drank. With the wine I swallowed cries I did not mean to utter, fury and woe I could not afford to express. Only my tale stood between me and death. And only my tale held back Obal's fall.

Bracing my heart, I continued.

"I awoke to a dazzle of illumination"—light as acute as my distress in the Duke's hall—"and the sound of screaming. I found myself seated erect, but my limbs were bound so that I could not move. The pain of damaged bone filled my head. And hunger— A considerable time must have passed since I had last fed. Two days? As much as three? I had not drawn sustenance the night before I was to have been baptized. Now the yearning to survive blazed in all my veins. My weakness was such that I could not have stood if my arms and legs had been free—could not have remained upright if my bonds had not held me.

"The voice that screamed was one I knew well. It had grown dear to me, a treasure of sweetness, now betrayed to agony.

"In frailty and desperation, I labored to clear my sight so that I might determine the nature of my plight."

Some among my auditors must have guessed what I would relate—and anticipated it with relish.

"I sat, secured by ropes, in a chair of iron which had been placed on a low dais against one wall of a stone chamber, windowless and cold. By its shape, the room was an oubliette. But if it was, then night had fallen on the world, for no hint of sun or sky showed above me. Instead the chamber was lit by torches and braziers by the score, leaving nothing unrevealed.

"Arrayed around the space and awaiting use were objects and devices which chilled my chest, instruments of torture— I saw racks and thumb-screws, an iron maiden, eye-gouges, flails and lancets and brands, flaying tables, cruel gibbets where a body might hang for days without death, castra-tors, rape-engines, alembics a-fume with acid. By such means was Hell made tangible, temporary flesh given its first taste of eternal excruciation.

"Clearly the room was a testing chamber, where the servants of Mother Church searched for truth among the wracked limbs and torn flesh of Heaven's foes. I had heard that clergymen and inquisitors employed such instruments against evil, but I had given the matter no thought—no credence. It had no place in Father Domsen's teachings, or in Irradia's beliefs, and I had put it from my mind.

"Now I saw that I must expand my understanding of Mother Church."

Bishop Heraldic might take offense at my words, but I did not care. Closing my eyes against illumination and memory, I went on.

"At the center of the room, a man stood beside a long table with his work displayed before me as though for my inspection. Despite my weak-ness, and my damaged head, I knew him at once for a clergyman. He wore the robes and chasuble, as crimson as anguish, of the lords of Mother Church, but he had set aside the miter of his office, leaving his head unrestricted, and his hands were flecked with blood. His features had been formed for piety, strict of mouth and nose, lean of cheek, his brow lined with denunciations. Rue and eagerness defined his gaze. Two ebon-clad men, bulky and muscular, awaited his commands, but did not put themselves forward to assist him.

"With each touch he lifted new screams from Irradia's raw throat.

"She lay naked on the table." The memory was vivid to me, etched so deeply into the passages of my brain that I believed it would endure when my flesh had fallen to worms and corruption. Merely closing my eyes did not shut it out. "Her arms had been drawn above her head and clamped in iron fetters, and her ankles were knotted to rings set into the wood. Thus outstretched, she might shift her hips and writhe, but could do nothing to avoid her tormentor's touch. Already blood and pain in profusion marked her helpless flesh.

"In one hand the clergyman employed a curiously serrated blade—in the other, pincers gripping a sponge damp with vitriol. As I watched, he stroked his blade tenderly across her belly toward her breasts, laying bare her nerves, then squeezed his sponge to drip acid into the streaming wounds. Her skin and tissues steamed with liquid fire as she shrieked out her hurt to the high ceiling and the unattainable sky.

"Appalled beyond bearing, I croaked, 'Stop'—and again, 'Stop.'

"Her tormentor lifted his head. Setting aside his implements, he seemed to regard me kindly. After a moment, he addressed me.

"'I see that you have regained consciousness.' His voice was husky and avid, a voice of passion—as well suited as his long fingers to caress or flay. 'That is well. You must attend what transpires here.

"'I am Straylish,' he continued, 'High Cardinal of Mother Church, and worldly suzerain of all this land in the name of Heaven. What you are'—he appeared to smile—'will be made plain to God's judgment.'

"He confused me. Living in Sestle, I had heard him spoken of often, yet I did not comprehend his power—or his intent. Did he not already know me? 'Father Domsen—' I began. But there my voice, or my heart, faltered. I meant to say that the priest had already betrayed me. Cardinal Straylish knew perfectly what I was.

"How had Father Domsen turned against me? And *why*? I had seen sorrow in him, but not distrust. His grief had given me no hint—

"And if Father Domsen had turned against me, why did the High Cardinal now inflict such suffering upon Irradia?

"'I am not done with him,' replied His Reverence sternly. 'Like this maid—her name is Irradia, I believe?—he also has countenanced the presence of evil among us.

"'It is true that he served me in the end. Repenting his folly—or so he said—he identified you to my men, so that you would work no more abomination. I doubt his sincerity, however. I do not know how long he was aware of you. Later you will confess the truth, so that I may pursue Heaven's judgment accurately.' The High Cardinal flexed his fingers in anticipation. 'But he did not come forward until after I had taken her.'

A gesture indicated Irradia. 'I fear for him that he was moved to aid my search, not by genuine repentance, but rather by a desire to spare this weak daughter of his congregation God's wrath.

"'That doubt I will resolve later, however. For the present, her guilt compels me.' He spoke as lovers do, in eagerness and intimacy.

"Now I understood Father Domsen, although His Reverence still baffled me. At the time, I gave the matter no further thought. I cared only for Irradia—cared only that I might find some means to halt her great pain.

"Nevertheless between that day and this I have ached with regret over the good priest's plight—yes, and burned with shame for my part in it. I find no fault with him that he chose to sacrifice me as he did. For Irradia's sake, I would have done the same.

"Yet he did betray me, and I am certain that his gentle heart bore the burden heavily. Irradia I had apparently doomed by the simple sin of accepting her goodwill. But if I had not revealed myself to Father Domsen, he would have been spared the necessity of denouncing me."

It seemed that my confession meant nothing to my auditors. Their silence had closed against me, unyielding as the doorstone of a sepulchre. Even the Duke and his adherents stood motionless, almost breathless, as though snared in dismay.

Sighing, I labored onward.

"As I say, however, such considerations came later. At the time, every faint scrap of my remaining energy and attention was concentrated toward His Reverence. I knew how I had come to be where I was. But I could not conceive why my captor continued to harm Irradia after I had fallen into his power.

"'Father Domsen has told you what I am,' I countered through my weakness. 'She is no longer needed. What do you want from her?'

"'What do I want?' My question appeared to pique the Cardinal. 'For myself, nothing.' With the tip of his tongue, he moistened his lips. 'For my God, however, I desire the utter extirpation of Satan and all his minions. And toward that end, one small step will be taken here.

"'It came to my attention,' he explained, 'that a vampyr preyed in Sestle—a vile spawn of Hell, devouring souls to feed its own damnation.

For some weeks I hunted him in vain. Infidels and scum, apostates and heretics I sifted without number, seeking Heaven's foe. And at last I gleaned the tale of a Leeside maid befriended by a stranger—a man without apparent homeland, history, employment, or domicile. By degrees I learned to believe that this stranger was indeed the abomination I sought—that this lost maid knew who and what he was—and that she had condoned his evil by concealing his identity. Therefore I gathered her to me.'

"Sadly he shook his head over her. 'Her sin is as great as her innocence. I suspect that she has been cruelly misled. By God's grace, however, her soul has been granted to my care. Guided by Heaven, I will win truth from her, purging her fault with pain.

"'Then,' he finished gently, 'I will deal with you.'

"Still I did not understand. I failed to comprehend his doctrine, as I had failed to grasp Father Domsen's. By nature I knew nothing of 'forgiveness' or 'repentance.' But Irradia's cries had at last subsided to quiet sobbing while the Cardinal spoke with me, and I could not endure to think that he would torment her anew—that she would scream again.

"'No,' I protested. 'Deal with me now.

"'I will confess,' I told him, gathering urgency as I went. 'Release her. *Stop* this cruelty. I will confess'—I hardly knew what—'everything. She was ignorant of me. I hid the truth. I tricked her—I will tell you how I practiced on her innocence, so that she learned to trust me. Whatever you wish—

"'Only release her,' I pleaded.

"The High Cardinal replied with laughter. 'You will surely confess,' he promised. 'In your turn, you will reveal the depth and breadth of your foulness in every particular. But first I must redeem this maid.

"'Without repentance she cannot hope for Heaven's forgiveness. She must see her sin and turn from it. She must turn from you. In mercy and love, I will not spare her one item or instance of agony until she surrenders her fault by speaking your name.'

"Smiling, he retrieved his implements. A stroke of the sponge wiped her blood from his blade, refreshing its serrations. His hands were those of an adept, certain of their purpose, and made cunning by experience.

"Confronted by Irradia's anguish, I lost all dignity, all restraint—all thought of myself. 'No!' I cried, wailed, shrieked, 'she has no fault, the fault is *mine*, I *confess* it, you must *stop!*'

"But His Reverence Straylish Beatified was not swayed.

"'Her fault is indeed yours,' he pronounced, 'and I will exact its penalty from you.' His hands lingered over her pale flesh, although his gaze held mine. 'Since you wish to confess, this will be your penance until I am ready for you—to witness the tortures which you will suffer eternally, and to be helpless against them.

"'With every breath in your lungs and pulse in your veins, you will struggle to oppose God's judgment in me, to resist the righteousness which damns you—and you will gain nothing. You are bound to my will, and to Hell. Your evil cannot prevail against Heaven. Inspired by Satan's cunning, you seek to restore this maid's life with your own, but it will not avail you. Rather you will bear her pain until I am ready for yours.'

"Then in charity and sorrow he turned with exquisite care to the labor of Irradia's redemption."

I knew not how I continued. My weakness itself, and the burden of Irradia's anguish, seemed to uphold me, for without them I would surely have fallen prostrate. My eyes were open now, but I gazed only at Duke Obal. The rest of Mullior's highborn had ceased to exist for me. Only his steady glower, angry and aggrieved—only his honesty or dishonor—retained any import that I could recognize.

"My lords," I said hoarsely, "I will not speak of what was done to her." When her eyes were burst from their sockets, I screamed myself until my throat was torn, and blood spewed from my mouth. "I will say only that under the High Cardinal's hands she cried out until she could cry no more. Thereafter her limbs and sinews enacted a wailing to which she could no longer give voice. Mute, her excruciation was more terrible to me than any howl."

I drew a long, shuddering breath. "But she did not surrender my name.

"By silence she believed that she might save me. Though His Reverence asked it and demanded it, prayed and pleaded for it, soothed and wracked her to obtain it, she held my name to herself. In that baptism of agony, she stood with me, as she had promised."

Dry-eyed now, for my pain had grown too great for tears, and the hall's brilliance no longer daunted me, I met the clenched attention of my audience.

"And at last," I sighed, "the High Cardinal set aside his implements in vexation. Informing his ebon-clad servants that he would return after an hour's rest to continue her redemption, he withdrew from the chamber.

"This, apparently, signaled that their turn had come. When he had closed the door, they advanced at once, jesting with each other. One approached Irradia's table. His hands fumbled at the ties of his breeches as he moved. The other began with me.

"Drawing near, he struck me a full-armed blow, and laughed as he swung. My head recoiled against the iron of my seat. Moments of darkness gnawed at my vision, so that sight itself appeared to mortify within me, announcing the corruption of the grave.

"In glee and malice, he thrust his visage close to mine. 'You are a great fool,' he informed me. His breath stank of garlic and stale wine, rotting teeth and unrestricted appetites— 'You thought yourself safe, didn't you?' he jeered. 'Hiding in a sanctuary. Sneaking into the skirts of a pretty maid. You thought—'

"His taunts died with him. Beyond him, I saw his companion climb open-breeched onto the table and Irradia. Leaning forward suddenly, I sank my teeth into the flesh of his lower lip.

"My bite drew blood. And blood drew life. Without pause or hesitation, he folded to the stone at my feet as though Heaven itself had stricken him.

"Immediately I received the benefit of his many lusts. His vitality became mine. His strength suffused my limbs. On the instant I ceased to be the weak and starving creature whom the Cardinal's ruffians had captured. Although I remained bound, I was no longer helpless.

"Shouting wordless threats to distract Irradia's assailant, I struggled to win free of my ropes.

"Curses answered me, guttural and dismayed. The man rolled from the table to his feet. Clutching at his breeches with one hand, he snatched a dirk from its sheath with the other, then lumbered furiously forward to stab at me before my bonds loosened.

"He succeeded well enough. His dirk he pounded into my shoulder with the force of a blacksmith's hammer. But it did not suffice. Irradia's tortures had driven me to madness. And I possessed all his companion's great strength.

"While his dirk thudded deeply into me, I turned my head enough to nip at his wrist.

"It was a small wound, no more—a drop of blood. I required nothing greater. He toppled, lifeless, onto the corpse of his companion, and I used what he had given me to snap my ropes.

"The dirk I must have plucked out, but I do not recall doing so. I kept it, hardly thinking that it might be of use to me.

"Then I was at Irradia's side."

Perhaps it was not weakness which upheld me. Perhaps wrath and sin had struck so deeply into my bones that they became a form of strength.

"I had no garment with which to cover her. But she was clad in blood, and did not need one. Yet for that very reason I dared not touch her, although I burned to lift her into my embrace. I did not wish to slay her.

"Blinded, she could not return my gaze. For a moment, however, she seemed to know me. Her lips shaped my name, and she strove to speak. Lowering my ear to her, I heard a word which may have been, 'Forgive—' But I could not ask whom she wished me to forgive—or why. Or how. When she had breathed her prayer, she succumbed to unconsciousness."

At last the end was near, and I hastened to meet it. I had forgotten my fear. For the moment, at least, the prospect of my death had lost its power to appall me.

"Then there came upon me a time of darkness—a time I have no courage to describe. I might have restored Irradia, as I restored Lord Numis. I might have given her the life which I had torn from the Cardinal's servants, and raised her whole from her ordeal.

"But what then, my lords? What then? We would be prisoners still—and I would be weak again, as I am now. What hope did we have of flight? In darkness and despair, I saw that we had none. And when we had been secured anew, His Reverence would return her to torment. The screams which had brought me to madness would be no more than a foretaste of those which would surely follow.

"I had learned to love Mother Church, as I loved Irradia. Under her sweet influence, and Father Domsen's teachings, I had dreamed that I had a soul. But in the High Cardinal's oubliette I abandoned it."

That pain—that sin—was mine. Mere revulsion and death could not bereave me of it.

"With a caress of my hand, I took her life, so that His Reverence Beatified would never harm her again. Her small scrap of vitality I added to the strength I had already harvested. Then I made my escape by ascending the walls until I came to the mouth of the oubliette, and so to the open night of the city.

"Sestle I fled as quickly as I could manage." I had explained enough. My tale required little more of me. "When I learned of my lord Duke's opposition to the High Cardinal's doctrine, I made my way to Mullior. After a time, I gained an opportunity to offer him my service."

It was finished.

"In his service, my lords, I carry out my penance. My sin is plain to me, and I expiate as Straylish Beatified instructed me. I bear Irradia's pain. I seek to restore life. I resist the righteousness which damns me. And I obey Father Domsen. I take no life which has not already been claimed by God.

"Do with me what you will. I am done. Perhaps it is true that I have no soul. Irradia whom I loved asked me to 'Forgive,' and I cannot."

Bowing my head, I fell silent.

—————

The distress in the hall echoed my own. So much I had gained, if no more. Lords and ladies wrestled with emotions which they must have abhorred. Priests murmured over their beads, telling prayers I did not choose to hear.

The Duke's heir gripped my arm convulsively. "Fear nothing, Scriven," he whispered. His voice caught. "Fear—nothing."

I did not heed him. Drained of fear and strength and supplication, I regarded only Duke Obal. Above his jaw's grim thrust, a gleam of moisture or regret pierced his gaze. His expression I was unable to read. But I would not have been surprised to hear him say that I had shown myself no fit ally of Mullior—that my sin and my nature justified the High Cardinal's enmity—that a man who had slain his only friend, his only love, could not claim clemency here.

Doubtless His Reverence the Bishop would assert as much, when he recovered his wits.

Slowly Duke Obal turned away. His features were hidden from me as he addressed the hall. In a voice husky with fervor, he announced, "There is one aspect of Scriven's tale which he did not mention—because he does not know it. He has already been given a sign of Heaven's acceptance.

"Before your eyes," he told the gathering, "he has been tested by holy water. Pure water blessed and sanctified by my confessor was mingled with Scriven's wine. You have seen that he drank of it—twice—and took no hurt.

"It is not baptism," he acknowledged. "But it will suffice for me."

Abruptly he raised his fists, and his voice lifted to a shout like the cry of an eagle. "Who speaks against him now?" he called fiercely. "Who *dares?*"

Bishop Heraldic cleared his throat. Shamefaced, he mumbled, "Not I, my lord."

Around him, lords and ladies added, "Not I." Merchants and guards, officials and priests, did the same, swelling a chorus of assent. Lord Numis might have protested, but two of the Bishop's confessors stilled him.

Lowering his arms, Duke Obal returned to me. With a few strides, he crossed the rugs between us until he stood near enough to place his hands like an embrace upon my shoulders.

"Then, Scriven," he proclaimed so that none would mistake him, "I say to you before all these witnesses that you are my trusted friend, and I am honored by your service. Be welcome in Mullior. Be at home. As you keep your vows, so will I keep mine. The House of Obal stands by you. While I live, you are safe among us."

In the grip of his strong hands, I straightened my back and met his gaze as best I could.

"Thank you, my lord. I will keep my vows."

He deserved better gratitude, but I had come to the end of what I could do. I had begun to weep, and had no heart to stanch it.

He was more than a good son of Mother Church. He was a man of faith.

Together the Duke's Commander and the Master of Mullior's Purse offered me escort in their lord's name, showing openly that they, too, honored me. With their support, I left the hall and the palace, and made my way accepted into the night.

The Woman
Who Loved Pigs

Fern loved pigs, but in all the village of Sarendel-on-Gentle she may have been the only woman who did not own one.

The Gentle's Rift down which the river ran was at once fertile and isolated. The wains of the merchanters came through in season, trading salt by the pound and fabric by the bolt for wheat and barley by the ton; there were no other visitors. And the good people along the river wanted none—especially after they had listened to the merchanters' tales of the larger world, tales of wars and warlocks, princes and intrigues. Their lives in the Rift were like the Gentle itself, steady and untroubled. Whether poor or comfortable, solitary or gregarious, the villages and hamlets had only four essential activities—their children, their farms, their animals, and their ale. Pleasure produced their children, work in the fields and with the animals produced their food, and ale was their reward.

Among the fields and meadows, cows were precious for their milk, as well as for their strength at the plow. And pigs made better meat. For that reason, sows and porkers were common.

It may have been because they were raised for meat—because they were such solid creatures, and so doomed—that Fern loved them, although they were not hers.

In Sarendel she knew them all by their size and coloring, their personalities and parentage. Recognizing her love, they came to her whenever they could. And she adored their coming to her, as though she were a great lady visited by royalty.

Yet she took nothing which was not granted to her, and so she returned them. Before she returned them, however, she pampered them as best she could in the brief time her honesty allowed her, tending their small sores and abrasions, offering them the comfits and comforts she was occasionally able to scavenge for them, scratching their ears when she had no treats to offer. She wept for the porkers and flattered the sows. Since she had no language of her own, their throaty voices were articulate enough for her; she knew how to warm her heart with their snorts and grunts of affection.

When they strayed among the hills, she could divine where they were, and so she was able to recover them. When they misplaced their piglets, she found the young and brought them home—her ear for the thin squeals of the lost was unerring. When the sows suffered farrowing, she came to them from wherever her scavenging took her, bringing poultices and caresses which eased the piglets out.

The good people of Sarendel could not comprehend the sounds which came from her mouth, but they understood the importance of gratitude and kindliness in a small village. When Fern had performed her small services for the creatures she loved, the farmwives and alemaids to whom they belonged thanked her with gifts of food, which did more to keep breath in her body than the sustenance she scavenged.

Indeed, in gratitude one of her fellow villagers would almost certainly have given her a pig, had she been capable of raising it. Alas, that steady nurturance would have been beyond her. In a village where poverty was common but active want was rare, Fern was destitute. If Yoel the aleman had not allowed her a disused storeshed to serve as her hovel, she would have had no place to live. If the farmwives had not given her scraps of weaving and discarded dresses, she would have had no clothes. If Sarendel-on-Gentle had not granted her the freedom of its refuse, she would have lacked food more often than she had it. Her parents had been poor—her father a farm laborer, her mother a scrubwoman—able to feed and clothe and shelter her, but little more; and they were long dead. From dawn to dusk she was friendless as only those to whom words meant nothing could be, comforted only by the affection of the sows and porkers.

If she owned a pig—so the village believed—she would have fed it before she fed herself; and so she would have died.

Even with only herself to keep alive, no one would have been surprised to find her dead one morning among the fields or beside the river. Her life was a small thing, even by the ordinary standards of Sarendel-on-Gentle. The village in turn was a small thing along the verdant Rift. And the Gentle's Rift itself was a small thing within the wide world of Andovale, where princes and warlocks had their glory.

No one took note—or had cause to take note—when Fern of Sarendel-on-Gentle was adopted by a pig.

He was not a handsome pig, or a large one. Indeed, she saw as soon as she looked at him that he was dying of hunger. His brindled skin showed splotches of disease, as well as of scruffy parentage. Stains and gashes marked his grizzled snout. One eye appeared to be nearly blind; the other was flawed by a strange sliver of argent like a silver cut. In the early dew of dawn, he shouldered his way into her hovel as though he had traveled all night for many nights to reach her, lay himself down at her feet, rolled his miscolored eyes at her weakly, and began at once to sleep like the dead.

Fern had only seen that sleep once before—a sleep without the twitches and snuffles, the unconscious rootings of a pig's dreams. She had no measure of time, and so she did not know when it was, but on some prior occasion she had found a lost sow far from the village. The sow had broken her leg crossing a streambed. The disturbance of the rocks and mud showed that she had struggled for hours, perhaps for days; then she had lost heart. She was asleep when Fern found her, and Fern could not rouse her; she slept until she died.

Fern understood instantly that the pig now asleep at her feet was like that sow—brokenhearted and near to dying.

As she looked at him, however, an image formed in her mind. It was unfamiliar because she was a creature of instinct and did not think in images.

Rueweed.

Rueweed and pigsbane.

Also carrots.

Rueweed was poison to both pigs and cattle, as everyone knew. And pigsbane was presumed to be poison, for the simple reason that pigs refused to eat it—and pigs were known to be clever in such matters. Nevertheless Fern did not hesitate. The images which had come into her head were like the voiceless promptings that told her when one of the pigs of the village was in need of her. She did not question them any more than she questioned why this pig had come to her—or where he had come from.

She had seen Meglan, one of the farmwives, working in her carrot patch yesterday. Perhaps there would be carrots in Meglan's refuse-tip today. And Fern knew where to find rueweed and pigsbane.

Hurrying because a pig had come to her for his life, she clutched the scraps which served as her cloak around her and ran from her hovel.

Along the one street which passed over the hills and became Sarendel-on-Gentle's link to the other villages of the Rift, past both alehouses, into a little lane which separated thatch-roofed shacks from more prosperous homes of timber and dressed stone, she made her way in a scurry of haste. An observer who did not know her would have thought she looked furtive. However, the villagers were accustomed to her crouching gait and her habitual way of keeping to the walls and hedges as if she feared to be accosted by someone who might expect her to speak, and so she passed as unremarked as a wraith among the dwellings to Meglan's home on the outskirts of the village.

Apparently unaware of Meglan spading her vegetables outside the house, Fern went directly to the refuse-tip beyond the fence and began rooting in her human fashion among the farmwife's compost.

Meglan paused to watch. She was a kindly woman, and Fern's haste suggested extreme hunger. When she saw how Fern pounced on the remaining peels and tassels of yesterday's stew, the farmwife unthinkingly pulled up a fresh handful of carrots, strode to the fence, and offered the carrots over the rails to Fern.

Too urgent to be gracious, Fern snatched the carrots, snuffled a piggy thanks, and scuttled away toward the hills as fast as her scrawny, unfed limbs could carry her.

Pigsbane. Rueweed. Meglan's generosity had already fallen into Fern's vague past, in one sense vividly remembered, in another quite forgotten. In her present haste she could not have formed any conception of how she had come by so much largesse as a handful of fresh carrots. Her head held nothing except rueweed and pigsbane and the need for speed.

It did not occur to her to fret over the fact that centuries of habitation had cleared all such plants away around the village for at least a mile in any direction. She did not fret over facts. They simply existed, unalterable. Yet she was afraid, and her fear pushed her faster than her strength could properly carry her. A pig had come to her, heartbroken and dying. She did not understand time, but she understood that when the pig's broken heart became cold death it would be a fact, as unalterable as the location of pigsbane and rueweed on the distant hillsides. Therefore she was afraid, and so she ran and stumbled and fell and ran again faster than she could endure.

Scarcely an hour had passed when she returned to her hovel, clutching the fruits of her scavenging in the scraps of her clothes. Sweat left streaks in the grime of her cheeks, and her eyes were glazed with exhaustion; she could have collapsed and slept and perhaps died without a moment's pause. Nevertheless she was still full of fear. And when she looked at the pig sprawled limp and hardly breathing in the dirt of her hovel, new images entered her mind.

She had no fire for heat, no mortar and pestle for grinding; she made do with what she had. First she tore the pigsbane to scraps. Scrubbing one stone over another, she reduced the scraps to flakes and shreds. Then she set them to soak in a bowl of water.

Shaking with tiredness and fear, she broke open the leaves of rueweed and rubbed their pungent odor—the tang of poison—under the pig's snout.

With a snort and a wince, the pig pulled his head back and blinked open his eyes. One of his eyes was unquestionably blind, but the other flashed its slice of silver at her.

At once, Fern set her bowl of soaking pigsbane in front of him. In relief rather than surprise—how could she be surprised, when all facts were the same to her?—she watched him drink.

When he had emptied the bowl, she gave him the carrots.

That was all she could do. If she had understood time, she would have known that she herself had eaten nothing for at least a day and a half. Her fear and strength were used up. Curling herself against the pig's back to keep him warm, she sank into sleep.

She did not think of death. Her heart was not broken.

Sleep was a familiar place for her, full of colors which might have been emotions and the affectionate snuffling of sows suckling their young. But after a time the colors and sounds became more images, and these were not familiar.

She saw the silver cut of the pig's eye rising like a new moon over the night of her mind.

She saw herself. How she knew it was herself was unclear, since her only knowledge of her appearance came from reflections in the moving waters of the Gentle, yet she did know it. And she knew also that it was herself beaten and weary, nearly cold with extinction.

Although the image was of herself, however, it did not disturb her. She gazed at it the same way that she gazed at all the world, as a fact about which there were no questions.

A crimson hue which might have been vexation or despair washed the image away, and another took its place.

In this image, she rose from her hovel and went to the nearest ale-house. There she scratched at the rear door until the aleman opened it. Then she dropped to her knees and made supplicating gestures toward her belly and mouth.

This image did disturb her. It came to her clad in the yellow of lament. She was Fern. She accepted gifts, but she did not ask for anything which was not hers. The image of pleading sent tears across the trails of sweat on her sleeping cheeks.

Nevertheless the thin sliver of argent in her mind and in the pig's eye bound her to him. He had come to her, adopted her: she was already his. When she awoke, she pulled her scraps of clothing about her and crept weeping along the street to Jessup's alehouse, where she scratched at the door behind the building until he answered. Filled with yellow and tears, she fell to her knees and begged for food with the only words she knew— the movements of her hands.

From his doorway Jessup peered at her and frowned. He was not known for Meglan's unthinking generosity. Stern and plain in all his dealings, he had used his father's alehouse to make himself wealthy—as such things were measured in Sarendel—and he liked his wealth. He made good ale and expected to be paid for it. Farmers and weavers, potters and laborers, men and women who wished to drink their ale today and settle their scores tomorrow were strictly required to take their custom to Yoel's alehouse, not Jessup's. In some other village, in some other part of Andovale, Jessup would have closed his door in Fern's face and thought no more about it.

But here, in Sarendel-on-Gentle, beggary was unknown. Jessup had not learned to refuse an appeal as naked as hers. Fern herself *was* well-known, however: both her destitution and her honesty were as familiar as the village itself. On this occasion, her plight was as plain as emaciation and grime, tears and rags could make it. And finally, at Jessup's back door there were no witnesses. No one would see what he did and think that he had become less strict.

With a black scowl, he retreated to his kitchen and brought out a jug of broth, a slab of bread, and an earthen flask of ale, which he thrust into Fern's unsteady hands.

Snuffling grief instead of thanks, she returned to her hovel.

She did not want to eat the bread or drink the broth and ale. She felt that a violation had taken place. She had been hurt in some way for which she had no words and no understanding. She took nothing which was not granted to her. But as soon as she reentered her dwelling the brindled pig fixed his eyes upon her. He could scarcely lift his head; he clearly had no strength to stand. His exhaustion was as profound as hers, and as fatal. The danger that he would starve had been only briefly postponed. And the scabs and splotches which marked his hide were plain signs of illness rather than injury. Yet he fixed his eyes upon her—the one blind, the other flawed with silver—and she found that she could not refuse to eat. Did she not love pigs? And had he not come to her in his last need?

Held by his gaze, she chewed the bread and drank the broth. With a pig's cleverness she knew that the ale was too strong for her, so she did not touch it. Instead she poured it out in a bowl and set it under his snout so that he could have it.

When he had consumed it all, he drew a shuddering breath which she interpreted as pleasure. And that in turn pleased her more than any amount of food or drink for herself.

Together they slept again.

So Fern became a beggar—and so her pig's life was saved. Each time she slept, the images came to her: more scratching at doors, more supplication. And each time she awoke she acted on them with less sorrow. The loss of her honesty had become a fact, unalterable. Instead of grieving, she used the strength of new sustenance to scavenge for her pig. She was able to roam more widely, root more deeply. She found grains and vegetables for him, as well as herbs from which she concocted healing poultices and balms. Steadily, if slowly, he drew vitality from her care and began to mend.

After several nights, the images stopped. They were no longer needed. In their place, her head was filled with the soothing cerulean and emerald which she had always gained from the affection of pigs, and occasionally she heard sounds—silent except within her head—which might have been, *My thanks.* She felt the gratitude in them; but the sounds themselves meant nothing to her, so at last she concluded that they were the pig's name, and she took to calling him "Mythanks." That was the first word she had ever spoken, the only word she knew. She hugged him morning and night, and caressed him whenever the mood came upon her, and whispered fondly in his ears, "Mythanks, Mythanks," and her regret for the woman she had once been became vague with the uncertainty of all time.

When perhaps a fortnight had passed, Mythanks was well enough to join her in her scavenging. Although he was still weak, he trotted briskly at her side, scenting the air and scanning the vistas like a creature which had come to a new world. Uncharacteristically for a pig, he sniffed and snorted at every grass and herb and shrub they encountered as though he were teaching himself to know them for the first time. He surveyed the hillsides as though he were measuring distances and possibilities. He shied away from passing herd-dogs and farmers as though they might be his enemies, despite the fact that no one in Sarendel-on-Gentle would harm a pig—until the time came to slaughter the porkers and the aging sows. And when the herd-dogs and farmers were gone, he rubbed his bristled back against Fern's legs with a pig's desire for reassurance.

Because he was not yet fully hale, he could not roam far; and so the day's scavenging found him less food than he wanted. This worried Fern. She thought she saw a look of discouragement—or was it calculation?—in Mythanks' strange eyes. However she petted and coddled him, he did not nuzzle her fondly, or fill her head with the hues of gratitude. He had adopted her. He was her responsibility, and her care of him was inadequate. When a tear or two of remorse caught and spread on her muddy cheeks, he ignored them.

But the next day he went with her while she begged.

Prompted by her instinct to creep from place to place, calling as little attention to herself as possible, she had taken her unwonted supplications to a different villager each day. After the gift of carrots, she had not dared return to Meglan. Certainly she had not approached Jessup again. Rather she had been to Yoel's alehouse, then to widower Horrik's tannery, then to Salla and Veil among the farmwives, then to Karay the weaver and Limm the potter; and so to a new benefactor on every occasion.

On this occasion, however, Mythanks had his own ideas. Directly, as though he had lived in Sarendel all his life and knew it well, he led Fern back to Jessup's alehouse.

Wordlessly alarmed, she could not put her hand to the door at the rear of the alehouse. Jessup's sternness frightened her. If she had not been so near to starvation on that first day, she would not have dared go there at all. She could only watch and wince as Mythanks lifted a foreleg and scratched at the door with his hoof.

When Jessup opened the door and saw her, he did not take the sight kindly.

"You!" he snapped. "Begone! Do not think you can take advantage of me a second time. All the village is talking about your beggary. You have acquired a pig, and now you beg. Did you beg him as well, or have you fallen as low as theft? I would not have fed you so much as once, but I believed that you were honest. I will not make that mistake again."

Fern understood none of his words, but his tone was plain. It hurt her like a blow. Cringing, she tried to shrink down into herself as she turned away.

Mythanks snorted once, softly, and fixed Jessup with his eyes, the one blind, the other flawed by silver.

Jessup made a noise in his throat which frightened Fern more than shouts and abuse. To her ears, it was the strangling gurgle of death.

As if he were stunned, Jessup moved backward into the alehouse and out of sight. Then he returned, carrying a bushel of barley and a large basket overflowing with bread and sausages. These he set at Mythanks' feet without a word. Backward again, he reentered the alehouse and closed the door.

Mythanks sniffed the barley, looked over at Fern where she crouched in alarm, and snorted a pig's laughter.

Fern was astonished. She had never seen so much food. "Mythanks," she murmured because she had no words with which to express her surprise. "Mythanks, Mythanks."

At once his laughter became vexation. New sounds formed in her mind. *My name is not Mythanks, you daft woman. It is Titus. Titus! Do you hear me? TITUS!*

"Ti-tus." Staring at him, she tried the word in her mouth. "Ti-tus. Titus." In her amazement, she failed to notice that she had understood him.

Blue pleasure and green satisfaction came into her head as she said his name. *That,* he replied, *is a distinct improvement.* But her instant of comprehension had passed, and she had no idea what the sounds meant.

"Titus."

Hardly aware of what she did, she set the basket of bread and sausages on his back, steadied it with one hand, then propped the bushel of barley on her hip and returned to her hovel.

That day they feasted and slept. And the next morning Titus nudged her awake with his snout. When she met his blind and piercing gaze, she heard more sounds in the silence of her mind.

It is time we began. Bread and sausages will feed your body, but they will do nothing to nourish your intelligence. I **must** *have intelligence. Also you are filthy—and filth wards away help. There are many lessons that a pig could teach you. Today we will make a start.*

This meant nothing to Fern. The sounds came from him—she accepted that as a fact—but they communicated less than the grunts of pigs. Nevertheless she hugged him happily because he seemed so brisk and whole. Yesterday's fear and surprise were forgotten. She was simply glad that Titus had come to her, and that she had been able to help him, and that she knew his name.

Never mind, he said while he nuzzled her neck. *Perhaps you will understand me in time. For the present, you are willing. I will make that suffice.*

Again he fixed her with the argent sliver of his good eye, and now in images she saw herself leaving her hovel and walking to a secluded bank of the Gentle, where she removed her shreds of clothing, immersed herself in the water, and scrubbed herself with sand until her skin became a color which she had never before seen in her own reflection.

It is a risk, he said as she rose to obey the image. *Change attracts attention, and attention is dangerous. But I need help. We must begin somewhere. Cleanliness will do much to improve your place in this misbegotten pigsty of a village.*

"Titus," she answered, dumbly pleased. "Titus."

Snuffling encouragement, he accompanied her down to the Gentle.

The image he had placed in her mind amazed her entirely, but her compliance did not. She had accepted her obedience to him as a fact. And she was not afflicted with modesty. Her impulse to cower, to avoid notice, grew from other fears than bodily shame. So it was not a hard thing for her to do as Titus directed. Hidden by the overarching boughs of a thirsty willow at the river's edge, she set aside her scraps and entered the water.

Here the Gentle was cool but not cold, and it had worn a fine sandy bottom for itself off the hard edges of time. Under Titus' watchful eye, Fern splashed and bubbled and rubbed until the color of her skin and the feel of her hair were transformed. As she did so, she was filled with a light blue pleasure as quiet and steady as the water. And the blue deepened to azure—she did not know or ask why—when the pig said to her like a promise, *Someday you will ask me what loveliness is, and I will tell you.*

Next he gave her an image in which she scrubbed her clothes as she had cleaned herself. Washing them did not make them whole, but it did give them a gentler touch on the unfamiliar tingle of her skin.

At last she rose from the water as if on this day she had been made new.

As she dressed, two of Yoel's small sons scampered past the willow, looking to avoid the chores which Nell alewife, their mother, had in mind for them. They may have seen Fern or they may not; in either case, their attention was elsewhere. Nevertheless she crouched instinctively against the bole of the willow, so that whatever the boys saw would be as unobtrusive as possible.

At once the pleasure in her head changed to the hue of vexation. Perhaps all the colors of her mind were no longer hers, but now belonged to Titus.

Blast you, he muttered, *you have too far to go. And I am helpless.*

Almost as if he wished to punish her for her timidity, he urged her to scavenge all day for wood. And the next day he pushed her to accost one of Yoel's small sons while the boys played truant from Nell's chores. Fern herself did nothing except to put out her hand to pause the boy as he ran, and that was enough to make her heart beat in her throat. Titus did the rest. After he had gazed at the boy for a moment or two with his silver-marred eye, he turned away. Snorting in satisfaction, he led Fern back to their hovel.

Because she loved his satisfaction, she hugged and caressed him and fed him barley-mash. When Yoel's small son and two of his brothers arrived at her storeshed a short time later carrying a firepot full of flame, her ability to grasp that they might have been doing the pig's bidding had already faded. She understood them only because the farmwives sometimes sent her a firepot as an act of kindness, knowing that she had no other flame to keep her alive if the night turned bitter across the Gentle's Rift.

Before she lost her honesty, she had been able to accept gifts. But now kindness dismayed her. She cowered away from the children as though they frightened her.

The youngest boy set the firepot in the dirt beside Fern's woodpile. Staring at her, he asked, "Is she sick, then?"

"You're daft," the middle brother snorted with the contempt of his greater age. "That ain't sick, that's clean."

"Cor!" breathed the oldest. "Who'd have thought she looked like that?" Then he flushed and ducked his head.

While Fern tried to sink out of sight against the wall, Titus stepped in front of her. Standing proudly in the center of the space as if the hovel were a mansion and his, he fixed his eyes on each of the boys until they all nodded in turn. Then he dismissed them with a grunt and a jerk of his head.

"Titus," Fern murmured because she had no other name for her dismay. "Titus."

He looked at her. As if her distress were a question, he said, *Yes, they would be easier—for a time. But then they would begin to fear me, and then I would be lost. However, I seriously doubt that any of these clods and clowns is capable of fearing you. And the children even less than the adults. So I will ask only children for help—and only for you. The rest must be kept between the two of us.*

Seeing that she was not comforted, he nuzzled at her until she came away from the wall to scratch his ears. Then he added, *I will take it as a personal triumph if you are ever able to say* **yes** *to me of your own accord.*

Yes, Fern thought to herself. Yes. It was a strange sound. If it had been the name of a pig, she would have understood it. As matters stood, however, the sound could only trouble her with hints of significance; it could not reach her.

Never mind, he told her again. *For today we have gained enough. When those whelps return, we will cast our net wider.*

She heard sadness in his voice, and so she hugged him with all her strength, seeking to reassure him.

You or no one, Titus whispered to her embrace. *You must suffice. I have no other hope.*

The boys did not return until evening. While Fern and Titus warmed themselves beside her unaccustomed fire—which she built and tended and kept small according to the images he placed in her mind—hands tugged at the burlap curtain that served as her door, and children entered her hovel. During the day the three had become five, and two of them were girls. They came to her carrying small sacks and tight bundles of herbs.

Here her acceptance of facts failed her. Herbs? For her and Titus? Children did not do such things. Her vague experience of time did not contain those actions. Typically children ignored her; on occasion they teased and tormented her; sometimes they were as kind as a warm breeze. But they did not bring her gifts of witch hazel and thyme, rueweed and coriander, sloewort, and marjoram, and vert. And Titus had not prepared her with images. Whatever she knew and needed in order to live seemed to totter when Yoel's familiar sons and daughters offered her herbs.

In order to grasp what had happened, to accommodate it so that it could be borne, she had to make a leap across time; for her, a profound leap. She had to connect the fact that Titus had looked into Yoel's sons' eyes at some point in the imprecise past with the fact that these children had come here now with herbs. This was a leap greater than understanding that a sow broached in farrow must be helped to release her piglets. It was a leap greater than knowing that the farmwife who offered her a cloak after she had eased the birth pangs of the farmwife's sow did so in thanks. Those events were self-contained, each within its own sequence. But *this*—

As though he sensed her distress, Titus began to fill her head with images.

One of them showed her herself as she nodded in thanks and smiled for the children; it showed her rising from the protection of the wall to surprise them with her cleanliness, and to touch each of them gratefully upon the cheek, and to let them know that it was time for them to return home.

But she obeyed without noticing what she did: her attention was on other images, images which explained what the children had done. In those images, he spoke to them, and they complied. When they brought the herbs he needed to her hovel, they were acting on his instructions.

Yes, Titus told her firmly, almost urgently, as soon as the children were gone, *there is a connection. You guessed that, and you were right. You do not understand time, but you can understand that it is no barrier to sequence. If you touch the flame, will you not be burned? If Jessup at the hearth of his alehouse touches the flame, will he not be burned, even though you do not see it? If I ask you to bathe, do you not go to the river and cleanse yourself? It is not otherwise with these whelps, or with time. One thing will lead to another because it must.*

Yes, Fern repeated because that was the only sound she recognized. Yes, Titus.

She meant neither *yes* nor *no*, but only that she knew no other response. Nevertheless she saw clearly what he gave her to see: he had spoken to the boys as he spoke to her, silent and silver; those sounds conveyed images to them, which they had heeded; obediently they had hunted the hills for herbs and brought them to her, telling no one what they did. Again and again the events played through her, showing her the links between them, until she fell asleep; sleeping, she dreamed of nothing else. And when she awakened, the connection had become secure.

Across time, and against all likelihood, Yoel's children had brought these herbs because Titus had asked it of them.

At her side, Titus snored heavily, sleeping as though he had been awake all night to weave images. He did not rouse when she scratched his throat; dreams and images were gone from her head.

But the connection remained.

"Yes," she said aloud, although he did not hear her. The sound *Titus* meant this pig. The sound *Yes* meant the connection. One thing will lead to another because it must.

She had no idea what all these herbs were for, so she left them where they lay. After a fine breakfast of bread and sausages and clear water, she spent the morning hunting wood; then she returned to her hovel to find Titus awake at last.

About time, he snorted. *Did you think I gathered all these herbs for my health?* But the hue of his mood was reassuring, and the images he wove for her had an itch of excitement in them.

She set to work promptly under his watchful gaze. When she had built up her fire from its embers, she turned to the gifts Yoel's children had brought. In a bowl of water she mixed marjoram (*Not too much*), vert (*Just so*), coriander and thyme (*More than that, more*), and sloewort (*Only a pinch, you daft woman, I said only a* **pinch**). This she settled in the flames to boil, and as it heated she crushed rueweed (*Better if it were dry, but it will have to serve*) and a little witch hazel into a smaller pot. Once she had ground the leaves as fine as she could, she stirred in enough water to make a paste with a smell so acute that her nose ran.

Wipe it on a rag, not your hand, he told her imperiously. *You already need another bath.* However, he gave her no images to compel her. His attention was on the bowl steaming among the coals.

At his behest, she stirred the herbs vigorously while they boiled; then she pulled the bowl from the flames and set it in the dirt to cool.

Hints of green and blue and a strange, raw crimson flickered at the edges of her mind while she and the pig waited. Titus was excited, she felt that. And expectant, awaiting another connection. And anxious—

Anxious? Was it possible for the connection to fail? Had he not told her that one thing will lead to another?

Because it must, he finished brusquely. *Yes. But it is possible to misunderstand or misuse the sequence. And it is possible for the sequence to be obstructed. It may be that you are too stupid, even for me.*

His tone saddened her, but she did not know how to say so.

Instructed by images, she stirred the herb broth again, then scooped a measure of the thick liquid into a broken-rimmed cup—the last container she owned. New images followed. Titus showed her drinking from the cup, showed her face twisting in disgust, showed her spitting the broth into the dirt. Then, so vehemently that her head rang and her limbs flinched, he forbade her to do what she had just seen. Instead she must swallow the broth, no matter how it gagged her. After that she must dip one finger into the paste of rueweed and witch hazel, and place a touch of it upon her tongue. That would cure her need to gag.

He was Titus, the pig who had adopted her; he was her only connection in all the world. She wished to shy away from the broth, but she did not do so. Thinking, Yes, with her peculiar understanding of the word, she gulped down the contents of the cup.

It felt like thistles in her throat; it stung her stomach like thorns and immediately surged back toward her mouth. Her face twisted; she hunched to vomit. Yet Titus' images held her. Obeying them, her finger stabbed at the paste, carried it to her tongue.

That flavor was as acrid as gall, but it accomplished what he had promised: instantly it stilled her impulse to gag. Her body felt that it had suffered another violation; however, the sensation faded swiftly. By the time her heart had beat three times, she was no longer in distress.

The pig rewarded her with a vivid display of pleasure and satisfaction, as bright as the sun on the waters of the Gentle and as comforting as dawn on her face. *Well done,* he breathed, although she did not know those words. *You are indeed willing. The fault will not be yours if I fail.* Then he added, *As you grow accustomed to it, it will become less burdensome.*

"Yes?" she murmured, asking him for the sequence, the connection. Without words or knowledge, she wished to comprehend what he did.

Now, however, he did not appear to understand her.

He required her to drink the broth again at sunset, and again at dawn and noontime. And when the sun had set once more, Yoel's children returned, bringing four or five of their young friends as well as more herbs and firewood. They also brought bread and carrots, corn and bacon, butter and apples and sausages and beans, which they had appropriated from their parents' kitchens. Now Fern was not a beggar: she was a thief. But she did not see the connection, and so she was not disturbed by it. Instead she was simply gladdened that she did not need to abase herself for so much good food.

For perhaps another fortnight, Titus impelled her to do nothing new or strange. Indeed, her life became simpler than it had ever been, so simple that she hardly regarded its unfamiliar ease. Apparently he was now content. Three times a day she drank the broth and touched her tongue with the paste. Often she bathed in the Gentle. And she stopped pressing her bones against the wall when the children—at least a dozen of them now at various intervals—came to her hovel. More than often, she smiled; once she was so filled by pleasure that she laughed outright. The rest of her days and nights were spent sleeping with Titus, roaming the hills with him, caressing and cozying him, or perhaps watching the games and play of the children, and then studying the images in her mind while Titus showed her the sequences which explained what the children did.

She owned a pig, and she was happy. Only her lack of self-consciousness prevented her from knowing that she was happy. If other pigs needed her, she failed to hear their cries or feel their distress. And they no longer came to her when they succeeded at wandering away from their homes. But her knowledge of time was still uncertain, and she did not notice the change.

Of course, the village noticed. With the selective blindness of adults, the farmers and farmwives, the weavers and potters declined to recognize the surreptitious activities of their children; but they had all known Fern long enough to mark the change in her. They saw her new cleanliness, her new health; they saw the gradual alteration in the way she walked. When she raised her head, the brightness in her eyes was plain. And all Sarendel could hardly fail to observe that wherever she went she was accompanied by a pig which belonged to no one else.

Strange things were rare in Sarendel-on-Gentle. They were worthy of discussion.

"A beggar!" Jessup protested in his taproom. "That pig has made her a beggar, I swear it."

"Be fair, Jessup," rumbled widower Horrik the tanner. He was a large man with large appetites. He still missed his wife, but because of Fern's cleanliness he had begun to see her in new ways, ways which did not altogether distress him. "She was only a beggar for a short time. Was it as much as a fortnight? Now she lives otherwise."

He looked around the taproom, hoping that someone would tell him how Fern lived.

No one did. Instead, Meglan's husband, Wall, said, "In any case, Jessup, you must be sensible." To counteract his softheartedness, Wall placed great store on sense. "The creature is only a pig—and not a prepossessing one, you must admit. How can a pig make her do anything?"

Jessup might have retorted sourly, Because she is daft and dumb. She cannot care for a pig with her own wits. However, Karay the weaver was already speaking.

"But where does he come from?" she asked. "That's what I wish to know. Pigs do not fall from the sky—or climb the sides of the Rift. No village is nearer than Cromber, and that is three days distant for a man in haste. At their worst pigs do not wander so far."

Wall and the other farmers nodded sagely. None of them had ever heard of a pig lost more than three miles from home.

Like Wall's, Karay's question was unanswerable. Glowering blackly, Jessup muttered, "I mean what I say. You mark me. That pig is an ill thing, and no good will come of him." He had no name for the silver compulsion which had caused him to give bread, sausages, and barley to Fern. "If she no longer feeds herself by beggary, it is because she has learned a worse trick."

"Be fair," Horrik said again, and Wall repeated, "Be sensible." Nevertheless the men and women gathered in the taproom squirmed uncomfortably at Jessup's words. All Sarendel had heard the tales of the merchanters on their annual drive down the Rift, tales of intrigues and warlocks and wonders. The villagers could adjudge with confidence any matter which was familiar along the Gentle, but who among them could say certainly what was and what was not possible in the wider world?

No more than a day or two later, the wider world offered them an opportunity to ask its opinion. Unprecedented on a white horse, with a rapier at his side and a tassel in his hat, a man entered Sarendel-on-Gentle from the direction of Cromber. In the center of the village, he dismounted. Stamping dust from his boots and wiping sweat from his brow, he waited until Limm the potter and Vail farmwife came out from their homes to greet him; until every child of the village had arrived as if drawn by magic to the surprise of a stranger; until Yoel and Jessup had left their alehouses, Horrik his tannery, Karay her weaving, and the other farmwives their kitchens and gardens to join the crowd he attracted. Then he swept off his hat, bowed with a long leg, and spoke.

His eyes were road-weary and skeptical, but he smiled and spoke cheerfully. "Good people of Sarendel-on-Gentle, I am Destrier, of the Prince's Roadmen. Lately it has come to Prince Chorl, the lord of all Andovale, that his domain would profit if its many regions and holdings were bound together by a skein of tidings and knowledge. Therefore he has commissioned his Roadmen to travel throughout the land. It is the will of my Prince that I spread the news of Andovale down the Gentle's Rift, and that I bear back to him the news of the Rift's villages and doings.

"Good people, will you welcome me in Prince Chorl's name?"

Yoel tugged at his leather apron. Because he was an affable man who had shown during the visits of the merchanters that he was not chagrined by strangers, he sometimes spoke on behalf of the village. "Surely," he replied in a slow rumble. "We welcome any man or woman who passes

among us. Why should we not? We mean no harm, and expect none."
He might have added, We do not require the bidding of princes to extend
courtesy. However, his good nature worked against such plain speaking.
Instead he continued, "But I fear I do not understand. What manner of
news is it that you seek?"

"Why, change, of course," Destrier replied as though he found Yoel's
affability—or his perplexity—charming. "I seek news of change. Any
change at all. Change is of endless interest to my Prince."

Yoel received this assertion with some concern. "Change?" He
dropped his eyes, and a frown crossed his broad face. Around him, people
shifted on their feet and looked away. Children stared at the Roadman
as though he might begin to spout poetry. At last Yoel met Destrier's
gaze again and shook his head.

"We are as you see us—as we have always been. Along the Gentle we
know little of change. Surely the other folk of the Rift have said the same?

"However, it is of no great moment," he went on more quickly. "You
are road-weary, no doubt thirsty and hungry as well. I must not ask you
to remain standing in the sun while I inquire in what way your Prince
believes we might have changed. Will you accept the hospitality of my
alehouse?" He gestured toward it with an open palm. "Your horse will
be cared for. We have no horses here, as you surely know, but the merchanters have taught us how to care for their beasts."

At once Wall stepped forward to place a hand on the reins of the
Roadman's mount. "I have a stall to spare in my barn." During the visits
of the merchanters, he often profited in a small way by tending their horses.

Smiling with less cheer and more skepticism, Destrier bowed and
answered, "My thanks." To Yoel he added, "Aleman, I will gladly accept
a flagon and a meal. I do not mean to overstay my welcome, but if you
will house and feed me until the morrow, you will earn Prince Chorl's
gratitude."

"In plain words," Jessup muttered softly to the farmwife standing
near him, "the Prince's Roadman does not propose to pay for his fare.
Let Yoel have his custom—and my gratitude as well."

If Destrier heard this remark, he did not acknowledge it. Instead he
followed Yoel to the alehouse.

In turn, a good half of the villagers—Jessup among them—followed the Roadman. They desired to hear the tales he would tell of the wide world. And his talk of "change" had made them apprehensive; they wished to know what would come of it. The rest of Sarendel's folk herded their children away and returned to their chores.

While these events transpired, Fern and Titus knew nothing about them. Together they had roamed farther than usual, and they came home late for her midday dose of herbs. However, during the afternoon some of the smaller children made their way to her hovel with the tidings.

The pig responded as though he had been wasp-stung. Fern saw flashes of anger and fear in the air as he turned his one blind eye and his marred one commandingly on the children. Unfortunately, they were too young to give a cogent account of what had happened. Strangers and strangeness caught their attention more than names or words. One child remembered "Roadman." Another babbled of "Prince Chorl." But none of them could say what brought a Roadman to Sarendel, or what Prince Chorl had to do with the matter.

Fools, Titus snorted bitterly. *Guttersnipes. Children. Why has that meddling Prince invented Roadmen? And what damnable mischance has brought this pigsty to his attention?*

Curse them, I am not ready. I need more time.

In a voice so harsh that Fern was shocked by it, he cried, *I need more* **time!**

"Yes," she murmured incoherently, trying to console him. "Yes, Titus."

The pig turned on her. Thin silver ran like a cut into her brain.

For an instant she saw an image of herself approaching Yoel's alehouse, entering it to witness what was said and done. She saw herself hearing voices and remembering what they said, remembering words— But before it was complete the image frayed away, tattered by despair.

You will understand nothing, he groaned. *And they will not allow a pig to enter. I must— I must—*

He did not say what he must.

But when he had fretted Fern to distraction through the afternoon and evening, his fortunes improved. Late enough to find her yawning uncontrollably and barely able to keep wood on the fire, more children came to her hovel and nudged the curtain to announce themselves. When they entered, she recognized two of the older boys, one Yoel's tallest son, the other Wall and Meglan's boy, who was nearly of a size to begin working in his father's fields. She knew without knowing how she knew that their names were Levit and Lessom.

Titus jumped up to face them. With the familiarity of frequent visits, they dropped to the dirt beside the fire. Fatigue and excitement burned on their faces; their eyes were on a level with his. As if they no longer noticed the oddness of what they did, they spoke to the pig rather than to the woman.

"They told us not to go," Lessom panted, out of breath from running. "We are too young for ale, and we had no business there. But we sneaked into the cellar—Levit knew the way—and found a crack in the floorboards where we could hear. Cor, my legs hurt. We stood for hours and hours.

"Do all grown men talk so, of everything and nothing in the middle of the day, as if they had no work—?"

Titus stopped the rush of words with a flash of his eyes. *Slowly*, Fern heard. *Be complete. I must know everything. Begin at the beginning. Who is he? Where does he come from? What does he want?*

Every line and muscle of the pig's body was tight with strain, as though he were about to flee.

"He is Destrier," Levit offered, "Prince Chorl's Roadman. He said Prince Chorl commissioned the Roadmen to carry news everywhere in Andovale. He said he wants to hear the news from all the villages in the Rift. And he told tales—"

"Cor, the tales!" Lessom breathed. "Better than the merchanters tell. Is it true that there are wars—that warlocks and princes fight each other for power beyond the Rift?"

No! Titus grunted. *Warlocks do not fight princes. The ruling of lands requires too much time and attention. Any warlock who neglects his arts for such things becomes weak. Warlocks reserve their struggles for each other.*

What "news" does this Roadman want?

"Change." Levit's eyes were as round and solemn as a cow's. "He said he wants news of change. Any change. For Prince Chorl."

Impelled by the pig's tension, Fern added more wood to the fire.

Titus held the boys with his gaze. *Now pay attention*, he insisted. *Make no mistake. My life depends on this. What did they tell him? Your fathers—all those self-satisfied clodhoppers who talk of everything and nothing when there is work to be done—what did they tell him?*

Did they betray me? Have I been betrayed?

Levit glanced sidelong at Lessom. "Your father talked about the weather. I've never heard so many words about wind and sun. The weather! I thought I would die of impatience. I wanted to hear what the Roadman would say."

"Yes." Lessom was too excited to take offense. "And your father repeated everything everyone has ever known about brewing ale."

Levit nodded. "And then Karay mentioned every birth or death in, cor, it must have been ten years. My knees were trembling before the Roadman so much as began his tales."

Continue.

"But the tales were worth it," Lessom said, "were they not?"

Again Levit nodded.

"You say that warlocks do not fight princes," Lessom continued, "but the Roadman said otherwise. He spoke of a time when the enemies of Andovale mustered a great army of soldiers and warlocks to march against Prince—"

"Prince Chrys," Lessom put in.

"—Prince Chrys, and were defeated by—"

Titus stopped him. *Old news. Ancient history. That war is why warlocks no longer meddle in the affairs of princes. Preparing for war, the warlocks of Carcin and Sargo neglected their true arts. They made themselves weak, and so were defeated by the warlocks of Andovale. In magic, those who do not grow must decline.*

Hearing another connection, Fern thought softly, Yes.

But, *Think!* the pig was saying. *This Roadman did not ride the length of the Rift to relate old news. He must have spoken of more recent matters—events which have transpired since the last visit of the merchanters. Tell me that tale!*

Titus' vehemence disconcerted Levit. "He spoke of a war among warlocks," the boy began. "But Prince Chorl was also involved—" He broke off as though he feared to displease the pig.

That *one*, Titus demanded.

"He was called Suriman," Lessom began abruptly. The small cut of silver in the pig's gaze seemed to take hold of him. His body tightened in ways which distressed Fern. From the corners of his mind he brought out the Roadman's tale just as Destrier had told it. "That was his title— men do not speak his name. He was a prince among warlocks, ancient in magic as well as years. That he was called Suriman shows the respect in which he was held by all his brother warlocks. When the masters of magic gathered in council, he was often the first to speak. When Prince Chorl or the other lords of Andovale needed either the help or the counsel of a warlock, they often approached Suriman first. Indeed, it was Suriman himself who devised the means by which the warlocks of Sargo and Carcin were defeated.

"Yet there were some in Andovale, warlocks as well as ordinary men, who spoke ill of Suriman behind his back. They were thought jealous or petty when they hinted that he practiced his arts in ways which the masters of magic in council had proscribed many generations ago. They said—though they were not believed—that he had violated the foremost commandment of the councils, which is that the study and practice of magic is the responsibility of warlocks and must not be imposed on ordinary men against their will. If a warlock requires a man for experimentation or study, he must perform his researches upon himself, or upon some other warlock, not on men who can neither gauge nor accept— and certainly cannot prevent—the consequences.

"Those who spoke ill against Suriman said that he had performed his studies upon ordinary men, making some less than they were and others more, but always depriving his victims of choice in his researches. By so doing, he had gained for himself powers unheard of among warlocks for many generations. Thus his might, his stature, and his very title were founded upon evil."

Titus snorted in disgust, but did not interrupt.

"At first, those who spoke ill against Suriman were ignored. Then they were criticized and scorned. From time to time, one or another of them died, perhaps because they erred in their own experimentation, perhaps because they were punished for their indiscretions, perhaps because Suriman himself took action against them. Such deaths belonged to the province of warlocks, however, not to the jurisprudence of princes, and the masters of magic found Suriman faultless in them.

"But Prince Chorl had a daughter. Her name was Florice, and she was renowned throughout Andovale for her beauty and her sweetness—and her simplicity. In truth, she was not merely simple. She was a child of perhaps eight or nine years in a woman's body, unfit for a woman's life. For some time this was a cause of great grief to Prince Chorl. But when his grief was done, he cherished her for her beauty, for her sweet nature, and also for her simplicity. Therefore she was unwed—and unavailable. The Prince kept her as a child in his household, both protecting and loving her for what she was."

Abruptly, Fern found that she could see Prince Chorl's daughter—a woman clad in white as pure as samite, with silken hair, eyes like sunshine, and a form which Titus might have called *lovely*. Her image in Fern's mind was as precise as presence. Yet Fern knew more of her through the colors of the image than from the image itself. They were the hues of a complex and insatiable hunger.

"So she would have remained," Lessom related in Destrier's tones, "until old age claimed her, if she had not caught Suriman's eye. To Prince Chorl's amazement, and all Andovale's astonishment, Suriman asked to wed Florice.

"'No,' said the Prince in his surprise.

"'Why not?' Suriman countered calmly. 'Do you fear that I will not cherish her as you do? I swear by my arts that her sweetness and happiness are as precious to me as my life, and I will find great joy in her.'

"Dumbfounded, Prince Chorl seemed unable to think calmly. 'It is absurd,' he protested. 'You do not know what you are asking. You—' Because he was not thinking calmly, he turned to his daughter. 'Florice, do you wish to wed this man?'

"Florice gazed at Suriman and smiled her sweetest smile. 'No, Father,' she said. 'He is bad.'

"Neither the Prince nor Suriman knew how to respond to such a remark. However, the warlock was less disconcerted than his Prince. Laughing gently, he said, 'Really, my lord, I am too old to be a jilted suitor. I have lost my appetite for appearing foolish. Please permit me to remain as your guest for a season. Permit me to speak to your daughter for a few minutes each day—in your presence, of course. If you see nothing ill in my comportment toward her, perhaps you will not believe that I am "bad." And if at the end of the season she does not desire me, I will accept my folly and depart the wiser.'

"This proposal Prince Chorl accepted. He is not to be blamed for his mistake—although he blames himself mightily. Suriman was held in high esteem throughout Andovale. And those who spoke ill against him could prove nothing."

The colors in Fern's mind were ones of hope and possession, of a grasped opportunity. She could not image why Titus showed them to her: they were simply a fact, as all his images were facts—or became facts. Perhaps they came from him involuntarily or unconsciously while he heard Destrier's tale in Lessom's mouth.

"Yet if the Prince erred, he did not err blindly. He made certain that Suriman had no contact with Florice outside his own presence. And he watched her closely while Suriman spoke with her, studying her dear face for understanding. Before a fortnight passed, he saw that her face had changed.

"Tightness pulled at the corners of her mouth, straining her smiles. Her eyes lost their forthright sweetness and turned aside from her father's gaze. She asked questions which the Prince had never heard from her before. 'Father, why do men and women marry?' 'Father, why do you treat me like a child?' By these signs, he understood that his beloved daughter was in peril."

The image Fern saw conveyed satisfaction and excitement, whetted desire. Nevertheless, unbidden, she made a connection which did not come to her either from the image or through its colors. Rather it came from her own emotions—and from her growing sense of time.

Yes, she thought, not in acceptance, but in dismay. What she saw on the face of the Prince's daughter was violation.

Florice was not willing.

Perhaps Titus wished her to understand this, so that she would understand what followed.

"Yet Suriman was Suriman, respected everywhere. Prince Chorl felt that he could not send the warlock from his house. Instead, he took other precautions. In secret he summoned one of the warlocks—a man named Titus"—again the pig snorted—"who was known to think ill of Suriman, and he told Titus of his fears. He gave Titus the freedom of his house, and charged Titus to find proof that Suriman wrought evil against Florice.

"With Prince Chorl's support and assistance, Titus did as he was charged. Before another fortnight was ended, Florice announced to her father her settled intention to wed the warlock who courted her—and Titus announced his accusation that Suriman had flouted the most urgent commandment of the councils, that he had betrayed Florice by using his arts to alter her to his will.

"Consternation! In an instant, the peace of Andovale became chaos and distress. Flinging defiance at her father, Florice sought to flee the house with Suriman." Fern saw a hunger on her face which echoed the hunger of the colors surrounding her—a hunger she had not chosen and could not refuse. "Prince Chorl countered by imprisoning her, his daughter whom he cherished. Suriman attacked her prison, wreaking havoc in the Prince's house, and was only prevented from freeing Florice by the foresight of Titus, who had prepared defenses against the greater warlock—and had also demanded the attention of the council in what he did. The masters of magic gave Titus their aid until they could learn the truth of his accusations, and so Suriman's onslaught was beaten back. Even as the masters of magic met in council to examine Titus' proofs, Suriman ran.

"Inspired by his loathing of the crimes he attributed to Suriman, Titus had found sure proof. With gossamer incantations and webs of magic, he had followed Suriman's movements throughout the Prince's house. He had traced Suriman daily to the kitchens, where the delicacies which Florice most loved were prepared. And in the foods she was given to eat he found the herbs and simples, the poisons and potions, which

Suriman would need to make Florice something other than she was against her will.

"Outraged, the council declared anathema on Suriman and went to war against him.

"He was mighty—oh, he was mighty! He could stand alone against any half dozen of his peers. And the dark tower where he studied his arts was mightily protected. But all the masters of magic in Andovale moved against him. They brought out fire from the air to crack his tower and drive him forth. Then he fled, and they gave chase. He took refuge in castles and towns. They scorched the very walls around him until he fled again. He hid himself in forests and villages. They shook the stones under his feet, so that he could not stand, but only run. And at last, on one of the farms at the end of the Gentle's Rift, they brought him to bay.

"The masters of magic do not speak of the final battle, but it was prodigious. In desperation, Suriman wove every power and trick at his vast command. Warlocks fell that day, and some never rose again. When the fire and passion had ended, however, Suriman lay dead among the wreckage of the farm. The beasts had scattered, and the fields were blasted, but the council had triumphed.

"That is to say, the masters of magic believed that they had triumphed. Suriman's corpse lay before them. Only Titus insisted that the evil was not done—Titus and Florice. Crying in wild hunger, the Prince's daughter claimed that the warlocks were too little to kill a man of Suriman's greatness. And Titus, whom loathing for Suriman had made cunning, spoke of texts and apparatus in Suriman's tower which pertained to the transfer of intelligences from one body to another. He told all who would hear him that Suriman could have escaped the last battle cloaked inside another man, or even concealed within a beast. If what he said were true, then Suriman might well remain alive—and might return.

"So the council watches for Suriman constantly, seeking any sign that the most evil of warlocks yet lives. And Prince Chorl watches also. His daughter is little better than a madwoman now, sorrowing over the loss of the man who changed her, and because the Prince blames himself his anger cannot be assuaged.

"All considered," the Roadman concluded his tale in Lessom's voice, "it has been a tumultuous time. Surely you have felt it here? Magic and battles on such a scale have repercussions. Has nothing changed at all— nothing out of the ordinary? Do not the cows talk, or the pigs sprout wings? Has no thing occurred which you might call strange? Is everything truly just as it has always been?"

With a gasp, Lessom sagged as the pig's gaze released him. Titus turned his eyes on Levit.

Now think! he demanded. *Make no mistake. What answer was this Roadman given?*

Yoel's son appeared to search his memory. "They were silent," he said slowly. "I could not see them, but I heard their boots on the floor, and the benches shifting. Then Horrik said, 'You came. That was strange. We have never seen a Roadman before.'

"Everyone laughed, and the Roadman with them. After that my father took Destrier to a room for the night, and people left the alehouse. I heard nothing else."

Think, Titus grunted urgently. *Nothing was said of me? Of Fern? Did not that clod-brain Jessup speak against me?*

Levit glanced at Lessom. "Nothing."

Lessom nodded and echoed, "Nothing."

For a time, the pig did not speak. Both boys slumped on the dirt, wearied by Titus' coercion. Beside them Fern tended the fire uncomfortably; she wanted sleep, but she was full of a fear she could not name. Images of Florice seemed to resonate for her like wind past a hollow in a wall, as though they might convey another connection; yet the connection eluded her. Such things were matters of time, and her grasp on them remained imprecise.

Then Titus snuffled, *Ah, but they squirmed. I can see it. They dropped their eyes and twisted in their seats. And this Destrier noticed it. He was sent to notice such things.*

Hell's blood! I must have time!

Like Titus, Lessom and Levit needed time. Their parents would not speak kindly to them for staying out so late. Yawning and shuffling, they left the hovel.

But Titus continued to fret. He paced the floor as though his hooves were afire. Fern tried to rest, but she could not be still when the pig she loved was in distress. "Yes?" she murmured to him, "yes?" hoping that the sound of her concern would comfort him.

No, he retorted harshly. *You do not know what you are saying. It is not enough.*

As though he had judged and dismissed her, he did not speak again that night.

The next morning, however, he ventured out early to watch Prince Chorl's Roadman ride away from Sarendel-on-Gentle. And when he returned to the hovel, he was full of grim bustle. *I must take action,* he informed her. *Any delay or hindrance now will be fatal.* And he showed her an image which instructed her to prepare a double—no, a treble—portion of the herbs and paste with which he fed her thrice daily.

She obeyed willingly, because he instructed her. When his concoctions were done, she bathed thoroughly; she combed out her hair and let the sun dry it until it shone. Then, guided by images, she draped her limbs with her scantest, most inadequate rags.

Cold, she thought when she saw how ill she was covered. A moment later, she thought another word, which might have been, Shame.

Shame? The pig's disgust was as bright as fire. *Shame will not kill you. My need is extreme. Extreme measures are required.* Nevertheless he allowed her to remain concealed in her hovel while he roamed the village; when he returned, they remained there together until the sun had set.

By that time, Sarendel had newer, more personal news to replace Destrier's unexpected visit. Meglan's husband, Wall, had fallen ill. According to the children who brought the tale, he writhed on his bed like a snake, vomiting gouts of bile and blood, and his skin burned as though his bones were ablaze. Meglan and her children were beside themselves, fearing his death at any moment.

Meglan? Fern had little impression of Wall, but Meglan farmwife was vivid to her. Meglan's kindnesses, of which Fern had known many, came to her through veils of time—carrots and shawls, cabbages and sandals and smiles. She felt tugging at her the same concern, the same impulse to respond, which she had often felt for Sarendel's pigs.

Good, Titus said. *Such concern looks well.*

And he showed her an image in which she went alone to Meglan's home, bearing small portions of her broth and paste. Alone she knocked at the door until she was answered. Alone she repeated Meglan's name until Meglan was brought to her. Then, still alone, she spoke to Meglan. In words, she explained how the broth and paste should be administered to save Wall.

Alone?

Spoke? In words?

Explained—?

Fern flinched against the wall of the hovel as though Titus had threatened to strike her.

I will teach you, Titus replied patiently. *If you are willing, you will be able to do it.*

"No," she protested in fright.

Come now, Fern, Titus went on, filling her mind with the colors of calm. *You will be able to do it. I have made you able. Did you not hear yourself speak just now? That was a word. You know both "yes" and "no." And you know names. Each new word will be a smaller step than the one before—and you will not need many to save Wall.*

Alone? she cried fearfully.

If you love me, you will do this. Meglan will have no tolerance for pigs at such a time.

Fern did not know how she understood him; yet she comprehended that he needed her—and that his need was greater than she could imagine. With her crumbling resistance, she gestured toward the rags she wore.

You will feel no shame, he promised her. *There can be none for you, when you do my bidding.*

There: another connection. Through her fright and distress, an involuntary excitement struck her. She had always contrived to cover herself better than this; but now she did not because Titus had instructed her. His bidding— She acted according to his wishes, not her own.

Other connections trembled at the edges of her mind, other links between what he wished and what people did. However, his urgency and his steady promises distracted her. While she readied her small portions of herbs and paste, he taught her the words she would need.

When she left the hovel, she went in a daze of fear and shame and excitement. No, not shame— *There can be none for you, when you do my bidding.* What she felt was the strange, uneasy eagerness of comprehension, the unfamiliar potential of language. Ignoring how her breasts and legs showed when she walked, she crossed the village and did as Titus had instructed her.

She was almost able to recognize what she gained by wearing her worst rags. They caught the attention of the farmer who opened the door, a friend of Wall's; they trapped him in pity, embarrassment, and interest, so that he was not able to send her away unheard. Instead, he went to fetch Meglan, thinking that Meglan would be able to dismiss Fern more kindly.

And when Meglan came to the door, Fern astonished her with words.

"I know herbs," said Fern, slurring each sound, and yet speaking with her utmost care, because of her love for Titus. "These can heal Wall. A spoonful of the broth. A touch of the paste on his tongue. Four times during the night. His illness will break at dawn."

Meglan stared as though the sounds were gibberish. All Sarendel knew Fern did not speak; she could not. Then how could these sounds be words?

But Titus had taught her one more: "Please."

"'Please'?" Meglan cried, on the verge of sobs. "My husband whom I love dies here, and you say, 'Please'?"

Fern could not withhold her own tears. Meglan's grief and the burden of words were too great for her to bear. Helpless to comfort the good farmwife—and helpless to refuse her pig—she could only begin again at the beginning.

"I know herbs. These can heal—"

Another woman appeared at Meglan's shoulder, a neighbor. "Is that Fern?" she asked in surprise. "Did I hear her speak?"

Grief twisted Meglan's face. If Fern could speak, the farmwife could not. Taking both broth and paste, she turned her back in silence and closed the door.

Fern went weeping back to her hovel.

Titus had no patience for her nameless sorrows. When she entered the hovel and stumbled to the scraps and leaves which she used as a pallet, he fixed her with his eyes, compelling her with silver and blindness until he had seen what was in her mind.

After that, however, his manner softened. *It was hard, I grant,* he told her. *But you have done a great thing, though you do not know it. The next steps will be less arduous. That is a better promise than the one I gave you earlier.*

Then he nuzzled and comforted her, and filled her head with solace, until at last she was able to stop crying and sleep.

While she slept, new connections swam and blurred, seeking clarity. She had gone to Meglan because Titus bade her. She had bathed her body and combed her hair and donned her worst rags on his instructions. She had prepared new stores of broth and paste at his behest. Were all these things connected in the same way? One thing will lead to another because it must. Had the pig foreseen Wall's illness? Was time no barrier to him, neither the past nor the future?

For a moment, as if time were no barrier to her as well, she seemed to see through the veils of the past. She saw that the ease and comfort and companionship of her life were new—that her life itself had changed. How did it come about that all her needs were supplied by children who had taken no notice of her until Titus adopted her?

What had he done? He had filled her with images. And she had done his bidding. One thing will lead to another— Did the children also find images in their minds, new images which instructed them in Titus' wishes?

These connections were like the surface of the Gentle. They caught the sun and sparkled, gems cast by the water, but they were too full of ripples and currents to be seen clearly.

And they vanished when the pig awakened her. *It is morning,* he informed her intently. *You must be prepared to speak again soon.* His concentration was acute; his eyes seemed to focus all of him on her. *Hear the sounds. They are words. When I have given them to you, they will be yours. At first, they will be difficult to remember. Nevertheless they will belong to you, and you will be able to call on them at need.*

Words? she thought. More words? But he left her no opportunity for protest. When she tried to say, "No," he brushed that word aside. *It will become easier, I tell you,* he snapped. *And I have no time for subtlety.*

She surrendered to his bidding scant moments before a tentative scratching at her door curtain announced a visitor.

Held by his gaze, she spoke the first of his new words.

"Enter."

Expecting children, she was filled with chagrin when she saw Meglan come into her hovel. Only the strength of her love for her pig—or the strength of his presence in her mind—enabled her to rise to her feet instead of cowering against the wall.

Meglan herself appeared full of chagrin. Fern could look at the farmwife because Meglan was unable to look at Fern. Her gaze limped aimlessly across the floor, lost among her pallid features, and her voice also limped as she murmured, "I know not what to say. I can hardly face you. My husband is saved. You saved him—you, who speaks when none of us knew you could—you gave no hint— You, whom I have treated with little concern and no courtesy. You, who came in rags to offer your help. You, whom I have considered at worst a beggar and at best a half-wit. You and no other saved my husband.

"I cannot— I do not know how to bear it. You deserve honor, and you have been given only scorn.

"Fern, I must make amends. You have saved Wall, who is as dear to me as my own flesh. Because of you, he smiles, and lifts his head, and will soon be able to rise from his bed. I must make amends." Now she looked into Fern's eyes, and her need was so great—as great as Titus'— that Fern could not look away. "I will tell the tale. That I can do. I will teach Sarendel to honor you. But it is not enough.

"I have brought—" Meglan opened her hands as if she were ashamed of what they held, and Fern saw a thick, woolen robe, woven to stand hard use and keep out cold. "It is plain—too plain for my heart—but it is what I have, and it is not rags. And still it is not enough.

"If you can speak—if you are truly able to speak—please tell me how to thank you for my husband's life."

Fern, who had never owned a garment so rich and useful, might have fallen to her knees and wept in gratitude. To be given such a gift, without begging or dishonesty—! But Titus' need was as great as Meglan's. He did not let her go.

Instead of bowing or crying, she answered, "Thank you." The words stumbled in her mouth; they were barely articulate. Yet she said them—

and as she said them she felt an excitement which seemed like terror. "I helped Wall because I could. I do not need tales."

That is safe, Titus commented. *She will talk in any case.*

"Or gifts," Fern went on. Belying the words, she gripped the robe tightly. "Yet it would be a kindness if I were given an iron cookpot and a few mixing bowls."

Damnation! Titus grunted. *That came out crudely. I must be more cautious.*

Ashamed to be begging again, Fern could no longer face the farmwife. Because Titus required it, however, she gestured at her fire and her few bowls. "My knowledge of herbs is more than I can use with what implements I have. If I could cook better, I could help others as I have helped your husband."

Tears welled in Meglan's eyes. "Thank you. You will have what you need." Impulsively, she leaned forward and kissed Fern's cheek. Then she turned and hurried from the hovel as though she were grieving—or fleeing.

There. Titus sounded like Jessup rubbing his hands together over an auspicious bargain. *Was that not easier? Did I not promise that it would be less arduous? Soon we will be ready.*

For the second time, Fern felt her own tears reply to Meglan's. "No." She had no recollection that she had ever been kissed before. Her surprise at Meglan's gesture startled another surprise out of her—an unfamiliar anger. "No," she repeated. Almost in words, almost using language for herself, she faced the pig's strange gaze and showed him her shame.

Titus shook his head. *You did not beg.* Now he sounded condescending and desirous, like Horrik the tanner. *You answered her question—a small act of courtesy and self-respect. Consider this.* He showed Fern an image of Meglan coming to the hovel to offer gratitude, carrying not a robe but a cookpot and some bowls. *Would you have felt shame then?* he asked. *No. You were not shamed by the gift she chose to give you. It is only because you named your own need that you think you have done wrong.*

But it was not wrong. It was my bidding.

Perhaps we will have enough time. Perhaps you will be able to save me. Take comfort in that, if you cannot forget your shame. Perhaps you will be able to save me.

As I saved Wall? she almost asked. Was that not also your doing?

But she lacked the language for such questions. And the pig distracted her, nuzzling her hand to express his affection and gratitude, wrapping her mind in azure and comfortable emerald; and so the connection was lost.

After that, her life changed again. The roaming and scavenging which had measured out her days came to a complete end. Feeling at once grand and unworthy in her new robe, she sat in her hovel while Titus went out alone and came back; while children supplied her with food and water and firewood and herbs; while first one or two and then several and finally all of Sarendel's good people came to visit her. Some scratched at her curtain and poked their heads inside simply to satisfy their curiosity or resolve their doubt. But others brought their needs and pains to her attention. Meglan's tale had inspired them to hope that Fern could help them.

Red-eyed from sleeplessness, and strangely abashed in the presence of a woman whom she had scarcely noticed before, Salla farmwife brought her infant son, who squalled incessantly with colic. Had the boy been a pig, Fern would have known what to do. However, he was a boy, and so it was fortunate that Titus stood at her side to instruct her. (*A bit of the paste, diluted four times. Mint and sage to moderate the effect. There.*) When Salla left the hovel, she added her son's smiles and his sweet sleep to Meglan's tale.

And later Salla brought Fern the gift which Titus had told Fern to request—a mortar and pestle, and a set of sturdy wooden spoons.

Horrik came, bearing an abscessed thumb. After Fern had treated it with a poultice which she had never made before, he lingered to stare and talk like a man whose mind drooled at what he saw. Yet he did not take it unkindly when at last Titus succeeded at urging her to dismiss him. Smiling and bowing, the tanner left; still smiling, he brought to her the gift she had requested, a keen flensing knife.

Karay's daughter had been afflicted with palsy from birth. The weaver was so accustomed to her daughter's infirmity that she would not have thought to seek aid, were it not for the strange fact that Fern could now speak. Perhaps if a mute half-wit could learn language and healing, a palsy could be cured. So Karay set her forlorn child in the dirt beside Fern's fire and asked bluntly, "Can you help her?"

In response, Fern prepared a broth not unlike the one she ate herself, a paste not unlike the one she had given Salla's infant. "And ale," she added. "Mix it in ale. Let her drink at her own pace until she has drunk it all."

Once Karay had seen that this rank brew indeed put an end to her daughter's palsy, she gave Fern a curtain of embroidered velvet to replace the hovel's burlap door. And also, because she was asked, she delivered to Fern a cupful each of all the dyes she used in her weaving.

Herded by his angry wife and four angry daughters, Sarendel's blacksmith entered her hovel, carrying so much pain that he could hardly move. He had fallen against his forge and burned away most of the flesh on one side of his chest; his wife and daughters were angry because they feared that he would die. Fern gave him a salve for healing, herbs to soften the hurt, and other herbs to resist infection.

When her husband began to mend, the blacksmith's wife at last allowed herself to weep. She cried ceaselessly as she brought Fern several small flakes of silver.

A farmer was given a cure for gout; he expressed his thanks with a lump of ambergris which he had treasured for years without knowing why. Over her father-in-law's vociferous objections, Jessup's eldest son's wife asked for and received an herb to ease the severity of her monthly cramps; her gratitude took the form of two pints of refined lard. One of the blacksmith's daughters believed that she was unwed because her beauty was marred by a large wen beside her nose; when Fern supplied her with a poultice which caused the wen to shrink and fall away, she— and her father—gave Fern an iron grill to hold Meglan's cookpot.

In the course of a fortnight, Fern seemed to become the center of all Sarendel-on-Gentle, the hub on which the village turned. Children cared for her needs, and adults visited her at any hour. Resplendent in her new robe—of all the gifts she had been given, this one alone warmed her heart—she sat in state to receive all who came to her. With Titus at her side, as well fed and well tended as herself, she made new concoctions and spoke new words as though those separate actions were one and the same, bound to each other in ways she could not see. She no longer cowered against her walls in fright or chagrin. Instead she gave her help with the same unstinting openheartedness which she had formerly shown only to pigs. Helping people made her love them. She disliked only the gifts she was given in thanks, never the efforts she made to earn that thanks.

Her life had indeed changed. This time, however, she recognized the change for what it was. She neither chose it nor resisted it, but she saw it. And when she watched the change, comparing it to what her life had once been, she made new connections.

She understood why she could speak, why she could understand the people around her and reply, why she could prepare complex salves and balms, why she could look her fellow villagers in their faces. It was because of the broth and paste which Titus caused her to eat three times daily. Those herbs had wrought a change within her as profound as the change in her life.

One thing will lead to another because it must.

And she understood that she did not deserve Sarendel's gratitude for her cures and comforts. That was why gifts gave her no pleasure, but only sorrow. She healed nothing, earned nothing. Like her new ability to speak, all the benefits she worked for others came from Titus: the credit for them was his, not hers.

She did not resent this. The pig had come to her in his extremity, and she loved him. Nor could she wish the lessons he had taught her unlearned. Nevertheless she grieved over her unworth.

In addition, she understood without knowing she understood that Titus himself caused a certain number of the hurts she treated. Too frequently to be unconnected, his forays away from her hovel coincided with the onset of injuries and illnesses in the village. The same powers with which he had raised her from her familiar destitution, he used to create the conditions under which Sarendel needed her.

He was trying to speed the process by which she accumulated gifts.

This troubled her. It offended her honesty more than begging; it seemed a kind of theft. But she did not protest against it. Other, similar connections crouched at the edges of her understanding, waiting for clarity. When she grasped one, she would grasp them all.

Ready, she thought to herself, using words instead of images. We must be ready. We are becoming ready.

We are, Titus assented. She could hear pride and hope in his voice, as well as anger and more than a little fear.

Before the end of another fortnight, Sarendel had learned to accept Fern in her changed state; the village had begun to live as though she had always been a healer rather than a half-wit. And Titus had finished accumulating the gifts he required.

Now she noted the passing of time. Around her the seasons had moved along the Gentle's Rift, turning high summer to crisp fall. Hints of gold and crimson appeared among the verdure; at their fringes the leaves of the bracken took on rust. Slowly the labor of tending fields and beasts eased. Soon would come a time she dreaded, a time she now knew she had always dreaded—the time when porkers were slaughtered for food and hide and tallow. She did not fear for Titus in that way: because he was hers, no villager would harm him. And yet she feared for him now, just as she had always feared for the porkers.

True, she could hear his own fear in the way he spoke. But she also saw it in the tension of his movements, in the staring of his flawed eyes; she smelled it in his sweat. It confirmed her apprehension for him when she might have been able to persuade herself that she had no reason for alarm.

One sharp fall morning, he poked his snout past her hovel's velvet curtain, scented the air—and recoiled as though he had been stung.

Hell's blood! he panted. *Damn and blast them!*

An unnamed panic came over her. She surged up from her pallet to throw her arms about his neck as though she believed that she could ward him somehow. He shivered feverishly, hot with dread.

"Titus?" She needed words for her fear, but only his name came to her. "Titus?"

He appeared to take comfort from her embrace. After a moment, his tremors eased. The confused moil of images and hues which he cast into her sharpened toward concentration.

Now we must hurry in earnest, he breathed. *There is a stink of princes and warlocks in the air. That damnable Roadman has betrayed me, and I have little time. As I am, I can neither flee nor fight.*

Oh, Fern, my Fern, if you love me, help me. Give me your willingness. Without it, I am lost.

"Who?" she asked with her face pressed to his neck. "Who comes to threaten you?"

Princes, warlocks, does it matter? he snapped back. *They are frightened, even more than I—therefore they will be enough. They would not come if they were not enough. I tell you, we must* **hurry!**

She could not refuse him. She gave him a last hug, as though she were saying farewell. After that, she dropped her arms and seated herself by the fire.

"Then tell me what to do."

She seemed to take his fear from him; he seemed to leach all calm and quiet out of her. The words and images which he supplied to instruct her were precise and unmistakable, as clear as sunlight on green leaves; yet her hands shook, and her whole heart trembled, while she obeyed. She was Fern of Sarendel-on-Gentle, a half-wit who loved pigs. What did she know of language or time, of magic or warlocks? Nevertheless Titus needed her, as he had needed her once before, and she did not mean to fail him.

Throughout the day she labored under his guidance, trying to do several things at once. As she heated her new cookpot until the iron shone red, she also ground rueweed and fennel and sloewort and garlic and vert and silver flakes to fine powder; at the same time, she gripped the lump of ambergris between her thighs to soften it. While she warmed lard to liquid in one of her mixing bowls, she also kneaded the ambergris until it became as workable as beeswax. And when her hands were too tired for kneading, she busied herself dividing her powders into ever more meticulous quantities and combining them with pinches of dried dyes.

Children came to scratch at her curtain, but she sent them away without caring whether she was brusque. She would have sent all Sarendel away. Horrik the tanner came as well; he seemed to want nothing more than an opportunity to sit and look at her. But she told him "No," calling the word past Karay's heavy curtain without raising her head from her work. "If you meant to speak to me, you should have done so long ago." She hardly heard herself add, "I am too far beyond you now."

Morning lapsed to afternoon; afternoon became evening. Still she worked. Now her hands were raw and her arms quivered, and sweat splashed from her cheeks to the dirt. Fire and red iron filled the hovel with heat until even the slats of the walls appeared to sweat. The smells of powders and dyes in strange combinations made her head wobble on her neck. But Titus did not relent. His instructions were unending, and she labored with all her willingness to obey them.

At last he let her pause. While she rested, panting, he surveyed her handiwork, squinting blind and silver at what she had done.

Now, he announced distinctly. *Now or never.*

With the hem of her robe, she mopped sweat from her face. Fatigue blurred her sight, so that she could no longer see the pig clearly.

"Have they come yet?" she asked in a whisper. "Are they here?"

I cannot tell, he responded. *Even a pig's senses cannot distinguish between those scents and what we do.*

But it does not matter. Whether they are poised around us or miles away, we must do what we can.

Fern, are you ready?

Because all his fear was hers, she countered, "Are you?"

To her surprise, he filled her mind with laughter. *No*, he admitted, *not ready at all.* Then he repeated, *But it does not matter. For us there is only now or never.*

"Then," she repeated in her turn, "tell me what to do."

Now his instructions were simple. She obeyed them one at a time, as carefully as she could.

The lump of ambergris she divided in two parts, each of which she molded with her fingers until it was shaped like a bowl. Into these bowls she apportioned the powders she had prepared, the mixtures of herbs and dyes and metal. Using Horrik's knife, she pricked at the veins in her forearm until enough blood flowed to moisten the powders. Then quickly, so that nothing spilled, she cupped one bowl over the other to form a ball. With water warmed in a pan at the edge of the fire, she stroked the seam of the ball until the ambergris edges were smeared together and sealed.

Good. Titus studied her hands while she worked as though he were rapt. His breathing had become a hoarse wheeze, and sweat glistened among the bristles on his hide. *The ball. The lard. My water dish. And some means to remove that cookpot from the fire.*

Fern flinched at the thought. The fatal glow of the iron seemed to thrust her back. She was not sure that she could go near enough to the pot to take hold of it.

A shaft of anger and fear broke through Titus' calm; he grunted a curse. But then, grimly, he stilled himself. Reverting to images, he made her see herself taking two brands from her dwindling woodpile and bracing them under the handles of the cookpot to lift it out.

She picked up the brands, set them in front of her beside the half-full water dish, the lard, and the ambergris ball.

The pig stood facing her as though nothing else existed—as though all the world had shrunk down to one lone woman. He had told her more than once to hurry, but now he gave her no instructions, and did not move himself.

Fear crowded her throat. "Titus," she breathed, "why do you delay?"

Like you, he told her, *I am afraid.*

After a moment, he added, *Do you remember your first name for me? It was Mythanks. At the time, I was not amused. But now I consider it a better name than Titus.*

So swiftly that she could not distinguish them, images rang through her head. In one motion, she rose to her feet and dropped the ball into the cookpot.

Ambergris hit the red iron with a scream of scalding wax. But before the ball melted entirely away, she snatched up the lard and poured it also into the pot.

Instantly the smoke and stench of burning fat filled the hovel. The walls seemed to vanish. Tears burst from Fern's eyes. She could no longer see Titus.

She could see his images still, however. They guided her hands to the brands, guided the brands to the cookpot; they made her strong and sure as she lifted out the pot and tilted it to decant its searing contents into the dish.

Gouts of steam spat and blew through the reeking smoke. Nevertheless Titus did not hesitate now. The potion would lose its efficacy as it cooled.

Plunging his snout into the fiery dish, he drank until he could no longer endure the agony. Then he threw back his head and screamed.

Fern cried out at the same instant, wailed, "Titus!" She had never heard such a scream. The pain of cattle was eloquent enough. And pigs could squeal like slaughtered children. But this was worse, far worse. It was the pure anguish of a pig and the utter torment of a man in one, and it seemed to shake the hovel. The walls bowed outward; smoke and stink filled the air with hurt.

And the scream did not stop. Shrill with agony and protest, it splashed like oil into the fire, so that flames blazed to the ceiling. The smoke itself caught fire and began roaring like the core of the sun. Conflagration limned each slat of the walls and roof, etched every scrap and leaf of her pallet against the black dirt. The scream became fire itself. Flames ate at Fern's robe, her face, her hair. In another instant it would devour her, and she would fall to ashes—

But it did not. Instead it seemed to coalesce in front of her. Flames left the walls to flow through the air; flames drained off her and were swept up into the center of the hovel. The fire she had made lost heat. Her pallet ceased burning. Every burst and blaze came together to engulf Titus.

At the same time, another fire burned in Fern's head, as though she, too, were being consumed.

Outside her, beyond her, he stood in the middle of the floor, motionless. Like wax, he melted in the flames. And like wax, he fed the flames, so that they mounted higher while he was consumed. From his pig's body they grew to a pillar which nearly touched the roof. Then the pillar changed shape until it writhed and roiled like a tortured man.

Abruptly he stopped screaming.

The fire went out.

A deep dark closed over Fern. The smoke and stench blinded her with tears; echoes of flame dazzled her. She could see nothing until he took hold of her arms and lifted her to her feet.

Lit by the last embers of her fire, a man stood in the hovel with her.

Clad only in a faint red glow and shadows, he released her arms and stepped back so that she could see him more clearly.

He was tall and strong. Not young—she saw many years in the lines of his face and the color of his beard. Prominent cheekbones hid his eyes in caves of shadow. Beneath a nose like the blade of a hatchet, his mouth was harsh.

Looking at him, she was hardly able to breathe. She knew him without question—he was Titus, the pig who had chosen her, the one she loved—and the sight of him struck her dumb, as though he had stepped out of her dreams to meet her. Was he handsome? To her, he was so handsome that she quailed in front of him.

"Fern," he murmured softly, "oh, my Fern, we have done it." His voice was the voice she had heard in her mind, the voice which had taught her words—the voice which had changed her life. "We have *done* it."

Before she could fall to her knees in hope and love and astonishment, another voice answered him. As hard as the clang of iron, it called out, *"But not in time!"*

"Damnation!" A snarl leaped across Titus' face; embers and silver flashed from his hidden eyes. His strong hands reached out and snatched Fern to him as though he meant to protect her.

In that instant, a bolt like lightning shattered the hovel. Argent power tore the air apart. A concussion too loud for hearing knocked the walls to shards and splinters, and swept them away. Embers and rags scattered as though they had been scoured from the dirt. Fern was only kept on her feet amid the blast by Titus' grasp. She clung to him helplessly while her home ceased to exist.

Then they found themselves with their arms around each other under the open sky at the edge of the village. This was the spot where her hovel had stood, but no sign of it remained: even her iron cookpot had been stricken from the place. Dimmed by glaring coruscation, a few stars winked coldly out of the black heavens.

A circle of fire the color of ice surrounded her and Titus. It blazed and spat from the ground as though it marked the rim of a pit which would open under their feet. At first it was so bright that her abused eyes could not see past it. But gradually she made out figures beyond the white,

crystal fire. On the other side of the ring, she and Titus were also surrounded by men and women on horseback, as well as by the people of
Sarendel-on-Gentle.

She saw Jessup and Yoel there, Veil and Nell and Meglan, Horrik
and Karay, all the folk she had known throughout her life. Only the
children were absent, no doubt commanded to their homes with the best
authority their parents could muster. The strange, chill light seemed to
leech the familiar faces of color; they were as pallid as ghosts. Their eyes
were haunted and abashed, full of shame or fear.

Among them towered the riders. These figures also were spectral in
the icy glow. Nevertheless they masked their fear and betrayed no shame.
Their eyes and mouths showed only anger and determination, an unremitting outrage matched by resolve.

Fern had never seen such men and women before. Their armor and
cloaks and caps, their weapons and apparatus, were outlandish, at once
regal and incomprehensible. Yet she seemed to recognize them as soon
as she caught sight of them. There was Prince Chorl—there, with the
blunt forehead, the circlet in his curling hair, and the beard like a breast-
plate. He was accompanied by his lords and minions, as well as by his
daughter Florice—her plain riding habit, wild hair, and undefended
visage made her unmistakable. And among the others were Andovale's
masters of magic, come to carry out the judgment of the council against
one of their own.

All of them had ridden here for no reason except that the people of
Sarendel had squirmed when Destrier had asked them about change. And
those people had squirmed because they had known of a change which
they had not wished to name. Out of loyalty or pity, they had declined
to mention that she, Fern, had been adopted by a pig none of them had
ever seen before. And yet their very desire to protect Fern had betrayed
the man who now held her in his arms. He was snared in this circle by
his enemies because of her.

She did not ask how she knew such things. She knew a great deal
which had been vague to her before: the fire which had transformed Titus
had altered her in some way as well. Or perhaps in his desperation for
her help he had altered her more than he intended. She made connections

easily, as though the pathways of new understanding had been burned clear in her brain.

One among the riders was fiercer than the others; his rage shone more hotly. He lacked the sorrow which moderated Prince Chorl's anger. Alone of the warlocks—the men who bore apparatus and periapts instead of arms were surely warlocks—he rode at his Prince's side, opposite Florice. He appeared to command the ring of riders as much as the Prince did.

"So, Suriman," this warlock barked across the fire, "you are caught again—and damned as much for new crimes as for old. How you escaped us to work your evil here, I do not fully understand. But we are prepared to be certain that you do not escape again."

Suriman? Fern thought. Suriman?

The man in her arms loosened his embrace so that he could bow. If he felt any dismay at his nakedness, he did not deign to show it. His lips grinned sardonically over his teeth, and silver glinted like a threat in his eye. "My lord Prince." His voice was as clear and harsh as the night. "My lady. Titus. You are fortunate to catch me. In another hour I would have been beyond the worst that you can do."

Fern felt a pang around her heart. "Titus?" she asked aloud. Connections twisted through her, as ghostly and fatal as the riders. "You said *your* name was Titus."

"He is called Suriman because we do not speak his name," the warlock barked. "I am Titus. If he told you his name is mine, that is only one lie among many."

"Titus?" Fern asked again. Surrounded by cold fire, she sounded small and lost. Ignoring the warlock, she faced the man who had been her pig. Unprotected from the cold, he had begun to shiver slightly. "Titus?"

He did not look at her; his gaze held the Prince and the warlock. When he spoke, his voice cut like a whip. "Her name is Fern, Titus. You will address her as 'my lady.' Regardless of your contempt for me, you will show her courtesy."

Fern flung a glance at this unfamiliar Titus in time to see him flinch involuntarily. All the power here was his—and still he feared his enemy.

Prince Chorl lifted his head. His eyes were as deep as the night. "Show her courtesy yourself, Suriman. Answer her."

For a moment, the man hesitated. But then, slowly, he turned in Fern's grasp so that he could face her. Again his eyes were hidden away in shadows. Yet he seemed abashed by her needy stare, as if he were more vulnerable to her than to any of the circled riders.

Tightly, he said, "I am Suriman."

She could not still the pain twisting in her. "Then why did you teach me to call you Titus?"

His brows knotted. "I feared such stories as the Roadman told. I thought that if I gave myself another's name I was less likely to be betrayed—and what name would protect me more than the name of the man who most wished me dead? But I misjudged you, my Fern. I misjudged your willingness. If I had known then what you are now, I would have risked the truth."

At his words, anger stirred the ring. Flames of ice leaped higher, as though the warlocks fed them with outrage. And Titus cried in a loud voice, "*Willingness?* She is not *willing*. She is a *half-wit*—the poorest and most destitute person in all the Rift. These folk love her—they do not speak against her—but at least one of them has told us what he knows."

Fern did not doubt that this was Jessup. The other villagers ached to have no part in her downfall. Yet they could not turn away. Fire and fury held them.

"We can surmise the rest," Titus continued. "She had no *choice*, Suriman. You took her life from her without her consent. You altered her for your own purposes, not knowing and not caring what she wished or desired. She is not willing because she chose *nothing*."

Suriman did not shift his gaze from Fern. She felt the appeal in his eyes, although she could not see them.

"That is false," he said softly. "She is willing because she *is*, not because I made her so. She was willing when I found her. She loves pigs, and I was a pig. She would have given her life for me from the first moment she saw me."

Then the Prince's daughter spoke for the first time. In a voice made old by too much weeping, she protested, "But *I* was not willing. When you first asked to wed me, I knew your evil. I told my father of it as best I could. You did not heed that, or anything I might have desired for myself. Now I crave you, I cannot stop desiring you, and I chose none of it.

"Was that not a crime, Suriman? Have you not betrayed me? Tell me that you have not betrayed me."

Like Suriman's fire, Florice's pain burned through Fern, making new connections.

He turned to face this accuser. "I did not betray you, my lady," he answered. He seemed to hold the lords and warlocks at bay with harshness. To Fern, he looked strong enough for that. "I failed you. The distinction is worth making. If I had not failed, you would have craved me utterly. Prince Chorl would have lost a half-wit daughter, and all Andovale would have gained a great lady. You would have been as willing as my Fern is now, and you would have regretted nothing.

"It was my folly that I could not win your father's trust—and his that he asked this Titus to act in his name."

Titus reared back to launch a retort, but Fern stopped him by raising her hand. All her attention was focused on Suriman; she hardly noticed that Titus had stopped, or that all the ring fell silent as though she were a figure of power.

"I was not willing."

Suriman swung back toward her like a man stung. "Not?" The word was almost a cry.

If she could have seen his eyes, she might have told him, Do not be afraid. I must say this, or else I will say nothing. But they remained shadowed, unreadable. She knew nothing about him except what he had chosen to reveal.

"You made me a beggar." Her voice shook with fright; she felt overwhelmed by her own littleness in the face of these potent men and women. Yet she did not falter. "Oh, I helped you willingly enough. As you say, I love pigs. But in all my life I have taken nothing that was not mine. That shamed me."

"We would have died!" he countered at once, urgently. "You lacked the means to keep us alive. It is not a crime to ask for help—or to need it. Do you think less of me because I came to you when I was in need?"

She shook her head. "But Jessup did not choose to feed us the second time. The children did not choose to feed us. You chose for them. You cast images into their minds which they did not understand and so could not refuse. You made me a thief."

"A thief?" Suriman sounded incredulous—and daunted. "You stole nothing!"

"But I lived on stolen things. I grew healthy and comfortable on stolen things. The fault is yours—but you feel no shame, and so the shame is mine."

"What are you saying?" His voice came close to cracking. "You did not know the food was stolen because you could not comprehend it." He had another nakedness, which signified more than his lack of garments. "It was beyond your abilities to see consequences which did not take place before your eyes—and you could not remember them when they were past.

"I do not say this in scorn, Fern. You simply were not able to understand. And now you are. I have given you that. You accuse me of a fault which would have meant nothing to you if I had not given you the capacity to see it."

His need touched her so deeply that tears came to her eyes, and the ring of fire blurred against the dark night. And still she did not falter.

"But you could see it," she replied. "You knew all that I did not, and more besides. You knew me—you saw into my mind. You saw the things which shamed me. And yet you caused the children of this village to go thieving for my benefit."

As though she had pushed him beyond his endurance, he snapped back, "Fern, I was *desperate*. I was a *pig*, in hell's name! If I did not die on the road to be devoured by dogs, I would be slaughtered in the village to be eaten by clods and fools!"

At the same time, she heard his voice in her mind, as she had heard it so often when he could not speak.

Fern, I implore you.

"So is the lady Florice desperate," she answered him. "So am I."

Florice could no longer keep silent. "Yes, desperate, Suriman—as desperate as you were. I am desperate for you, though it breaks my heart. But more than that, I am desperate to understand.

"What is this *willingness* you prize so highly? Why must you extract it from women who can neither comprehend nor refuse? You do not desire us as women—you desire only tools, subjects for research. Why must you make us to be more than we were, when what you wish is that we should be less?"

Suriman did not turn from Fern. He concentrated on her as though the circle of riders and villagers and fire had ceased to have any import. When he responded to Florice, his words were addressed to Fern.

"Because, my lady, no woman but a half-wit is able to give herself truly. You say I do not desire you as women, but I do. If I had not failed, you would have lost your flaws—the limitations which prevent you from sharing my dreams and designs—but you would have retained your open heart, your loveliness of form and spirit.

"If that is a crime, then I am guilty of it." Finality and fear ached in his tone. "Do what you came to do, or leave me be. I am defenseless against you."

At the same time, his silent voice said beseechingly, *Oh, my Fern, tell me I have not failed.*

"We will," Titus announced loudly. And Prince Chorl echoed, more in sorrow than in anger, "We will.

"I care nothing for your protests or justifications, Suriman," the Prince continued. "We are not here to pass judgment. That has been done. Our purpose is only to see you dead."

"Dead," the warlocks pronounced. "Finally and forever."

"Yes," growled the lords and minions on their mounts.

The silver fire leaped up, encircling Suriman more tightly.

"Do not harm Fern!" a farmwife cried out. It was Meglan. Fern could no longer see her: all the villagers were hidden by flames of ice. "She has done nothing wrong!" Then, abashed by her own audacity, she pleaded more quietly, "My lords and ladies, if you say that he is evil and must die, we do not protest. We have no knowledge of these matters. But she is ours. There is no harm in her. Surely you will not hold her to account for his crimes?"

Titus might have answered, but Prince Chorl stopped him with a gesture. "Good woman," he replied to Meglan, "that is for her to say. Until now, she has made no choices. Here she will choose for herself.

"My lady Fern," the Prince said across the fire, "the warlock at your side is condemned for precisely such crimes as he has committed against you. Knowing what he has done, and having heard his answers, would you stand between him and his punishment? Or will you stand aside?"

Fern had been changed by fire. Even now, she could not stop making connections which had never occurred to her before. She had said what she must: that was done. Now she took the next step.

Letting go of Suriman, she backed away.

"No!" At the sight of her withdrawal, he flinched and crouched down as though his destruction had already begun; he covered his face with his hands. Spasms of cold shook and twisted his naked limbs.

To abandon him wrung her heart. Softly, so that he only might hear her, she murmured, "My thanks."

He must have heard her. A moment later, he lowered his arms and drew himself erect. For the first time in the ring of fire, she saw his eyes clearly—the one almost blind, the other marred by a slice of silver. Shivers mounted through him, then receded. He could not smile, but his voice was gentle as he said, "I regret nothing. You were worth the risk. You have not asked me what loveliness is—in that I was wrong, as in so many other things—but still I will tell you.

"It is you."

Because he did not try to compel her with images or colors or supplications, Fern answered, "Yes."

"*Suriman!*" Florice wailed in despair.

She was too late. The masters of magic had already raised their periapts and apparatus, summoned their powers. In silence the white fire raged abruptly into the heavens: mutely the flames towered over the ring and then crashed inward, falling like ruin upon the warlock.

He did not scream now, as he had when he was transformed. The force mustered against him surpassed sound. As voiceless as the conflagration, he writhed in brief agony while retribution and cold searched him to the marrow of his bones, the pit of his chest, the gulf of his skull.

Then he was lifted out of the circle in a swirl of white embers and ash. The fire burned him down to dust, which the dark swallowed away. Soon nothing remained of him except the riders in their triumph, the shocked faces of the villagers, and Florice's last wail.

As though bereft of language, images, and will, Fern sprawled on the ground with her face hidden in her arms. Her heart beat, her lungs took air. But she could not speak or rise or uncover her face—or she would not. At Prince Chorl's bidding, two of his minions and one of the warlocks came forward to offer their assistance. Meglan, Karay, and others had already run to Fern's side, however, and they spurned help. Unexpectedly dignified in the face of lords and magic, Meglan farmwife said, "She is ours. We will care for her."

"I understand," said the Prince sadly. "But I give you this promise. At any time, in any season, if you desire help for her, only send to me, and I will do everything I can."

"And I," Florice added through her grief. "I promise also."

Titus was too full of fierceness and vindication to find his voice; yet he nodded a promise of his own.

When the riders were gone, Meglan and the others lifted Fern in their arms. Like a cortege, they bore her to Wall's house, where a clean room with a bed and blankets was made ready for her. There she was comforted and cosseted as she had once cared for Sarendel's pigs. Unlike the pigs, however, she did not respond. She lay with her face covered—as far as anyone knew, she slept with her face covered. And before dawn, she left the house. Meglan searched for her, but to no avail, until the farmwife thought to look out toward the refuse-tip beyond her garden.

There she saw Fern scavenging.

After Meglan had wept for a time, she bustled out to the village. She told what she had seen; men and women with good hearts—and no knowledge of warlocks—heard her. Before Fern returned from her scavenging, a new shed had been erected on the exact spot of her former hovel. A new curtain swung as a door; a new pallet lay against one wall; new bowls and cups sat on the pallet. And the bowls were full of corn and carrots, cured ham and bread.

Fern did not seem surprised to find her hovel whole. Perhaps she had forgotten that it was gone. Yet the sight of Meglan and Horrik, Veil and Salla, Karay and Yoel standing there to greet her appeared to frighten her. With a familiar alarm which the village itself had forgotten, she cowered at the nearest hedge, peering through her hair as though she feared what would happen if she were noticed.

In rue and shame, the villagers left the hovel, pretending that they had not noticed her. At once she took the fruits of her scavenging inside and closed the curtain.

From that moment onward, her life in Sarendel-on-Gentle became much the same as it had been before she had been adopted by a pig. From dawn to dusk she roamed the village refuse-tips and the surrounding hills, scavenging scraps and herbs, and storing them against the coming winter. The changes which marked her days were few—and no one spoke of them. First out of kindness, then out of habit, Sarendel's folk gave her as many gifts as she would accept. The children learned to ignore her; but if any of the younger ones thought to tease or torment her, the older ones put a quick stop to it. As the days became fortnights, even Horrik forgot that he had once desired her. And she no longer seemed to know or care anything about pigs. Her love for them had been lost among the stars and the cold white fire. By slow degrees the present became so like the past that men and women shook their heads incredulously to think the continuity had ever been disturbed.

In this way she regained the peace and safety which had been lost to her.

If the villagers had looked more closely, however—if Fern had worn her mud-thick and straggling hair away from her face, or if she had not ducked her head to avoid meeting anyone's gaze—they might have noticed one other change.

Since the night when she had transformed her only love from a pig to a man, just in time to see him caught and taken by his doom, one of her eyes had grown warmer, brighter, belying her renewed destitution. The other bore a strange mark across the iris, a thin argent scar, as though her sight had been cut by silver.

What Makes
Us Human

Aster's Hope stood more than a hundred meters tall—a perfect sphere bristling with vanes, antennae, and scanners, punctuated with laser ports, viewscreens, and receptors. She left her orbit around her home-world like a steel ball out of a slingshot, her sides bright in the pure sunlight of the solar system. Accelerating toward her traveling speed of .85c, she moved past the outer planets—first Philomel with its gigantic streaks of raw, cold hydrogen, then lonely Periwinkle glimmering at the edge of the spectrum—on her way into the black and luminous beyond. She was the best her people had ever made, the best they knew how to make. She had to be: she wasn't coming back for centuries.

There were exactly three hundred ninety-two people aboard.

They, too, were the best Aster had to offer. Diplomats and meditechs, linguists, theoretical biologists, physicists, scholars, even librarians for the vast banks of knowledge *Aster's Hope* carried: all of them had been trained to the teeth especially for this mission. And they included the absolute cream of Aster's young Service, the so-called "puters" and "nicians" who knew how to make *Aster's Hope* sail the fine-grained winds of the galaxy. Three hundred ninety-two people in all, culled and tested and prepared from the whole population of the planet to share in the culmination of Aster's history.

Three hundred ninety of them were asleep.

The other two were supposed to be taking care of the ship. But they weren't. They were running naked down a mid-shell corridor between the clean, impersonal chambers where the cryogenic capsules hugged their occupants. Temple was giggling because she knew Gracias was never going to catch her unless she let him. He still had some of the ice cream she'd spilled on him trickling through the hair on his chest, but if she didn't slow down he wasn't going to be able to do anything about it. Maybe she wasn't smarter or stronger than he was, better-trained or higher-ranking—but she was certainly faster.

This was their duty shift, the week they would spend out of their capsules every half-year until they died. *Aster's Hope* carried twenty-five shifts from the Service, and they were the suicide personnel of this mission: aging at the rate of one week twice every year, none of them were expected to live long enough to see the ship's return home. Everyone else could be spared until *Aster's Hope* reached its destination; frozen for the whole trip, they would arrive only a bit more mature than they were when they left. But the Service had to maintain the ship. And so the planners of the mission had been forced to a difficult decision: either fill *Aster's Hope* entirely with puters and nicians, and pray that they would be able to do the work of diplomats, theoretical physicists, and linguists; or sacrifice a certain number of Service personnel to make room for people who could be explicitly trained for the mission. The planners decided that the ability to take *Aster's Hope* apart chip by chip and seal after seal and then put her all back together again was enough expertise to ask of any individual man or woman. Therefore the mission itself would have to be entrusted to other experts.

And therefore *Aster's Hope* would be unable to carry enough puters and nicians to bring the mission home again.

Faced with this dilemma, the Service personnel were naturally expected to spend a significant period of each duty shift trying to reproduce. If they had children, they could pass on their knowledge and skill.

And if the children were born soon enough, they would be old enough to take *Aster's Hope* home when she needed them.

Temple and Gracias weren't particularly interested in having children. But they took every other aspect of reproduction very seriously.

She slowed down for a few seconds, just to tantalize him. Then she put on a burst of speed. He tended to be just a bit dull in his love-making—and even in his conversation—unless she made a special effort to get his heart pounding. On some days, a slow, comfortable, and just-a-bit-dull lover was exactly what she wanted. But not today. Today she was full of energy from the tips of her toes to the ends of her hair, and she wanted Gracias at his best.

But when she tossed a laughing look back over her shoulder to see how he was doing, he wasn't behind her anymore.

Where—? Well, good. He was trying to take control of the race. Win by tricking her because he couldn't do it with speed. Temple laughed out loud while she paused to catch her breath and think. Obviously, he had ducked into one of the rooms or passages off this corridor, looking for a way to shortcut ahead of her—or maybe to lure her into ambush. And she hadn't heard the automatic door open and close because she'd been running and breathing too hard. Very good! This was the Gracias she wanted.

But where had he turned off? Not the auxiliary compcom: that room didn't have any other exit. How about the nearest capsule chamber? From there, he'd have to shaft down to inner-shell and come back up. That would be dicey: he'd have to guess how far and fast, and in what direction, she was moving. Which gave her a chance to turn the tables on him.

With a grin, she went for the door to the next capsule chamber. Sensing her approach, it opened with a nearly silent *whoosh*, then closed behind her. Familiar with the look of the cryogenic capsules huddled in the grasp of their triple-redundant support machinery, each one independently supplied and run so that no systemwide failure could wipe out the mission, she hardly glanced around her as she headed toward the shaft.

Its indicators showed that it wasn't in use. So Gracias wasn't on his way up here. Perfect. She'd take the shaft up to outer-shell and elude him there, just to whet his appetite. Turn his own gambit against him. Pleased with herself, she approached the door of the shaft.

But when she impinged on the shaft's sensor, it didn't react to her. None of the lights came on: the elevator stayed where it was. Surprised, she put her whole body in front of the sensor. Nothing. She jumped up and down, waved her arms. Still nothing.

That was strange. When Gracias had run his diagnostics this morning, the only malfunction anywhere was in an obscure circuit of food-sup's beer synthesizer. And she'd already helped him fix it. Why wasn't the shaft operating?

Thinking she ought to go to the next room and try another shaft, find out how serious the problem was, Temple trotted back to the capsule-chamber door.

This time, it didn't open for her.

That was so unexpected that she ran into the door—which startled more than hurt her. In her nearly thirty years, she had never seen an automatic door fail. All doors opened except locked doors; and locked doors had an exterior status light no one could miss. Yet the indicators for this door showed open and normal.

She tried again.

The door didn't open.

That wasn't just strange. It was serious. A severe malfunction. Which didn't show up on diagnostics? Or had it just now happened? Either way, it was time to stop playing. *Aster's Hope* needed help. Frowning, Temple looked for the nearest speaker so she could call Gracias and tell him what was going on.

It was opposite her, on the wall beside the shaft. She started toward it.

Before she got there, the door to the chamber slid open.

A nonchalant look on his dark face, a tuneless whistle puckering his mouth, Gracias came into the room. He was carrying a light sleeping pallet over one shoulder. The door closed behind him normally.

"Going somewhere?" he asked in a tone of casual curiosity.

Temple knew that look, that tone. In spite of herself, she gave him a wide grin. "Damn you all to pieces," she remarked. "How did you do that?"

He shrugged, trying to hide the sparkle in his eyes. "Nothing to it.

Auxcompcom's right over there." He nodded in the direction of the comp-command room she had passed. "Ship motion sensors knew where you were. Saw you come in here. Did a temporary repro. Told the comp not to react to any body mass smaller than mine. You're stuck in here for another hour."

"You ought to be ashamed." She couldn't stop grinning. His ploy delighted her. "That's the most irresponsible thing I've ever heard. If the other puters spend their time doing repros, the comp won't be good for alphabet soup by the time we get where we're going."

He didn't quite meet her happy gaze. "Too late now." Still pretending he was nonchalant—in spite of some obvious evidence to the contrary—he put the pallet on the floor in front of him. "Stuck here for another hour." Then he did look at her, his black eyes smoldering. "Don't want to waste it."

She made an effort to sound exasperated. "Idiot." But she practically jumped into his arms when he gave her the chance.

They were still doing their duty when the ship's brapper sounded and the comp snapped *Aster's Hope* onto emergency alert.

————————

Temple and Gracias were, respectively, the nician and puter of their duty shift. The Service had trained them for their jobs almost from birth. They had access, both by education and through the comp, to the best knowledge Aster had evolved, the best resources her planners and builders had been able to cram into *Aster's Hope*. In some ways, they were the pinnacle of Aster's long climb toward the future: they represented, more surely than any of the diplomats or librarians, what the Asterins had been striving toward for two thousand years.

But the terms themselves, *nician* and *puter*, were atavisms, pieces of words left over from before the Crash—sounds which had become at once magic and nonsense during the period of inevitable barbarism that had followed the Crash. Surviving legends spoke of the puters and nicians who had piloted the great colonization ship *Aster* across the galactic void from Earth, light-years measured in hundreds or thousands from the homeworld of the human race. In *Aster*, as in all the great ships which

Earth had sent out to preserve humankind from some now-forgotten crisis, most of the people had rested frozen through the centuries of space-normal travel while the nicians and puters had spent their lives and died, generation after generation, to keep the ship safe and alive as the comp and its scanners hunted the heavens for some world where *Aster*'s sleepers could live.

It was a long and heroic task, that measureless vigil of the men and women who ran the ship. In one sense, they succeeded; for when *Aster* came to her last resting place it was on the surface of a planet rich in compatible atmosphere and vegetation but almost devoid of competitive fauna. The planet's sun was only a few degrees hotter than Sol; its gravity, only a fraction heavier. The people who found their way out of cryogenic sleep onto the soil and hope of the new world had reason to count themselves fortunate.

But in another sense the nicians and puters failed. While most of her occupants slept, *Aster* had been working for hundreds or thousands of years—and entropy was immutable. Parts of the ship broke down. The puters and nicians made repairs. Other parts broke down and were fixed. And then *Aster* began to run low on supplies and equipment. The parts that broke down were fixed at the expense of other parts. The nicians and puters kept their ship alive by nothing more in the end than sheer ingenuity and courage. But they couldn't keep her from crashing.

The Crash upset everything the people of Earth had planned for the people of *Aster*. The comp was wrecked, its memory banks irretrievable, useless. Fires destroyed what physical books the ship carried. The pieces of equipment which survived tended to be ones which couldn't be kept running without access to an ion generator and couldn't be repaired without the ability to manufacture microchips. *Aster*'s engines had flared out under the strain of bringing her bulk down through the atmosphere and were cold forever.

Nearly nine hundred men and women survived the Crash, but they had nothing to keep themselves alive with except the knowledge and determination they carried in their own heads.

That the descendants of those pioneers survived to name their planet Aster—to make it yield up first a life and then a future—to dream of the stars and spaceflight and Earth—was a tribute more to their determination than to their knowledge. A significant portion of what they knew was of no conceivable value. The descendants of the original puters and nicians knew how to run *Aster*; but the theoretical questions involved in how she had run were scantly understood. And none of those personnel had been trained to live in what was essentially a jungle. As for the sleepers: according to legend, a full ten percent of them had been politicians. And another twenty percent had been people the politicians deemed essential—secretaries, press officers, security guards, even cosmeticians. That left barely six hundred individuals who were accustomed to living in some sort of contact with reality.

And yet they found a way to endure.

First they survived. By experimentation (some of it fatal), they learned to distinguish edible from inedible vegetation; they remembered enough about the importance of fire to procure some from *Aster*'s remains before the wreckage burned itself out; they organized themselves enough to assign responsibilities.

Later they persisted. They found rocks and chipped them sharp in order to work with the vegetation; they made clothing out of leaves and the skins of smaller animals; they taught themselves how to weave shelter; they kept their population going.

Next they struggled. After all, what good did it do them to have a world if they couldn't fight over it?

And eventually they began to reinvent the knowledge they had lost.

The inhabitants of Aster considered all this a slow process. From their point of view, it seemed to take an exceptionally long time. But judged by the way planetary civilizations usually evolved, Asterin history moved with considerable celerity. Five hundred years after the Crash, Aster's people had remembered the wheel. (Some theorists argued that the wheel had never actually been forgotten. But to be useful it needed someplace to roll—and Aster was a jungle. For several centuries, no wheel could compare in value with a good ax. Old memories of the wheel failed to take hold until after the Asterins had cleared enough ground to make its value apparent.) A thousand years after the wheel, the printing press came back into existence. (One of the major problems the Asterins had throughout their history to this point was what to do with all the dead lumber they created by making enough open space for their towns, fields, and roads. The reappearance of paper offered only a trivial solution until the printing press came along.) And five hundred years after the printing press, *Aster's Hope* was ready for her mission. Although they didn't know it, the people of Aster had beaten Earth's time for the same development by several thousand years.

Determination had a lot to do with it. People who came so far from Earth in order to procure the endurance of the human race didn't look kindly on anything that was less than what they wanted. But determination required an object: people had to know what they wanted. The alternative was a history full of wars, since determined people who didn't know what they wanted tended to be unnecessarily aggressive.

That object—the dream which shaped Asterin life and civilization from the earliest generations, the inborn sense of common purpose and yearning which kept the wars short, caused people to share what they knew, and inspired progress—was provided by the legends of Earth and *Aster.*

Within two generations of the Crash, no one knew even vaguely where Earth was: the knowledge as well as the tools of astrogation had been lost. Two generations after that, it was no longer clear what Earth had been like. And after two more generations, the reality of space-flight had begun to pass out of the collective Asterin imagination.

But the *ideas* endured.

Earth.

Aster.

Nicians and puters.

Cold sleep.

On Aster perhaps more than anywhere else in the galaxy, dreams provided the stuff of purpose. Aster evolved a civilization driven by legends. Communally and individually, the images and passions which fired the mind during physical sleep became the goals which shaped the mind while it was awake.

To rediscover Earth.

And go back.

For centuries, of course, this looked like nonsense. If it had been a conscious choice rather than a planetary dream, it would have been discarded long ago. But since it was a dream, barely articulate except in poetry and painting and the secret silence of the heart, it held on until its people were ready for it.

Until, that is, the Asterins had reinvented radio telescopes and other receiving gear of sufficient sophistication to begin interpreting the signals they heard from the heavens.

Some of those signals sounded like they came from Earth.

This was a remarkable achievement. After all, the transmissions the Asterins were looking at hadn't been intended for Aster. (Indeed, they may not have been intended for anybody at all. It was far more likely that these signals were random emissions—the detritus, perhaps, of a world talking to itself and its planets.) They had been traveling for so long, had passed through so many different gravity wells on the way, and were so diffuse, that not even the wildest optimist in Aster's observatories could argue these signals were messages. In fact, they were scarcely more than whispers in the ether, sighs compared to which some of the more distant stars were shouting.

And yet, impelled by an almost unacknowledged dream, the Asterins had developed equipment which enabled them not only to hear those whispers, sort them out of the cosmic radio cacophony, and make some surprisingly acute deductions about what (or who) caused them, but also to identify a possible source on the star charts.

The effect on Aster was galvanic. In simple terms, the communal dream came leaping suddenly out of the unconscious.

Earth. EARTH.

After that, it was only a matter of minutes before somebody said, "We ought to try to go there."

Which was exactly—a hundred years and an enormous expenditure of global resources, time, knowledge, and determination later—what *Aster's Hope* was doing.

Naturally enough, people being what they were, there were quite a few men and women on Aster who didn't believe in the mission. And there were also a large number who did believe, who still had enough common sense or native pessimism to be cautious. As a result, there was a large planetwide debate while *Aster's Hope* was being planned and built. Some people insisted on saying things like, "What if it isn't Earth at all? What if it's some alien planet where they don't know humanity from bat dung and don't care?"

Or, "At this distance, your figures aren't accurate within ten parsecs. How do you propose to compensate for that?"

Or, "What if the ship encounters someone else along the way? Finding intelligent life might be even more important than finding Earth. Or they might not like having our ship wander into their space. They might blow *Aster's Hope* to pieces—and then come looking for us."

Or, of course, "What if the ship gets all the way out there and doesn't find anything at all?"

Well, even the most avid proponent of the mission was able to admit that it would be unfortunate if *Aster's Hope* were to run a thousand light-years across the galaxy and then fail. So the planning and preparation spent on designing the ship and selecting and training the crew was prodigious. But the Asterins didn't actually start to build their ship until they found an answer to what they considered the most fundamental question about the mission.

On perhaps any other inhabited planet in the galaxy, that question would have been the question of speed. A thousand light-years was too far away. Some way of traveling faster than the speed of light was necessary. But the Asterins had a blind spot. They knew from legend that their ancestors had *slept* during a centuries-long, space-normal voyage; and they were simply unable to think realistically about traveling in any other way. They learned, as Earth had millennia ago, that *c* was a theoretical absolute limit: they believed it and turned their attention in other directions.

No, the question which troubled them was safety. They wanted to be able to send out *Aster's Hope* certain that no passing hostile, meteor shower, or accident of diplomacy would be able to destroy her.

So she wasn't built until a poorly paid instructor at an obscure university suddenly managed to make sense out of a field of research that people had been laughing at for years: c-vector.

For people who hadn't done their homework in theoretical mathematics or abstract physics, *c-vector* was defined as *at right angles to the speed of light*. Which made no sense to anyone—but that didn't stop the Asterins from having fun with it. Before long, they discovered that they could build a generator to project a c-vector field.

If that field were projected around an object, it formed an impenetrable shield—a screen against which bullets and laser cannon and hydrogen torpedoes had no effect. (Any projectile or force which hit the shield bounced away "at right angles to the speed of light" and ceased to exist in material space. When this was discovered, several scientists spent several years wondering if a c-vector field could somehow be used as a faster-than-light drive for a spaceship. But no one was able to figure out just what direction "at right angles to the speed of light" was.) This appeared to have an obvious use as a weapon—project a field at an object, watch the object disappear—until the researchers learned that the field couldn't be projected either at or around any object unless the object and the field generator were stationary in relation to each other. But fortunately the c-vector field had an even more obvious application for the men and women who were planning *Aster's Hope*.

If the ship were equipped with c-vector shields, she would be safe from any disaster short of direct collision with a star. And if she were equipped with a c-vector self-destruct, Aster would be safe from any disaster which might happen to—or be caused by—the crew of *Aster's Hope*.

Construction on the ship commenced almost immediately.

And eventually it was finished. The linguists and biologists and physicists were trained. The meditechs and librarians were equipped. The diplomats were instructed. Each of the nician and puter teams knew how to take *Aster's Hope* down to her microchips and rebuild (not to mention repro) her from spare parts.

Leaving orbit, setting course, building up speed, the ship arced past Philomel and Periwinkle on her way into the galactic void of the future. For the Asterins, it was as if legends had come back to life—as if a dream crouching in the human psyche since before the Crash had stood up and become real.

But six months later, roughly .4 light-years from Aster, Temple and Gracias weren't thinking about legends. They didn't see themselves as protectors of a dream. When the emergency brapper went off, they did what any dedicated, well-trained, and quick-thinking Service personnel would have done: they panicked.

But while they panicked they ran naked as children in the direction of the nearest auxcompcom.

In crude terms, the difference between nician and puter was the difference between hardware and software—although there was quite a bit of overlap, of course. Temple made equipment work: Gracias told it what to do. It would've taken her hours to figure out how to do what he'd done to the door sensors. But when they heard the brapper and rolled off the pallet with her ahead of him and headed out of the capsule chamber, and the door didn't open, he was the one who froze.

"Damn," he muttered. "That repro won't cancel for another twenty minutes."

He looked like he was thinking something abusive about himself, so she snapped at him, "Hold it open for me, idiot."

He thudded a palm against his forehead. "Right."

Practically jumping into range of the sensor, he got the door open; and she passed him on her way out into the corridor. But she had to wait for him again at the auxcompcom door. "Come on. Come *on*," she fretted. "Whatever that brapper means, it isn't good."

"I know." Leftover sweat made his face slick, gave him a look of too much fear. Grimly, he pushed through the sensor field into the auxcompcom room and headed for his chair at the main com console.

Temple followed, jumped into her seat in front of her hardware controls. But for a few seconds neither of them looked at their buttons and readouts. They were fixed on the main screen above the consoles.

The ship's automatic scanners showed a blip against the deep background of the stars. Even at this distance, Temple and Gracias didn't need the comp to tell them the dot of light on the phosphors of the screen was moving. They could see it by watching the stars recede as the scanners focused on the blip.

It was coming toward them.

It was coming fast.

"An asteroid?" Temple asked mostly to hear somebody say something. The comp was supposed to put *Aster's Hope* on emergency alert whenever it sensed a danger of collision with an object large enough to be significant.

"Oh, sure." Gracias poked his blunt fingers around his board, punching readouts up onto the other auxcompcom screens. Numbers and schematics flashed. "If asteroids change course."

"Change—?"

"Just did an adjustment," he confirmed. "Coming right at us. Also"— he pointed at a screen to her left—"decelerating."

She stared at the screen, watched the numbers jump. Numbers were his department; he was faster at them than she was. But she knew what words meant. "Then it's a ship."

Gracias acted like he hadn't heard her. He was watching the screens as if he were close to apoplexy.

"That doesn't make sense," she went on. "If there are ships this close to Aster, why haven't we heard from them? We should've picked up their transmissions. They should've heard us. God knows we've been broadcasting enough noise for the past couple of centuries. Are we hailing it?"

"We're hailing," he said. "No answer." He paused for a second, then announced, "Estimated about three times our size." He sounded stunned. Carefully, he said, "The comp estimates it's decelerating from above the speed of light."

She couldn't help herself. "That's impossible," she snapped. "Your eyes are tricking you. Check it again."

He hit some more buttons, and the numbers on the screen twisted themselves into an extrapolation graph. Whatever it was, the oncoming ship was still moving faster than *Aster's Hope*—and it was still decelerating.

For a second, she put her hands over her face, squeezed the heels of her palms against her temples. Her pulse felt like she was going into adrenaline overload. But this was what she'd been trained for. Abruptly, she dropped her arms and looked at the screens again. The blip was still coming, but the graph hadn't changed.

From above the speed of light. Even though the best Asterin scientists had always said that was impossible.

Oh, well, she muttered to herself. One more law of nature down the tubes. Easy come, easy go.

"Why don't they contact us?" she asked. "If we're aware of them, they must know we're here."

"Don't need to," Gracias replied through his concentration. "Been scanning us since they hit space-normal speed. The comp reports scanner probes everywhere. Strong enough to take your blood pressure." Then he stiffened, sat up straighter, spat a curse. "Probes are trying to break into the comp."

Temple gripped the arms of her seat. This was his department; she was helpless. "Can they do it? Can you stop them?"

"Encryption's holding them out." He studied his readouts, flicked his eyes past the screens. "Won't last. Take com."

Without waiting for an answer, he keyed his console to hers and got out of his seat. Quickly, he went to the other main console in the room, the comp repro board.

Feeling clumsy now as she never did when she was working with tools or hardware, she accepted com and began trying to monitor the readouts. But the numbers swam, and the prompts didn't seem to make sense. Operating in emergency mode, the comp kept asking her to ask it questions; but she couldn't think of any for it. Instead, she asked Gracias, "What're you doing?"

His hands stabbed up and down the console. He was still sweating. "Changing the encryption," he said. "Whole series of changes. Putting them on a loop." When he was done, he took a minute to double-check his repro. Then he gave a grunt of satisfaction and came back to his com seat. While he keyed his controls away from Temple, he said, "This way, the comp can't be broken by knowing the present code. Have to know what code's coming up next. That loop changes often enough to keep us safe for a while."

She permitted herself a sigh of relief—and a soft snarl of anger at the oncoming ship. She didn't like feeling helpless. "If those bastards can't break the comp, do you think they'll try to contact us?"

He shrugged, glanced at his board. "Channels are open. They talk, we'll hear." For a second, he chewed his lower lip. Then he leaned back in his seat and swung around to face her. His eyes were dark with fear.

"Don't like this," he said distinctly. "Don't like it at all. A faster-than-light ship coming straight for us. Straight for Aster. And they don't talk. Instead, they try to break the comp."

She knew his fear. She was afraid herself. But when he looked like he needed her, she put her own feelings aside. "Would you say," she said, drawling so she would sound sardonic and calm, "that we're being approached by somebody hostile?"

He nodded dumbly.

"Well, we're safe enough. Maybe the speed of light isn't unbreakable, but a c-vector shield is. So what we have to worry about is Aster. If that ship gets past us, we'll never catch up with it. How far away is it now?"

Gracias turned back to his console, called up some numbers. "Five minutes." His face didn't show it, but she could hear in his voice that he was grateful for her show of steadiness.

"I don't think we should wait to see what happens," she said. "We should send a message home now."

"Right." He went to work immediately, composing data on the screens, calling up the scant history of *Aster's Hope*'s contact with the approaching ship. "Continuous broadcast," he murmured as he piped information to the transmitters. "Constant update. Let Aster know everything we can."

Temple nodded her approval, then gaped in astonishment as the screens broke up into electronic garbage. A sound like frying circuitry spat from all the speakers at once—from the hailing channels as well as from intraship. She almost let out a shout of surprise; but training and recognition bit it back. She knew what that was.

"Jammer," Gracias said. "We're being jammed."

"From this distance?" she demanded. "From *this distance*? That kind of signal should take"—she checked her readout—"three and some fraction minutes to get here. How do they do that?"

He didn't reply for a few seconds; he was busy restoring order to the screens. Then he said, "They've got faster-than-light drive. Scanners make ours look like toys. Why not better radio?"

"Or maybe," she put in harshly, "they started broadcasting their jammer as soon as they picked us up." In spite of her determination to be calm, she was breathing hard, sucking uncertainty and anger through her teeth. "Can you break through?"

He tried, then shook his head. "Too thick."

"Damn! Gracias, what're we going to do? If we can't warn Aster, then it's up to us. If that ship is hostile, we've got to fight it somehow."

"Not built for it," he commented. "*Aster's Hope*. About as maneuverable as a rock."

She knew. Everything about the ship had been planned with defense rather than offense in mind. She was intended, first, to survive; second, not to give anything away about her homeworld prematurely. In fact as well as in appearance, she wasn't meant as a weapon of war. And one reason for this was that the mission planners had never once considered the idea of encountering an alien (never mind hostile) ship this close to home.

She found herself wishing for different armament, more speed, and a whole lot less mass. But that couldn't be helped now. "We need to get their attention somehow," she said. "Make them cope with us before they go on." An idea struck her. "What've the scanners got on them?"

"Still not much. Size. Velocity." Then, as if by intuition, he seemed to know what she had in mind. "Shields, of course. Look like ordinary force-disruption fields."

She almost smiled. "You're kidding. No c-vector?"

"Nope."

"Then maybe—" She thought furiously. "Maybe there's something we can do. If we can slow them down—maybe do them some damage—and they can't hurt us at all—maybe they won't go on to Aster."

"Gracias, are we on a collision course with that thing?"

He glanced at her. "Not quite. Going to miss by a kilometer."

As if she were in command of *Aster's Hope*, she said, "Put us in the way."

A grin flashed through his concentration. "Yes, sir, Temple, ma'am, sir. Good idea."

At once, he started keying instructions into his com board.

While he set up the comp to adjust *Aster's Hope*'s course—and then to adjust it continuously to keep the ship as squarely as possible in the oncoming vessel's path—Temple secured herself in her momentum restraints. Less than three minutes, she thought. Three minutes to impact. For a moment, she thought Gracias was moving too slowly. But before she could say anything, he took his hands off the board and started snapping his own restraints. "Twenty seconds," he said.

She braced herself. "Are we going to feel it?"

"Inertial shift? Of course."

"No, idiot. Are we going to feel the impact?"

He shrugged. "If we hit. Nobody's ever hit a c-vector shield that hard with something that big."

Then Temple's stomach turned on its side, and the whole auxcomp-com felt like it was starting into a spin.

The course adjustment was over almost immediately: at the speeds *Aster's Hope* and the alien were traveling, one kilometer was a subtle shift.

Less than two and a half minutes. If we hit. She couldn't sit there and wait for it in silence. "Are the scanners doing any better? We ought to be able to count their teeth from this range."

"Checking," he said. With a few buttons, he called a new display up onto the main screen—

—and stared at it without saying anything. His mouth hung open; his whole face was black with astonishment.

"Gracias?" She looked at the screen for herself. With a mental effort, she tightened down the screws on her brain, forced herself to see the pattern in the numbers. Then she lost control of her voice: it went up like a yell. "Gracias?"

"Don't believe it," he murmured. "No. Don't believe it."

According to the scanners, the oncoming ship was crammed to the walls with computers and weaponry, equipment in every size and shape, mechanical and electrical energy of all kinds—and not one single living organism.

"There's nothing—" She tried to say it, but at first she couldn't. Her throat shut down, and she couldn't unlock it. She had to force a swallow past the rigid muscles. "There's nothing alive in that ship."

Abruptly, *Aster's Hope* went into a course shift that felt like it was going to pull Temple's heart out of her chest. The alien was taking evasive action, and *Aster's Hope* was compensating.

One minute.

"That's crazy." She was almost shouting. "It comes in faster than light and starts decelerating right at us and jams our transmissions and shifts course to try to keep us from running into it—and there's nobody *alive* on board? Who do we talk to if we want to surrender?"

"Take it easy," Gracias said. "One thing at a time. Artificial intelligence is feasible. Ship thinks for itself, maybe. Or on automatic. Exploration probe might—"

Another course shift cut him off. A violent inertial kick—too violent. Her head was jerked to the left. Alarms went off like klaxons. *Aster's Hope* was trying to bring herself back toward collision with the other ship, trying—

The screens flashed loud warnings, danger signs as familiar to her as her name. Three of the ship's thrusters were overheating critically. One was tearing itself to pieces under the shift stress. *Aster's Hope* wasn't made for this.

Temple was the ship's nician: she couldn't let *Aster's Hope* be damaged. "Break off!" she shouted through the squall of the alarms. "We can't do it!"

Gracias slapped a hand at his board, canceled the collision course.

G-stress receded. Lights on Temple's board told her about thrusters damaged, doors jammed because they'd shifted on their mounts, a locker in the meditech section sprung, a handful of cryogenic capsules gone on backup. But the alarms were cut off almost instantly.

For a second, the collision warnings went into a howl. Then they stopped. The sudden silence felt louder than the alarms.

Gracias punched visual up onto the screens. He got a picture in time to see the other ship go by in a blur of metal too fast for the eye to track. From a range the scanners measured in mere hundreds of meters, the alien looked the size of a fortress—squat, squarish, enormous.

As it passed, it jabbed a bright red shaft of force at *Aster's Hope* from point-blank range.

All the screens in the auxcompcom went dark.

"God!" Gracias gasped. "Scanners burned out?"

That was Temple's province. She was still reeling from the shock, the knowledge that *Aster's Hope* had been fired upon; but her hands had been trained until they had a life of their own and knew what to do. Hardly more than a heartbeat after she understood what Gracias said, she sent in a diagnostic on the scanner circuits. The answer trailed across the screen in front of her.

"No damage," she reported.

"Then what?" He sounded flustered, groping for comprehension.

"Did you get any scan on that beam?" she returned. "Enough to analyze?" Then she explained, "Right angles to the speed of light isn't the same direction for every force. Maybe the c-vector sent this one off into some kind of wraparound field."

That was what he needed. "Right." His hands went to work on his board again.

Almost immediately, he had an answer. "Ion beam. Would've reduced us to subatomic particles without the shield. But only visual's lost. Scanners still functioning. Have visual back in a second."

"Good." She double-checked her own readouts, made sure that *Aster's Hope*'s attempts to maneuver with the alien hadn't done any urgent harm. At the same time, she reassured herself that the force of the ion beam hadn't been felt inside the shield. Then she pulled her attention back to the screens and Gracias.

"What's our friend doing now?"

He grunted, nodded up at the main screen. The comp was plotting another graph, showing the other ship's course in relation to *Aster's Hope*.

She blinked at it. That was impossible. Impossible for a ship that size moving that fast to turn that hard.

But of course, she thought with an odd sensation of craziness, there isn't anything living aboard to feel g-stress.

"Well." She swallowed at the way her voice shook. "At least we got their attention."

Gracias tried to laugh, but it came out like a snarl. "Good for us. Now what?"

"We could try to run," she offered. "Put as much distance as possible between us and them."

He shook his head. "Won't work. They're faster."

"Besides which," she growled, "we've left a particle trail even *we* could follow all the way back to Aster. That and the incessant radio gabble— If that mechanical behemoth wants to find our homeworld, we might as well transmit a map."

He pulled back from his board, swung his seat to face her again. His expression troubled her. His eyes seemed dull, almost glazed, as if under pressure his intelligence were slowly losing its edge. "Got a choice?" he asked.

The thought that he might fail *Aster's Hope* made panic beat in her forehead; but she forced it down. "Sure," she snapped, trying to send him a spark of her own anger. "We can fight."

His eyes didn't focus on her. "Got laser cannon," he said. "Hydrogen torpedoes. Ship like that"—he nodded at the screen—"won't have shields we can hurt. How can we fight?"

"You said they're ordinary force-disruption fields. We can break through that. Any sustained pounding can break through. That's why they didn't build *Aster's Hope* until they could do better."

He still didn't quite look at her. Enunciating carefully, he said, "I don't believe that ship has shields we can hurt."

Temple pounded the edge of her console. "Damn it, Gracias! We've got to try! We can't just sit here until they get bored and decide to go do something terrible to our homeworld. If you aren't interested—" Abruptly, she leaned back in her seat, took a deep breath, and held it to steady herself. Then she said quietly, "Key com over to me. I'll do it myself."

For a minute longer, he remained the way he was, his gaze staring disfocused past her chin. Slowly, he nodded. Moving sluggishly, he turned back to his console.

But instead of keying com over to Temple, he told the comp to begin decelerating *Aster's Hope*. Losing inertia so the ship could maneuver better.

Softly, she let a sigh of relief through her teeth.

While *Aster's Hope* braked, pulling Temple against her momentum restraints, and the unliving alien ship continued its impossible turn, she unlocked the weaponry controls on her console. A string of lights began to indicate the status of every piece of combat equipment *Aster's Hope* carried.

It wasn't supposed to be like this, she thought to herself. She'd never imagined it like this. When/if the Asterin mission encountered some unexpected form of life, another spacegoing vessel, a planetary intelligence, the whole situation should've been different. A hard-nosed distrust was to be expected: a fear of the unknown; a desire to protect the homeworld; communications problems; wise caution. But not unprovoked assault. Not an immediate pitched battle out in the middle of nowhere, with Aster itself at issue.

Not an alien ship full of nothing but machinery? Was that the crucial point?

All right: what purpose could a ship like that serve? Exploration probe? Then it wouldn't be hostile. A defense mechanism for a theoretically secure sector of space which *Aster's Hope* had somehow violated? But they were at least fifty light-years from the nearest neighbor to Aster's star; and it was difficult to imagine an intelligence so paranoid that its conception of "territorial space" reached out this far. Some kind of automated weapon? But Aster didn't have any enemies.

None of it made any sense. And as she tried to sort it out, her confusion grew worse. It started her sliding into panic.

Fortunately, Gracias chose that moment to ask gruffly, "Ready? It's hauling up on us fast. Be in range in a minute."

She made an effort to control her breathing, shake the knots of panic out of her mind. "Plot an evasive course," she said, "and key it to my board." Her weapons program had to know where *Aster's Hope* was going in order to use its armament effectively.

"Why?" he asked. "Don't need evasion. Shield'll protect us."

"To keep them guessing." Her tension was plain in her voice. "And show them we can hit them on the run. Do it."

She thought he was moving too slowly. But faster than she could've done it he had a plot up on the main screen, showing the alien's incoming course and the shifts *Aster's Hope* was about to make.

She tried to wipe the sweat from her palms on her bare legs; but it didn't do much good. Snarling at the way her hands felt, she poised them over the weapons com.

Gracias' plot stayed on the main screen; but the display in front of her gave her visual again, and she saw the alien ship approaching like a bright metal projectile the galaxy had flung to knock *Aster's Hope* out of the heavens. Suddenly frantic, as if she believed the other ship were actually going to crush her, she started firing.

Beams of light shot at the alien from every laser port the comp could bring to bear.

Though the ship was huge, the beams focused on a single section: Temple was trying to maximize their impact. When they hit the force disruption field, light suddenly blared all across the spectrum, sending up a rainbow of coruscation.

"Negative," Gracias reported as *Aster's Hope* wrenched into her first evasion shift. "No effect."

Her weight rammed against the restraints, the skin of her cheeks pulling, Temple punched the weapons com into continuous fire, then concentrated on holding up her head so that she could watch the visual.

As her lasers turned the alien's shields into a fireworks display, another bright red shaft of force came as straight as a spear at *Aster's Hope*.

Again, the screen lost visual.

But this time Gracias was ready. He got scanner plots onto the screen while visual was out of use. Temple could see her laser fire like an equation on a graph connecting *Aster's Hope* and the unliving ship. Every few seconds, a line came back the other way—an ion beam as accurate as if *Aster's Hope* were stationary. "Any effect yet?" she gasped at Gracias as another evasion kicked her to the other side of her seat. "We're hitting them hard. It's got to have an effect."

"Negative," he repeated. "That shield disperses force almost as fast as it comes in. Doesn't weaken."

Then the attacker went past. In seconds, it would be out of reach of Temple's laser cannon.

"Cancel evasion," she snapped, keying her com out of continuous fire. "Go after them. As fast as we can. Give me a chance to aim a torpedo."

"Right," he responded. And a second later g-stress slammed at her as all the ship's thrusters went on full power, roaring for acceleration.

Aster's Hope steadied on the alien's course and did her best to match its speed.

"Now," Temple muttered. "Now. Before they start to turn." Her hands quick on the weapons board, she primed a whole barrage of hydrogen torpedoes. Then she pulled in course coordinates from the comp. "Go." With the flat of her hand on all the launch buttons at once, she fired.

The comp automatically blinked the c-vector shield to let the torpedoes out. Fired from a source moving as fast as *Aster's Hope* was, they attained attack velocity almost immediately and went after the other ship.

Gracias didn't wait for Temple's instructions. He reversed thrust, decelerating *Aster's Hope* again to stay as far as possible from the blast when the torpedoes hit.

If they hit. The scanner plot on the main screen showed that the alien was starting to turn.

"Come on," she breathed. Unconsciously, she pounded her fists on the arms of her seat. "Come on. Hit that bastard. Hit."

"Impact," he said as all the blips on the scanner came together.

At that instant, visual cleared. They saw a hot white ball explode like a balloon of energy rupturing in all directions at once.

Then both visual and scan went haywire for a few long seconds. The detonation of that many hydrogen torpedoes filled all the space around *Aster's Hope* with chaos: energy emissions on every frequency; supercharged particles phasing in and out of tardyon existence as they screamed away from the point of explosion.

"Hit him," Gracias murmured.

Temple gripped the arms of her seat, stared at the garbage on the screens. "What do you think? Can they stand up to that?"

He didn't shrug. He looked like he didn't have that much energy left. "Wouldn't hurt us."

"Can't you clear the screens? We've got to *see*."

"The comp's doing it." Then, a second later: "Here it comes."

The screens wiped themselves clear, and a new scanner plot mapped the phosphors in front of him. It showed the alien turning hard, coming back toward *Aster's Hope*.

The readout was negative. No damage.

"Oh, God," she sighed. "I don't believe it." All the strength seemed to run out of her body. She sagged against her restraints. "Now what do we do?"

He went on staring at the screens for a long moment while the attacking ship completed its turn. Then he said, "Don't know. Try for collision again?"

When she didn't say anything, he gave the problem to the comp, told it to wait until the last possible instant—considering *Aster's Hope*'s poor maneuverability—and then thrust the ship into the alien's path. After that, he keyed his board onto automatic and leaned back in his restraints. To her surprise, he yawned hugely.

"Need sleep," he mumbled thickly. "Be glad when this shift's over."

Surprise and fear made her acid. "You're not thinking very clearly, Gracias." She needed him, but he seemed to be getting farther and farther away. "Do you think the mission can continue after this? What do you think the chances are that ship's going to give up and let us go on our way? My God, there isn't even anybody *alive* over there! The whole thing is just a machine. It can stay here and pound at us for centuries, and it won't even get bored. Or it can calculate the odds on Aster building a c-vector shield big enough to cover the whole planet—and it can just forget about us, leave us here, and go attack our homeworld because there won't be anything we can do to stop it and Aster is *unprotected*. We don't even know what it *wants*. We—"

She might have gone on; but the comp chose that moment to heave *Aster's Hope* in front of the alien. Every thruster screaming, the ship pulled her mass into a terrible acceleration, fighting for a collision her attacker couldn't avoid. Temple felt like she was being cut to pieces by the straps holding her in her seat. She tried to cry out, but she couldn't get any air into her lungs. Her damage readouts and lights began to put on a show.

But the alien ship skipped aside and went past without being touched.

For a second, *Aster's Hope* pulled around, trying to follow her opponent. Then Gracias forced himself forward and canceled the comp's collision instructions. Instantly, the g-stress eased. The ship settled onto a new heading chosen by her inertia, the alien already turning again to come after her.

"Damn," he said softly. "Damn it."

Temple let herself rest against her restraints. We can't—she thought dully. Can't even run into that thing. It can't hurt us. But we can't hurt it. *Aster's Hope* wasn't built to be a warship. She wasn't supposed to protect her homeworld by fighting: she was supposed to protect it by being diplomatic and cunning and distant. If the worst came to the very worst, she was supposed to protect Aster by not coming back. But this was a mission of peace, the mission of Aster's dream: the ship was never intended to fight for anything except her own survival.

"For some reason," Temple murmured into the silence of the auxcompcom, "I don't think this is what I had in mind when I joined the Service."

Gracias started to say something. The sound of frying circuitry from the speakers cut him off. It got her attention like a splash of hot oil.

This time, it wasn't a jammer. She saw that in the readouts jumping across the screens. It was another scanner probe, like the one that had tried to break into the comp earlier. But now it was tearing into the ship's unprotected communication hardware—the intraship speakers.

After the initial burst of static, the sounds began to change. Frying became whistles and grunts, growls and moans. For a minute, she had the impression she was listening to some inconceivable alien language. But before she could call up the comp's translation program—or ask Gracias to do it—the interference on the speakers modulated until it became a voice and words.

A voice from every speaker in the auxcompcom at once.

Words Temple and Gracias understood.

The voice sounded like a poorly calibrated vodor, metallic and insensitive. But the words were distinct.

"Surrender, badlife. You will be destroyed."

The scanner probe had turned up the gain on all the speakers. The voice was so loud it seemed to rattle the auxcompcom door on its mounts.

Involuntarily, Temple gasped, "Good God. What in hell is that?"

Gracias replied unnecessarily, "The other ship. Talking to us." He sounded dull, defeated, almost uninterested.

"I *know* that," she snapped. "For God's sake, *wake* up!" Abruptly, she slapped a hand at her board, opened a radio channel. "Who are you?" she demanded into her mike. "What do you want? We're no threat to you. Our mission is peaceful. Why are you attacking us?"

The scanner plot on the main screen showed that the alien ship had already completed its turn and caught up with *Aster's Hope.* Now it was matching her course and speed, shadowing her at a distance of less than ten kilometers.

"Surrender," the speakers blared again. "You are badlife. You will be destroyed. You must surrender."

Frantic with fear and urgency, and not able to control it, Temple pounded off her mike and swung her seat. "Can't you turn that *down*?" she raged at Gracias. "It's splitting my eardrums!"

Slowly, as if he were half-asleep, he tapped a few buttons on his console. Blinking at the readouts, he murmured, "Hardware problem. Scanner probe's stronger than the comp's line voltage. Have to reduce gain manually." Then he widened his eyes at something that managed to surprise him even in his stunned state. "Only speakers affected are in here. This room. Bastard knows exactly where we are. And every circuit around us."

That didn't make sense. It made so little sense that it caught her attention, focused her in spite of her panic. "Wait a minute," she said. "They're only using *these* speakers? The ones in this room? How do they know we're in here? Gracias, there are three hundred ninety-two people aboard. How can they possibly know you and I are the only ones awake?"

"*You must surrender,*" the speakers squalled again. "You cannot flee. You have no speed. You cannot fight. Your weapons are puny. When your shields are broken, you will be helpless. Your secrets will be lost. Only surrender can save your lives."

She keyed her mike again. "No. You're making a mistake. We're no threat to you. Who are you? What do you want?"

"Death," the speakers replied. "Death for all life. Death for all worlds. You must surrender."

Gracias closed his eyes. Without looking at what he was doing, he moved his hands on his board, got visual back up on the main screen. The screen showed the alien ship sailing like a skyborne fort an exact distance from *Aster's Hope.* It held its position so precisely that it looked motionless. It seemed so close Temple thought she could have hit it with a rock.

"Maybe," he sighed, "don't know we're the only ones awake."

She didn't understand what he was thinking; but she caught at it as if it were a lifeline. "What do you mean?"

He didn't open his eyes. "Cryogenically frozen," he said. "Vital signs so low the monitors can hardly read them. Capsules are just equipment. And the comp's encrypted. Maybe that scanner probe thinks we're the only life-forms here."

She caught her breath. "If that's true—" Ideas reeled through her head. "They probably want us to surrender because they can't figure out our shields. And because they want to know what we're doing, just the two of us in this big ship. It might be suicide for them to go on to Aster without knowing the answers to questions like that. And while they're trying to find out how to break down our shields, they'll probably stay right there.

"Gracias," her heart pounding with unreasonable hope, "how long would it take you to repro the comp to project a c-vector field at that ship? We're stationary in relation to each other. We can use our field generator as a weapon."

That got his eyes open. When he rolled his head to the side to face her, he looked sick. "How long will it take you," he asked, "to rebuild the generator for that kind of projection? And what will we use for shields while you're working?"

He was right: she knew it as soon as he said it. But there had to be something they could do, *had* to be. They couldn't just sail across the galactic void for the next few thousand years while their homeworld was destroyed behind them.

There had to be *something* they could do.

The speakers started trumpeting again. "Badlife, you have been warned. The destruction of your ship will now begin. You must surrender to save your lives."

Badlife, she wondered crazily to herself. What does that mean, badlife? Is that ship some kind of automatic weapon gone berserk, shooting around the galaxy exterminating what it calls badlife?

How is it going to destroy *Aster's Hope*?

She didn't have to wait long to find out. Almost immediately, she felt a heavy metallic thunk vibrate through the seals that held her seat to the floor. A fraction of an instant later, a small flash of light from somewhere amidships on the attacking vessel showed that a projectile weapon had been fired.

Then alarms began to howl, and the damage readouts on Temple's board began to spit intimations of disaster.

Training took over through her panic. Her hands danced on the console, gleaning data. "We've been hit." Through the shield. "Some kind of projectile." *Through the c-vector shield.* "It's breached the hull." All three layers of the ship's metal skin. "I don't know what it was, but it's punched a hole all the way to the outer-shell wall."

Gracias interrupted her. "How big's the hole?"

"About a meter square." She went back to the discipline of her report. "The comp is closing pressure doors, isolating the breach. Damage is minor—we've lost one heat exchanger for the climate control. But if they do that again, they might hit something more vital." Trusting the c-vector shields, *Aster's Hope*'s builders hadn't tried to make her particularly hard to damage in other ways.

The alien ship did it again. Another tearing thud as the projectile hit. Another small flash of light from the attacker. More alarms. Temple's board began to look like it was monitoring a madhouse.

"The same place," she said, fighting a rising desire to scream. "It's pierced outer-shell. Atmosphere loss is trivial. The comp is closing more pressure doors." She tapped commands into the console. "Extrapolating the path of those shots, I'm closing all the doors along the way." Then she called up a damage estimate on the destructive force of the projectiles. "Two more like that will breach one of the mid-shell cryogenic chambers. We're going to start losing people."

And if the projectiles went on pounding the same place, deeper and deeper into the ship, they would eventually reach the c-vector generator.

It was true: *Aster's Hope* was going to be destroyed.

"Gracias, what is it? This is supposed to be impossible. How are they doing it to us?"

"Happening too fast to scan." In spite of his torpor, he already had all the answers he needed up on his screen. "Faster-than-light projectile.

Flash shows after impact. Vaporize us if we didn't have the shields. C-vector brings it down to space-normal speed. But then it's inside the field. She wasn't built for this."

A faster— For a moment, her brain refused to understand the words. A faster-than-light projectile. And when it hit the shield, just enough of its energy went off at right angles to the speed of light to slow it down. Not enough to stop it.

As if in mockery, the speakers began to blast again. "Your ship is desired intact. Surrender. Your lives will be spared. You will be granted opportunity to serve as goodlife."

So exasperated she hardly knew what she was doing, she slapped open a radio channel. "Shut up!" she shouted across the black space between *Aster's Hope* and the alien. "Stop shooting! Give us a chance to think! How can we surrender if you don't give us a chance to think?"

Gulping air, she looked at Gracias. She felt wild and didn't know what to do about it. His eyes were dull, low-lidded: he might've been going to sleep. Sick with fear, she panted at him, "Do something! You're the ship's puter. You're supposed to take care of her. You're supposed to have ideas. *They can't do this to my ship!*"

Slowly—too slowly—he turned toward her. His neck hardly seemed strong enough to hold his head up. "Do what? Shield's all we've got. Now it isn't any good. That"—he grimaced—"that thing has everything. Nothing we can do."

Furiously, she ripped off her restraints, heaved out of her seat so that she could go to him and shake him. "There has to be something we can do!" she shouted into his face. "We're human! That thing's nothing but a pile of microchips and demented programming. We're more than it is! Don't surrender! *Think!*"

For a moment, he stared at her. Then he let out an empty laugh. "What good's being human? Doesn't help. Only intelligence and power count. Those machines have intelligence. Maybe more than we do. More advanced than we are. And a lot more powerful." Dully, he repeated, "Nothing we can do."

In response, she wanted to rage at him, We can refuse to give up! We can keep fighting! We're not beaten as long as we're stubborn enough to keep fighting! But as soon as she thought that she knew she was wrong. There was nothing in life as stubborn as a machine doing what it was told.

"Intelligence and power aren't all that count," she protested, trying urgently to find what she wanted, something she could believe in, something that would pull Gracias out of his defeat. "What about emotion? That ship can't care about anything. What about love?"

When she said that, his expression crumpled. Roughly, he put his hands over his face. His shoulders knotted as he struggled with himself.

"Well, then," she went on, too desperate to hold back, "we can use the self-destruct. Kill *Aster's Hope*"—the bare idea choked her, but she forced it out—"to keep them from finding out how the shield generator works. Altruism. That's something they don't have."

Abruptly, he wrenched his hands down from his face, pulled them into fists, pounded them on the arms of his seat. "Stop it," he whispered. "*Stop* it. Machines are altruistic. Don't care about themselves at all. Only thing they can't do is feel bad when what they want is taken away. Any second now, they're going to start firing again. We're dead, and there's nothing we can do about it, *nothing*. Stop breaking my heart."

His anger and rejection should have hurt her. But he was awake and alive, and his eyes were on fire in the way she loved. Suddenly, she wasn't alone: he'd come back from his dull horror. "Gracias," she said softly. "Gracias." Possibilities were moving in the back of her brain, ideas full of terror and hope, ideas she was afraid to say out loud. "We can wake everybody up. See if anybody else can think of anything. Put it to a vote. Let the mission make its own decisions.

"Or we can—"

What she was thinking scared her out of her mind, but she told him what it was anyway. Then she let him yell at her until he couldn't think of any more arguments against it.

After all, they had to save Aster.

Her part of the preparations was simple enough. She left him in the auxcompcom and took the nearest shaft down to inner-shell. First she visited a locker to get her tools and a magnetic sled. Then she went to the central command center.

In the cencom, she keyed a radio channel. Hoping the alien was listening, she said, "I'm Temple. My partner is crazy—he wants to fight. I want to surrender. I'll have to kill him. It won't be easy. Give me some time. I'm going to disable the shields."

She took a deep breath, forced herself to sigh. Could a mechanical alien understand a sigh? "Unfortunately, when the shields go down it's going to engage an automatic self-destruct. That I can't disable. So don't try to board the ship. You'll get blown to pieces. I'll come out to you.

"I want to be goodlife, not badlife. To prove my good faith, I'm going to bring with me a portable generator for the c-vector field we use as shields. You can study it, learn how it works. Frankly, you need it." The alien ship could probably hear the stress in her voice, so she made an extra effort to sound sarcastic. "You'd be dead by now if we weren't on a peace mission. We know how to break down your shields—we just don't have the firepower."

There. She clicked off the transmitter. Let them think about that for a while.

From the cencom, she opened one of the access hatches and took her tools and mag-sled down into the core of Aster's Hope, where most of the ship's vital equipment operated—the comp banks, the artificial gravity inducer, the primary life-support systems, the c-vector generator.

While she worked, she didn't talk to Gracias. She wanted to know how he was doing; but she already knew the intraship communication lines weren't secure from the alien's scanner probe.

In a relatively short time—she was Aster's Hope's nician and knew what she was doing—she had the ship's self-destruct device detached from its comp links and loaded onto the mag-sled. That device (called "the black box" by the mission planners) was no more than half Temple's size, but it was a fully functional c-vector generator, capable from its own energy cells of sending the entire ship off at right angles to the speed of light, even if the rest of Aster's Hope were inoperative. With the comp links disconnected, Gracias couldn't do anything to destroy the ship; but

Temple made sure the self-destruct's radio trigger was armed and ready before she steered the mag-sled up out of the core.

This time when she left the cencom she took a shaft up to the mid-shell chamber where she and Gracias had their cryogenic capsules. He wasn't there yet. While she waited for him, she went around the room and disconnected the chamber's communications gear. She hoped her movements might make her look from a distance like one furtive life-form preparing an ambush for another.

He was slow in coming. The delay made her fret. Was it possible that he had lapsed back into half-somnolent panic? Or had he changed his mind—decided she was crazy? He'd yelled at her as if she were asking him to help her commit suicide. What if he—?

The door whooshed open, and he came into the chamber almost at a run. "Have to hurry," he panted. "Only got fifteen minutes before the shield drops."

His face looked dark and bruised and fierce, as if he'd spent the time she was away from him hitting himself with his fists. For a second, she caught a glimpse of just how terrible what she was asking him to do was.

Ignoring the need for haste, she went to him, put her arms around him, hugged him hard. "Gracias," she breathed, "it's going to work. Don't look at me like that."

He returned her embrace so roughly he made her gasp. But almost immediately he let her go. "Keep your suit radio open," he rasped while he pushed past her and moved to his capsule. "If you go off, the comp will take over. Blow you out of space." Harshly, he pulled himself over the edge into the bed of the capsule. "Two-stage code," he continued. "First say my name." His eyes burned blackly in their sockets, savage with pain and fear. "If that works, say 'Aster.' If it *doesn't* work, say 'Aster.' Whatever happens. Ship doesn't deserve to die in her sleep."

As if he were dismissing her, he reclined in the capsule and folded his arms over his chest.

But when she went to him to say good-bye, he reached out urgently and caught her wrist. "Why?" he asked softly. "Why are we doing it this way?"

Oh, Gracias. His desperation hurt her. "Because this is the only way we can persuade them not to blow up *Aster's Hope*—or come storming aboard—when we let down the shields."

His voice hissing between his clenched teeth, he asked, "Why can't I come with you?"

Tears she couldn't stop ran down her cheeks. "They'll be more likely to trust me if they think I've killed you. And somebody has to stay here. To decide what to do if this all goes wrong. These are the jobs we've been trained for."

For a long moment, he faced her with his dark distress. Then he let go of her arm. "Comp'll wake me up when you give the first code."

She was supposed to be hurrying. She could hardly bear to leave him; but she forced herself to kiss him quickly, then step back and engage the lid of his capsule. Slowly, the lid closed down over him until it sealed. The gas that prepared his body for freezing filled the capsule. But he went on staring out at her, darkly, hotly, until the inside of the lid frosted opaque.

Ignoring the tears that streaked her face, she left him. The sled floating on its magnetic field ahead of her, she went to the shaft and rode up to outer-shell, as close as she could safely get to the point where the faster-than-light projectiles had breached *Aster's Hope*'s hull. From there, she steered the mag-sled into the locker room beside the airlock that gave access to the nearest exterior port.

In the locker room, she put on her suit. Because everything depended on it, she tested the suit's radio unit circuits four times. Then she engaged the suit's pressure seals and took the mag-sled into the airlock.

Monitored automatically by the comp, she cycled the airlock to match the null atmosphere/gravity in the port. After that, she didn't need the mag-sled anymore. With hardly a minute to spare, she nudged the black box out into the high metal cave of the port and keyed the controls to open the port doors.

The doors slid back, leaving her face-to-face with the naked emptiness of space.

At first, she couldn't see the alien ship: everything outside the port was too dark. But *Aster's Hope* was still less than half a light-year from home; and when Temple's eyes adjusted to the void she could see that

Aster's sun sent out enough illumination to show the attacking vessel against the background of the stars.

It appeared too big and fatal for her to hurt.

But after the way Gracias had looked at her in farewell, she couldn't bear to hesitate. This had to be done. As soon as the alarm went off in the port—and all over *Aster's Hope*—warning the ship that the shields were down, she cleared her throat, forced her taut voice into use.

"All right," she said into the radio. "I've done it. I've killed my partner. I've shut down the shields. I want you to keep your promise. Save my life. I'm coming out. If we're within a thousand kilometers of the ship when the automatic self-destruct goes, we'll go with it.

"I've got the portable field generator with me. I can show you how to use it. I can teach you how to make it. You've got to keep your promise."

She didn't wait for an answer: she didn't expect one. The only answer she'd received earlier was a cessation of the shooting. That was enough. All she had to do was get close to the alien ship.

Grimly she tightened her grip on one handle of the black box and fired her suit's small thrusters to impel herself and her burden past the heavy doors out into the dark.

Automatically, the comp closed the doors after her, shutting her out.

For an instant, her own smallness almost overwhelmed her. No Asterin had been where she was now: outside her ship half a light-year from home. All of her training had been in comfortable orbit around Aster, the planet acting as a balance to the immensity of space. And there had been light! Here there were only the gleams and glitters emitted by *Aster's Hope*'s cameras and scanners—and the barely discernible bulk of the alien, its squat lines only slightly less dark than the black heavens.

But she knew that if she let herself think that way she would go mad. Gritting her teeth, she focused her attention—and her thrusters—toward the enemy.

Now everything depended on whether the alien knew there were people alive aboard *Aster's Hope*. Whether the alien had been able to analyze or deduce all the implications of the c-vector shield. And whether Temple could get away.

The size of the other vessel made the distance appear less than it was, but after a while she was close enough to see a port opening in the side of the ship.

Then—so suddenly that she flinched and broke into a sweat—a voice came over her suit radio.

"You will enter the dock open before you. It is heavily shielded and invulnerable to explosion. You will remain in the dock with your device. If this is an attempt at treachery, you will be destroyed by your own weapon.

"If you are goodlife, you will be spared. You will remain with your device while you dismantle it for inspection. When its principles are understood, you will be permitted to answer other questions."

"Thanks a whole bunch," she muttered in response. But she didn't let herself slow down or shy away. Instead, she went toward the open port until the dock yawned directly in front of her.

Then she put the repro Gracias had done on the comp to the test.

What she had to do was so risky, so unreasonably dangerous, that she did it almost without thinking about it, as if she'd been doing things like that all her life.

Aiming her thrusters right against the side of the black box, she fired them so that the box was kicked hard and fast into the mouth of the dock and her own momentum in that direction was stopped. There she waited until she saw the force field which shielded the dock drag the box to a stop, grip it motionless. Then she shouted into her radio as if the comp were deaf, "*Gracias!*"

On that code, *Aster's Hope* put out a tractor beam and snatched her away from the alien.

It was a small industrial tractor beam, the kind used first in the construction of *Aster's Hope*, then in the loading of cargo. It was far too small and finely focused to have any function as a weapon. But it was perfect for moving an object the size of Temple in her suit across the distance between the two ships quickly.

Timing was critical, but she made that decision also almost without thinking about it. As the beam rushed her toward *Aster's Hope*, she shouted into the radio, "*Aster!*"

And on that code, her ship simultaneously raised its c-vector shields and triggered the black box. She was inside the shield for the last brief instants while the alien was still able to fire at her.

————

Later, she and Gracias saw that the end of their attacker had been singularly unspectacular. Still somewhat groggy from his imposed nap, he met her in the locker room to help her take off her suit; but when she demanded urgently, "What happened? Did it work?" he couldn't answer because he hadn't checked: he'd come straight to the locker from his capsule when the comp had awakened him. So they ran together to the nearest auxcompcom to find out if they were safe.

They were. The alien ship was nowhere within scanner range. And wherever it had gone, it left no trace or trail.

So he replayed the visual and scanner records, and they saw what happened to a vessel when a c-vector field was projected onto it.

It simply winked out of existence.

After that, she felt like celebrating. In fact, there was a particular kind of celebration she had in mind—and neither of them was wearing any clothes. But when she let him know what she was thinking, he pushed her gently away. "In a few minutes," he said. "Got work to do."

"What work?" she protested. "We just saved the world—and they don't even know it. We deserve a vacation for the rest of the trip."

He nodded, but didn't move away from the comp console.

"What work?" she repeated.

"Course change," he said. He looked like he was trying not to grin. "Going back to Aster."

"What?" He surprised her so much that she shouted at him without meaning to. "You're aborting the mission? Just like that? What the hell do you think you're doing?"

For a moment, he did his best to scowl thunderously. Then the grin took over. "Now we know faster-than-light is possible," he said. "Just need more research. So why spend a thousand years sleeping across the galaxy? Why not go home, do the research—start again when we can do what that ship did?"

He looked at her. "Make sense?"

She was grinning herself. "Makes sense."

When he was done with the comp, he got even with her for spilling ice cream on him.

By Any Other Name

I had wealth—an enviable villa graced by servants and soothing grounds, courtesans both imaginative and compliant, and a thriving merchantry, coupled with social standing just below that of the Thal himself. I had friends, well placed and gracious, who might have come to my aid—if they could have done so without inconvenience. I had a substantial, if somewhat overfed, cohort of guards sworn to my service and, presumably, to my protection.

But necromancy and the fatal arts were Sher Abener's province, and at last I fled from them.

The nature of his quarrel with me was at once mystically arcane and stupidly practical. The caravans of my merchantry extended their travels to Sher Abener's distant homeland, from whence his occult passions and powers derived. In hushed whispers, it was often said that there men trafficked openly with the dead, while here such practices are only feared and shunned.

On the day when Sher Abener's enmity toward me was set in motion, he approached me, asking that I command my caravans to obtain various necrotic objects and potencies for him from his homeland. Naturally, I acquiesced. I had never sought conflict with any man. Indeed, during the years since my kind and indulgent father had succumbed to the plague, and I had inherited his villa, his riches, and his merchantry, I had studiously avoided contention of any kind. I saw no purpose in it. I desired no alarms and apprehensions to trouble my satisfied life. The manly skills appropriate to my station—primarily the saber and lance, supported by some few techniques of unarmed combat, and a smattering of theurgy—I had learned without interest as a youth, and forgotten as swiftly as I could. My business dealings were marked more by pleasure and comradeship than by profit. My sport with my courtesans and friends accommodated no discomfort. No doubt Sher Abener had come to me because he could be certain of my acquiescence.

Unfortunately, the man whose duty it was to carry out my assent refused. He was Tep Longeur, the overseer of my merchantry—the man who both commanded and represented the drovers and carters and warehawks of my caravans. Two days after Sher Abener's request, he approached me with his unwelcome reply.

"Sher Urmeny," he informed me stiffly, "it won't be done. We won't do it."

"My good man, why ever not?" I responded in protest. Truth to tell, I had at that moment no notion what he meant. My transaction with Sher Abener—ominous though it was—had already vanished from my mind.

"The men won't do it," Tep Longeur explained. "And I won't force them. I wouldn't do it myself in their place. That trek is already dangerous enough. These things—" The neat scrim of his beard lifted in disgust. His eyes flashed a careless anger past the sun-belabored leather of his cheeks. "They're evil, Sher Urmeny."

"'Things,' Tep Longeur?" I made no attempt to conceal my bewilderment. He had served my family longer than I had been alive, and knew me too well to be misled by feigned certainty. "'Evil'? Have you dismissed your senses?"

"No, I haven't, Sher." My overseer brandished before me a parchment marked by Sher Abener's crabbed hand. A thrust of his finger indicated one illegible item. "This is a mechanism used to suck the blood from a man while he still lives. And *this*"—Tep Longeur pointed again—"keeps a man's member rigid after death, so he can still be used for fornication. For those," he sneered bitterly, "who enjoy that sort of amusement."

I found that I needed to seat myself. I had been cognizant of Sher Abener's reputation, certainly. And a moment's thought might have informed me that the objects and potencies he desired were of unpleasant application. Yet I had not considered that I might become an unwitting participant in some dire rite.

"But I have accepted Sher Abener's request," I informed Tep Longeur. "It must be carried out. That is the nature of merchantries. The alternatives"—I could hardly suppress a shudder—"are disagreeable."

Indeed, my overseer himself had always insisted that a merchant must stand by his word.

Now, however, he jutted his jaw stubbornly. "The men won't do it," he repeated. "They'll leave your service first." Then he added, "I'll leave it myself. We're decent folk, all of us. We'll have nothing to do with necromancy."

Had I been of a less dignified temperament, I would have groaned aloud. Here was a choice for which I had no taste thrust upon me. The prospect of informing Sher Abener that I must decline his requirements appeared unpleasant in the extreme. At the same time, I had no answer for the threat of Tep Longeur's defection. I was entirely dependent on him. I could no more have filled his place myself than survived a contest of necromancy. If he abandoned me, I would be forced to rebuild my entire merchantry. And that burdensome task might prove impossible. If men who had grown fat in my service refused my commands, others would likely do the same.

Wracked by concerns I did not enjoy, I concluded eventually that my need for Tep Longeur's forthright service outweighed other considerations. Sher Abener must take his requirements elsewhere. He was a reasonable man, was he not? Doubtless he would be vexed by my decision—but he would accept it. And I could offer him a number of valuable compensations. I alone controlled the price of my goods, regardless of their cost of procurement, or their exotic origins. Surely he would not disdain to profit at my expense?

This decision contented me in the privacy and comfort of my villa. Unfortunately, I began to doubt it when I ventured forth to announce it to Sher Abener in person. His reputation for darkness, like the memory of his bitter visage, contrasted uncomfortably with the gracious avenues along which I strolled in the direction of his walled manor. Benedic, the seat and chief municipality of our Thal's demesne, was a sun-drenched and soothing town. Locust trees overarched the avenues, shaping the sun's kindness with an artist's hand. Whitewashed villas nearly as attractive as my own gleamed among their grounds and gardens on each side. Ladies and courtesans displayed their gowns and charms in open phaetons drawn by the fine steeds which were the source of the Thal's personal wealth. Prosperous laborers tended the walks and intersections, the gates and carriageways. And above my head a flawless sky held Benedic like the setting for a rare and grace-bedizened gem. I conceived that I had been born for the enjoyment of such days in such a place, and images of Sher Abener's dour countenance disturbed my satisfaction.

His manor was of grim granite, undressed, naked of plaster, and high-walled to foil any unwelcome attention. As it stood, it formed a blot on one of Benedic's most harmonious vistas, and I wondered as I approached why the Thal had permitted it to be built as it was. The light of the sun shunned it, and the locusts leaned askance. Its stone spoke of secrets and practices dangerously protected. Indeed, it appeared strangely ominous, as though it threatened the whole of the town. Nearing it, I became concerned that its owner and architect might not prove as reasonable as I desired.

I had with me no more retinue than one servant and a guard. Considering the nature of my errand, I had no wish for ostentation. Yet I found now that I would have preferred a greater company around me. I would have liked Sher Abener to know that I was not a man to be threatened or harmed, despite my compliant nature.

But these were fancies, I assured myself, suggested by the hard stone and unfamiliar style of the manor. Thoughts of threat and harm had no place in such sunlight, under such a sky. Benedic was not a municipality in which a man of my wealth, charm, and pleasantness need fear the ill will of his fellows. Surely the Thal would not have granted Sher Abener leave to dwell among us if his arts or his intentions were as dread as his abode.

Assuming a good face, I sent my servant to announce me at the manor's portal.

The gates opened before us, though I saw no servants drag them aside. A dreary voice instructed us to proceed to the doors of the manor itself, but I saw no speaker. And when we gained the doors, we found them wide, despite the fact that they had been unmistakably shut, and we had not seen them move.

"Sher," my guard murmured to me, "this is an unwholesome place." A pallor had come over his plump features. Sweat stood on his brow. "Do not enter."

I wished to scoff at his apprehensions, but I found that my own assurance had sunk too low. Turning to bid my servant advance ahead of me, I saw only the miscreant's back and heels as he fled between the portal gates at a run.

"Sher—" my guard quavered piteously.

Devoutly, I desired the man to display more fortitude. He had accepted good coin in my service for years, and had been asked little or nothing in return. I felt entitled to his courage. At the same time, however, I considered it unseemly for a man of my stature to appear more timorous than his underlings. Cursing the honorable intentions which had brought me to this discomfort, I took pity on him and ordered his return to my villa.

Perhaps he would spread the tale of my courage, beneficence, and forbearance, and Benedic's esteem for me would be enhanced by this otherwise distressing adventure.

Escorted by that cold comfort, I entered Sher Abener's disconcerting abode alone.

As outside, so within—my host appeared to have no servants or retainers, and need none. The manor doors admitted me to a vestibule as remarkable for its emptiness of occupants as for its dreariness of design. To one side a vast stair rose toward regions too ill lit to betray the use their master made of them. They appeared so clenched with gloom, however, that my fancy unwillingly supplied hosts of fiends pouring from them to assail me. Yet the prospect opposite the stair was hardly more pleasing. There beyond a heavy archway one featureless chamber succeeded another into the obscurity, each apparently more vacant and unadorned than the one before it. Sher Abener had scant use for windows—or the light of day. His rooms gathered darkness as a well does water.

Again an unseen speaker addressed me. "This is the present dwelling of Sher Abener in exile. His friends may enter freely. Others may not. Reveal your name and purpose."

The dour tones appeared to issue from the walls themselves—an utterance of the very stones. Once more I wondered why our Thal had permitted such an edifice to be constructed. It shed a chill into the marrow of my bones.

Striving to portray an assurance I lacked entirely, I replied, "I am Sher Urmeny. I wish to speak to Sher Abener concerning his recent transactions with my merchantry."

"Very well," assented the walls, or some other unnatural agency. "You may approach Sher Abener as he breaks his fast."

No one appeared to guide me—and I did not relish the notion of simply blundering about the manor until I chanced upon my host. After a moment or two, however, a lamp in the chamber beyond the immediate archway appeared to take light of its own accord. Finding the darkness dispelled to that extent, I ventured beyond the vestibule toward the source of illumination.

The room in which I found myself was indeed featureless—naked of adornment and windows, or of any lamps save the one now blazing necromantically before me. Yet as I neared it, another lamp took flame in the next chamber. And when I approached that light yet another announced itself ahead of me. Clearly, this unnatural display was intended to lead me to Sher Abener.

I obeyed. But I disliked progressing in that fashion. I disliked it extremely. Its impersonality and power diminished me. And what was worse, it heightened my sense of alarm. I found now that I distrusted my host. A man who treated his neighbors and associates thus violated the social ease and graciousness which characterized Benedic, and upon which I depended for much of my pleasure in life. Our Thal had erred grievously when he had granted Sher Abener a place among us. Virtuously, I resolved to tell the Thal this in person at my earliest convenience.

Such intentions steadied me somewhat, but they could not quell my growing apprehension. As I advanced through the manor, I became quite certain that its master was not a man who would respond reasonably to disappointment.

I reached him after I had crossed some eight or ten chambers which varied only in their size and in the height of their ceilings. By then I was positively relieved to discover him engaged in an activity as ordinary as breaking his fast. Truth to tell, I was even relieved by the sight of the plain trestle table at which he dined, the stool on which he sat, the blunt plate and mug which held his food and drink. During my trek, my fancies had conjured the image of a man who feasted on the dead and drank from the veins of sheep. At another time, I might have said that his rejection of physical comfort and service was both absurd and ostentatious, but in my relief I was simply glad to discern that his meal was not monstrous.

"Sher Urmeny." He inclined his head to me without rising. "It is not your custom to visit your friends in order to discuss a merchant's transactions. I fear you have come with bad tidings. What is amiss?"

Without realizing that I had stopped and fallen silent, I stared at him as though we had never met before. He was Sher Abener and no other—not a man who might be mistaken for someone else—and yet he appeared to have altered himself in some fashion. The urbane citizen of Benedic who had brought his requirements to my merchantry was gone. A stranger had assumed his face and name.

I had not noticed in our previous dealings that his voice was abrasive, as rough to the ear as new rope to the touch. Not had I observed that the sleek beard lying tightly along his cheeks and jaw appeared to have been oiled with blood and clotted in place. A look in his eyes which I had earlier taken for pleasantry now seemed feral and avid, eager to demonstrate its strength.

A moment passed before I understood that I had not answered him. I had lost my voice. Indeed, I could hardly swallow. On the instant, I determined to assure him that all his needs would be met. If this displeased Tep Longeur and my caravaneers, I would replace them as best I could. The utter ruin of my merchantry and fortunes appeared less fearsome than Sher Abener's displeasure.

Yet my resolve failed as quickly as it formed. It was impossible. Without Tep Longeur—without his honest service, and the support of men who believed as he believed—I was helpless to satisfy Sher Abener. Then I would be forced to deliver the same tidings I now bore. And the necromancer's ire would not be made less by delay.

Therefore I performed what I considered the most difficult action of my life. I swallowed my fear.

"Sher Abener," I began awkwardly, "pardon my discourtesy. I find myself disconcerted by your manor." I did not add, And by your person.

"That is its intent." His manner was grave, but also ominous. "*I* find that disconcertion inspires truthfulness in those who approach me."

His response suggested a criticism which irked me. My own manner stiffened.

"Then I will be truthful, Sher. As you surmise, I come with tidings which will be as unpleasant for you to hear as for me to relate. Recently you honored my merchantry with several small requests. I regret that I will be unable to satisfy them."

At this my host arose from his stool. I had not previously marked that he was so tall—for some reason, I had thought him shorter. Now, however, he appeared to impend over me. And the grim displeasure in his gaze only served to augment his stature.

"Sher Urmeny," he pronounced with fatal care, "that is not acceptable. I am precluded from obtaining in person the items I have requested. Therefore you must obtain them for me."

My heart quailed within me. I was inclined to accept his view of the circumstance. He was precluded. Therefore I must. His looming darkness conveyed conviction.

With some difficulty, I replied, "I am saddened on your behalf. I have no wish to distress or inconvenience you. However, I have encountered a difficulty I cannot surmount." I sought to phrase my dilemma delicately. "It appears that the objects and potencies you desire disturb those who serve my merchantry. They decline——" I shrugged to communicate my discomfort.

"That does not concern *me*," the necromancer retorted. "The unhappiness of your slaves and lackeys signifies nothing."

Despite the difficulties of my situation, I found that I was shocked. My host's comportment ill suited the good grace which characterized transactions in Benedic, and on which I had long relied. Yet his manner was not less incondite than the disdain it expressed. From the reports and gossip of my caravaneers, I was naturally aware that in some lands beyond the demesne of our Thal human flesh was considered a commodity, to be bought and sold for profit or sport. I had thought as little on the notion as possible, however. It afflicted me with queasiness, like the taste of tainted meat.

I may have attained a moment of indignation as I answered, "There is the difficulty, Sher. They are not 'slaves and lackeys.' They are men such as yourself——"

"Surely not," Sher Abener interposed blackly.

"——citizens of Benedic," I insisted, "and if they do not choose to do a thing, they cannot be compelled to it. We are a civilized people, Sher. We do not possess each other, either men or women."

Much to my chagrin, I saw a yellow light, which I took to be tongues of flame, lick at the corners of the necromancer's eyes. His ire verged on conflagration. In haste, I added, "Since I cannot satisfy you, I offer recompense. I cannot obtain that which you desire——but I can obtain much. And the cost does not concern me, since I consider that you have been ill-used. Name other wishes, Sher Abener, and I will endeavor to ensure that you are not again disappointed."

Thus I strove to appease him. He could hardly complain of me now. He might well enjoy his own displeasure——at that moment, he appeared dire enough to revel in any perversity——but he would not be able to accuse me of defalcation.

At first, his mouth twisted on the taste of bitter ruminations. The hint of flame in his gaze did not abate. He regarded me as he might have scrutinized a noxious rodent. Then, however, he nodded at the outcome of his thoughts.

"Very well, Urmeny." His neglect of my honorific suggested scorn. "You say that you do not possess men or women. That inconveniences me. In time, I will see the lack amended in this land of fops and sycophants. But for the present, a few 'slaves and lackeys' will suffice to deflect my wrath from your foolish head. Deliver to me half a dozen, three male, three female—adult, but young—and I will forget that I have been ill-used."

To my dismay, he shocked me further. In an instant, I saw my vaporous hopes for his acquiescence dissipate.

"Have I understood you, Sher Abener?" My own voice had become an unseemly croak, but I could not master it. "You wish me to procure *slaves*? You mean to practice that custom *here*?"

A sneer curled his lip. "You will find it salutary. It will teach you to spend your days otherwise than on trifles."

Trifles? Had the fitted stone of the floor shifted beneath my feet, I would not have felt more distress. How otherwise should a man conduct his life, except as I did?

"Sher—" I cast about me for some refuge, but none was apparent. "The Thal will not permit it. He will be outraged. In his demesne, such practices are shunned. Indeed, his own wives and consorts—" I faltered to silence under the bale of my host's burning censure.

"You are mistaken," he snorted. "Your 'Thal' will propose no objection. He has learned already that it does not profit him to thwart me."

Now indeed the plain stone failed to provide an adequate foundation. I was quite unable to doubt the necromancer's word. The suggestion of flame in his gaze, hinting at destruction like a blaze glimpsed within the windows of a villa, convinced me entirely. I did not believe that Sher Abener would err at any point which touched upon his arts.

"Then, Sher—" With an effort which wracked me, I swallowed at the dry dread clogging my throat. "Sher Abener, *I* am outraged. The purchase and sale of men or women is not a transaction I am inclined to countenance. You presume too far upon my goodwill." In desperation more than daring, I concluded, "Perhaps if you were sold and purchased yourself you would consider the matter in another light."

At this rebuff, my host spread his hands. Disdain sharpened his bitter mouth. From his eyes, the impression of fire began to gather and spill as though it were tears.

"If you imagine that you have the strength," he sneered, "I invite you to make the attempt."

Off his cheeks and beard, slow flame ran to his chest. He opened wide his jaws, and fluid fire bubbled in his gullet to drain past his teeth. Across his shoulders it spread in consuming runnels, and thence along his arms to his hands. There it pooled and blazed, mounting higher as it fed.

Flinching, I recoiled involuntarily. Though I stood five paces from him, his heat seemed to scorch my features, and I feared for my beard and brows. Around me, the chamber appeared to contract as darkness gathered against the light.

In the voice of a furnace, Sher Abener roared, "Begone from my sight! Obey me! *Satisfy* me! If you do not, I will render the marrow from your bones, and drink it while you *die!*"

Raging, he raised his arms to fling fierce shafts of conflagration at my defenseless head.

Until that moment, I had not considered myself a coward. My valor had never been tested. Therefore I had no cause to doubt it. In that instant, however, all illusion fell from me. My folly and weakness became plain. I had no substance of any kind—no wealth, no position, and no courage—which might enable me to stand against a man whose eyes and mouth and hands held flames of ire. Forgetting the dignity and comportment which but a short time ago I had foolishly deemed inherent to my station, I fled for my soul.

Unable to think, for my mind held only fear, I ran headlong through the unadorned chambers toward the manor's vestibule. Yet I did not flee unaccompanied. Shouts which issued from no human throat harried me on my way, as if the very stones uttered their master's displeasure.

"Obey!" the walls commanded with the lost urgency of ghouls. "Satisfy!" And the floors and ceilings echoed, "You must!"

Fortuitously, the manor doors remained open, as did the portal gates. Had I found them closed, I might have lost my wits altogether. Heedless of how I might be regarded by the passersby beyond the walls, I ran in frenzy and despair until my lungs could no longer support my exertions. And still I seemed to hear the wailing of Sher Abener's rooms, although they were now some way behind me.

"Obey! Satisfy!"

If you do not, the necromancer repeated amid the labor of my pulse and the straining of my chest, I will render the marrow from your bones—

Nevertheless by degrees the avenues embraced by locusts moderated my trepidation. Eventually, the sun's gracious light drew away a portion of my distress. The open porticoes on either hand appeared to invite me back to men and transactions and courtesies which were within my compass. Remembering the safety which had swaddled all my days, I amended somewhat the indignity of my haste.

Before I gained the sanctuary of my villa, I attempted to apply a measure of reason to my plight.

Here, under the benison of a warm breeze, I might have found it congenial to dismiss the dire necromancer's requirements and threats. But his confidence in our Thal's acquiescence to his cruel designs raised an uncomfortable echo within me. Privately, I had always considered the Thal a weak ruler—too quick to profit when he could, and too quick to retreat when he could not. More than the well-being of his citizens, he coveted the bliss of augmenting his riches. Thus I could all too easily imagine that Sher Abener had offered some rich accommodation which would inspire our lord to turn his back toward the blot of necromancy upon his demesne. The Thal was rather like myself in that regard. Trusting Tep Longeur's honesty, I had never previously troubled myself over the nature of my merchantry's transactions.

Now, however, I understood clearly that I could not recall my refusal to fulfill Sher Abener's demands. My overseer would never countenance the acquisition of slaves. And nor could I.

Therefore it was plain that I must contrive some means to defend myself.

This I determined to accomplish with little delay, once I had regained the familiar solace of my villa. My gates I would seal—although I did not expect such an obstacle to hamper my enemy. More to the point, I meant to procure assistance from my friends, associates, and neighbors, several of whom maintained in their employ theurgists of no small repute. The wards, glamours, and periapts of theurgy might secure my person. And my cohort of guards I might strengthen greatly by enlisting Tep Longeur's righteous caravaneers. If necessary, I could pay large sums for such aid—and begrudge not one saludi of the expense. Beyond all question, I could not stand against the necromancer without help.

Fear gave my resolve all the vigor it required. Despite the discomfort of speed, I advanced briskly.

Yet my resolve was folly—as much an action of fancy and moonshine as the prescient alarms which had frighted me upon first entering Sher Abener's manor. Despite our encounter, I still failed to grasp how entirely the necromancer surpassed me. For when I reached my villa, I found the ornamented welcome of the gates barred and guarded to refuse me.

Though the home I cherished was now in plain view, I could not reach it. Men whom I had known for years obstructed my way with pikes clutched in their sweating hands. Strange fears glistened whitely from their eyes. Though I ordered them to admit me—though I called loudly for succor—though I entreated them with curses—they only tightened their ward against me.

I might have screamed at them in the open street, as much in frustration as in apprehension, but before I was reduced to that indignity I saw Tep Longeur approaching the gates. He was the overseer of my merchantry—more completely in command of it than I had ever been—and his courage as well as his rectitude were unshakable. Truth to tell, the wealth I had harvested so negligently since my father's passing derived from his judgment, determination, and integrity, not from any virtue of mine. He would retrieve me from the incomprehensible terror of my guards. He would know how to defend me from Sher Abener.

When he drew near, however, he did not order the gates unbarred.

I have said that his features were sun-toughened and hardy, that his beard was trimmed as straight as his ledgers, that his gaze was quick to anger. All these things I had trusted to compensate for lacks in myself. But never had I seen his eyes burn with such fanaticism and disgust as they did now.

Without preamble, he informed me, "Urmeny, you must flee." The harshness of his voice appeared to strain his throat, although he spoke softly. "Benedic is done with you. Your life won't be tolerated. I can't hold back your death beyond the next hour."

I gaped at him. "Tep——" He appalled me to such an extent that I could scarcely form words. "What is this? Admit me. Admit me at once. I must enter or die. Sher Abener means to destroy me." My voice broke. Pointing urgently past his shoulder, I cried, *"That is my villa!"*

My overseer confronted me, unmoved. "The Sher won't destroy you if you flee. It's your merchantry he means to take."

Was this the man who had served me, and my father before me, with such fidelity for so many years? I could not credit my ears—or master my dismay. "Have you lost your wits?" I protested. "Are you drunk? Tep Longeur, I command your obedience. It is my right. You are not yourself." Clenching the bars of the gates, I pressed my appeal as near to him as I could. "Sher Abener wishes us to procure slaves for him. *Slaves*, Tep! He means to introduce that vile practice *here.*"

Though I had little acquaintance with such extremes, I saw madness in Tep's stare. Bitterly, he answered, "So it will be. He's already taken me. He'll take as many as are required to produce the outcome he intends.

"Do you think I *choose* to serve a master such as him?" Whips of fury and loathing flayed in the overseer's tone. "*I,* who refused to acquire his foul mechanisms and serums for him? I would prefer death by my own hand. As he well knows. But he cares nothing for my choices or desires. I'm only allowed to let you flee."

Foundering as though I were a swamped coracle, I strove to counter, "The Thal——"

Tep Longeur spat at my feet. "If you appeal to the Thal, you'll be laughed away. If you attempt to approach any of your friends, I must bind you and deliver you to the Sher." The mad glaring of his gaze hinted at Sher Abener's fire. "No theurgy in Benedic can preserve you. No force of arms will rise to your aid. The Sher was driven from many lands before he came among us, but he's drawn profit from those defeats. He's grown wise in the uses of power. He wouldn't have declared himself to you if he hadn't first secured his grasp upon this demesne."

My hands clutched the graceful bars of the gate, while within myself I floundered, gasping. Sher Abener had indeed surpassed me. With fire and coercion, he had altered the foundations of my life. My dilemma appeared before me in terms I could neither recognize nor understand. I did not ask how Tep Longeur could speak with such surety of the Thal's attitudes, or of Sher Abener's history. I did not think to ask. The eerie distress in the overseer's eyes sufficed to convince me that he spoke truth.

Yet if he spoke truth, then it was also true that I could not oppose him. No appeal or argument of mine would impinge upon the transformation of my circumstances. My life depended utterly upon the presumption that Tep Longeur would accept my instructions and carry them out. My merchantry and all my wealth derived from that conviction. If he refused me now, I was powerless to compel him.

In that way, he bereft me of dignity even more thoroughly than did his new master. I might have preferred to face the necromancer's power again. Tep Longeur's forced madness was as fatal to me—and far more hurtful to my self-regard.

"Yet you are not such a man, Tep," I panted, although my resistance was broken. "You have said it yourself. How do you carry out his wishes?"

His teeth set against each other as on a bit. Between them, he answered, "With great pain."

To that I could make no reply. Beyond question, I was powerless.

Yet where could I go? I had no other home than Benedic. And the nearest municipality where I might obtain temporary lodging was some ten leagues distant, too far for even a hardy man—which I was not—to journey afoot under this sun. Indeed, my feet were better suited to being massaged with perfumed oils than to arduous treks. I would cripple myself within a league. Within two, I would perish of thirst.

Helpless to do otherwise, I cast my fate abjectly upon the overseer's mercy. "Tep," I beseeched him, "I must have a horse. I will die upon the road without a horse."

His anguish wrung my heart, although I was its victim. Unlike myself, he was accustomed to responsibility and action. Doubtless he had taken pride in the necessary authority of his place as my overseer. Perhaps he had gone so far as to take pride in my dependence upon him. By his own admission, his plight was an excruciation to him. The cost of his distress was ledgered in his face.

"That's not permitted." He spoke so thickly that he seemed to choke himself. "The Sher desires only your immediate departure. He doesn't care that you die."

My dignity was gone. I made no effort to reclaim it now. "Tep," I groaned, "I am lost. Without you, I am naught." A well-meaning fool, empty of hope. "I have no power to save myself." Though I saw how my words pained him, I did not hold them back. "If you do not succor me, I must abandon myself where I stand, and accept whatever ill Sher Abener intends for me."

The prospect of being enslaved—*taken* as Tep Longeur had been *taken*—horrified me. Yet I saw no alternative to it.

Despite Sher Abener's tyranny, the overseer retained some vestige of the man he had been. Anguish glared from his gaze, but he did not refuse me again. Instead, he raised one strong hand before him, leather palm inward, and struck himself a resounding blow across the cheek.

Thus compelled, he informed me in bitten words, "I'll do it."

At once, he turned to the guards. "A horse for Urmeny," he demanded. "Quickly. Before the Sher stops us."

Apparently, it was fear rather than necromancy which commanded the guards. Tep Longeur ruled them with his own authority as much as with Sher Abener's. Together, they pelted in disarray toward the stables.

Though my life hung on the delay, I turned my back to the gates while I waited. The Tep struck himself again, and yet again, and I could not bear the sight. Truth to tell, I did not mean to look at him ever again, if I could avoid it. My own catastrophe consumed me. I could not attend to his.

Nevertheless he demanded my notice. In a voice which must surely have drawn blood from the soft flesh of his throat, he pronounced, "Urmeny, it's your place to help us."

Involuntarily, I flinched as though he had slapped at me. Turning my head, I directed my dismay toward him.

"The merchantry was yours," he continued cruelly. "The villa was yours. We were yours. The burden is yours. If you don't rescue us, we'll never be free. Even death won't redeem us from the Sher."

Rescue them? *I?* At another time, I might have laughed my scorn into his face. Only the open agony of his regard restrained me.

I lowered my gaze. "You have mistaken me for my father," I answered in a groan. At that moment, I loathed myself. Nevertheless I spoke the truth. "I am not such a man."

There Tep Longeur could not gainsay me. Though he continued to stand against me, he did not speak again. No other farewell passed between us, regardless of our years together. When his men brought the beast they had selected—a tired, old nag with a gait like a broken wheel—he opened the gates for it, but took care to ensure that I could not attempt to enter.

His men had cinched a traveling saddle to the beast's back. Pitifully, I set my foot to the stirrup and pitched upward. Gripping the reins in both hands—I did not trust my seat otherwise—I hauled my horse's head around and departed from my home and my life at a wrenching canter.

So it was that I left Benedic on a mount I could scarcely endure, lacking both water and food, with no coin beyond the few saludi I chanced to carry in my purse, no destination except to reach a place where I might gain lodging, and no purpose other than to escape Sher Abener.

I could not say whose voice haunted me more as I rode, the necromancer's or Tep Longeur's.

I will render the marrow from your bones, and drink it while you die!

If you don't rescue us, we'll never be free.

Under the shade and locusts of Benedic, the sun's warmth had seemed kindly, beneficent. But when I had left behind the washed plaster of the municipality's walls and risen among the hills which bordered Benedic to the west, I learned that a benison may also be a curse. In my merchant's finery, I was foolishly attired for a journey, and the trees which graced the hillsides—olive, locust, and feather-leafed litchi—gave no cover to the dusty roadway. Before my trek was truly commenced, I had begun to ooze like a squeezed pomegranate.

Within a league, I had shed my formal cloak. Within two, I had bundled my robe behind my saddle, leaving myself clad in naught but a loose blouse, my flowing underbreeches, and a fop's ornate sandals. Still the weight of the sun accumulated on my head and shoulders, bearing down like the threat of Sher Abener's malice. Under its pressure, I soon saw difficulties and dilemmas throng the shimmering heat before me.

Thirst was the most immediate of my discomforts, although it was among the least of my concerns, for I knew that beyond the next ridge of hills lay the river Ibendwey. Hunger would assume larger proportions as my journey extended itself. However, the lack of substance in my purse posed a far greater peril. Doubtless there were men and women in the wide world who would have called my few saludi wealth, but I did not. With the coin I carried, I could purchase lodging in an austere inn for a brace of days, no more. Then they would be gone.

Worse still was the fact that I could not long call upon the credit of my merchantry to sustain me. Beyond Benedic's boundaries, men with whom I had indirectly shared many transactions would perhaps make me welcome—briefly—in the name of our joint ventures. Yet I hardly knew their names. I did not know the men themselves at all. While Tep Longeur had cared for my interests, I had paid them a profound inattention. And it was certain those men would refer their curiosity concerning my circumstances to Benedic, and would learn that I could no longer command my own riches.

What would they do then, those men whose names I could scarcely recall? Why, naturally they would be overtaken by pity for my helpless plight, as well as by righteous indignation on my behalf. Being strong, forthright, wise, and above all generous, they would devise some means— I could not imagine what—to quash my dire foe, restoring what I had lost. Would I not have done the same in their place?

Honesty and thirst, and the burnished pressure of the sun, compelled me to admit that I would not. I had enjoyed wealth too much, and contention too little, to bestir myself against any injustice which did me no personal harm.

Clearly, I must prepare myself for the likelihood that men with whom I had once shared profit would simply turn their backs upon me, once they discovered the truth of my condition.

Then what would I do?

I had no idea at all.

If you don't rescue us, we'll never be free.

Tep Longeur's appeal galled my sore heart. I was not fit to carry such burdens—as he well knew. If I could not prolong my life with alms in the days ahead, I would die as surely as if I had given myself over to Sher Abener's mercy.

Daunted by such considerations, I was in a state approaching despair as my nag crested the intervening ridge, and I saw below me the course of the river Ibendwey.

Eager to slake my thirst, I amended my pace. As I descended, however, I soon observed that the river was swollen and swift, troubled with silt. Quantities of rain must have fallen in the mountains which fed the water-course, for the current surged and frothed uncomfortably. Even my inexpert eye could discern that a customarily placid ford had become turbulent and uncertain.

In dismay, my heart sank still lower. Here was another obstacle I could not surmount. Not only had the crossing become impassable, but the water appeared undrinkable as well. Now I must either suffer from thirst or make myself ill with unclean drink—and yet neither choice would improve my lot, for I would remain within reach of the necromancer's power.

Surely a malign fate had stirred my stars when Sher Abener had first selected my merchantry to serve him. My doom had been fixed from that moment, and nothing I might do would alter it.

Thus consumed by my own difficulties, I did not immediately notice that there appeared to be a man caught in the midst of the tumultuous stream.

Blinking against the perspiration of my brow, I peered downward. There, beyond question—a man perched on a jutting boulder midway between the banks of the Ibendwey. How he had come to place himself in such straits I could not at first imagine. Had he attempted the ford afoot, despite the force of the river? If so, he was either a fool or a madman. Or perhaps the Ibendwey had risen suddenly, surprising him with its rush. My caravaneers had often described similar misadventures. Taken unaware, the man below me had gained the only sanctuary within reach before the current could bear him away.

Madman, fool, or unfortunate, he was well stranded. Until the Ibend-wey eased its spate—or until some rescue chanced upon him—he remained ensnared, as helpless to correct his plight as I was to answer Sher Abener's ire.

Whipping the reins, I belabored my mount to a brisker pace.

The man crouched upon his boulder with his knees against his chest, his head downcast. He seemed unaware of my approach—certainly he did not react to it. Instead he appeared to stare vacantly into the current as though he studied the swift tumble of silt for auguries.

At first, I could see little of him. Rudely cropped hair was his head's only covering. Boots clogged with mud, an unmarked and indefinite brown shirt, worn leather breeches—so much was visible. To that extent, his apparel suggested that he was a traveler. Yet he had no sack or satchel for a traveler's belongings and supplies. His possessions must have been lost when the rising of the river overtook him. In every particular, he was indistinguishable from the grime and wear of his sojourns.

Nevertheless as I neared the marge where the Ibendwey's rush gnawed at my road, and halted to scrutinize the man more closely, I discovered that despite his lowered head and dull raiment he seemed more *vivid* than his circumstances or surroundings. He drew my gaze as though he made all other things illusory by comparison. An air of significance resembling a hint of the sun's own fire defined him against the far verge of the river. In some fashion, he was more truly *there* than any man I had ever met.

How he achieved this effect mystified me. Whatever the cause, how-ever, its result was to convey the disturbing impression that his crouch upon the boulder was the only aspect of the Ibendwey's spate which held any importance.

Hardly thinking what I did, I shouted, "Ho, fellow! Do you require aid?"

He seemed unable to hear me—still unaware of my presence. I told myself that my call had not carried over the loud grumble of the river in its ragged banks. Yet I was troubled by the eerie conviction that he would have heard me easily if I had not lacked the *vividness* to attract his notice. Like the peril in which he found himself, I had no importance. If my pampered and pleasant life in Benedic had owned any real substance, Sher Abener could not have stripped me of it with so little difficulty.

This belief was unreasonable as well as unexplained. The traveler's need was obvious—and there was no one else to help him.

In response, a sudden, unwonted fury overcame me. My composure had passed its limits. I had suffered altogether too much thirst and heat and humiliation.

"Ho, fellow!" I shouted again. "Do you take pleasure in your plight? Heed me, fool! There is no other rescue! I have seen no one else on the road."

When he did not so much as raise his eyes, I added, "I will abandon you where you sit!" As I myself had been abandoned by those who held my life in their hands.

For the moment, I had forgotten that I had nowhere else to go.

Yet I did not forget that I possessed a horse. The man trapped before me had none. Contemptible though my nag undoubtedly was, the beast might be able to brave a current which I could not confront myself.

And this deaf traveler was indeed trapped. The Ibendwey's spate gave no sign that it might abate. In time, of course, the waters would recede, as they must. But that might not occur for days. Indeed, the river might swell still more while the storm in the mountains ran its course—might swell until it swept the man from his perch and carried him to his death. Already I seemed to see the torrent thrash higher against his rock.

Apparently, my mind had ceased to perform its functions. I could neither gauge the dangers nor estimate my chances of success. Without thought or circumspection, I pounded my mount with my heels until the beast plunged unwillingly down the slope into the swift tumble of the stream.

The chill shock of the waters, and the instant frenzy of my nag's efforts to keep its footing, restored me at once to a saner state of mind. I was no hardy drover or muscled caravaneer to attempt such feats. And I lacked the skills to aid my mount in its struggles. With every heave on the reins, I threatened to overbalance the nag or unseat myself. Quickly, I resolved to retreat while I could—

Yet to turn seemed as perilous as to advance. I kept my beast surging forward. Together, we strove toward the traveler's rock with all our strength.

Soaked and gasping, scarcely able to breathe amid my efforts to retain my seat, I saw within the space of a few heartbeats that my task was impossible. I had crossed no more than a third of the distance, and already I felt my mount's hooves skid and stumble beneath me. In another moment, I would cause us both to capsize. The horse squealed in terror. I may well have wept.

As my heart quailed, however, and I began to slip helplessly from my saddle, the trapped man at last lifted his head and looked at me.

For an instant, his gaze held mine, and a sense of dislocation came over me, as though the wheel of time had jumped its rut and run briefly astray. Although I was about to founder and drown, I ignored my plight, for I had never seen eyes as *blue* and piercing as those of the man I sought to aid. They seemed at once deeper and more uncompromising than the very heavens—eyes which might stare into the heart of the sun as easily as into the pit of my cowardice and futility, without squinting.

During that instant, he appeared to keep me in my seat, and my nag upright on its legs, by the simple force of his gaze.

Then I found that I had covered more than half the distance. I remained in my seat, and my mount had gained better footing—retreat had become pointless. The beast and I had finally achieved a measure of unanimity in our efforts. Though we still plunged and stumbled frantically, we continued toward our goal.

After its brief dislocation, time's wheel hastened in compensation. Events became a rush as urgent as the writhing of the river. My mount and I gained the traveler's boulder on its downstream side. By some miracle, the froth-filled eddy there enabled us to turn, and then to press closely against the stone, so that the man might lower himself to us with less risk of a fall. Swiftly, he stretched out a leg and shifted his limbs downward until he straddled the nag behind me. As suddenly as we had reached him, we bore him back the way we had come.

My mount seemed stronger now, despite its extra burden. Doubtless the traveler's weight improved its footing, and the sight of safety before us gave the beast vigor. Nevertheless I imagined that the nag drew substance from the man's strange intensity—that the beast's strength reflected its new rider. I felt the effect myself. Though he kept his seat by gripping my shoulders, he did not overbalance me, as anyone else would surely have done. Indeed, his grasp kept me steady, when I would have floundered without it.

Scant moments later, blowing spume like a creature of the vast sea, the horse heaved us recklessly up the drowned road to higher ground and dry dirt.

There the man squeezed my shoulders as if in thanks, then slid over the beast's rump to the roadway. At once, all my fear was transformed to weakness. Urgency drained from me as though I were a cistern holed at its base, and a profound lassitude took its place. The day had held too many terrors, too much heat and thirst—more than I could endure. Helpless to do otherwise, I slipped from my saddle and folded to the ground. Supine, I closed my eyes and felt myself swept away by a spate of abject weariness.

I was not aware of sleep. To the best of my knowledge, I rested for a short time only. Yet when I looked up again the sun had moved noticeably toward midday, and my garments were dry. Truth to tell, it was the discomfortable sensation that I was being baked which had roused me.

Blinking rapidly to moisten my parched eyes, I propped my torso upright and peered about me.

By chance my head was turned toward the Ibendwey. The sight troubled me vaguely, but at first I could not name the cause. Was it because I had nearly perished there? No— For a moment or two I regarded the river stupidly. Then I grasped the truth.

Some distance below me, the stream chuckled placidly over a shallow ford. The tumult in which I had risked my life was gone, leaving no sign of its passage—neither debris nor dampness upon the verges, nor erosion of the banks. Tall as a man, the boulder on which the traveler had perched jutted calmly from the ford, unassailed by torrents, the stone as dry as dust.

If I had merely waited for an hour or perhaps two, the endangered man would have needed no rescue, and I could have spared myself—

Stung by a peculiar sense of alarm, I stumbled to my feet and wheeled to look for my mount, as well as for the traveler I had so foolishly aided.

Asked to account for my quick fright, I might have said I feared that the man had taken my nag and deserted me. The truth was otherwise, however—more obscure as well as more disturbing. In fact, I seemed chiefly to fear that he had *not* left me alone.

Too soon, I found that he had not.

Some small distance uphill from me, he sat my mount as though he owned the beast. Both he and the nag faced me in the light of the sun. By some weird theurgy, the horse had been transfigured. In every particular, it remained the decrepit nag Tep Longeur had granted me—and yet its manner had become regal. It appeared to consider itself one of the Thal's coursers, avid for show or contest. It held its head up, snorting from flared nostrils and champing its bit. Its eyes regarded me contemptuously.

In contrast, the traveler was unchanged. His apparel had dried cleanly, and his boots had shed their mud as if they resisted mire and murk. He seemed untouched, untouchable—beyond the reach of Thals and sovereigns. His seat showed the natural poise of a born horseman. One hand controlled the reins with negligent ease. The sun shone full upon his face—and yet I received no impression of his features. They might have been aquiline or equine for all I knew. His gaze consumed me to the exclusion of other details.

My apprehension grew, and I squirmed under the discomfiting precision of his scrutiny as though I were a misbehaved boy. For a long moment, he studied me, considering what he saw. Then he announced, "I am in your debt."

His voice was mild enough. Yet it hinted at the clangor of iron—a sound which both dismayed and stirred me, as if those responses were indistinguishable.

Still mildly, he instructed me, "Tell me your name."

My thirst had renewed its force, accentuated by exertion. My throat clenched, and I could not swallow. Suddenly I feared this man as though he were another like Sher Abener, fatal and malign.

Yet I did not find it possible to refuse an answer. With an effort, I croaked, "Urmeny. Massik Urmeny. Sher Urmeny. Of Benedic." Awkwardly I concluded, "A merchant."

The man upon my horse appeared to consider my reply adequate. He nodded once with an air of unalterable resolution. Then he turned the nag and headed away up the slope at a gliding trot.

I was at once so amazed and so appalled that I could not immediately react. He took my mount— Comprehension failed me. I could not grasp what had just transpired. Instead of running or raging after him, I gaped at his back in stupefaction. I did not wonder at what he did. Rather, I wondered where my nag had learned that light-hoofed gait.

After a moment, however, the fact that he had just stolen my horse penetrated my thoughts.

Stolen my horse and abandoned me—

Without considering my actions, I pitched my worn limbs into a laborious run. In my mind, I shouted after him, Ho, fellow, fool, thief! Is this how you repay a debt? *That is my horse!* Nevertheless my lips released neither indignation nor protest. I could not voice what filled my heart. He was too substantial to be touched by my accusations.

Yet I required some outcry—I could not remain silent. Like a madman, I wailed at his back, "At least tell me *your* name! You are in my debt. Tell me who repays me."

At that, he turned. The jarring beast I had ridden from Benedic pranced a neat curvette, then struck a pose of disdain while it awaited its rider's next command. I stopped to hear him, and his answer reached me as clearly as a curse.

"I am Sher Urmeny."

I was no longer certain of what I saw. My nag may have reared, pawing scorn into the air, before it bore its rider away.

Slack-jawed with astonishment, I stared after them. Had I been bereft of my wits? Perhaps so. Did the traveler mean to ride my horse to Benedic, calling himself by my name? *My name?* I wished to believe that I had misheard him, but his announcement conveyed too much certainty. First he stole my horse. Then he took my *name?* Because he was in my *debt?*

Briefly I became so incensed that I fumed at the sky, stamping my feet and flailing my fists. However, I lacked the energy for such displays, and the heat of the day chastened them. Soon I grew calmer.

It was necessary for me to choose my course.

I could not remain where I was—so much was plain. When I had done railing at dark necromancers and thieving travelers, I would be left alone under the hard sun, hungry and friendless. Therefore I had no alternative but to continue my journey—or to return to Benedic. Wearily, I considered the matter.

In the name of my sanity, if not of my survival, I wished to increase my distance from Sher Abener—and from the traveler as well. I could have crossed the Ibendwey easily now—trudged footsore and beaten as a mendicant along the way I had begun this morning. The journey might slay me, however, unaccustomed as I was to such travel. I had no strength for the task. I also had no robe to protect me when the night grew cold. The man in my debt had taken it with my horse. If I wished to live, I must turn toward my lost home.

The prospect filled me with a dread bordering upon nausea. Yet it seemed unavoidable. Striving to summon courage enough for the hazard, I concentrated my attention, not upon Sher Abener, but upon the madman I had rescued.

Never before had I undertaken an action as perilous as broaching the Ibendwey's spate. At another time, I might have prided myself on it. But my debtor repaid me by stealing my horse and pretending to my name.

In one sense, I had not the slightest comprehension of what had passed between us. In another, however, I found that I understood it well enough. Stripped of my life, degraded by friend and foe alike, dismayed by sun and thirst and futility, I had become somewhat mad myself. I could account for the behavior of madmen.

Perhaps he sincerely considered that he might repay his debt by confronting the difficulties which had driven me from my home. For that reason, he meant to ride into Benedic upon my nag, proclaiming himself with my name. But he would be laughed to scorn. I was too well known to be replaced by an impostor. If he were fortunate, he would merely receive ridicule and disregard—or perhaps expulsion from the municipality. Otherwise, he might find himself imprisoned by the Thal—or, worse, noticed by Sher Abener.

So it seemed to me that if I followed him I might eventually gain an opportunity to reclaim my horse.

This appeared my best hope. Certainly, I could not imagine another.

Therefore I swallowed my visceral alarm, mustered the remains of my strength, and set out upon the course I had chosen.

Sadly, the vitality of decision soon deserted me. By the time I had crested the ridge and put the river behind me, I knew that even this road might prove too arduous. I should have drunk from the Ibendwey when I could. A furnace of thirst had come to fire in the parched tinder of my throat, and my tongue had swollen beyond speech. Yet that distress was no more than a dull misery beside the state of my feet. My sandals had been made for decoration rather than travel—already they had galled my skin to blisters and blood. Yet when I removed them I learned that the roadway was rougher than I had realized. Pebbles and shards gouged at my soles until I donned my sandals again. Then the straps of the sandals ate like acid at my flesh until I removed them again. Though the sun threatened to scald my face and neck and hands, I hardly noticed that hurt through the pain of my abused feet.

Benedic was the only destination I could hope to gain. Any farther goal would have seen me sprawled by the roadway in despair. Only the thought that I might retrieve my mount kept me upright.

Even so, I might have faltered and failed, were it not for the curious fact that the stranger seemed unable to outdistance me. Though the nag moved at a light trot, horse and rider remained in view. Indeed, I appeared to gain on them. By some means which baffled me, my abject trudge closed the distance. I made no effort to hasten after them. Yet I shortened their lead stride after stride.

Thus they lured me on through my misery. By the time they gained the walls of the municipality, they were no more than a pike's cast ahead of me.

At other times, I had enjoyed the vista of those walls. Their clean and sweeping lines proclaimed Benedic's kempt grace to all who approached. Now, however, they served principally to restore my apprehension. My feet were so bloody, and my skin so burned—my unhappiness so complete—that I had not thought myself still capable of fear. Yet I valued my survival enough to dread Sher Abener.

I wished to reclaim my mount *here*, outside the walls—away from the necromancer.

Stumbling, I strove to improve my pace, so that I might draw nearer to the impostor.

It was customary that Benedic's open gates were guarded. It was *not* customary that the guards attended to their duties. The municipality had been a place of placid commerce and easy wealth for many years. Guards watched the gates only to inform strangers that they must pay their courtesies to the Thal, both in respect and in coin. When I had ridden outward, I had seen no sign that anyone marked my passing. Indeed, I had assumed that both pikemen slept in the gatehouse.

Yet now they stood against the traveler and my nag, their pikes crossed and clenched between them in righteous trepidation.

"Halt!" one of them called in a voice which may have quavered.

The stranger sat my mount with an air of authority. "What is the meaning of this indignity, fellow?" he responded. "I am Sher Urmeny. Benedic is my home. I am known here. Admit me at once."

I was near enough to hear him. Nevertheless I believed for a moment that I had mistaken his reply. He could not be such a fool. I was indeed known here. In another moment, he would be answered with mockery.

But he was not. "Still you must halt, Sher," the guard retorted. His voice gathered the force of duty. "We are commanded to apprehend you. Your offenses have displeased the Thal, Sher Urmeny, and you must appear before his judgment."

For the space of several heartbeats, I stopped in dismay. The pikeman had called the stranger *by my name?* He could not see the truth? I felt as though the hard dirt and stone of the roadway had lurched beneath my feet, causing me to totter for balance. I beheld my usurper and the guards, the gates and the wall, distinctly in the heavy light of the sun—and yet they appeared to dissipate as I stared, sacrificing their substance to moonshine and guesswork. I almost expected them to become mist and disappear before me—mirages cast by heat and thirst, and by nothing else that I had ever known.

Nevertheless the man on my nag dared disdain. "This is unjust," he countered sternly. "I am ignorant of any offense. Why is the Thal displeased?"

His mode of address daunted the guards. Attempting hauteur, the one who spoke achieved mere surliness as he stated, "If you are ignorant of your own actions, Sher Urmeny, you will be reminded of them before the Thal. Dismount, and we will convey you there."

Without warning, I staggered out of my immobility. This was intolerable! That man claimed my name—and the Thal pikemen *acknowledged* him? Did they mean to visit the Thal's—and Sher Abener's—*displeasure* at me upon his demented head? His madness had overtaken them as well as himself.

"Fools!" I cried. My parched throat permitted only a harsh croak, but I gave it what vehemence I could. "Has the sun baked your wits? Have you been bedazzled?" Unsteadily I hastened forward. "I am Sher Urmeny. I am *known* to you!

"*That* is a madman." My arm trembled with indignation as I indicated the traveler. "I am clad in sweat and grime, and close to death from thirst, but *I am known to you!*"

The man I had rescued paid no heed to my protest—indeed, he appeared not to have heard it—but both guards turned from him to regard me balefully. The one who had yet spoken addressed me.

"Have a care, fellow," he pronounced. "This man has been apprehended, it's true—but he's no wandering caitiff to be insulted by the likes of you. He is a Sher of Benedic, and holds a respected place among us. Be off, or we will cast you to the outer middens. Seek alms elsewhere. Beggary and destitution are unwelcome here."

This reproof shocked me so entirely that I halted my advance and closed my mouth. Because I could not comprehend what I had just heard, my mind shied from it. Staring aghast at the guards and my pretended self, I thought of nothing except the surprising revelation that Benedic repulsed the ruined and the poor. I had not known our Thal ruled so. I had always conveniently believed that the gates and opportunities of the municipality were open to all who came this way.

By some means I could not explain, the stranger appeared to solidify himself against the guards. His tone assumed an ominous hue—a color of warning. "Nevertheless," he vowed, "I will not dismount for men who perform such duties. Attend me to the Thal if you must, and I will answer his displeasure. But do not pretend that you compel me."

Seconding its rider, the nag arched its neck regally and stamped its hooves as though the decrepit, broken-gaited beast had been bred to battle.

Although they sneered at me, the guards blanched visibly before my usurper. They must truly have credited his assumption of my name. Together, they bowed. "As you wish, Sher Urmeny," said the first, nearly fawning where but a moment earlier he had been peremptory. "If you will ride between us, we will escort you."

The man inclined his head in condescension. Proud as a suzerain, he rode my mount through the gates into Benedic. Quickly the guards took their places at his sides, but he ignored them.

They appeared to forget me at once when they turned their backs— why, I did not know. Yet forget me they did. Although they had warned me away, they did not close the gates against me, or give any sign that they noticed me as I followed.

The lunacy of my circumstances frightened me more with every stride. Bloody of foot and broiled of body, I lurched after my horse and my name, as lost in what transpired as this eerie traveler had been in the Ibendwey's spate. I had no recourse but to follow, however. My need for a mount remained unaltered. And I had received a blow which seemed to compel me.

That the stranger claimed my name was merely madness. He did not know the peril it conveyed. But that the guards who knew me *believed* him—ah, that was the stuff of dismay and nightmares. It shook me to my heart, chiefly because it seemed to remove me from existence, depriving me of substance entirely, but also because it implied theurgy, a glamour to confuse the senses of the pikemen. And theurgy could not stand against necromancy.

If the stranger's power to assume my place held, he would suffer harm meant for me.

I found that this appalled me as much as the loss of my identity. It reft me, not only of my name, but of my value to myself. *I* had refused Sher Abener's demands and incurred his wrath—I and no other. If the consequences fell upon the stranger in my stead, my refusal was diminished to the point of triviality.

Even Tep Longeur's plight had not so thoroughly effaced the worth of my life.

Despite my helplessness to direct events, I must somehow persuade my usurper to give over his charade before he reached the Thal's estate, or he would find himself at Sher Abener's mercy.

Fearing each step I took, I clutched at any hope I could conceive. Perhaps my usurper's glamour would fail before more sophisticated witnesses. If we encountered someone acquainted with theurgy, that individual might pierce and dispel the confusion. Then my name would be restored to me—and I might be able to reacquire my horse.

Thus we passed along the benign avenues of Benedic, the roadways and prospects I had loved throughout my life—he on my mount, the Thal's guards beside him, and I wincing behind them, so weary and worried that I could hardly keep my feet out of the nag's droppings.

At first, we passed only a few streetsweepers, a day laborer or two, the occasional artisan abroad in the municipality to procure or fulfill a commission—no one who might meet my need. Soon, however, I saw ahead of us a new test of the stranger's power to displace me. A sterner test—or so I imagined hopefully. Along the avenue came an open phaeton bearing none other than Sher Obalist and his lady. They knew me well, for they were my neighbors. Their grounds edged mine on the less propitious side of my villa. And they employed a theurgist to entertain, advise, and defend them. Surely they were familiar with the arts and actions of theurgy.

From their route and the time of day, I concluded that Sher and Sharna Obalist were homeward bound from one of the racing festivals at which our Thal celebrated his latest steeds. If so, it was apparent that Sher Abener's enmity and my flight had not altered ordinary events in Benedic by so much as a shrug.

I reacted without forethought. To the extent that I was still capable of sane intent, I considered that I might help penetrate the stranger's glamour if I acted promptly. With as much dignity as my damaged feet permitted, I rushed ahead of my usurper and his escort in order to accost Sher Obalist.

His garb and that of his lady confirmed that they had indeed come from the races. On another occasion, I might have taken a moment to compare his raiment with mine—and to congratulate myself upon my better taste. Now, however, the contrast was all to his advantage. Sweat- and road-stained as I was, I compared unfavorably with his grooms and lackeys.

Plump and portentous, he peered out from his phaeton as though he were uncertain of what he saw. Unfortunately, his regard was fixed, not on me, but on the stranger. He might have been unaware of my presence.

Bowing politely to my usurper, he pronounced, "Sher Urmeny," like a man who felt constrained to deliver unpleasant tidings.

The stranger bowed in response, but did not speak.

I made an attempt to intrude between them. "Sher Obalist." Although dust and thirst threatened to choke me, I forced words from my abused throat. "Sharna. You must help me."

His lady noticed me before he did. Her gaze dropped to mine, and at once a look of fright disturbed her lacquered countenance. Around her eyes and mouth, the paints and polishes which concealed her years cracked as she shrank back into her cushions. One hand clutched urgently at her husband's forearm.

The Sher turned a perplexed frown toward her. He seemed unable to see me until she pointed me out. When he had followed her trembling indication to its target, however, he noticed me at last.

His expression became a scowl of disapproval. Jowls quivering, he commanded, "Stand aside, fellow. You have come between your betters. Here is Sher Urmeny, and I must speak with him."

Even in my unbalanced state, I observed that he did not refer to me as "my esteemed neighbor, Sher Urmeny," as was his custom. No doubt his familiar fulsomeness had been cooled by the knowledge that the Thal was displeased with me.

"No, Sher Obalist," I insisted with more ardor than he was accus- tomed to hearing. "You must speak with *me*. *I* am Sher Urmeny.

"Gaze upon me closely," I urged. "You will see that I speak truth. That man"—I flung an unsteady accusation toward the stranger—"is a charlatan who seeks to impose upon your credulity." Certainly he failed to resemble me in any particular.

When the Sher did not respond—did not in fact appear to comprehend what I said—I appealed to his lady, with whom I had often flirted out of courtesy, dissembling personal distaste. "Sharna. You know me. You know—"

My supplication went no farther. Without warning, one of the guards dealt me a cuff to the ear, which caused me to stumble against Sher Obalist's near horse and then fall, tumbling like refuse to the roadway.

I did not lose consciousness, despite my exhaustion. I heard what passed above my head. To some extent, I retained my sight. However, the capacity for movement deserted me entirely. If my neighbor's horses had stepped on me, I might have been unable to cry out.

Sher Obalist's voice reached me through a clamor of pain. "Such a fellow has no place here," he informed the guards indignantly. "He must be ejected from Benedic."

"He will be, Sher," one of them answered. "We will return for him when we have conveyed Sher Urmeny to the Thal."

"See that you do so."

"You wished to speak to me," the stranger interjected mildly. He betrayed no interest in my condition.

Disconcerted, Sher Obalist huffed, "Indeed. So I did." Apparently he could not at first recall what he had intended to say. "That is"—with an effort he mastered the disturbance of his thoughts—"I meant to express my concern, and that of my lady." He patted the Sharna's hand as though to console her. "The Thal's displeasure is severe. It must be appeased. But I trust that you will answer the difficulty for the benefit of us all." His tone suggested the reverse of this pious sentiment. "And indeed of all Benedic," he concluded portentously.

I wished to inquire, And how shall I accomplish this miracle of resolution? By necromancy? However, my throat and tongue declined to obey me.

"Fear nothing," my usurper responded. His confidence was pleasant to hear. "I will repay my debts."

"Then I will wish you good fortune, Sher Urmeny," said my neighbor. His relief was evident. Doubtless he was pleased that he had found means to break off the exchange before the pretender on my nag thought to request his support or assistance. At his command, the phaeton rolled into motion.

The supposed Sher Urmeny and his guards resumed their progress toward the Thal's estate. I was left alone and derelict in the road, still unable to shift my limbs or raise my head.

For a moment or two, I could not imagine why I should trouble to rise. The stranger's glamour sufficed to baffle even experienced observation. Wrapped in mystification, he proposed to replace me before the Thal—and Sher Abener. Well and good. I would be spared the Thal's displeasure—and Tep Longeur's doom.

In other ways, my continued endurance from this day to the next had become purely conjectural. I had not the smallest idea how I might achieve it. But even if I perished of thirst or exposure before the wounds on my feet turned to putrefaction, I would not go to my death with Sher Abener's grasp upon my soul.

While the guard's blow still throbbed in my head, I was content. As the pain receded, however, images of Tep Longeur intruded on my thoughts. In memory, I saw him turn a gaze tormented by horror and disgust toward my ineffectuality. Again I heard him say, *Urmeny, it's your place to help us.*

He had addressed his appeal to me, not to the impostor in my place.

Here again, I found that my usurper had diminished me grievously. He had imposed himself between me and my own actions. I did not suffer the possession Tep Longeur experienced. Nevertheless I could no longer choose what I did—or what was done in my name. I could only watch while another Sher Urmeny made choices and accepted hazards which appalled me.

To be so entirely deprived of myself filled me with a horror and chagrin which compelled me to my feet. Groaning, I pried my battered flesh from the roadway and stumbled after the stranger. The matter had become more urgent to me than my simple need for a mount. I had grown desperate to recover my name.

Therefore I required some means by which I might preserve my usurper from the consequences of his folly.

Thus driven, I pursued him grimly along the avenues.

As before, his escorts appeared to have forgotten my existence. Although they had promised to expel me from the municipality, they spent not a glance in my direction. And again my usurper had somehow failed to gain much distance. Surely he should have passed out of sight by now—yet there he rode, no more than a loud hail ahead of me. My nag's tail flared like a pennon from its rump.

So I limped and groaned behind him. Through a haze of weariness, I saw him nod courteously to all he passed, men of rich birth and low, women both comely and plain. Some greeted him with my stolen name. Others avoided him by veering to the far side of the avenue. Clearly opinion in Benedic was divided regarding the safety—or the wisdom—of acknowledging my acquaintance.

The Thal's estate formed the center of the municipality, and was highly esteemed for both its luxuriance and its artistry. In my view, its grounds and furnishings were too profusely opulent to be truly tasteful. As matters stood, however, I cared nothing for aesthetic considerations. Instead I concentrated on the task of overtaking my usurper before he passed through the gates onto the estate. Once he entered there, and the gates were closed against me, my last chance to distract him would be lost. The wall which encircled the estate was high enough to prevent observation of what transpired beyond it—entirely too high for me to climb even in my dreams, still more so in my present condition. I must succeed now or accept failure.

The finest locusts in all Benedic overarched those gates, offering those who approached a swath of shade so soothing and precious that it left me giddy. I tottered as though I were in my cups as the stranger and his escort paused to gain admittance.

Unfortunately, they were allowed inward before I could reach them. And I feared to raise my voice after them—I could not bear to be struck again. With my arms outstretched in mute supplication, I lurched to the gates as the Thal's pikemen drew them shut.

Seeing ruin before me, my eyes filled with helpless tears, and I made a forlorn sound which might have been a sob. I was exhausted beyond endurance, and lacked the dignity to bear either my frustration or my alarm.

So that I would not fall, I gripped the bars of the gate. Pressing my face there, I muttered piteously to the pikemen, "Stop him," although I could hardly have expected them to understand me. "He must not go on. Sher Abener will destroy him."

At first, both men flinched from me. They were resplendent in the Thal's livery, and may have feared that my touch would sully them. But then they rallied. "Ho, fellow," one of them snorted, "begone. This is the estate of the Thal of Benedic—no place for the likes of you. Go at once. Do not compel us to cast you away."

My mind had been heavily battered by the sun, abused by a day without food or drink or kindness. Dirt and sweat soiled my garments. My feet were caked with blood and mud. Much of my skin had been burned to fine blisters. I could not say that I had suddenly become cunning. Rather I seemed to fall more deeply into madness. Facing the pikemen, I sobbed more elaborately. "Oh, help me, help me," I wailed. "Take pity on me. Have mercy." My voice rose and cracked as I pleaded. "I am ruined utterly, and only the good Thal of Benedic can succor me."

The pikemen regarded me briefly, then consulted with each other. One of them shrugged, sneering. The other smirked darkly, handed his pike to his companion, and stepped to open the gates.

Grinning over his teeth, he informed me, "You were warned, fool. Now I will teach you to profit from such courtesies when they are offered."

Prompted by a form of lunacy, I fluttered my hands and wailed still more loudly.

With the deliberation of great strength, the pikeman lifted a fist like a chunk of stone and swung it at my head.

Had it struck, that blow would have poleaxed me where I stood. And at any other time it would have struck, for I had willingly forgotten those manly arts which my father had required me to learn in my youth. Now, however, I remembered to duck.

Scrambling away with my back to the pikeman, I found a loose stone as large as my hand ornamentally placed among the shrubs which edged the wall. As my assailant advanced to pummel me, I lifted the stone and pitched it at the hostile expanse of his forehead.

Stunned as much by surprise as by the impact, he toppled backward.

His companion emitted a shout of indignation. Feigning unconcern, I approached the open gate.

Apparently the Thal's pikemen were selected for their brawn rather than their wit. The remaining guard stared at me with his jaw hanging slack. His hands still gripped both pikes, their butts braced at his feet.

Before he could recollect that pikes were weapons, made for the purpose of skewering madmen and assailants, I stumbled into him as though I had consigned myself to his embrace. Doubtless he could have crushed me easily. But my arms confused his. While the pikes hampered him, I summoned my strength and jerked my knee up into his groin.

Gasping, he hunched down, dropping his weapons. Quickly I retrieved one of them and struck him a blow on the temple, which dropped him to the ground.

All this was errant folly of the most fatal sort. I had surprised both men, but done them no real harm—I had neither the skill nor the force to damage such stalwarts. When they recovered their legs, they would teach me the cost of my demented actions. Therefore I discarded the pike and hastened away, limping on my wounded feet.

The guards might have pursued me, but there was no need. If they wished, they could sound the alarm against me, alerting other pikemen to effect my capture. However, I had passed beyond such considerations. Thoughts of that ilk did not enter my head because I no longer possessed a mind capable of entertaining them. I merely ran as best I could. And when at last I glanced behind me, I saw that both men had resumed their duty at the gates, as though they, too, had forgotten me.

Apparently no one was able to recall my existence unless I stood directly before him. The stranger's glamour effaced me entirely. He had enhanced his own substance by depriving me of mine.

In my new lunacy, I meant to demand recompense for that theft. It was too personal to be suffered.

Around me, manicured lawns defined by ornamental gardens, flagstoned walks, well-kept stables, and gay pavilions swept gently downward to the Thal's mansion. Widely spread rather than built high, the mansion rested in a hollow among gradual slopes—a vantage from which our Thal could look out and see nothing which he did not own.

Throngs of Benedic's highest citizens must have trodden the grass earlier. The Thal's racing festivals were always multitudinous occasions, attended by every man of rank and woman of beauty or birth in the municipality. And the citizens were joined by the Thal's chosen assortment of sycophants, relatives, advisers, and theurgists, as well as by a considerable number of lesser folk, aspirants and favorites of one kind or another, who augmented a veritable army of breeders and attendants, trainers and riders, stable hands, grooms, and farriers for the horses. However, all such guests and servants had departed now, or withdrawn to duties elsewhere. The grounds were empty—with the occasional exception of a gardener or sweeper here and there—and the engraved mahogany of the mansion's portal stood closed.

Ahead of me, the stranger still rode my nag as though he had become inseparable from the beast, approaching the portico which framed and sheltered the doors. Indeed, his escort had already hailed the pikemen standing guard, who had in turn announced "Sher Urmeny" to the doormen. As the stranger paused under the portico, the doors opened to admit him to the mansion and the Thal's presence.

Here was a difficulty greater than the outer gates. A tradesman could not have gained the servants' entrance in my state. At the formal portal, I would surely be refused. Furthermore, the pikemen here must have observed the manner in which I had passed the gates. These men would be forewarned against my poor cunning—and uninclined to treat with me graciously.

Beneath the portico, my usurper dismounted. His tone hinted at severity as he consigned my mount to the care of his escort. Another man might have taken a moment to brush some of the dust from his raiment before hazarding the Thal's hospitality. But no other man would have dared to enter there clad as he was. Untouched by such concerns, he advanced on the doormen.

My extremity and weariness had become a form of frenzy. Having no other recourse, I swallowed the remnant of my pride and called him by my stolen name. "Sher Urmeny, wait but a moment!" I urged weakly. "I must speak with you."

Doubtless his escort should have recognized me. However, their glaring eyes betrayed only hostility and incomprehension. They had forgotten me again. They said nothing to warn the men who warded the Thal.

The pikemen gave no sign that they had watched me assault their comrades at the gates. Nevertheless they interposed themselves between me and the stranger. "Stand away, fellow," they warned. "Sher Urmeny has been summoned by the Thal, and may not be delayed by the likes of you."

In my distress, I ignored them. "Sher Urmeny!" I cried past their obstruction. "Only a moment! Please!"

One boot upon the portal stair, the stranger turned to regard me. Although I had seen it before, the complete clarity of his gaze shocked me as though I had been doused in springwater. Infernally mild, he stated, "I am in your debt. Interfere at your peril." Without awaiting a response, he ascended the stairs and passed between the carved doors.

Sadly, the shock of his gaze—or of his words—did not diminish my desperation. Frantic and unthinking, I attempted to force my way past the shoulders of the pikemen.

They repulsed me roundly, so that I staggered and nearly fell. Then they aimed their pikes at my hollow belly.

Since my earlier cunning would not serve me here, and every vestige of my dignity had been lost, I shrugged aside the last scraps of sanity as well. Drawing myself as erect as I could, I feigned hauteur.

"Have care, fools," I advised the pikemen scornfully. "I serve Sher Abener the necromancer. He has commanded me to observe both Sher Urmeny and the Thal. Do not be deceived by my appearance. If you thwart me in my master's service, you will confront consequences greater than you can either imagine or bear."

All Benedic knew who had brought about my ruin. Certainly Sher Obalist's manner had indicated as much. The pikemen lost their composure as swiftly as their contempt. Both retreated a step, and their weapons wavered in their hands.

Still they made some attempt to outface my threat. "A scruffion such as you?" protested one of them unsteadily. "What use has a great necromancer for *your* service?"

"My appearance suits my duties," I retorted without hesitation. Reasonable doubts and reconsiderations were no longer of any use to me. "Stand aside while you may."

My clarity of purpose—or perhaps my equally obvious lunacy—conveyed conviction. Shuffling their boots, the pikemen opened my way to the portal, where the doormen admitted me with uncertain courtesy to the mansion of the Thal.

I entered as though I could still claim a welcome there, in the name of my wealth, and of my father's honor, if not of respect for my person or reputation.

At another time, the shaded cool and comfort within would have been bliss to my aggrieved flesh, balm for my abraded nerves. Now, however, I hardly noted such sensations. The urgency of my mission outweighed them.

In its furnishings and appointments, the mansion lacked only a certain restraint and subtlety to be exquisite. By any lesser standard, it was delicious to both eye and ear, soothing of scent, plush and pleasant to the touch. From the bedecked atrium where I had entered, high halls and chambers followed each other ahead of me and to either side—rooms for display or assignation, ballrooms public or intimate, galleries where musicians or charlatans might perform. Great candelabra charmed the ceilings, garlands and tapestries graced the walls, rugs of imponderable depth consoled the floors. Yet I wasted no time on admiration. I cared only to descry which way the stranger had gone.

When I caught sight of him and the servants guiding him, he was nearly beyond recall ahead of me.

By passing the Thal's guards and breaching his sanctuary, I had already accomplished a seemingly impossible feat. However, I had so far gained nothing of significance, other than a dramatic increase in the hazards of my plight. I had entirely failed to deflect my usurper from his purpose. Worse, my enemy himself might attend this audience with the Thal, biding the outcome of his wishes. That was a threat I could not confront, no matter how profoundly it imperiled the stranger. Yet even if Sher Abener were not present the dangers of my position increased with every step.

Pikemen guarded each room and passage. They did not thwart my progress now, but they would certainly act against me if they were ordered to do so. And the audience to which the stranger strode with such impenetrable confidence would include the Thal's counselors and theurgists, as well as Sher Abener's malice. Any of those greedy, grasping men was more than a match for me. A counselor might denounce me at his whim. The theurgists could strike me to salt where I stood.

My task was too great for me. Bitterly, I abandoned all hope of redeeming my name by suasion or appeal. I did not call out after the stranger, or hasten to overtake him. Instead I merely followed at a distance. As best I could, I strove to project the impression that I must not be interrupted in my course. However, I had no higher intention than to await events.

Yet at the last I diverged from my aim. I was well familiar with the mansion, for I had attended fetes and celebrations without number here. And I was soon certain that I knew the chamber toward which my usurper was guided. It was a broad space, parquet of floor and gilt of wall, which the Thal called his "hall of wisdom," perhaps because a dais to one side, and an odd concentration of light caused by the domed ceiling, gave him stature. I also knew of other, less public approaches to that chamber. Seeking to avoid peril, I drifted into a side passage, and there followed a sequence of smaller rooms connected by archways in the direction of my goal. Because they were less frequented, these rooms were unguarded.

Barefoot, I made no sound as I moved. Thus it was that I heard men ahead of me without warning them of my presence.

Instinctively timorous, I slowed my pace in order to approach the entryway to the last room sidelong and unseen.

Like the other arches through which I had just passed, the one before me held a heavy velvet curtain which could be closed for purposes of discretion, but which was at present drawn aside. The room ahead of me joined on the hall of wisdom, however, and that entry curtain had been pulled shut.

At the velvet hunched two men, peering past its edges into the hall where the Thal and his adherents gathered against me.

From their drab apparel and rude features, I might have guessed that they were caravaneers. They had the sturdy frames, blunt movements, and insolent eyes which I associated with Tep Longeur's drovers and carters. But no caravaneer of my acquaintance moved freely about the Thal's mansion. And both of these men held in their fists long, evil blades so well whetted that reflected illumination grew sharper along their edges.

In alarm, I studied the men from the covert of the archway behind them. For my life, I could not imagine why the Thal's guards had admitted armed ruffians to the mansion.

They spoke softly, but their words were plain. Velvet protected them from being overheard in the hall of wisdom.

"I dislike it, Rowel," one of them whined. A misfocused squint in one eye suggested that his wits were not as keen as his blade. "Does our lord mean us to murder this Urmeny in full view of all these folk?"

Murder— I could hardly credit my hearing. Did Sher Abener intend to slay me outright? Had his malice toward me grown so extreme that only butchery would appease it?

I trembled in dismay.

How had I become so dangerous to the necromancer?

The man called Rowel continued his scrutiny of the hall. "If needed, Scut," he answered his duller companion with practiced patience. "If needed. One of our lord's theurgists is there"—he pointed cautiously past the curtain—"do you see? And he has bribed another to aid him. They will cast a mood for blood upon the gathering."

These tidings were fearsome to me, but the speaker said more. "Benedic's brave Thal is already in a muck sweat, lathered with fear." His tone conveyed a feral pleasure. "Our lord has given him certain hints concerning the price of opposition. Likely our work will be done for us, with his command or without it."

Scut remained stubbornly uncertain. "Yet we are instructed—"

"And wisely so," answered Rowel. "Fear is an imprecise tool." The man was a philosopher. "As is theurgy, when it must be worked in secret. Our lord is not ready to declare his mastery of this demesne. He seeks to daunt opposition indirectly. Therefore—" He left his study of the hall to regard his companion. "If it becomes clear that we are needed," he stated in cold tones, "we will act. The theurgists will provide for our escape, and our lord will reward us."

Scut spat his disgust. "It is filthy work, Rowel. I prefer honest killing at night in solitary alleys, when the moon is dark—and no pikemen in earshot.

"Still, I would not displease our lord," he added more conscientiously. "My blade follows yours."

Holding my breath, I drew back. For a moment, I could not conceive what I would do. My desperation so nearly resembled stupidity that I saw no alternative but to assail these ruffians with my fists, hoping to raise enough clamor so that aid would find me before I was slain. However, the thought of theurgists halted me. If miraculously I foiled Rowel and Scut—and survived—I would still have gained little, for Sher Abener's other servants would remain to work his will.

Theurgy could deliver wounds as fatal as any knife cut or sword thrust—and could do so secretly, as Rowel had intimated. A man might perish without knowing who had harmed him, or how. Yet for that very reason, those who served Sher Abener in the hall of wisdom were a greater danger than these ruffians.

Clearly, I must find some other path to my goal.

Flinching on damaged feet, I retraced my passage from room to room with the most elaborate caution until I had regained the passage where I had turned aside from the stranger's progress.

Here were guards aplenty, stationed wherever a corridor joined the larger chambers. I approached the nearest pikemen. They eyed me mistrustfully. Doubtless I did not appear to be a man who should walk freely within the Thal's domicile. They must have wondered who had admitted me to these halls—and how that error would be punished. Nevertheless I did not hesitate to accost them. My manner was one of assurance, which was entirely feigned, and urgency, which was quite sincere.

"Heed me well," I instructed before they could challenge me. "My time is short, and I must act quickly." I meant, Ask no explanation, for I have none. "Assassins have entered the mansion. I overheard two men—

armed men—plotting murder. In those rooms adjoining the hall of wisdom." I indicated the archway from which I had just emerged. "They did not make it clear whom they mean to slay. But I fear for the Thal.

"Do not shout," I added, "or you will forewarn them before they may be apprehended."

This intelligence would have perplexed even the cleverest of the Thal's guards. Plainly, the men I addressed were not among them. Their hands assumed readiness on their pike shafts, but no comprehension illuminated their eyes. My words struggled against the distrust on their blunt features.

I recognized their confusion, however. Indeed, I relied upon it. Sharper-witted men would surely have troubled me with questions. But these dullards might obey almost any command issued in a peremptory tone.

Therefore I snapped, "Fools! Will you bring death down on this house? Go! Otherwise the deed will be done, and all who serve here will be held accountable."

Then I turned and hastened away.

Behind me, I heard the clatter of their boots as they began to run. Glancing over my shoulder, I saw them race toward the rooms I had indicated.

I feared that they would forget me—and my words—as soon as they lost sight of me. The stranger's glamour threatened death to us both. I could only pray that my desperation would inspire the guards with a lingering alarm persistent enough to outlast my immediate presence. I did not doubt that Scut and Rowel would soon shed blood, if they were not interrupted.

Swallowing thirst and dread, I directed my steps to the Thal's misnamed "hall of wisdom."

Soon it became apparent that I had correctly guessed the chamber where Benedic's sovereign meant to express Sher Abener's displeasure. I heard a gathering of voices, hushed but numerous, and ahead of me a laggard or two hurried toward the hall. As they took no notice of me, I spared myself all pretense of stealth. In any case, the effort would have been wasted, for the last corridors offered no concealment. They were at once open and guarded. Nothing remained to assist my approach except a demented confidence in my strange insubstantiality.

Yet when I gained the polished parquet and condensed illumination of the hall of wisdom, I did not push forward to the center, but rather lurked back against the walls. They were behung with plush draperies, a few of which concealed entries, although most were entirely decorative. Praying that I might encounter no more assassins, I positioned myself as near as practicable to hangings behind which I might hide at need. The chamber held a throng of the Thal's counselors and sycophants, courtesans and near relations, guards and theurgists, in addition to retainers, servants, and interested spectators, and I had no wish to be snared among them. My madness was not yet so extreme. By mischance or intent, someone would certainly remark upon my presence, and then I would be lost. For that reason, I kept to the walls, and fretted.

For the moment, the stranger faced no visible peril. Forty or fifty citizens of Benedic were in attendance, but Sher Abener was not among them. And none of them approached the supposed Sher Urmeny. While the throng awaited the Thal's appearance, even those who wished me well distanced themselves from my usurper. He stood silent in a clear space before the dais, his arms folded upon his chest, his features composed to mildness, his confidence plain.

Undistracted, I gnawed anxiously upon the daunting challenge of identifying those who meant to work Sher Abener's will.

One of our lord's theurgists is there, Rowel had told Scut. *And he has bribed another to aid him. They will cast a mood for blood upon the gathering.*

There lay the chief danger, as I conceived it. Benedic had no history of dire punishments. During our prolonged years of wealth and indolence, we had grown unfamiliar with the bloody-handed practices which reportedly characterized other demesnes and lands. When apprehended, pickthieves were compelled to honest labor. Bolder burglars risked incarceration. A vandal might suffer flogging. However, expulsion from the municipality was the worst retribution exacted upon miscreants. We lacked the vehemence for more fatal measures. If Sher Abener sought to snuff my life, he must first overcome decades of tradition, habit, and sloth. Beyond question *a mood for blood* would be necessary.

That, among other practices, was the work of theurgists.

As Rowel had remarked, however, theurgy was often imprecise. Especially *when it must be worked in secret*—for surely the necromancer's henchmen would not wish their labors known. Even in fright, our Thal might withhold action against me if he suspected that he had been urged to it by arcane means.

I had been taught that the farcasting of glamours and suasions—indeed, of any theurgy—was chancy at best, liable to run wild. To control the effects of their arts, those who served Sher Abener must be present. But they would not put themselves forward. Rather they would feign uninvolvement, doing all they could to remain unremarked among the gathering.

Thus I reasoned to myself—if what passed through a mind in such straits as mine could be named "reason." Unfortunately, my dilemma remained unresolved. If Sher Abener's theurgists disguised themselves, how could I identify them in order to interrupt their power? By custom, theurgists did not attire themselves as men of rank, but instead wore symbolistic robes, bore amulets and talismans. That gave me no aid, however. Without searching the hall, I saw no fewer than six such individuals. Four of them were known to me—yet that signified nothing, since my knowledge did not extend to the private details of bribery and conscience. Furthermore, one or both of the necromancer's henchmen must surely have set aside traditional garb, as an added disguise for their intentions. My enemies might wear the raiment of honored merchants, favored relations, or even trusted retainers.

In frustration, I fretted like a steed at once reined and goaded, driven ahead and restrained—tormented by conflicting commands. Was the Thal truly *lathered with fear*? No more so than I. The insanity of my presence here was exceeded only by that of the stranger who had taken my name, and my doom. As I had assured Tep Longeur, I was not the man to effect bold salvations. Too late—*years* too late—I asked myself why I had not attended more closely when my tutors had striven to teach me a wellborn young man's polite knowledge of theurgy. Had I but *listened* then, I might now be able to act.

An apprehension resembling my own accumulated in the hall. Tense muttering sank to silence amid the folds of the draperies. Men shuffled their feet. Courtesans and ladies plucked the lint of anxiety from their purses and sleeves. The Thal had not yet made his entrance, and the assembly grew ever more restive at the delay. Doubtless the men and women before me were disturbed by my usurper's air of inviolable confidence. None of them would have met the prospect of our sovereign's displeasure with such a mien. And doubtless also their concern was enhanced by their awareness of the true threat looming before this Sher Urmeny. If a merchant of my wealth, charm, and complaisance might be threatened thus, who among them could consider himself safe?

At last, however, a flourish struck upon a tabla announced the Thal, and he swept past hangings into the hall, accompanied not by his usual coterie of ladies, but by a phalanx of pikemen. He arrived directly upon the dais, where the light concentrated to augment his stature, for he was not by nature an imposing figure. For that reason, I saw him clearly, although I cowered nowhere nearby. Rowel had described him aptly. A sheen of perspiration accentuated his fleshy visage, and his eyes stared widely, so that the whites of the orbs gleamed. He might have been an overwrought gelding—or a stallion maddened by the presence of too many mares. Indeed, he was palpably afraid.

Observing him, I deemed that he understood his own plight. The rule of Benedic had already slipped from his grasp, whether he willed it or not. His "displeasure" was entirely the necromancer's. His sole concern here was not to punish me, but rather to preserve some residue of his own riches and standing against Sher Abener's designs. As Tep Longeur had suggested, my enemy aimed at all Benedic.

Sadly, this altered nothing. Those who opposed Sher Abener would suffer for it nonetheless.

From the side of the dais, an oblivious chamberlain, immune to the mood of the gathering, recited the tally of the Thal's titles, possessions, and honorifics thoroughly, but no one heeded him. Our ruler himself chafed under the delay. When the proclamation of his significance was complete, he spoke without further ceremony.

"This has become a dark day," he complained, "when it should have been pleasant for us all, blessed by festivity and acquisition." His voice was high and unstable, like a mistuned theorbo. His white gaze rolled about the hall, avoiding only my usurper. "One among us, Sher Urmeny himself, an esteemed and prosperous merchant, has transgressed the standards of conduct observed by all Benedic since the time of my father, and of his father before him.

"We are a municipality of commerce." In his distress, the Thal allowed himself petulance. "On commerce we all depend. Without it, we would sink to rabble and poverty. Furthermore, we are a compliant people, generous and acquiescent in all our dealings. By this virtue, we conduct commerce without ill will or jealousy, and every honest transaction is sanctified.

"Yet Sher Urmeny has offended against one among us, a respected neighbor and honored citizen, by refusing commerce."

As I have said, our Thal was a weak ruler, self-interested to the point of greed, and easily led. At an earlier period of my life—yesterday, perhaps—I would have listened witlessly to his words, nodded bland assent to their import, and given them no further thought. Now, however, I seemed to hear them with new senses, a new knowledge of pain—with my damaged feet, for example, bleeding through their own crust, or with the scorched wasteland of my mouth and throat. Thus I understood that the Thal's speech itself meant nothing. Its only real purpose was to muster his courage for the denunciation Sher Abener required of him—and, if I heard him rightly, to beg the forgiveness of his people. He wished Benedic's citizens to understand what he did, and hold him blameless.

Well, he was a weakling. And I was a madman. Although I heard him with new ears, I did not attend to him. Instead I wracked my peculiar insanity for some means by which I might divert what would follow.

Others around the hall were more present in their alarm, more concerned for the immediate appearance of events. A grumble of assent rose uncertainly to meet the Thal's displeasure. I heard such descriptives as "insult" and "dishonor." Sher Abener's theurgists may have already begun to work upon the gathering.

Beyond question, I should have given my tutors better attention than I had ever accorded the Thal.

Emboldened by his own peroration, perhaps, or by the murmuring of his supporters, he turned at last to confront the stranger unrepentant before him. In his manner, he strove to convey a virtuous indignation which his manifest fright undermined.

"Sher Urmeny, you have disgraced Benedic. You have disgraced me."

In response, my usurper smiled. The effect was less than amiable. "You are mistaken," he replied so that all could hear him. "The facts are otherwise. You have disgraced yourself."

The sheer audacity of this affront struck the Thal so that he gaped like a fish. For the space of several heartbeats, I forgot my own concerns to gape as well. A stinging tension afflicted the entire assembly. Men and women whom I had known from my youth turned rigid with apprehension, or retreated to increase their distance from the stranger. Pikemen gripped their weapons expectantly. Retainers and relations withdrew from the reach of harm, while theurgists fumbled for talismen hung about their necks or secreted in pouches at their belts.

In his consternation, the Thal spoke without considering what he said. "How so?" he asked fearfully, thereby granting the supposed Sher Urmeny leave to distress him further.

My usurper showed neither hesitation nor doubt. He did not raise his voice, yet his strength grew as he answered the Thal.

"A citizen of this municipality has accused me of improper dealing. You do not name him." The stranger lifted one finger as though to enumerate a list. "And you do not inquire whether the accusation is accurate." A second digit joined the first. "You do not inquire whether there might be circumstances which explain my conduct." A third. "Indeed, you do not inquire whether there might be circumstances which would cast my dealings in an altogether more favorable light." And a fourth. "This is unjust."

Standing vividly in the enhanced illumination, he closed his list into a fist. "You are the sovereign of this demesne," he concluded. "The responsibility of justice is yours. If you choose to set it aside, you disgrace yourself, and your demesne as well."

Now the Thal achieved the indignation he had feigned a moment earlier. Doubtless he borrowed its force from his fear of Sher Abener. He reminded me uncomfortably of Tep Longeur as he protested, "Choose? Do you think I choose?"

Yet the difference between him and my former overseer was palpable. By the necromancer's arts, Tep Longeur had been deprived of volition. Our Thal had not.

Supporting the Thal, my friends and associates and neighbors protested vociferously. Outright anger mounted against the stranger, warning me of theurgy and bloodshed. He spoke simple truth. Therefore Benedic's citizens took offense. I felt my own ire rise, as though I, too, had been insulted.

And still I could think of no means to deflect what transpired.

My usurper remained undaunted, however—secure in his imponderable confidence. "Surely you *do* choose," he countered. "You are a man, free of heart and mind." Briefly he lifted his head and appeared to scent the air like a hound trained to the hunt. Then he remarked, "If I am not mistaken, there are those in your demesne who experience a coercion which is beyond their strength to overthrow"—I could not conceive how he had acquired this knowledge—"but you are not among them. Each word you speak, and each breath with which you speak it, is a choice. You are self-disgraced, and must bear the stain yourself."

In response, *a mood for blood* swelled across the assembly, gaining force as it deepened and grew. Sher Abéner's theurgists were at work, I was certain of it, although I could see no sign of the baffling arts. At any other time, Benedic's Thal and citizenry would no doubt have been similarly offended by the stranger's words, but their reaction would have been otherwise. They would have disarmed his accusation with jests, dissipated it with laughter—and declined to heed it. In their place, I would have done the same.

On the present occasion, however—

The Thal's round face and fleshy features quivered like those of a man in the throes of apoplexy. Threats gleamed in the sweat of his brow. Vehement punishments stared from his wide eyes.

"You dare?" he gasped. "You dare insult me so?"

The indignation of the gathering appeared to feed his—or to feed on it. Ladies and courtesans cried shame on the impostor. Merchants of high birth and low offered uncharacteristic imprecations. Retainers, relations, and sycophants posed themselves as though only decorum restrained them from rushing to their lord's defense. Unbidden, pikemen advanced a step or two on my usurper. Even I was overtaken by an accumulating wish for retribution. A fury which consorted ill with my plain terror thickened my throat. Involuntarily, I yearned to call for my own destruction.

Surely, I told myself while unwilling wrath and quick dread opposed each other in my veins, surely there must be *some* means by which I might determine who had cast this mood upon us.

"You are a *merchant*, Urmeny," the Thal continued on the strength of his people's support. "It is not your place to judge *me*. Like your father, and his father before him, you dwell among us and acquire wealth and enjoy your ease because the *Thal of Benedic* permits it!"

Another man might have accepted this reprimand—might at least have mustered a decent silence—while he still retained his life. However, the man who had bereft me of my name was relentless. "Again you are mistaken," he stated in clarion tones. "It is the place of every honest citizen to name injustice whenever it occurs, and to reject it honestly."

The Thal brandished his fists. "Insult!" he roared. "Outrage!" Spittle splashed from his lips. "This merchant threatens the Thal of Benedic. He threatens me! Did you hear him? Is this to be endured?"

"No!" a man quavered from the assembly—none other than decrepit Sher Vacompt himself, as vacant a fop as ever strode the avenues of Benedic. *"No!"*

At once, he was seconded by his elderly Sharna, as well as by the twin courtesans Milne and Vivit, with whom he had carried on an ineffectual dalliance for some years. "No! Never!"

They were the first to encourage the Thal's wrath. And they encouraged others. New voices quickly joined theirs. Nevertheless they had done me an oblique service. The sight of Sher Vacompt's flaccid jowls and Sharna Vacompt's powdered bosom straining with vehemence restored my sense of discrepancy. The Sher and his lady were altogether too vapid to convey intense emotion credibly, and their incongruous outrage had a salutary effect upon me. My own ire did not fall away. However, it ceased to mislead me. To some extent, I recovered my comprehension of events.

Theurgy—not passion—gripped the hall. And any art could be countered, by one means or another.

If I could but *remember*—

Not to be outdone, more citizens named their disapproval. A queasy hunger for harm filled the chamber. Men and women who would not have lifted their hands to strike a pillow called for Sher Urmeny's disgrace—even for his death. At the same time, the guards answered their lord's outrage by surrounding the stranger. Ingrained custom or indolence caused them to withhold their pikes, but they did not withhold their hands. Some of them clutched at my usurper to secure him. Others struck him about the head and body. I heard the sodden pounding of hard bone on undefended flesh. In moments, he had received more blows than I had ever imagined.

Still I could not aid him. This fate had befallen him in my name, *my name*, and I could do nothing.

I found, however, that need and despair had at last improved my recollection.

As a youth, I had been taught the merest scraps of theurgy, nothing more than the sort of small acts and invocations which might prove useful or appropriate for a young merchant of high birth who chanced to find himself in unfamiliar circumstances, confronted by men and purposes he had cause to mistrust. And one of those minor skills was an easy and unobtrusive exercise in—so my tutor had named it—*demystification*. It was used, I now remembered, to detect the presence of theurgy, and to determine its source, so that the young merchant might be wary of bafflement.

Fortuitously, I also recalled how this *demystification* was done.

I feared I had regained my memory too late. The stranger had already been accorded punishment enough to flatten a stallion. Pikemen pummeled his face and body. Merchants and retainers delivered weaker blows to his shoulders and back. Among them, I recognized Sher Ablute and his personal scrivener, Tep Jacard, as well as Vivit, Teppin Sommenie, and others. And those who were not near enough to strike called in compelled voices for his death. Some may have demanded dismemberment. In his place, I would no doubt have died where I stood—slain by fear if not by pain.

Nevertheless I set to work without hesitation. My own urgency tolerated no delay.

The beauty of *demystification*, as my tutor had explained it, was that it
required neither talent nor apparatus, for it drew on the preexisting energy
and exercise of theurgy. Therefore it might be within my abilities, despite
my rather wan condition. It demanded of me only that I utter certain
arcane syllables in certain ways, accompanying them with subtle but
appropriate gestures.

The gestures I recalled well enough. They were performed *thus* and
thus, using only the fingers and a small rotation of the wrist. I could repeat
them as often as needed without attracting notice. The words, however,
came to mind less distinctly. Did the invocation speak of *cataphract* or
cataphracsis? Did it make reference to *abeminil* or *abemanol*? I could not
remember.

Sweating feverishly, I struggled to achieve my aim. Every blow suffered
by the stranger in my name caused my heart to labor with more violence.
How he remained on his legs I could not conceive. In haste, I attempted
every imaginable variation of sound and stress, repeating my gestures
with greater and greater emphasis.

Through the rising tumult, I heard the Thal shout, "Let him be
beheaded!"

Swallowing curses, I exercised my invocation once more, performed
my tense gestures—and saw an eerie spangling punctuate the air of the
hall. Small, misshapen flashes resembling sunlight a-dance upon disturbed waters stretched and broke above the heads of the gathering. They
were apparent only to me—so my tutor had assured me—accessible only
to the man who had invoked them. Nevertheless I saw them plainly. At
first, they covered all the chamber, shattered gleamings, rough fragments
of illumination, indicating theurgy at work upon the entire assembly.
Soon, however, they concentrated toward the sources of their effect.

The milling and clamor of the crowd had grown so strenuous that I
could not immediately identify Sher Abener's theurgists. There were two,
as Rowel had indicated, one near at hand, the other somewhat apart. But
who—?

There! The nearer one became clear to me—a theurgist in the Thal's service, a gaunt, haughty man by the name of Bandonire. I had been acquainted with him for years, but knew little about him except that he had practiced sneering until his contempt had acquired the refinement of fine weaving or sculpture. Spangles flurried about his bald pate, marking him for me. One hand he held deep in the pouch hung from his belt. The other clutched an amulet at his throat. His lips moved incessantly, murmuring words without sound.

As a theurgist, he was impervious to me. My unreliable memories held nothing which might obviate his arts. Still I did not hesitate. Ordinary doubt and caution had deserted me. Rushing forward, I pounced upon Sher Vacompt for the simple reason that he supported his years and infirmities upon a cane.

The Sher's cane had caught my eye on more than one occasion. Its polished and luminous teak shaft was surmounted by a crown of inlaid bronze sculpted to suit its owner's fingers. I snatched it from him and swung it high in one motion. Gripping it by its shaft, I aimed its heavy head and my own desperation at the curve of flesh between Bandonire's neck and shoulder, and struck.

He collapsed under the blow like a man who had been shattered within his robes. I felt a sudden alteration in my hearing, as though I had lifted my ears from submersion in a basin of water. At once, the spangles which had echoed Bandonire's arts faded.

Around me, the entire gathering staggered, overtaken by uncertainty. Between one heartbeat and the next, the grip of imposed passion weakened. Some few of my fellow citizens may have wondered what they were about. Others merely paused in their avarice for dire actions.

I had felled one threat. So much was good. Yet there was another. I discovered him easily now. His attire resembled that of a retainer—a scrivener such as Tep Jacard, perhaps, or an estatesman—but he could not be other than a theurgist, for my *demystification* swirled about him, marking him beyond mistake, and the curious position of his hands was identical to Bandonire's.

Unlike Bandonire, however, he had been forewarned.

Fool that I was, I had not considered this danger. My gaze met his past the consternation of the gathering, and I saw at once that his own hostility was directed at me rather than at my usurper. He may have known who I was, despite the stranger's impenetrable glamour. Or he may have intended my hurt simply because I had impeded the designs of his master, and had thereby declared myself his enemy.

He was a theurgist in Sher Abener's service, whatever his disguise—trained to his arts, and to the support of necromancy. And I was nothing more than a sun-beaten merchant, too parched and foot-worn and hungry to retain my sanity. Nevertheless I had come too far to falter now.

Stooping to Bandonire's stunned form, I snatched the amulet from his neck, the pouch from his belt. These objects I raised in one hand as though I understood their uses. In the other, I flourished Sher Vacompt's cane. Impelled more by lunacy than by any reasonable purpose, I strode the parquet toward my foe.

Apparently, he had not expected my advance—or my acquisition of Bandonire's periapts. At once, his wrath became concern. Alarm twisted his features. Before I had taken three steps, he began to retreat, turning his head as he did so to howl through the heedless hubbub, "Rowel! *Scut!* Aid me!"

Then his hand swept from his pouch to perform a flinging gesture. He might have pitched a stone at my head, although I saw nothing.

Instead the air before me—indeed, the very hall—seemed to ripple and waver as though the calm surface of a pool had been disturbed. Immediately the air itself, or my opponent's arts, struck the center of my chest so heavily that the breath was driven from my lungs, and I lurched backward, blundering to the side as I staggered.

By chance, or by the theurgist's intent, I stumbled toward the drapes which covered the entry where I had last seen Sher Abener's ruffians.

They surged past the hanging before I could right myself. Still unable to breathe, I saw the fear and fury in their faces, the bloodshed ready on their blades. Clearly my attempt to bring about their capture had gone astray. The pikemen I had sent must have forgotten my warning as well as my existence. Or they had been ensnared and distracted by the mood imposed on the hall. The assassins would have time to gut and fillet me before any guard drew near enough to intervene.

In an airless frenzy, I swung Sher Vacompt's cane. Fortuitously, my efforts to recover my balance had the effect of increasing the force of my blow. The cane landed across Rowel's shoulder, causing him to stumble in his turn, away from me.

Toward the stranger—and the dais.

Witlessly obedient, Scut veered to follow.

Thus my life was spared.

Defending himself against me, Sher Abener's theurgist had necessarily loosed his hold upon the assembly. In consequence, the *mood for blood* had disappeared like quenched flame. When an instant later armed miscreants appeared, bearing their blades toward the Thal, his pikemen were able to respond. They may have understood nothing else, but they understood this. Without hesitation, they wheeled from the supposed Sher Urmeny to ward their sovereign.

By the time I had urged a thin breath into my stunned chest, Rowel and Scut had been stretched supine upon the parquet, disarmed and unconscious.

During the scuffle, Sher Abener's theurgist fled the hall, no doubt hastening to apprise his master of what had occurred.

Around me, my fellow citizens stared at the ruffians, and at each other, in astonishment and shock, disturbed by the proximity of keen-edged harm—as well as by the intensity of their brief passion for blood-shed. They hardly spoke, although a Sharna or two and several Teppin panted and moaned, preparing to faint at an appropriate moment. If they had not been so shaken, the gathering might have wondered what had inspired Rowel and Scut's attack, or why Bandonire lay sprawled in their midst, or indeed why I wielded Sher Vacompt's cane as a bludgeon. As matters stood, however, they required a moment in which to regain their wits before they could become hysterical.

I might cheerfully have indulged in hysteria myself, but could not afford the energy. I was exhausted to the heart. And my sense of urgency did not abate, although the immediate crisis had passed.

Sher Abener would receive warning. And he would know where to direct his enmity.

Trembling between difficult respirations, I dropped Sher Vacompt's cane, thrust Bandonire's pouch and amulet into my blouse, and turned to determine my usurper's condition.

Throughout the contest for his life, he had lifted no finger in his own defense. Although he had been bloodied and battered, he remained standing, motionless and inviolate, as though such trivial details as his own peril and my efforts to save him could not trouble his essential calm. Released now, he did not deign to wipe his face. Instead, he folded his arms upon his chest and confronted the Thal once more as though the true contest lay between them, still unresolved.

Borne down by the weight of the stranger's regard, our sovereign sank slowly to his knees, apparently poised to weep. The nature of his apprehension had been transformed. He had more now to dread than Sher Abener's displeasure alone. He had cause to fear himself. Perhaps more to the point, he had cause to distrust the people assembled before him. If they could be so easily swayed against one of their own number, how readily would they abandon their fealty to their lord?

Kneeling, he raised his fists. I thought that he might beat his breast, but he contented himself with shaking his arms in a gesture of distress.

"I am undone," he wailed piteously. "We are all ruined."

"How so?" inquired my usurper. No one else had the wit to speak.

"You have offended Sher Abener."

The Thal's tone was thick with abjection. Whatever dignity he had once possessed was gone. Poor man. I felt an odd moment of kinship with him, as though we had shared a bereavement.

"Do you not understand?" he continued. "He is a *necromancer*. His power is great and fatal. Already he has shown me arts which my theurgists can neither counter nor inhibit. And he has hinted at atrocities which chill my soul." The Thal shuddered extravagantly. "He instructed me to 'deal with you.' If I do not, he will perform—"

Our sovereign flinched into silence.

The stranger remained unimpressed. "Threats do not excuse injustice," he pronounced without mercy. "If they chill you, you must oppose them. No other response can save you. When you bow to them, their demands increase."

Then he lifted his shoulders in a shrug. "You need fear nothing, however." He appeared to dismiss the Thal from his consideration. "There is a debt I must repay. I will confront this necromancer."

Calmly, he left his place before the dais. Despite his injuries, he strode with confidence through the assembly. No one hindered his passage. Neither the pikemen nor the Thal himself remarked on the fact that this Sher Urmeny had not been granted leave to depart.

At last, I saw my chance. The Thal and I appeared to be the only men in the hall who grasped the extremity of Benedic's peril. Before my usurper could avoid me, I accosted him directly.

"Stop this," I demanded past cracked and burning lips. My hands clutched at the front of his shirt. "Stop now.

"Are you entirely mad? Did you comprehend nothing that happened here? Sher Abener is a necromancer. He treats with the dead. And he is not alone. He is served by theurgists and assassins, as well as by horrors—" My raw throat closed on the memory of Tep Longeur. Ignoring the dismayed stares of the gathering, I strove to turn the stranger aside from my fate. "He *possesses* those who do not choose to serve him, and compels them to his will. My own overseer drove me from my villa in Sher Abener's name—"

There I faltered. I found that I could not withstand my usurper's searching gaze. I saw no disdain in his eyes. Indeed, his expression suggested anger at Tep Longeur's fate more than contempt for me. Yet I felt profoundly disdained. Of their own volition, my frail fists dropped from his shirt. Although we were of similar height, he appeared to tower over me—too strong, and too certain of his purpose, to be impeded by a weary, thirst-maddened, compliant weakling like myself.

With an effort, I concluded, "You must flee. Restore my name to me, and flee while you can."

I already knew, however, that my appeal would be rebuffed. This man could not be swayed by such paltry considerations as pain, death, and abomination.

Several of the pikemen had drawn near as I spoke. "Sher Urmeny," one of them asked the stranger solicitously, "does this fellow disturb you?"

Some glamour had transformed my usurper from an object of animosity to a favored guest.

"Not at all," he replied without a glance at the guards. "Your concern is misplaced. He will attend me to my villa.

"Come," he commanded me. Without awaiting a reply, he departed the hall.

Unable to imagine what else I might do, I stumbled after him. Certainly, I had no wish to remain where I was. The men and women around me had begun to recover themselves. They shook their heads, fanned their brows, shuffled their feet, muttered softly. Soon some of them would question what had transpired, while others swooned. Inevitably, a few would take note of my rude appearance. They might conclude that I was another like Rowel and Scut, scruffy and murderous.

Hobbling, I followed my feigned self.

One thing I had accomplished. Despite his stated intent to confront Sher Abener, he meant first to visit my villa. He would not be safe there—not while Tep Longeur remained possessed—but he would be safer than in the necromancer's manor. And if he contrived to break Sher Abener's grasp on the overseer's soul, Tep Longeur might provide him with more assistance than I could manage. Indeed, Tep Longeur might be of more use to him than all the Thal's pikemen together, for at need he could muster a large company of caravaneers—travel-toughened men with hard eyes and harder fists—men who met peril, ambush, and disaster with resourcefulness and strength rather than with accession.

If he freed Tep Longeur, the stranger might then find it possible to act effectively against my enemy.

As I pursued him from the Thal's mansion, I permitted myself these optimistic musings, although I might have guessed that they were purest folly. In truth, he baffled me. Clearly he was a figure of some power. I knew of no theurgist potent enough to assume so entirely another's name and place. And the glamour with which he had bereft me of my identity had to some extent protected me as well. I would have been rendered helpless hours ago if men who gazed upon me with hostility had not been induced to forget my existence so promptly. Yet in the hall of wisdom—as in the spate of the Ibendwey—he had lifted neither hand nor power for his own protection.

I had no cause for optimism. The plain fact was that I did not understand anything the stranger had done. If I told myself that he now meant to free Tep Longeur, I did so only because I wished devoutly to believe it, not because his actions had made the notion credible.

He spoke bravely. I could not forget the clarion conviction with which he had announced, *It is the place of every honest citizen to name injustice whenever it occurs, and to reject it honestly.*

In other respects, however, he was a complete lunatic.

No one interrupted us as we ascended in sharp midafternoon sunlight to the wall encircling the mansion and passed through the gate. At every step, I watched apprehensively for ruffians and malice, but none was manifest. The guards regarded us with some confusion, but offered neither inquiry nor opposition. Soon we were out upon the locust-shrouded avenues of Benedic, where I had walked with pleasure throughout my life until this day.

There the danger of assault presumably increased. Beyond question, Sher Abener could more easily send harm against us now. Nevertheless my trepidation receded. To some extent, I was comforted by the familiarity of the municipality. And I was distracted from fear by a refreshed awareness of my road-torn feet, cooked flesh, and parched throat. With all my heart, I desired to spare my bleeding soles further abuse.

Yet I was sure that if I halted or paused, the stranger would leave me behind. Judging by the forthright certainty of his steps, he did not need my guidance to find my villa. His uncanny gifts apparently spared him the indignity of wandering astray or losing his road.

More because I wished to slow his pace than because I felt any urge to hear him speak, I called out, "Sher Urmeny." In a mood to match his madness with my own, I granted him my name. When he turned his head, I continued, "Sher Urmeny, what will you do? Are you acquainted with necromancy? How will you unbind my overseer from Sher Abener's possession?"

For a moment, he did not reply. Instead he considered me with a penetrating frown, then returned his gaze to the avenue ahead of him.

As though to taunt me, he lengthened his strides. Nevertheless I heard him distinctly.

"You do not yet grasp the nature of the debt I mean to repay."

Alarmed by this obscure utterance, I endeavored to hasten after him. I could not, however. My feet and limbs would not bear me more swiftly.

On the roadsides, villas and manors spread their walls and lawns as though in welcome, yet Benedic seemed strangely deserted. We met no one upon the avenue, saw no one in the distance. Even the street-sweepers and day laborers had withdrawn. The rumor of Sher Abener's enmity must have carried ahead of us, traveling with the speed of lightning, the force of thunder. Without apparent exception, the populace had retreated to safety.

I might have done the same, if I could. By mastering Tep Longeur, however, the necromancer had also taken possession of my home. I owned no sanctuary where I might hide myself until the crisis had passed.

My full trepidation returned, whetted and ready, when at last I drew near enough to see my gates. I dreaded the prospect of my overseer's distress—and the recall of his bitter appeal.

If you don't rescue us, we'll never be free.

Some distance ahead of me, the stranger gained the gates. Without hesitation or delay, he opened them and entered the grounds of my villa.

In surprise, I limped to a halt. Earlier those same gates had been closed against me. Why now did not one impede my usurper?

Had some new disaster befallen my home?

Urgency drove me forward. Spurred by fright, I managed an unsteady trot until I reached the gates.

There I saw that the grounds appeared as deserted as Benedic. No one attended the gates. No one except the stranger walked the carriage-way curving gracefully toward the villa. No one moved upon the kempt greensward, or among the discreet outbuildings. No guard showed his pike, no courtesan enjoyed the sunlight or the clear air, no servant followed the behest of duty or leisure.

They must, I told myself frantically, they must all have secreted themselves within the villa, fearing the thwarted necromancer's ire. Yet that explanation was as inadequate as my attire. Sher Abener had already claimed Tep Longeur. In effect, he ruled here. What remained for my servants, ladies, and guards to fear—or to avoid?

Staggering weakly, I began to run.

I was no more than three or four steps behind my usurper as he ascended the villa's marble portico and approached its high doors. Though my breath gasped and rattled in my chest, tearing at my throat, I rushed to reach the doors before him. Shouldering him aside, I flung the doors wide and stumbled inward, crying out for attendance as I entered.

My call echoed from the polished tile of the floor, but no voice answered. For a moment, the comparative darkness within the entry hall seemed to strike me blind, and I saw only gloom and shadows on every side, vague shapes cowering against the walls, fear crouching in the corners. Then, however, my sight cleared, and the emptiness of the villa made itself plain.

Never in my life had I passed those doors without being admitted by retainers assigned to that duty. A ragged shout brought no response. A feverish tug on a satin bellpull by the doors produced chiming echoes muffled by distance, but no other result.

Filled by horror and chagrin, I understood what had occurred.

Sher Abener had indeed been forewarned.

His theurgist had failed to penetrate the stranger's glamour. Believing my usurper to be Sher Urmeny, the man had been shocked and shaken by my interference. He had fled the Thal's mansion, bearing to the necromancer a confused tale of unguessed and unrecognized opposition.

Hence the abandonment of my villa.

That knowledge defeated me, and I fell to my knees. Only my palms upon the cool tiles spared me from striking my head. The foolish hopes with which I had nurtured my heart evaporated from my eyes, and I saw that all was lost.

The stranger gazed about him, frowning slightly. "Is this customary?" he asked. With a gesture, he indicated the entry hall's emptiness.

I shook my head. Still panting, I answered, "Sher Abener has been given warning. He has called all who serve him to his manor." I was certain of what I said. "Tep Longeur is there. Perhaps others. Everyone else has fled."

"Tep Longeur?" My usurper appeared to require confirmation. "Your overseer? The man this necromancer has possessed?"

"Yes." I raised a hand to wipe my eyes. Abjectly, I explained, "Sher Abener was surprised that his theurgist met resistance. He is unsure of your power. Therefore he fears it. He seeks to gather all his might against you.

"He has suffered defeats elsewhere." Tep Longeur had revealed this. "He does not mean to do so here."

"Then he will be disappointed," stated the stranger firmly. His tone had changed. Its former mildness had been replaced by hinted iron and determination. "I do not condone possession."

Deliberately he turned toward the doors.

He astonished me so greatly that I forgot myself. Weariness, burning, and thirst all dropped from my mind. I felt nothing except a trembling and avid fury.

In an instant, I had regained my feet. Before my feigned self had taken two steps, I sneered at his back, "And do you believe he *cares* whether you do or do not condone it?"

The stranger paused to face me. Briefly he scrutinized me as he had once before, on the banks of the Ibendwey. Then he nodded as though he had been reassured.

"That does not concern me," he replied. "You have not described how you incurred this necromancer's enmity, and I do not ask. The answer is plain. Still I am in your debt. It is your dread of possession which caused you to abandon your home and your life. It caused you to abandon Tep Longeur, who served you. Is that not so? In order to repay you, I must confront this necromancer. As I have already said.

"I am," he concluded, "a man of my word."

I found his confidence maddening. I had in fact done all that he said. Yet my fear was the fear of a reasonable man, a sane man, and I did not merit blame for it. Certainly I did not deserve to be held responsible for my usurper's lunacy.

Did he mean to suggest that I should have stood by my word to Sher Abener?—that having accepted a commission I should have held to it? Then what would I have done when Tep Longeur declined to obey me?

Would the stranger have found my actions honorable if I had enlisted the necromancer's aid to compel my caravaneers?

My position was intolerable. I could not stomach Sher Abener's demand for *slaves*.

"You intend to seek him out?" I protested, fuming. My indignation seemed to expand until I could no longer contain it. "In his manor? With all his powers and servants about him?"

My usurper regarded me sternly. "I am a man of my word," he repeated.

His eyes had lost none of their clarity. Events had not diminished his *vividness*, or his air of substance. Indeed, he seemed more potent than ever—beyond suasion or compromise. Now, however, he did not daunt me. Instead he fed my ire.

"You are also a great fool," I shouted at him, "and soon you will be a dead one! But that will not end your usefulness to Sher Abener. He is a *necromancer*. His strength is *drawn* from the dead!

"Heed me," I pleaded. "Hear me. I do not understand this *debt* of which you speak, or your notion of repayment, but I release you from it. It is accomplished, forgotten. Restore my name, and I am satisfied.

"Here is my villa." I flung out my arms, including all my riches in their sweep. "Raiment aplenty. Food and drink. Horses to bear us. Coin to pay our way." My strongboxes held a considerable sum of saludi. If Tep Longeur had not taken them for Sher Abener's use— "All this will enable us to flee with some prospect of success."

My usurper frowned. "As I have said, I am a—"

"You are a man of your word!" I cried in fury and dismay. I could not bring myself to strike him. Rather, I flailed at the empty air. "You are a man of your word. *I heard you!* But you are also *deaf*. Do *you* hear nothing? Mere fools and madmen are wiser than to confront necromancers with nothing more than their virtue to protect them.

"Have you entirely failed to notice that you would have *died* in the hall of wisdom if I had not rescued you? I *fought* for you. In all my life, I have never lifted my hand in anger against another living man, and *I fought for you.*

"I will not do so again!" There I lowered my voice. My shouts meant nothing to him, and I wished him to understand that I, too, would not be swayed. "I will not dare enter Sher Abener's manor." I could not. The mere thought caused my heart to quail utterly. "If you go there, you will learn that I have spoken the truth. Doubtless your power to assume my name and place amuses you. Perhaps the master of that dwelling will be amused as well.

"Go if you must. You will go alone."

In reply, my usurper shrugged. My failure to discourage or save him was complete. Quietly he answered, "I did not ask you to accompany me."

Then he turned his back and strode away. In a moment, he had passed the doors and was gone from my sight.

He left me trembling at the extent to which I had been diminished. Although he went to oppose a *necromancer*, he placed no value upon my aid. All that he desired of me was my name.

Very well, I thought as I shook with anger. *I did not ask you to accompany me.* Nor had he asked me to defend him in the Thal's mansion. I had done so because I had persuaded myself to the hazard, hoping to reclaim some vestige of myself.

Now, for the same reason, I meant to abandon him to his chosen fate. Whatever the cost of his usurpation, he had incurred it himself. While he repaid his *debts*, I would at last provide for my own survival.

To do so seemed simple enough. Despite my long reliance upon servants, I knew my own home sufficiently to obtain what I needed from it. Food, apparel, saludi, a mount—I could dispense with everything else. The stranger had given me one gift—a respite, an interval during which Sher Abener's attention would necessarily be concentrated elsewhere. If that interval lasted as long as an hour, I would be safely beyond his reach.

As I set about my purpose, however, I found that it was not so simple as I had imagined.

The villa was my *home.* *My* home. Each room and hallway raised memories to teach me the cost of flight. Pangs of loss set their teeth into my heart at every turn. And wherever I went, the same voices echoed in my mind.

If you do not save us, we will never be free.

I am a man of my word.

I will render the marrow from your bones, and drink it while you die!

The entire domicile seemed ghost-ridden and forlorn, reft of life by Tep Longeur's ruin. Malice and supplication haunted me as I readied my final departure.

You have mistaken me for my father. I am not such a man.

Go if you must. You will go alone.

Aching in pained recollection, I visited my kitchens, where I drank several flagons of water and eased my hunger with bread, cheese, and olives. Then I limped to my private chambers. After washing and tending my damaged feet, I shod them in sturdy boots. I selected garments for travel, including a dark-hued cloak which might serve as a blanket at need. When I had considered the contents of the theurgist Bandonire's pouch, I affixed it to my belt. I equipped myself with a hardwood staff, which I could employ as either support or weapon. A well-honed dirk I hung at my side.

Thus I prepared myself, to the accompaniment of voices and remembered anguish.

It is the place of every honest citizen to name injustice whenever it occurs, and to reject it honestly.

At last, I was ready to depart. I had already chosen the road which would lead me away from my life in Benedic.

And yet—

And yet I could not do it. My resolve failed me—or was transformed. When I bid farewell to my villa, I took no coin, and no horse. I carried neither food nor drink. I had no need of them.

From my gates, I directed my steps, not away from Benedic, but toward Sher Abener's dark abode.

My course horrified me. Indeed, I felt that my mind had failed altogether. Still I did not turn aside.

I did not ask you to accompany me.

The choice was mine to make. Therefore I made it.

I could perhaps have borne abandoning the stranger to possession and death. He had disregarded both my warnings and my attempts to save him. Somewhere during this long day, however, I had lost my capacity to endure Sher Abener's wish to practice his cruel arts in Benedic. He did not merit my compliance.

If my usurper yearned for doom, I would require him to seek it in his own name, not in mine.

Midafternoon had turned toward evening, for I had spent more time in preparation—or in the Thal's mansion—than I realized. The sun spread tall shadows upon the roadway before me so that they led me into darkness. Along the avenues to the necromancer's manor, I questioned my resolve a thousand times. But I did not alter it. The easy comfort of my former life could not be reclaimed. Therefore I let it go.

All too soon, I reached the grim granite which enclosed Sher Abener's manor.

In the walls, the black iron of the gates stood shut, as they had early this morning. Perhaps they would have opened themselves for me again if I had spoken my name, but I left the experiment untried. Although I could not hope to take the necromancer unaware, I had no wish to proclaim my approach. Instead I thrust my staff between the bars above the lock and levered until the bolt twisted from its seat. Then I stepped between the gates.

As I passed, I heard no voices, bodiless or otherwise.

Upon reflection, I was surprised by my success. I would have expected Sher Abener's arts to hold more securely. However, I did not complain. If he believed that no one other than the supposed Sher Urmeny would come against him, so much the better. His inattention might work to my benefit.

The doors to the manor were likewise closed. Rather than seek another entrance, which might have served me ill in any case, I forced the door bolt with the point of my dirk. Easing the portal open, I slipped into the manor.

The vestibule remained as I recalled it—large and empty, furnished only with gloom, a wide stair rising toward midnight on one hand, an archway clutching its secrets on the other. Here at last I was forced to acknowledge the folly of my intentions. A lifetime ago—a lifetime measured in mere hours—when I had approached Sher Abener to recant my acceptance of his commission, I had been guided by lamps which appeared to light and extinguish themselves of their own accord. How would I find him now? By what means could I hope to discover him in this dire place?

While I fretted over the question, however, I heard the sound of a step upon stone. In alarm, I wheeled toward the stair and saw a gloom-shrouded figure descending. Some man or fiend slowly paced the treads to confront me.

I contemplated screaming. I considered flight. Neither alternative seemed likely to procure Sher Abener's defeat. With an effort of will, I held my tongue and stood my ground.

Partway down the stair, the figure paused. "Who are you?" a man's voice demanded. "Why are you here? I have seen you—" His tones faded into uncertainty, then returned. "Where have I seen you before?"

Apparently the stranger's glamour shielded me yet. In contrast, my own recollection was precise. I recognized the voice, and knew the man. *Rowel!* I had heard him shout. Scut! *Aid me!* He was the disguised theurgist who had labored with Bandonire to bring about my usurper's death.

On impulse, I ducked my head and replied in a frightened gibber, "If it please your worship. Your mightiness. I am a mate of Rowel's. Not that fool Scut. Maybe you saw me when we were employed, Rowel and Scut to slaughter that fop Urmeny, me to watch their backs." In a show of deference, I dropped my staff. Hunching abjectly to conceal what I did, I put one hand into the pouch at my belt. With the other, I gripped my dirk. "I would have done the deed myself, but pikemen prevented me," I whimpered abjectly. "I came when the way was safe—to ask how I can serve—"

"Be silent, fellow!" snapped the theurgist. "You lie. Such ruffians as you do not force entry to their master's homes. And that is not where I have seen you.

"Come to the light," he commanded. As though by incantation he produced a lamp from the darkness and set it alight. "I will look at your face."

The sudden illumination dazzled me. For a moment, I could scarcely discern my boots, or distinguish the stair. Fortunately, I did not need to see my hands. Touch alone sufficed.

In Bandonire's pouch, I had found a sackette of rough powder like grains of sand—white, rough to the touch, and faintly malodorous. I could not for my life recall the powder's proper use. However, I remembered clearly one of the lessons it had taught me in my youth.

Cringing and shuffling, and blinking furiously as I did so, I approached the theurgist. At the same time, I withdrew the sackette from Bandonire's pouch and secreted it in my fist.

"If it please your worship," I whined repeatedly. "If it please you."

"But it does not," retorted my antagonist. "Lift your head, you cowering fool. I will see your face."

As an inattentive youth exasperating my tutor, I had once—and only once—inadvertently sneezed a similar powder into my own eyes. For an hour afterward, I had believed myself blinded by fire. Nearly a week had passed before my sight was fully restored.

When the theurgist had fixed his gaze on my features, I fumbled open the sackette and flung its contents into his face.

At once, he stumbled backward, roaring in pain. As he did so, his heel struck against a tread, and he fell. His hands slapped at his eyes in a belated attempt to protect them.

His lamp dropped to the stair. Fortunately, it continued to burn.

Before he could restore his sight with theurgy, or heal his eyes by any other means, I snatched out my dirk and aimed its butt at the side of his forehead.

Groaning, he slumped aside.

Tears streamed from his eyes as though he dreamed of grief. By that sign, I knew I had not struck too hard. Despite my fears, I did not wish to do murder.

But I was no nearer to discovering my enemy's whereabouts. I could not begin to guess how long the stranger might withstand Sher Abener's arts—or how extremely the necromancer might wish to protract my usurper's death—but I believed that I could afford neither uncertainty nor delay.

Since the theurgist had approached me from above, I chose to think that my goal lay there. Retrieving the lamp, I ascended the stair and cast about me for some sight or sound of habitation.

At first, I saw and heard nothing. The gloom was deeper here. Despite the lamp, I could scarcely discern the walls which enclosed the wide chamber at the head of the stair. My own unsteady respiration seemed to baffle my hearing, so that no other noise reached me. To left and right, hallways held featureless midnight. Sher Abener's dwelling was apt for fiends and bloodshed. I felt sure now that he did not drink the blood of sheep when he broke his fast. He quenched his thirst with darker fluids.

Holding the lamp before me, I ventured toward the nearer hallway. My small flame revealed only blunt stone and bare walls. When I had advanced a few steps, however, I heard a sound that might have been a human cry, stifled as it issued from the throat of the hall.

As if involuntarily, I quickened my pace. I had never known a man less likely to scream than the stranger. Independent of my mind, my limbs and flesh believed that no pain sufficient to draw a wail from his lips should be suffered to continue.

That hall ended in another perpendicular to the first. Apparently these passages followed the outer wall of some large chamber or suite. Yet no door gave admittance inward, just as no window offered any view beyond the manor.

Striding ahead, I rounded another corner—and lurched to a frightened halt so suddenly that I nearly dropped my lamp. In the hallway before me stood Tep Longeur. Although shadows muffled his features, I was certain of him. I had known his hardened cheeks and forthright gaze all my life.

He showed no surprise—indeed, he appeared to expect me. One arm cocked its fist grimly on his hip. His other hand rested on the hilt of a saber with its point braced on the stone at his feet. Lamplight gleamed along the blade, implying bloodshed. Clearly he had been set to guard his master.

"Come no farther," he commanded me. Authority and desolation complicated his tone. "You have committed crime enough by trespassing in Sher Abener's home. Do not compound your offense."

In response, I gazed my misery at him and wondered how I could dream of freeing him.

By what means was possession broken? I did not know. I was a fool, indolent and compliant, and I had neither weapon nor art which might accomplish my purpose. Truth to tell, I did not understand my overseer's plight. How then could I hope to restore that which had been reft from him?

He had served me, and my father before me, faithfully through all the years of his life. I should not have imperiled him for the sake of my efforts to appease the necromancer.

I required aid.

In this place, there was no one who might help me except my usurper. He did not *condone possession*. And he was a man of strange strengths—as well as of unwavering determination. He might perhaps know what was needed.

Therefore my first task was to reach him, despite Tep Longeur's—and Sher Abener's—opposition.

That was an endeavor which might lie within my compass.

Clearing my throat uncomfortably, I asked, "Tep Longeur, do you know me?"

He answered without hesitation. "Well enough." Bleak intent left his voice as parched as a wilderland. "You're a fool in Sher Urmeny's service. You're trying to aid your condemned master.

"But you won't. You will not pass here."

At his reply, my heart lifted against its burden of dread. While the stranger retained my name and station, no one knew me for who I was. His glamour baffled even the overseer of my merchantry. Sher Abener himself might not discern the truth—

"You are mistaken," I countered more strongly. "Grievously mistaken. I serve the necromancer. And I must give him warning. Why otherwise was I admitted this far?"

Apparently the condition of Tep Longeur's mind permitted doubt. "What warning?" he demanded.

My circumstances inspired shameless invention. "The Thal has recanted his earlier submission," I explained in haste. "He means to expel Sher Abener from Benedic. Even now he marches on the manor with all his pikemen. If he is not met and halted, he will drive our master away, and tear this dwelling to the ground."

The overseer raised his saber. His jaws worked as though he were disgusted by the taste of my words—or of his own. "You lie."

That I could answer. Holding my lamp beside my face to aid his sight, I repeated imperiously, "*Do* you know me? Look well."

He leaned slightly forward to peer at me. The doubt I invoked troubled him despite his weapon—and his subjugation to Sher Abener's will. After some consideration, he shook his head. "No."

"Then," I snorted, feigning scorn, "you do not know that I lie.

"Escort me to the necromancer," I instructed him. "He will distinguish truth from falsehood."

Tep Longeur deliberated within himself a moment longer. However, my suggestion proved too plausible to be dismissed. "Very well," he muttered abruptly. Brandishing his saber, he stepped aside. "Go ahead of me. Give me cause, and I'll hack you down where you stand."

I obeyed. In a few steps, I passed him cautiously to advance along the hall. Involuntarily I held my breath, fearing that he would strike me from behind—that his acquiescence was like my prevarication, a ruse. But he did me no harm, although I was entirely defenseless.

Guided by the threat of sharp steel, I led him to another corner, beyond which I finally saw an entry to the region enclosed by the passages I had traversed. The entry had no door. In fact, I had yet to encounter any door within the manor. Every hall and chamber I had visited opened on the next without restriction. Apparently Sher Abener wished his fiends to roam freely, his forces to expand without hindrance. Or perhaps his manor served as the body, the flesh, of his arts, through which necromancy flowed as though it were blood, and the passages and rooms were veins.

I did not doubt that beyond this entry I would encounter Sher Abener himself. From it, illumination reflected outward, ruddy as fire, unsteady as flame. And muffled gasping emerged at intervals, choked groans of a sort that suggested torment.

There I faltered, hampered by old terrors and new alarms, until Tep Longeur gestured with his blade, instructing me forward. Even then I could scarcely place one step ahead of the other. If he had not set a hand on my shoulder to thrust me along, I might have fled screaming rather than enter there.

I had no wish in the world to witness the pain which wrung those gasps and groans from any human throat.

I seemed to have no choice, however. Once Tep Longeur had set me in motion, the light drew me toward it. I felt the grasp of its heat and horror before I reached the chamber of its source—the heart of the manor, where my enemy exercised his arts.

Ahead of me, extracted anguish rose to a wail, then fell silent as though it had been stifled or strangled.

The room was large—more hall than chamber—but at first my sight failed to receive its details. After the gloom of the outer passages, the intensity of the light dazzled me. A pyre would not have blazed more brightly. Perhaps, I thought with the oblique concentration of the truly mad, this explained the absence of doors. Flame on such a scale must require vast quantities of air.

To my sun-cooked flesh, the heat might have been the direct touch of coals. Within my cloak, sweat squeezed from my ribs and back. I felt slick moisture upon my face.

Yet I heard no roar of devoured wood. And I smelled no smoke. Instead the bitter reek of a charnel assailed my senses. Soon the odor seemed to sting the dazzlement from my sight. I found now that I could see—and wished that I could not.

The chamber was round, encircled by walls of blunt stone. It held no lamps or torches. None were needed. Larger fires provided illumination. The fitted granite of the floor sloped somewhat downward from the walls to the center of the circle, where a blaze nearly the height of a man capered and spat from what appeared to be a shallow pit. At first, I could not guess how the flame was fed, if not with wood. But then I observed four servants around the chamber, at the points of the compass near the walls. Each had a look of possession in his eyes. And each attended a piled mess of flesh and bone, sinew and offal. I feared to imagine the slaughter which had produced so much hacked and bloody tissue. With the slow regularity of half-wits, the four bent in unison to their piles, lifted up gobbets of dripping meat or bone, and tossed them ponderously into the fiery pit.

Butchered animals fueled the conflagration. Or butchered men.

I might have stared at the necromancer's servants longer, transfixed by the nature of their task. However, another choked outcry snatched my attention away.

A quarter turn of the circle beyond my entrance stood a rude trestle table like the one at which Sher Abener had broken his fast during our earlier encounter. There the light was augmented by four iron braziers braced on tri-stands and set to brighten the corners of the table without interrupting movement. On the sides of the braziers, a bloody glow described the flames within them.

Stunned by the stench and the heat, I made no sound—either of surprise or of protest—when I saw my usurper outstretched upon the table.

He lay on his back, chin jutting fiercely at the ceiling. Leather thongs bound his wrists and ankles to rings of black iron set into the edges of the table. Pain corded his muscles and strained his limbs as though he lay upon a rack.

His shirt had been torn open, exposing his chest. And over his bared skin hunched Sher Abener. Like his servants, the necromancer had not noted my arrival. Fervor lit his eyes, echoing the braziers. In one hand, he held a thin blade, curved and cruel—an arthane. While I watched, aghast, he bent to his victim and drew a fine, precise cut across the helpless flesh. Anguish clenched the stranger's frame, but Sher Abener paid no heed to it. Instead he slowly lowered his head to lick up the welling blood.

The action of his tongue forced me to see that he had already cut his victim a number of times—too many to count. Wounds wove a tapestry of pain across the stranger's chest.

When the blood was gone, Sher Abener whispered avidly, "Endure, Urmeny." Husky passion rasped in his tone. "Endure if you can. I will teach you to fear death."

"This is no true death," the stranger gasped. The touch of Sher Abener's lips and tongue appeared to cause him more hurt than the arthane. "With every use of your arts, you slay yourself, necromancer."

His tormentor snorted. "Do you still believe you have the power to judge me?"

"No power is needed. The truth"—my usurper choked as he spoke—"suffices."

Sneering, Sher Abener poised his blade to slice again.

Fed by death, the central fire clawed upward, reaching higher and higher.

I could not move. I might have been one of the necromancer's servants, overtaken by a possession I could neither define nor counter. If the stranger had wailed for my aid, I would not have answered him. Sensations of fire searched within my garments to discover and consume my courage—and my purpose. Horror enclosed my soul. No other need could touch my own.

You have mistaken me for my father. I am not such a man.

I felt a pluck at my belt as Tep Longeur removed Bandonire's pouch, a tug as he claimed my dirk, but I did not regard him. I abandoned my lamp to him. No act of his could pierce my dismay. Only Sher Abener's fatal arts held any significance to me.

Leaving my side, Tep Longeur approached the table. At the base of the nearest brazier, he dropped my paltry weapons.

"Master," he intruded bluntly, "this fellow requires your attention." He showed no reluctance to interrupt his master's pleasures. Nothing remained for him to fear. "He claims he must warn you. He claims the Thal moves against you.

"I think he lies."

At once, the necromancer looked sharply toward me. Feral hungers lay naked upon his face. Blood from his lips smeared into the darkness of his beard.

I could neither move nor breathe. In terror, I begged the Heavens to grant that my usurper's glamour would withstand Sher Abener's gaze.

For a moment, he frowned as though he had glimpsed something which perplexed him—some hint of my true name. But then the danger passed. Scornfully, he dismissed me from his attention.

"Without question he lies," he informed Tep Longeur. "Like all his fine folk, the Thal has been bred to cowardice. He may flee. He will not fight."

Indicating me with a nod, the necromancer instructed, "Hold him there. I will enjoy discovering the truth from him when I have extracted"— he licked his lips over the stranger's flesh—"everything from Urmeny."

Tep Longeur glared at me with his hand on the hilt of his saber as though daring me to attempt escape.

I might have risked flight. I could not imagine the means by which Sher Abener would discover any "truth" from me, but I feared that his methods would surpass my deepest nightmares. Before I could summon heart or panic enough to move my legs, however, the necromancer's victim stopped me.

He did so by the simple expedient of turning his head so that his eyes met mine.

For the second time that day, I felt myself dislocated from time and comprehension. As before, the blue penetration of his gaze transcended any scrutiny I had ever endured. Indeed, it appeared to transcend my fate as well as my fears. As plainly as language, it seemed to promise that if our places had been reversed he would have spent his life to aid me.

No, I was wrong. His assertion went farther. In his eyes, I saw that he had *already* spent his life to aid me.

His sacrifice alone would have sufficed to unman me—but again I was wrong. Pierced by dislocation, I discerned that the particular hue of his gaze had changed. This morning, his eyes had expressed an unflinching resolve, a willingness to face any peril. Now they suggested another courage altogether—the valor, not of pleading or self-sacrifice, but of compassion.

Mutely, the stranger seemed to announce that he understood—and forgave—my inability to rescue him.

A moment later, he shifted his head away, and I felt myself snatched back to urgency. Sher Abener had chosen the place for his next cut, and had poised his blade to begin. My usurper turned to watch as though he meant to restrain the necromancer by the unassisted force of his will.

His efforts would fail—of that I was certain. While I lived, nothing the stranger did in my name would stay Sher Abener's hand.

Gasping with dread, I stumbled forward a step, then braced myself against the heat, coughed fire from my throat, and raised my voice.

"You are a fool, Sher Abener," I croaked fervidly. "You disdain theurgy—yet you have been baffled by it, and you notice nothing. The simplest glamour confuses you. While you blind yourself with pleasure here, your defeat is already accomplished."

In surprise, the necromancer jerked up his head to face me. For an instant, his perplexity returned, and a stronger doubt twisted his features. Then he spat a curse in a rough language beyond my grasp.

Setting aside his arthane, he made a weird gesture my eyes could not follow. At once, the braziers guttered, while the flames in the center of the chamber spouted higher. Before I could flinch, a fist of necromancy seized the front of my cloak, lifted me from my feet, and slapped me to my back upon the floor.

The impact drove the air from my lungs. Fire seemed to swirl about my head, bearing sight away.

Between one heartbeat and the next, Sher Abener appeared at my side. From his eyes, power spilled like dark blood to his hands. Swiftly, he stooped to splash burning drops of force onto my forehead and across my cheeks. Then he peered at me more closely.

Another raw curse abraded my ears. Staring, the necromancer snarled as though in protest, "*You* are Urmeny."

For no reason except that I was entirely insane, I nodded.

Wrenching himself upright, Sher Abener wheeled toward the stranger. "Then who are *you?*"

My usurper was insane as well. He replied with a grin as fierce as his tormentor's blade.

Muttering necrotic imprecations, Sher Abener strode to the table and retrieved his arthane. Without a glance in my direction, he pointed me out to Tep Longeur. "*Watch* him," he commanded. "I have questions which this impostor will answer."

Tep Longeur bowed slightly. Drawing his saber, he confronted me across the distance between us. His hard glare held my face as though he were enraged—as though he needed only a small excuse to strike my head from my shoulders.

The necromancer stood now with his back toward me. I could not see his visage as he addressed the stranger. Perhaps that was well. I would not have been able to bear the sight as he abandoned his former delicacy and hammered his malice into his victim's ribs.

Betrayed by his vulnerable flesh, my debtor cried out. As promptly as he could, he stilled his pain. But then Sher Abener put his mouth to the wound, and the stranger wailed again, unable to do otherwise.

That also I could not bear.

Ignoring the threat of Tep Longeur's saber, I pried my legs under me and lurched to my feet. His gaze roared at me, but he did not move.

I shrugged the cloak from my shoulders, swept it into my arms. One weak step and then another carried me forward. My overseer's fist corded on the hilt of his saber. A paroxysm of fury distorted his features. Still he did not advance to thwart me.

I chanced another step. Tep Longeur slapped his free hand across his mouth, clamping his voice to silence.

Now I understood his wrath. It was directed not at me, but at himself—at his involuntary submission to my enemy. Sher Abener had commanded him to *watch*, not to *warn*. Not to *act*. Despite the necromancer's grip upon his soul, Tep Longeur opposed his master by the only means available to him—by mere, literal obedience in the place of true compliance.

With ire and courage, he gave me all the assistance his possessed spirit could supply.

Like the stranger's pain, Tep Longeur's struggle was more than I could endure. Two more steps brought me to the nearest brazier. Within reach of his saber. He could have struck me there, slain me easily. Still his resistance held.

My weapons lay at the base of the tri-stand—Bandonire's pouch and my dirk—but I ignored them. My intentions were too extreme for such implements. Only my cloak could serve me now.

A sane man would have attacked without warning. I did not. I had left ordinary reason and sense far behind. I knew only heat and sweat—the excruciating fire of the damned, and the drawn blood of my mortality.

With my cloak swathed over my outstretched arms, I positioned myself across the brazier from Sher Abener. From its iron sides shone heat enough to shrivel my organs and scorch the marrow of my bones.

Nevertheless I stood near it. When I was ready, I called out hoarsely, *"Release him!* While you can!"

In a whirl of darkness, the necromancer turned.

At the same moment, the servants who fed the central fire ceased that task. As one, they strode slowly toward me, moving with the silent inexorability of figures in dreams. Their hands reached for me across the space between us.

Sher Abener's bloody scowl measured me briefly, then shifted to Tep Longeur. He spat at what he saw. "Lout!" Anger streamed from his eyes, dripped from his hands. "I have no patience for your puny opposition.

"Kill him." The necromancer pointed at me so that there would be no mistake. "Kill him *now!"*

Possessed and appalled, Tep Longeur clenched his fists upon the hilt of his saber and raised the blade above his head. A cry of denial which he could not utter filled his mouth as he aimed a long blow at the tender flesh where my neck met my shoulder.

I knew what I meant to do, but I was too slow, too slow. The slash of Tep Longeur's saber left too little time for me.

Yet I was not slain.

With an ease more swift than I could have imagined, the stranger shrugged the bonds from his wrists and ankles. Swinging his legs over the edge of the table, he set his boots to the floor. Despite the wounds woven across his chest, he caught Tep Longeur's hands so that the overseer could not strike.

Tep Longeur's physical strength was formidable. In addition, his subjugated soul had been commanded to murder. Still my usurper restrained him as though he were infirm, or ill.

That was all the opportunity I required. In another moment, the nearest of Sher Abener's other servants would reach me, but the man's progress was too ponderous to deflect me now.

Before the necromancer could master his surprise, I put my arms to the sides of the brazier.

There the true scale of my madness revealed itself. My cloak was thickly woven and heavy, yet it might as well have been parchment against the ruddy iron of the brazier. It caught fire instantly. Through it, a terrible incineration blazed into my arms. Flame beyond bearing seemed to strip away my flesh, so that nothing remained to me except nerves and agony. No doubt I screamed, although I could no longer hear myself.

Yet my resolve or my insanity endured long enough to lift the brazier from its stand and tip its contents onto the necromancer.

His garments and his power seemed to take fire as though they had been drenched in oil. At once, he became a torch, burning brightly enough to light the path to damnation. A howl which might have been anguish rose among the flames.

While he blazed, I slumped to the floor, cradling pain which consumed my senses. I scarcely saw what transpired. I felt nothing when Sher Abener's possessed servant raised me in his embrace in order to crush out my life. I did not understand when I heard the necromancer's shout echo about the chamber as though the fire had been given voice.

"Fools!" he raged with the passion of a pyre. *"Do you think you are strong enough to stop me?"*

While he roared, his hands seemed to shape the fire so that it might be hurled at his assailants. His eyes defined the blaze like glimpses into the heart of a furnace. Although he was immersed in conflagration, his power preserved him, transforming pain and flame to weapons.

The stranger did not shout. Nevertheless his reply matched Sher Abener's resounding fury.

"Yes," he promised. "We are strong enough."

Deliberately, he released Tep Longeur's hands.

Freed from constriction, the overseer struck as though he had been coiled and pent to the breaking point. His saber flashed crimson, reflecting the flames, as the blade buried itself to the guards in Sher Abener's blaze.

The necromancer's howl turned to shrieks, and he stumbled backward, away from the blow. For a long moment, he appeared to totter on the brink of dissolution, imponderably balanced between the strength of his arts and the damage of his wounds. Then he toppled.

As he plunged into the devouring heat of the central fire, his servant released me as though I had lost all significance.

I knew that I fell again, although the prospect did not trouble me. I had no attention to spare for minor impacts and bruises. I was more keenly aware that I could breathe once more, and that the stone under me felt comparatively cool.

After some consideration, I concluded that I would be content to rest on kind granite until my life reached its end.

Thereafter time passed in a fashion I could not fathom. Certain moments came to me clearly. Others evaded my notice. Tep Longeur spoke my name, his voice fraught with concern—so much was plain. The stranger seemed to stroke my arms, applying some balm or theurgy which comforted my suffering. He and Tep Longeur attended to Sher Abener's servants, left unconscious by the shock of their master's death. Deprived of fuel, the blaze which had consumed the necromancer receded into its pit. By degrees, the thick heat succumbed as well.

Other details eluded me, however. Presumably, Tep Longeur and the stranger spoke to each other—or to me. They must have made decisions. Yet I took no part in those interactions. Perhaps I simply forgot them when they were done.

Later, I found myself on my feet outside the manor's gates in the first light of a new day. How I had regained the strength to stand, I did not know. Nevertheless I was now able to hold up my head and breathe deeply. The dawn caressed my features with its cleanliness. And the distress of my burns had declined to bearable proportions. When I looked at my arms, I saw whole flesh beneath a covering of clear unguent. Where the stranger had obtained this ointment I could not guess—and did not ask. I did not wish to contemplate anything which threatened to amaze me.

Tep Longeur and my rescuer stood with me to ensure that I did not fall again. The overseer appeared haggard in the early light, haunted by harsh recollections. From time to time, however, he smiled—wanly, perhaps, but without coercion.

The stranger's shirt hung in strips from his shoulders, revealing the aftermath of Sher Abener's bloody work. But his wounds had been treated with the same balm which eased my hurts, and had already begun to heal. I suspected that before this day ended his chest would show new scars rather than recent cuts. If his power could grant me such a swift recovery from my burns, it could surely relieve him of the necromancer's malign weaving.

Despite the damage he had endured, his gaze as he greeted the dawn suggested eagerness.

No one moved upon the avenue. The day lay before us, rich with untouched possibilities.

My rescuer raised his features to the sun and seemed to scent the air. Then he informed us, "The Thal has indeed fled. Apparently his fears were too strong for him, as the necromancer suggested."

How he gained this knowledge was another amazement into which I did not inquire.

After a glance in my direction, he continued, "His departure opens the way for a new master. I do not doubt that the man who defeated Sher Abener will be able to assume the rule of Benedic without opposition."

I nodded as though I understood. "You mean yourself, of course." It might be pleasant to have a Thal who deserved respect.

But the stranger laughed. "I do not." He turned more fully toward me, so that I had some difficulty avoiding the vividness of his gaze. "I mean you. You need something to *do*, my friend. You waste yourself on ease.

"In any event"—again he laughed—"Tep Longeur is a far better merchant than you will ever be. The Thal's palace would be more suitable for you, I think. You have the makings of a ruler much superior to the last one."

I considered this notion foolish in the extreme. Perhaps for that reason, I did not scorn it.

Without awaiting a reply, the stranger announced, "Farewell. I have repaid my debt."

At once, he left my side and walked away. As he strode off into the dawn, a spring lifted his steps, and his arms seemed to swing him along as though his veins were full of anticipation.

When he had passed beyond sight along the avenue, Tep Longeur asked gruffly, "Did that make any sense to you at all, Sher Urmeny?"

"Not a whit," I admitted. Then I shrugged. "But no matter. Sense, I find, is too highly regarded."

Certainly I valued the memory of my own madness. And I enjoyed the sound of my own name.

"Come, Sher Longeur," I proceeded. Despite my lingering hurts, I was overtaken by an immense contentment. Had I felt less weary, I might have burst into song. "If you consent to accept ownership of my merchantry and villa, you have much to do."

Before he could protest, I explained, "Thal Urmeny of Benedic will have no time for such concerns." I lacked the strength for outright laughter, but I managed an easy chuckle. "And doubtless he will demand compliance for his desires."

My former overseer frowned until he saw that I jested. Then he relaxed. "Oh, very well, my lord," he muttered in feigned vexation. "If you insist."

Supporting me companionably upon his shoulder, he helped me find my way homeward.

Photo by Petra Hegger

Stephen R. Donaldson is the author of the six volumes of *The Chronicles of Thomas Covenant*, a landmark in modern fantasy. Every volume, beginning with *Lord Foul's Bane* in 1977, has been an international bestseller. Donaldson returned to the series with *The Runes of the Earth* in 2004. He lives in New Mexico. Visit his website at stephenrdonaldson.com.